Guardian of the Lamp

To Joan & Nick,
I wish for you -
a cozy fire,
a comfy chair, and
a good book to read
Best wishes,
LaRee Hindman Bryant
3/8/2003

GUARDIAN OF THE LAMP

Laryce Henderson Rybka
10/06/02

LARYCE HENDERSON RYBKA

ISBN:	Library of Congress Number:	2002093151
	Hardcover	1-4010-6612-7
	Softcover	1-4010-6611-9

This book was printed in the United States of America.

To order additional copies of this book, contact:

Xlibris Corporation

1-888-795-4274

www.Xlibris.com

Orders@Xlibris.com

15127

Contents

DEDICATION

TO MY BELOVED PARENTS, ENOS AND DOROTHY HENDERSON, WHO ALWAYS HAD FAITH IN ME, AND WHO REARED A VERY PLAIN LITTLE GIRL WITH AVERAGE INTELLIGENCE, TO BELIEVE THAT SHE WAS PRETTY, EXTREMELY SMART, AND COULD ACCOMPLISH ANYTHING TO WHICH SHE SET HER HEAD...AS LONG AS SHE NEVER GAVE UP! THANK YOU, MOTHER AND DADDY.

LOVE, LARYCE . . .

FOREWORD

The writing of this book was a four-year-long labor of love. Realizing, from the beginning, that some of the subject matter would be sensitive, I carefully weighed the wording. I wanted it to convey the message of the story in a way that was realistic for the time and place in which it was set. However, I did not want any reader to be offended. I debated whether or not to use the dialect common to the southern slave. After much deliberation, I finally decided that my not using the dialect would only serve to weaken the story. So I chose to write the dialogue, to the best of my ability, as it was spoken. I hope that no one will be offended by my efforts, for that was never my intention.

This book is completely fictional, as are all names, characters, and incidents; and although the idea which spawned this story is based on the line of strong women in my family, especially my maternal grandmother, any resemblance to names, incidents, or actual persons, living or dead, is purely coincidental.

CHAPTER ONE

THE ARRIVAL

Summer 1816 was a scorcher down home; of course that's not really unusual in the Charleston low country. But the first of August that year, the middle of what we call "dog days," felt like a record, especially to those struggling in the master bedroom of Fairlawn Plantation. It was early afternoon and sweltering. Fairlawn was located on the Ashley River, a few miles outside Charleston. However, the breezes off the river, that had cooled the evening before, had died. There was little sound in the beautiful old home except the interminable buzzing of the flies and the screams of Rebecca Prendle, suffering her twenty-first hour of labor with her sixth child. Becca, as her husband John called her affectionately, was a tiny woman with extremely narrow hips; so the midwife and slaves in attendance were not surprised at her suffering; for thus it had been with all her previous children, five strapping sons. This was a late baby; the boys were all in their teens or early twenties. Becca was forty-three and John, forty-eight; so they assumed that all danger of pregnancy had probably passed. Nevertheless, they had not complained when they learned that she was expecting. They would welcome this baby with open arms as they had their first five. They never questioned the will of God. The midwife, although very experienced, was becoming more than a little concerned. Having assisted Becca in the delivery of her first five babies, she realized that rather than proceeding down into the birth canal as labor progressed, this baby seemed to be moving upward. At this point, as a usual thing, a midwife would be ready to take the ground pepper she had at hand and use it to *sneeze* the mother to give the final push to force the birth. She finally told Delilah, "You better send one of the boys for Doctor Gilmore; I'm afraid we're in trouble with this one!"

Delilah, the old slave woman who had been Becca's personal maid since she was a girl, ran from the room calling, "Mistuh John, Mistuh John, send one of de boys for Doctuh Gilmore quick!" She then collapsed at the foot of the stairs, burying her face in her apron and sobbing, "Lawd, I ain't nevuh asked for much, but please Suh', don' take my Becca baby. I jus' don' think I can stan' it!" She finally pulled herself together as she climbed wearily up the stairs to help as much as she could until the doctor arrived.

The boys were all in the fields supervising the picking of the cotton. It had been a perfect year for cotton. The crop was at its peak now; and at this point, first priority on a cotton plantation was getting the crop in. The field slaves were hard at work, sweat glistening on their backs like black pearls in the hot August sun. Owners who wanted to get top dollar for their crops went to the fields to be sure the slaves stayed hard at it. John Prendle had the advantage of having five strong, intelligent, and hard working sons to help run the plantation. This was no accident; he and Becca had planned it that way from the day of their marriage. What they had not planned was to have another baby at this stage of their lives, and certainly not being delivered at cotton picking time! On horseback, the five boys rode from field to field in the heat, covering the entire plantation and encouraging their slaves to stay with the work. The Prendle slaves were always well-treated by their masters. They were well-fed, neatly-clothed, decently-housed, and never knew the sting of the whip. They took great pride in their work and only sought to please. Many slave owners regarded their slaves as working breed-stock and treated them much as they treated the other livestock they owned.

John was an adoring husband with Becca always his first priority. So he had kept the vigil all night long in the study beneath their bedroom, listening to the screams and growing more frightened by the minute. At this point, the cotton crop was of little importance to him; and he was leaving all the field work to the boys. When Delilah came with the call for the Doctor, not at all surprised, he bolted out the front door, across the broad piazza to his horse, already saddled and waiting, tied to the blackamoor which stood at the edge of the big circular drive. The drive led to an avenue of live oak trees, heavily draped with beautiful spanish moss, leading away from Fairlawn to the river road. With his riding crop, he frantically whipped Selam, his white Arabian, to full gallop as he covered the five miles between Fairlawn and Meadows, the plantation of Dr. Alan Gilmore. Once he had alerted the Gilmore household to the situation at home and was satisfied that the doctor would follow close behind, he wheeled Selam and headed back at full gallop. As he rode, he prayed, bargaining with God, making all the inane, back-to-the-wall promises people have a tendency to make at such critical times.

Back at Fairlawn, Becca's labor continued without progress. As the midwife looked on in helpless frustration, Delilah, weeping, swabbed her mistress's sweating body with cool cloths in a futile effort to bring her some small measure of comfort. Mandy, Delilah's daughter, fanned the relentless flies away from the bed as the tears streamed down her beautiful ebony face. She had grown up knowing Becca almost as an older sister, and she loved her deeply. She could empathize with her agony, having just delivered her first baby, a very difficult delivery also. Becca had brought the midwife in to deliver Mandy's baby, and had stayed in attendance herself to assist there in the household slaves' quarters behind the plantation kitchen. John had arrived back at Fairlawn and was pacing the piazza impatiently. Finally Dr. Gilmore's buggy could be heard, racing down the lane. He dismounted, medical bag in hand, and turned the reins over to Samuel, Delilah's husband and head of the household slaves at Fairlawn. Taking Doctor Gilmore's bag, John led him hastily up the grand stairway to the master bedroom. The doctor motioned John to remain outside as he took the bag and entered the room. He was in the room only a few minutes when he came back out to inform John of the gravity of the situation. "John, I must have your permission immediately to perform a Caesarian if there is to be any hope for Rebecca or the baby."

"Becca's my only concern, Doctor Gilmore. At this point, that baby doesn't matter!"

With a look of profound regret, Dr. Gilmore replied, "John, it's not a matter of choice; we'll be lucky if either one comes through. I can't make you any promises." John nodded his understanding and approval, he knew that Dr. Gilmore, in his many years of practice, had performed the procedure before; and that if anybody could save Becca, he could. "Bring me a bottle of brandy or the strongest thing you have to drink in the house. Unfortunately, something to help lessen pain during surgery is only in experimental stages," Dr. Gilmore said.

"There is a small cabinet of spirits that I keep on hand there in our bedroom. I think you will find what you need there."

"Now get out of the house; it is pointless to torture yourself listening to this. Pray that she will pass out quickly from the pain."

"Oh please God, please!" John replied in horror. "I'll be right here waiting!" Dr. Gilmore reentered the bedroom.

Waiting outside the door, John could hear the sounds of bustling activity inside the room. Becca's agonized screams continued, then subsided somewhat after she was given the brandy, and finally rose to an unbearable pitch as Dr. Gilmore began the surgery, John listened with mounting concern and wept. "Oh Dear Lord, how I wish I could bear this in her place." Suddenly there was silence; John knew the surgery was underway and thanked God that Becca had apparently lost consciousness.

As he paced the hallway, John looked from the balcony down into the foyer below. The late afternoon sun shone through the facets of the beautiful cut glass entrance doors and side panels, playing a rainbow of color across the marble floor and up the majestic staircase. His mind drifted back across the happy years of his life with Becca. Scene after scene threaded its way through his treasury of memories.

John's mother, daughter of a socially prominent Charleston family, and always a lady of fragile health, had only borne the one child who survived more than a few months. Finding life too difficult on a plantation which always struggled for survival, she had died at fifty-three. John and his father, Josiah Walton Prendle, had lived alone at Fairlawn with the few slaves they could afford to help them run the place. John had fallen in love with the youngest daughter of Judge Matthew David James and his wife, the former Lydia Barton. The beautiful Rebecca Gilbert James had been sought after by all the eligible young bachelors of the area; and John had considered it quite a coup to be the chosen one. John and Becca had honeymooned in Savannah. While there, they had visited in the home of his cousin Theodore Magwood. Becca had fallen in love with Theodore's beautiful mansion, which was a somewhat modified Greek Revival. A stairway on either end of the facade curved up to the veranda above. Becca had said that the stairways looked like welcoming arms. Her dream was to someday remodel Fairlawn to duplicate this style.

The sumptuous mansions of Charleston's most prosperous upper-class citizenry reflected the architectural evolution of the sedate old city. In the late seventeenth century, federal architecture had been most prevalent; in the early to mid eighteenth century, Georgian architecture had become more popular. However following the Revolution, Charleston, having been referred to as "Little London" in early years, had sought to acquire a more American persona; consequently, Greek Revival architecture had become the style of choice.

After their honeymoon, John had brought his young bride of eighteen home to become the new mistress of the large plantation. She brought with her—rather like a dowry—her personal maid, Delilah, and Delilah's husband Samuel, and their daughter Mandy. This well-trained little family aided immeasurably in her transition to mistress of the house. John's father had never regained any enthusiasm for life after the death of his wife; and, had passed away a few years after John and Becca had married, leaving the plantation to his only child, John. Those early years had been very difficult; the plantation was always struggling it seemed. Its cotton crops, at the mercy of the capricious Charleston weather—droughts at one extreme, and violent hurricanes at the other—were always meager. Each year or two Becca had suffered through the birth of another baby; while through it all, she had cooked, sewn, attended to the training of the household slaves as they could afford to purchase them, and had helped him with the field slaves when time had permitted.

She had insisted, however, no matter how hard the times were, that money be allocated for the boys' education. A classroom had been set up in the large plantation study; and a tutor had been given free room and board at Fairlawn in exchange for his services three days each week. The boys had been educated there at home from early childhood until they reached the age to be enrolled at the excellent College of Charleston, the first city school in America. In addition,

Becca had insisted that their formal religious training be as thorough as their formal education. As a result, the Prendle family had always been considered one of the pillars of St. Michael's Episcopal Church in Charleston. In recent years when everything had fallen into place for them, they had become truly prosperous—their five sons grown, the plantation running smoothly with a full complement of slave labor, and even the weather cooperating for several years in a row. Finally they could afford to make Becca's dream of renovating Fairlawn come true. John had allowed her free rein to fulfill her every whim, and this beautiful mansion that they now enjoyed had been—suddenly his reverie was shattered by the sound of a slap and the strong first cry of an infant. "Well, I guess the baby made it through. God why can't I really care one way or the other," John thought with honest regret.

In a few minutes, Delilah emerged from the bedroom with a screaming bundle, wrapped in one of the dozen or so receiving blankets which Becca herself had hemstitched in preparation for the baby's arrival. "We's finally got us a baby girl, Mistuh John; but Miss Becca is mighty weak and . . ." her words trailed off as she choked back the tears and rushed into the nursery adjoining the master bedroom, cuddling the baby to her heart.

After what seemed an eternity, the door again opened; Mandy and the midwife, who had both assisted in the delivery, came out of the bedroom; and avoiding John's eyes, they went down the stairs. Dr. Gilmore followed them out, shoulders slumped and head bowed, and spoke quietly to John, "I did everything I could, John; but I don't think Rebecca can possibly make it; she's lost a lot of blood; I'm so very sorry. She's asking for you; you'd best go on in."

John felt as if his heart would explode; but he squared his shoulders, slowly opened the door, and entered the room. Becca lay there in their big bed, pale and drawn, eyes closed.

He dropped to his knees beside the bed; and taking her small hand in both of his, he dropped his head to the bed and sobbed, "Oh Becca, my beloved, I'm so sorry, why couldn't you have been spared instead of her?"

In a voice stronger than John would have thought possible, Becca responded, "No Jonathan, never say or even think that again! Do you understand me, never! It isn't her fault. It isn't anybody's fault. It's just the will of God. We have never questioned His will in all our years together; and we're not going to start now! I have some things to say to you that are very important; and I have only a little time left to say them; so listen carefully and promise to honor my wishes."

"Anything, love, I promise!"

"First, my darling Jonathan, I have loved you and every minute of our lives together with every fiber of my being. I wouldn't change one moment of it. I have loved building this beautiful home with you, sharing a love sweeter and more passionate than any other woman could ever have known, and, above all, carrying and bearing your children, all six of them! Now for the promises. First, please love our little Lillianna Prendle—yes, that is her name, first name and last name, no middle name, no more, no less, no nickname, just Lillianna! Hold her, touch her, kiss her, adore her. Make her your own little princess and encourage her big brothers to do the same. Remember, I can't be here; so I'm counting on you, the boys, Delilah, and Mandy to be her mother. Will you give me your sacred promise to do this, please?"

"Yes beloved, yes, always," John sobbed.

"Now for one last promise, and don't ask me for any explanation as to why I ask it. Give Mandy and her baby Mattie their papers of freedom, all legally drawn; build them a nice little house on a plot of land, enough for a small farm; and deed it to Mandy. Furnish her house neatly and completely; then hire her to continue at her same job, and pay her a decent wage. Will you promise to do this?"

"Yes, my sweet, I promise. Whatever your reasons, I am sure they are good. What about Delilah and Samuel; do you want me to free them also? I'll be happy to if that is your wish."

"No, Delilah is aware that you are going to do this; and I offered her and Samuel their freedom also; but they declined my offer. They both are accustomed to their way of life, and they feel, at this stage of their lives, that they prefer to remain as they are. Now kiss me goodnight, sweetheart; I'm so tired. I'll see you in the morning."

"Yes darling, I'll see you in the morning," John replied. As he kissed her, she slipped quietly away. John then permitted himself to sob aloud until all the tears were spent; then he rose to go downstairs to tell his sons their mother was gone. John vowed never again to permit himself to weep. Before he went down, he went into the little nursery and took his daughter from Delilah, who sat rocking and crooning a lullaby to the baby through her own tears. "Hello, my precious little Princess Lillianna," John cooed as he kissed her button nose, "Your mama said goodnight. Delilah, you need to see if there is a wet nurse down in the quarters."

"Never worry, Mistuh John, my Mandy has 'nuff milk for her little Mattie and our little Lilli too."

"That's just fine, Delilah." As John returned the baby to her arms, he added, "By the way, her name is Lillianna, Lillianna Prendle—first name and last name, no middle name, no more, no less, no nickname, just Lillianna." Then he set his chin and strode purposefully down the stairs with his sad news.

John lost all track of time as he stood beside the grave, deep in the anesthesia of reminiscence. Family and friends had long since left the little fenced cemetery where Rebecca now rested with the generations of Prendles who had gone before. Suddenly he was back in the present where his grief was almost unbearable. One last time before leaving, he read aloud the passage of scripture from Proverbs which he had selected for the stone marking her grave. “Who can find a virtuous woman for her price is far above rubies? Her husband has full confidence in her and . . . she brings him good and not harm all the days of her life. . . . And her lamp does not go out by night . . . Her children rise up and call her blessed; her husband also, and he praises her: ‘Many women have done excellently, but you surpass them all.’ Oh, my darling Becca, the lamp of your life has been our guide for all these years. Who could ever be worthy to become guardian of that lamp?” John stood but a moment longer, choking back the tears he refused to shed. “Goodnight, my love, until I join you. Now take the rest that you have earned.” He kissed his fingers and touched the stone as he turned and walked away.

CHAPTER TWO

CHILDHOOD

August 1, 1826, the sunlight of the beautiful morning fell across the counterpane of Lillianna Prendle's big bed and peeked under the canopy to fall on her pretty young face, framed with auburn ringlets and boasting a freckled nose, which she hated. She awakened with a smile; and as always said, "Good morning new day." She stretched languidly, looked at the canopy above, and counted the kittens cavorting there. There were exactly thirty-two kittens dancing among the flowers; she had counted them many times before. Today it didn't seem as much fun as usual; "Guess I'm getting too old to play that baby game; after all, I am ten years old today!" She lay there thinking of all the things she should thank the Lord for in her morning prayer. Delilah, her "Wilah," had taught her from babyhood to begin and end each day with a prayer. Her morning prayer was always one of thanks to God for bringing her safely through the night, and then she thanked Him for all the wonderful blessings of her life. "First things first," she thought: "My angel Mama, looking over me in Heaven; Papa; Matt; Day, his wife Martha, and their baby Warry; Diddle, his wife Ellen, and their baby Eddie; Dilly; Wookey; Wilah; my Mandy Ma; and my best friend, Mattie."

These were the people around which Lillianna's world revolved. These were, of course, not their formal names; but they were Lillianna's version of the pet names given them by Delilah.

Rebecca always felt that she had earned the right through labor and delivery to name all her babies; John, as always, honored her wishes. She disapproved of diminutives and insisted that each be called by his formal name. Only John and Delilah were permitted to break that rule, in calling her Becca. She loved the way John had of saying Becca; it almost seemed a caress. She knew full well that it was useless to try to force Delilah not to call the babies, whom she considered her own, by whatever name she chose to call them. The babies' names, in order of birth, were Matthew James Prendle (Matt), Jonathan Warren Prendle, Jr. (Jay), David Lawrence Prendle (Little Davey), Gilmore Seth Prendle (Gilly), Lucas Aaron Prendle (Lukey), and Lillianna Prendle (the one formal name Delilah accepted).

Lillianna hopped out of bed and knelt on the step stool beside it. With the smell of her birthday cake drifting up to her bedroom as it baked in the kitchen out back, she began her prayer. "Thank You dear Lord for bringing me safely through the night, and for all my folks who love me and take care of me and whom I love so very much, and for my big birthday picnic this afternoon. In Jesus' name I offer this prayer, Amen. Oh, and by the way, Lord, since I am a big girl now, I have to stop all this baby talk; and just so You will be prepared, the next time I talk to You I'll call all my folks by their real names. I know You will recognize whom I'm talking about when I say Matt, Jay, Little Davey—nope,just Davey I think—Gilly, Lukey, and Mattie. If You are wondering why I didn't include Delilah, I just can't give up my Wilah—I'm sorry. Now, amen again, Sir."

With a bound, Lillianna sprang from the step stool, skipped across to her lounge, and took her white stockings and pantaloons from her picnic outfit laid out neatly there in readiness for her to put on later. As was her routine every morning, she went back to the step stool, sat down, and pulled on her stockings and pantaloons, pulling the latter up underneath her nightgown as she stood up. She stepped into her bedroom slippers, slipped into her robe, which lay across the foot of her bed, and ran to the top of the grand staircase. She surveyed the foyer below carefully; and seeing no one there, she straddled the banister and slid down gleefully.

"Ha! Cotched you agin! Dat Mistuh Lukey needed his pants warmed for teachin' you dat trick," Delilah complained, appearing unexpectedly from the dining room. "How Miss Clara Finch ever gonna' make a proper lady outn' you when you insists on doin' tricks like dat, and catchin' tree toads, and ain' no tellin' what all? You jus' tell me dat! Mistuh Matt drivin' all de way to Meetin' Street three times a week to fetch her out here to edicate you and Miss Jane with your readin', writin', numbers, and proper mannuhs. Lawsy me, what is we gonna' do with you?" She trailed off as she returned to the dining room to finish setting up breakfast.

"Oh Wilah, please don't *fuss me* today; it's my birthday. Besides it's the last time I'll ever do any of those things again. Today I am ten years old; and from now on, I'm going to act like a proper young lady." Lillianna promised.

"Uh huh, we jus' see 'bout dat," Delilah muttered from the dining room.

Lillianna ran across the foyer to Papa's big study, her favorite of all the rooms in the mansion. The study had been designed larger than the usual study in order that it might serve as a classroom for the Prendle children. The book-lined walls fascinated Lillianna; she was a precocious child and read far above her age level. On rainy days or extremely hot afternoons, she loved to go into the study to read; where any breeze that existed wafted into the large front window of the study. Five small desks were lined up in front of the window in order to afford the best light for the students working there. Above Papa's desk hung a beautiful life-sized portrait of Mama, wearing a lovely dark green velvet dress, which complemented her dark brown eyes and auburn hair—an adult version of the little face that gazed up at the portrait adoringly. Around her neck was the beautiful emerald-studded cross John had given her as a wedding gift, her favorite piece of jewelry. It now rested in its velvet box in Lillianna's armoire, but she was not yet allowed to wear it for fear she might lose it.

Lillianna crossed the study to gaze out the big front window, as she frequently did. The panorama before her was like a big beautiful painting. The trees across the Ashley River, the bright ribbon of the river as it wound its way toward Charleston in the morning sunlight, and the River Road, which hugged the near bank, all served as a lovely backdrop for the sweeping lawn of the plantation, from which Fairlawn took its name. Down the center of the lawn was the long tree-lined drive leading down to River Road. In the foreground was the big oval drive, centered in front of the mansion. The neatly landscaped oval, circled with boxwoods, had a marble bench on either end. Lillianna loved to sit on one of the benches and gaze down at her beloved river. Sometimes she strolled down to sit in a secluded little alcove beside the river. In this special place, she could ponder the how and why of life as she witnessed it each day—deep thoughts for such a little girl. Far to the left of the huge lawn she looked at last at Mandy's neat little home, with its front porch facing the river, and its short drive leading to River Road. She thought of all the hours she and Mattie had spent, sitting on those front steps and making up stories about the river. Their favorite was always of pirates and their derring-do.

At last Lilllianna crossed the study and sat down in Papa's big swivel chair and began her morning talk with Mama, which had been her practice as long as she could remember. The master bedroom was just above the study; and there was a little private stairway from the bedroom down to the study with a door that entered at the rear corner. Occasionally John would crack the door and peek in to listen as Lillianna talked with her Mother. He especially wanted to hear her birthday conversation. As always, his eyes would grow misty at the sight of his precious little girl, so tiny and lost looking in his big chair, yet always so serious and somehow grownup sounding.

"Good morning, Mama dear, course you know today is my tenth birthday; and we are having a picnic to celebrate; I am so excited. Papa says he has a special gift for me, and I can't wait to see what it is! Is it very selfish for me to be thinking so much of gifts I am going to receive? I think maybe it is; I think I should ask God to forgive me for that. You know, I just realized that even though this is a happy day, it is also an unhappy day for all of our family. After all, it is the day we all lost you. I have never thought of that before; maybe being ten years old just made me grownup enough to realize that everyone must feel a little sad at the thought of that. I know I do. Oh Mama, how I wish you could talk to me, and I could know the sound of your voice and all the things you think and feel! Papa said that you used to sit in the little alcove beside the river and read stories to the boys. Oh, I wish that I could sit with your arm around me and listen to you read. I love you so very much. Even though I have never really known you; I feel somehow that I do and that you look down from heaven and love me too."

At hearing this, John closed the door quietly. He knew that if he listened longer, the tears, which he never permitted himself, would surely come. He crept back up the stairway and made his way down to the little breakfast alcove where he and Lillianna always shared breakfast and his cherished Papa/Daughter talk.

"Oh Mercy Mama, look at the time; it's almost nine; and I know Papa must be waiting breakfast for me. See you in the morning, Mama," Lillianna called over her shoulder as she ran out of the study, across the foyer, through the big dining room, into the cozy breakfast alcove behind, and plopped down into her chair across the table from Papa, who was already seated and waiting. Then, as if there were a spring in her rump, she hopped back up; and standing properly beside her chair, as she glanced in the direction of Delilah's disapproving stare, she said, "Oops, I almost forgot, today I am ten, and I must seat myself like a proper young lady." Seeing Delilah's nod of approval, she then seated herself properly in the chair, adjusted herself comfortably, placed her napkin in her lap, folded her hands in her lap, and waited to be served.

"I am very impressed, Princess," John said with a little chuckle, in spite of himself. "Well, today is your big day. I have already figured out some of your thoughts this morning, with all this talk of being ten years old. Are there other ones you would share with me this morning?"

"Oh Papa, there's so much; I don't know where to start. I was just telling Mama all about my birthday doings and how excited I am about your surprise gift for me; and I suddenly thought what a selfish girl I must really be! After all, even though it is a happy day for me, it is also really a sad day in a way for all of us—'cause it's also the day Mama died! How could I have gone all these years and never thought about that before?" she said, as tears filled her eyes.

"No, no, no, Princess. You must never feel that way," John replied, "The day you were born was one of the happiest days of your Mama's life. She was so proud of her little girl and loved her so very much. Besides, Mama didn't die; she just went to live in a different place, a very beautiful place. From there she is watching over us and loving us all. I am sure she will enjoy your birthday quite as much as we all shall."

"But Papa, I so wish I could have Mama talk back when I

talk to her. I would love to know the sound of her voice, to feel her kiss on my face, and to see her smile at me."

"Oh Princess, you can. One of Mama's favorite spots was that shady nook down by the river. When the boys were small, she would take them down there on pretty days, sit on a comfortable quilt, and read to them. She loved doing that; and they did too, especially Matthew, as I remember. The next time you walk down by the river, think of the bubbling of the water as the sound of Mama's voice, the breeze off the river as a kiss on your sweet nose, and the sunlight peeping over your bonnet as her beautiful smile. Now put all the sad thoughts out of your mind; finish your breakfast; and get ready for the fun we're all going to have today!" So John and Lillianna finished breakfast as Delilah wept silently in the butler's pantry nearby.

After breakfast, Lillianna, who usually ran or skipped everywhere she went at breakneck speed, strolled back through the beautiful dining room, reaching up to rub the backs of the massive mahogany chairs and caressing the rest of the room with her eyes. She seemed to view it all in a different way than she ever had before. She went out into the elegant foyer; and as she walked across the polished marble, she looked up at the rainbow of beautiful colors that played on the crystal chandelier. She breathed in sharply and thought, "What a truly beautiful world I live in!" As she meandered slowly up the stairs, she ran her little hand up the shining banister and enjoyed the feel of the smooth wood, which had often felt the seat of her pantaloons.

About that time, Delilah walked out into the hall and said gently, "Honey, you best hurry up and git up to your room and dress; your guests will be gittin' here before you know it. I'll be up to help wif' your hair soon as I clear the breakfast table."

Suddenly, in typical Lillianna style, she flew up the stairs to her bedroom to start dressing. As she donned her new outfit, she admired it lovingly. She put on her under petticoats and hoop and slipped the pretty pale green voile dress, dotted randomly with tiny white buttercups, over her head. About that time, Delilah came in and crossed the room to hook the back of the dress. She brushed the child's auburn hair into beautiful ringlets and tied it back with a green ribbon with expert hands born of years of practice first with Becca and now with her daughter. She then reached for the broad brimmed sun hat, banded with fabric that matched the dress, tied in a neat bow with streamers hanging down from the back. Lillianna said, "Wait Wilah, let me put on my hat and tie it." She picked up the hat, perched it on the crown of her head, tied the under-chin bow to one side, then arranging it neatly, she admired the effect of the whole ensemble in the long mirror. She smiled and nodded her approval, thanked Delilah for her help, and skipped happily out of the room. She paused at the top of the steps and walked sedately down the grand staircase like a really grown-up Southern Belle.

Delilah, looking on, chuckled to herself and thought, "Maybe they's hope yit."

John, waiting at the foot of the staircase, looked up with adoring eyes. As Lillianna reached the bottom, he offered her his arm and said, "Miss Prendle, may I escort you to the stable where your birthday gift awaits?"

Taking his arm, Lillianna looked at him puzzled. She thought, "I already have a pony; what could it be?" As they walked around the house to the back and down the long marl drive to the stable, her mind was abuzz with possibilities.

Seth, the stable boy, waited for them beside the big stable doors. He was decked out in one of his jockey outfits for the occasion of Lillianna's birthday; and looked rather like a living, breathing blackamoor. He was not much larger than Lillianna, and was the eldest son of Zeke, a mulatto, who was Fairlawn's stable manager and chief horse trainer. Seth's job as jockey would pass down to a younger brother as he grew too large for the job and for the colorful outfits. Although John always rode Selam in the races himself; he had other horses which were trained to race; and as was the custom on local plantations, there was a small jockey trained as mount for racing stock other than the Master's horse, which was usually, as in John's case, ridden by the owner himself. As John and Lillianna reached the stable, Seth opened the big door; and as they entered, she took a deep breath, taking in the sweet smell of the hay. She loved the smells in the stable; she didn't even mind the rich fragrance of the manure. Papa led her down to Abra's stall—Lillianna always referred to Abra as Selam's wife. Papa opened the door of the stall; Abra rolled her big eyes around and looked protectively at the little white foal; and Lillianna gave a squeal of delight as she realized that this precious baby was her birthday gift from Papa.

"There she is, Princess; how do you like her?"

"Oh Papa, I love her," she replied, as she gave him a big hug and ran to the foal. "Papa, when she's all grown-up, I want to race her at the track in Charleston, like you do Selam."

"We shall have to give that some serious thought, Princess; I have never before seen a lady race at the track. That just isn't permitted. Besides, it will be some time before she is really turned over to you for the two of you to train together. Zeke is our expert. He will be in charge of her training until he feels both of you are ready for that. Of course, you will be able to pet her all you wish and help Zeke with currying and feeding her. Now it's time for you to give her a name; do you have any ideas?"

"Sheba, that's her name," replied Lillianna without hesitation, "And we'll just see about that racing," she said, with her lips pursed and chin firmly set. John knew from that look that it was useless to argue the point now.

Zeke was busy polishing Lillianna's bright red pony cart as the stable boy curried her pony, Grayboy, in preparation for the pony cart rides, which would be a part of the entertainment for the birthday guests following the big birthday picnic. One last hug for little Sheba, and John and Lillianna strolled out of the stable arm-in-arm. Suddenly the exuberant little girl broke away and into a run, shouting over her shoulder, "Look Papa, there's a buggy coming up the drive; it's Will bringing Jane to my party."

Although the other party guests would arrive in buggies driven by slaves, who would visit down in the slave quarters until their young charges were ready to go home, Jane Pinkston was being delivered by her big brother, Will Junior, who at fifteen would join in watching the birthday fun with the Prendle boys. The Pinkstons strongly disapproved of slavery and had tenant farm families running their plantation, Pink Hill. Slavery was such an integral part of southern life that the other plantation owners rather resented the Pinkston stand against this tradition, albeit an unspoken resentment for the most part.

Lillianna, panting for breath and face flushed, arrived at the blackamoor beside the piazza at the same time Will and Jane pulled up in the buggy, Will handed over the reins to one of several slaves waiting there to help the little guests step down as they arrived and to take their birthday gifts and place them on the gift table there on the piazza. "Happy Birthday," Jane sang out, as the two little girls embraced.

Will teased, "Hey, you with the carrots hanging out from under your bonnet, don't I get a hug too?"

"Oh Will, you're such a pesky teaser," retorted Lillianna as she gave him a hug and batted her brown eyes at him. She wondered to herself why her heart always seemed to skip a beat whenever Will tousled her auburn curls or gave her a brotherly hug, after all he really was such a pest!

When all the neighboring boys and girls had arrived, the festivities began with games of tag on the big lawn, dancing of reels to the twang of Luke's fiddle playing, pony cart rides around the big oval drive then down to the River Road and back, and last, but by no means least, the eating of the huge picnic spread. Then Delilah came out with the big birthday cake, its eleven candles aglow, one for each year and one to grow on. She placed it on the picnic table in front of the birthday girl. "Make a wish, baby, 'scuse me, I mean young lady, and blow 'em all out, so's ya'll can git on with the cake and custard eatin'!"

Lillianna cut her eyes around at Mattie, who stood against the wall on the piazza with her heart in her eyes, longing to be a part of the fun, but waiting to be in attendance when the gifts were opened. Mattie lived in a puzzling world, a world in which she knew that she and her mother were free, but that her grandparents were slaves. A world in which, though free, she, nevertheless, felt like a slave. Lillianna smiled at Mattie, closed her eyes, and silently wished, "I wish for a time when my sweet Mattie can join in all the fun of my birthday party with the rest of us, a time when everyone would be happy to include her, a time when I can tell all the world openly, 'This is my best friend!'" With that, Lillianna opened her eyes, and, with one big breath, blew out all the candles. There was then, of course, a chorus of the Happy Birthday song and much hand-clapping and giggling by all.

During all the happy partying, John and the other adults had watched the fun from comfortable peacock chairs on the shady veranda above. As Lillianna made her birthday wish, John found himself making the futile wish that she would never grow up and that the childish laughter and happiness which pervaded this day could go on forever.

After the gifts were all opened, thank you's and good-bye's said, and the last of the buggies had pulled away and headed for River Road, Will came down the stairs from the veranda to send for his buggy. Lillianna implored him to wait awhile so that they could all go down to the stable to see Sheba. Will agreed; and he, Jane, and Lillianna started to walk down to the stable. Lillianna said, "Come on Mattie and go with us; I want you to see her too." Mattie joined the little group shyly as they strolled down to the stable.

They all saw and admired the beautiful little foal with excitement; and as Lillianna confided her plan to someday race Sheba herself at the racetrack in Charleston, they all laughed at this ridiculous idea. Will said, "Yes, I can just see you astride that big white horse, racing around the track, skirts and petticoats flying, and those carrots sailing behind from beneath your bonnet!"

"Oh shush, that's all you know Will Pinkston. I'll have a beautiful side saddle, a proper riding habit, hat and all; and I'll race her myself; and I'll win; you'll see," she snapped petulantly.

"Oh I'm sorry, my little auburn-haired girl; I've made you angry, and on your birthday. I never intended to; it was all in jest. Tell you what, I'll just wait for you to grow up and marry you; and the day you win that race, I'll be cheering you on as your husband, waiting for you at the finish line with a victory bouquet of magnolias and wisteria. Is it a deal, Mrs. Lillianna Prendle Pinkston to be?"

"Oh Will, silly," she replied blushing. Will walked back up to the mansion laughing, as the three little girls strolled hand-in-hand down to the river bank and sat in Becca's shady nook, looking at the peaceful river flowing by, wishing that they could somehow capture this moment and make it last forever.

The last month of their summer vacation seemed to fly by. September 1 found Lillianna and Jane in the big study at Fairlawn awaiting the arrival of their tutor, Miss Clara Finch. On every Monday, Wednesday, and Friday, Will Junior and Jane would drive the buggy into Charleston to pick up Miss Finch and bring her to Fairlawn to tutor the two girls in the *three R's* and in proper ladylike behavior for every occasion. This had been the arrangement since the two little girls had turned six. Since it was well known that Miss Finch would have refused to include Mattie in her class, and since Lillianna was determined that she would be included, Lillianna and Jane conspired from the first day to find a way to have Mattie be a part of the class unbeknownst to Miss Finch.

The little stairway from the master bedroom down to the study was the perfect hiding place for Mattie to see and hear the lessons. Lillianna saw to it that Mattie had a slate, chalk, eraser, and all other materials necessary to actively participate in class work. Lillianna re-situated the blackboard so that Mattie would have full view of it through the slightly cracked door of the stairway. Every Monday, Wednesday, and Friday, without fail, Mattie was situated in her own little study by the time Jane and Miss Finch arrived. On the few occasions when Miss Finch might venture toward the stairway, either Jane or Lillianna would find a way to require her attention at the front of the study where their desks were situated. When academic instruction was finished for the day, Lillianna, Jane, and Miss Finch moved into the dining room or drawing room for etiquette instruction; then Mattie left her hiding place in the stairwell to return to her daily chores.

On Tuesday, Thursday, and Saturday afternoons, Lillianna and Mattie would meet in Mattie's room at Mandy's house to prepare the next class assignment and to give Lillianna the opportunity to instruct Mattie in the etiquette lessons she had received. They were sure that Mandy would be away and unaware of what they were doing. Lillianna could always make one excuse or another for not being at the plantation house, maybe reading or walking down by the river or down at the stable with Sheba. Sometimes Mandy and Delilah would take some time off on a Saturday afternoon to sit on Mandy's front porch and chat. On these occasions, Lillianna would slip out the back door to go home. This system of education for the girls continued for four more years.

When Lillianna and Jane were fourteen, Miss Finch told John that the time had come for the girls to be enrolled in

The Charleston Finishing School for Young Ladies, which was owned and operated by Miss Audrey Hockaday. This change would lead to a turn in Lillianna's life which no one anticipated.

CHAPTER THREE

COMING OF AGE (AWAKENING)

Coming of age—a difficult term to define. If asked, most people would probably define it as the time in ones life when he or she was finally permitted to participate in activities in which only adults were allowed. Not so with Lillianna Prendle. At fourteen, she was still considered a child by her family; however, events were about to occur which would forever set this year apart as the year she came of age, if not in the opinion of her family, certainly in her own opinion. This would be the year in which she would assume the privilege, even the moral responsibility, of thinking for herself regarding all the issues she would consider important for the rest of her life—regardless of the opinions of her father, the rest of her family, or even the rest of the world around her.

Midmorning September 1, 1830, a month after Lillianna's fourteenth birthday, John Prendle stood before the mirror in his bedroom, straightened the waistcoat of his riding habit, surveyed his still trim, sixty-two year old physique, picked up his hat and riding crop, and strode out of the room and down the stairs. Samuel was busy watering the plants in the foyer when John addressed him, "Samuel, have you seen Miss

Lillianna since breakfast? She and I have some business to attend to in Charleston this afternoon."

Samuel replied, "Yassuh, Mastuh John. I saw her ridin' Sheba down toward the river while ago. If you is a goin' to Charleston, I wish you'd consider buyin' a young man slave for me to train to take my place when I'se gone. I ain't gettin' no younguh Suh."

"Oh come now, Samuel, you've got years left ahead of you. Nevertheless, I'll see what I can do while we're in Charleston."

After breakfast, John had asked Samuel to see to it that Selam was saddled and waiting out front by eleven o'clock. He went outside, gave the big stallion a fond pat, mounted, and headed down toward the river in search of Lillianna. He saw her in the little alcove beside the river, riding slowly along the bank as she frequently did. John slowed his pace so as not to startle horse and rider, and to allow himself a few extra moments to savor the pleasure of the peaceful scene. He could hear Lillianna talking gently to her beloved companion as she allowed the horse to graze along the bank. "Oh Sheba girl, isn't that tender grass delicious. Soon I'll be back in school, and we won't have the time together that we've had all summer. Sometimes I wish that I never had to grow up, that I could just make time stand still, and that every minute could be just like this one."

"Amen," thought John. He hated even to speak and shatter this beautiful moment for them. "Hello ladies, the river is peaceful and serene today, isn't she? I hate to break this up; but we have to go into Charleston this afternoon to enroll you in Miss Hockaday's school. Classes start in a couple of weeks, and we can't put it off any longer. I think the Pinkstons went in this morning to enroll Jane. Will Junior will be taking some advanced courses at Charleston City College; and since you and Jane prefer not to be enrolled as boarding students, he will be taking you girls in to school each morning and bringing you home in the afternoon. The Pinkstons and I are in full agreement with your decisions about not boarding. We shall be leaving for town right after lunch, Princess; so you had better hasten up to the house to get ready before we eat."

"Yes sir, Papa," Lillianna answered as she reined Sheba around and headed toward the stables at a gallop.

The buggy ride into Charleston that afternoon was such a pleasure, especially for John. As he grew older and, as most older people, more jaded, he seemed to draw some small rejuvenation from Lillianna's fresh, young, and exuberant view of everything. As they drove along River Road, her youthful chatter about everything and nothing, interspersed with girlish laughter, warmed his heart. For that reason, he made their trip into Charleston a leisurely drive.

As they drove along, they first passed the huge Middleton Place to their left, with its beautiful gardens and twin lakes. "Wonder if they swim in the lakes, Papa? Bet that would be fun, since they are probably not too cold with the sun warming them up all summer." Lillianna reasoned.

"Could be; but I doubt it, since neither one has a dock." Papa responded.

"Well, I surely would if I lived there." Lillianna insisted. "What's that little thing like a lake on the left?" She asked.

"That's the rice mill pond. They grow rice here rather than cotton, like we do. The water from the mill pond is used to flood the rice fields or paddies, as they are called. That's the way rice is grown, in flooded paddies."

A few miles farther along, they passed the impressive Drayton estate with its Magnolia Plantation and Gardens, followed by lovely Drayton Hall. "They must really be rich; but I tell you what, I like our plantation much better. I think we have a much prettier view of the river; don't you, Papa?"

"Indeed I do, Princess! You're quite astute for such a young lady."

"Hmmm," she thought, "I'll look that one up when we get back."

A little farther along they passed the turnoff to the Washington Race Course. "It surely is quiet at the track today," Lillianna observed, "You usually can hear the horses hooves pounding and the crowd shouting. Aren't they racing today? I thought they'd be racing on a nice Saturday afternoon like this. Oh, I guess that was stupid of me. If they were racing, you would be there racing Selam."

"Oh, no indeed, Princess, nothing in the world could take precedence over our business in Charleston today," John reassured his daughter.

"Anyway, may I go to the next race to watch you, Papa, please. Matthew could bring me; or maybe Jane and Will, Jr. would like to come."

"We'll see, Sweetheart, a little closer to race time."

As they neared the turnoff for Charles Towne Landing, John flicked the reins to pick up their pace; Charleston was just ahead. "Princess, I think we had better go to Miss Hockaday's school straightway and take care of your enrollment; then we'll go order your new saddle for Sheba—fitted out exactly like you want it. Then you can shop for a grown-up riding habit while I attend to the purchase of a slave for Samuel to train for the house."

They headed up Meeting Street on the way to Miss Hockaday's. As they drove, they passed the beautiful gardens and home of Nathaniel Russell. "Papa, when Will brought Jane and me to see Miss Hockaday's school the first time, he told us that the Russell house has a free-flying stairway. Is that true; and if it is, what in the world is it?"

"Princess, I'm not honestly sure; but it is said that the Russell house does indeed have one. As I understand it, the staircase spirals upward in such a way architecturally that there is no need for visible structural support for it. I have not seen it; but those who have say it is impressive—looks like it is free-flying, and is quite beautiful."

"Guess I'll have to apologize to Will then. I accused him of fibbing, but it sure sounds like a fib! I tell you, I'll still have to see it to believe it!"

They proceeded from Meeting Street to Broad and then turned onto Legare where Miss Hockaday's school was located in a large and lovely old home, behind massive iron gates, and surrounded by an imposing high wall. As they entered the gates, Lillianna had to admit to herself feeling a little apprehensive; however, with outward bravado, she said, "Well, let's get this done. Just sign the papers, pay the fees, and let's get to the important things we have to do this afternoon."

"Sweetie, I imagine Miss Hockaday will want you to tour the school. She will probably tell you some things you should expect, and also some of her rules. She will doubtless give you something like a Student Handbook to study."

"Oh sakes alive, I'm sure Jane and I will learn about all that soon enough!"

John was right; the enrollment procedure, school tour, and instruction about rules, etc. took about an hour and a half. As they drove back down Meeting Street, Lillianna admitted, "You know, Papa, Miss Hockaday's school is really beautiful; and she is so nice. Now I am really sort of anxious for school to start. Did you notice she called me Miss Prendle; suppose she'll do that all the time?"

"I imagine so, Miss Prendle," replied John, with a smile and obvious pleasure at her enthusiasm.

Their next stop was in the ever busy shop of the saddler, Junius Pinkston, one of the few freedmen in business anywhere in the South. Junius had been a slave at Pink Hill when William Pinkston, Sr. had inherited the plantation at the death of his father. The elder Pinkston had owned a few slaves, and William had freed them all when he took over the plantation. Junius Pinkston had learned his trade on the Pinkston Plantation; and when William freed him, he also helped to set him up in the saddlery business in Charleston. At first, he had only a few customers; but as time passed and his reputation for expertise had grown, he soon had a busy and lucrative trade. As soon as he could afford to, he insisted on repaying his former master.

After a brief consultation with the Prendles, Junius was satisfied that he knew exactly what Lillianna wanted, to the smallest detail. He promised to deliver the saddle to Fairlawn in a week.

As they left the saddlery, John told Lillianna that he would drop her at The Charleston Mercantile, where Mrs. Robert Connor, the owner's wife, would help her select her new riding habit. He said that while she did that, he would go purchase the new slave and would then return to pick her up. "No Papa, please come in with me and help me select it. You always seem to know what looks best on me; and besides, I want to go with you to the slave market. I have never been there before."

"Lillianna, I don't feel comfortable with your accompanying me there. It isn't really a place for young ladies; and I don't believe it is something you would enjoy."

"Please, Papa, I want to go," she insisted. "I'll just watch from the buggy." John reluctantly agreed to allow her to go, as they tied up in front of the mercantile and went in together.

As they entered, they were greeted immediately by a smiling Maureen Connor, the proprietor's plump, but nonetheless beautiful wife. Even though she had been born in Charleston, Mrs. Connor still had a charming Irish accent, a leftover of having been reared by immigrant parents straight from the old country. She actually seemed to make a special effort to perpetuate the accent. "And a good day to you, Mr. Prendle and Miss Lillianna. My how you have grown, child, since last I saw you. And what can I do for you today?" Mrs. Connor inquired.

"We have come to select your prettiest and most grown-up riding habit for this young lady, Mrs. Connor," John responded.

"Well, Lillianna, I'll tell you what; we shall take you back to the dressing room; and I'll bring in the outfits. You can try them on and model each one for your father." As they went back to the dressing room in the rear of the large store, Lillianna's eyes scanned the counters displaying every sort of merchandise imaginable, from nuts and bolts to yard goods by the bolt. After they entered the dressing room and closed the door behind them, Mrs. Connor asked Lillianna to remove all of her outer garments so that she could take measurements to determine her size. When the young girl was finally down to her shift, Mrs. Connor looked at her young figure approvingly. "My what a lovely figure of a woman you are developing into, Lillianna," Mrs. Connor commented, as she began to take Lillianna's measurements. "You are such a wee girl in height; some alterations will probably be necessary. Now, what is your preference as to color?"

"Well, Papa always seems to prefer me in green, a dark shade I think will be better for riding. I like a deep, rich blue or a dark brown."

"I think that I might have one of each in stock; but the brown might be a bit lighter than you would like. I'll bring them all in, and you can try them for your father's approval."

"Mrs. Connor, I shall make the final decision; however, I do value Papa's opinion," Lillianna responded, with a slight raise of one eyebrow, a facial expression that she had, had since babyhood. The greater her resolve, the higher the eyebrow!

As she went out into the store to fetch the outfits, Mrs. Connor chuckled to herself at the implication that the young girl was quite grown-up enough to make her own decisions. She thought to herself that she surely didn't envy a father with the lone responsibility of trying to tame this headstrong little filly. "I fear it can't be done!" she thought.

Lillianna tried on the outfits one by one and went out to model them for John. The doting father "oooed and aaahed" over each one as she came out. She modeled a royal blue one, trimmed out in light gray, with a gray feather on the hat, set at a rakish angle on the left of her head, with the front point of the hat just above what John referred to as her rebellious eyebrow. John's breath caught in his throat when he first saw her. "Oh God, how much you look like my Becca," he thought. The wise father, knowing this to be Lillianna's favorite by the expression on her young face, commented, "I rather prefer this one, Princess, it looks beautiful on you; but the decision is entirely up to you, of course." Mrs. Connor smiled at his wisdom and agreed wholeheartedly.

"This is the one, Papa, without a doubt. I love it." After all the disrobing, redressing, packaging, and paying for the purchases had been completed, Mrs. Connor thanked them and wished them a good-day as they left the store. As John helped Lillianna up into the buggy and loaded the packages behind the seat, she bubbled, "Thank you for my beautiful, new outfit, Papa. Do you really like it?"

"Indeed I do, sweetheart. I truly think it is quite the most beautiful riding habit I have ever seen!"

As they approached the slave market, the busy harbor glistened in the sunlight. Majestic clipper ships borne on the outgoing tide, their crisp white sails unfurled in the wind like flying clouds, headed for faraway places with excited passengers seeking adventure or fortune or perhaps even escape. Dozens of cargo ships of varying tonnage lay at anchor in the harbor, waiting to load, unload, sign on a new crew, or to allow an old crew shore leave before shipping out with cargoes of rice, cotton, indigo, or other merchandise for Liverpool or other distant ports. Lillianna's eyes sparkled as she bubbled, "Oh Papa, look at the beautiful ships. I would love to sail to some romantic port, far across the ocean someday; wouldn't you? Think we ever could?"

"Well, Princess, I don't know about across the ocean; but maybe we could sail up to Boston or New York sometime."

As they drew in closer to the slave market, the more uneasy John became; but Lillianna was actually flushed with excited anticipation. As John reined-in the buggy somewhat back from the unusually small group of buyers, Lillianna urged him to pull in just behind the crowd. John did so, commenting that at this distance he could remain in the buggy with her, yet still participate in the bidding. The auction had already begun; and on the block, stood a handsome ebony toned couple, she with an infant at her breast. The young man glanced anxiously at his young wife and baby as the auctioneer chanted, "And now we have a fine offering for your consideration. They are offered at auction either separately or as a unit. You may be assured that from the loins of this strong, healthy, young stud much more fine stock will be issued. We also have this fine female specimen with many childbearing years ahead of her. The male pickaninny is a bonus you'll get with this one, as it is still at the breast."

Lillianna gazed in revulsion at the shackles and shuddered at the inhumane and degrading chant of the auctioneer. John, however, thinking only in terms of the sort of slave he was seeking, looked on the young black man as perfect for his purposes—handsome, strong, and appearing intelligent of eye. He started to raise his hand to open the bid. Lillianna caught his arm and held it down. With tears in her eyes, she pleaded, "Papa please don't bid on him. If you win the bid, it will separate this family. Please, Papa, please don't" John acquiesced, but determined that he would get this thing over with as quickly as possible, and get Lillianna away from the slave market.

"Damn, you knew you shouldn't bring her here in the first place, John. Why didn't you follow your better judgment?" he chastised himself. The little black family was finally sold as a unit. Lillianna was relieved, as was John, for her sake.

The next slave offered for sale was a light-skinned young black. The young man stood straight and tall, with head held proudly erect, though not in a defiant manner. He scanned the crowd slowly with intelligent looking eyes. As his eyes met John's, John determined to purchase him regardless of the cost. He opened the bidding with a more than reasonable bid. The bid was raised once; but his second bid stood; and the slave was his. He excused himself as he stepped down from the buggy and hastened to the table where final transactions were handled. He quickly made payment and signed the papers of ownership of the slave, whose name was given as Virgil. John made arrangements for the slave to be delivered the following day and was relieved to have this unsavory business behind them as he mounted the buggy and turned it toward the River Road and home.

Lillianna was quiet as their ride began. She was still wiping the tears that continued to flow despite her efforts to stop them. Finally, when she once again felt that she had her emotions under control, she said, without looking at John, "Papa, I never want to go there again; it was horrible! No matter what you say or anyone else says, I know in my heart that it is wrong—no, it is sinful—for anyone to buy or sell or own another human being. They *are human beings*; you know that, Papa!"

After a long pause, John replied, with hesitation, "Sweetheart, in an agricultural economy, such as ours here in the South, slaves are necessary for a plantation owner to be successful."

"The Pinkstons are successful, and they don't own slaves!" She responded angrily.

"Lillianna, I really don't think it wise for us to discuss this further," John said, his anger beginning to rise.

"As you wish, Papa," she replied icily. They rode the remainder of the way home in silence.

As they turned off River Road into the drive approaching Fairlawn, Lillianna said softly, "Papa, I want you to know that even though we don't always agree on everything, I respect you and love you with all my heart; and I always shall. If I hurt you or made you angry, or if I sounded disrespectful, I apologize."

"I know, Princess; and I accept your apology. It should go, even without my saying so, that I adore you now and forever shall! You are a very intelligent young lady. I respect your right to your own opinions. I would like to add though, my dear, don't be surprised if time and maturity find your opinions changing."

She started to reply in denial of that eventuality, but thought better of it as she gave John a kiss on the cheek and smiled at him.

COMING OF AGE (FACING REALITY)

Fall came on apace and found Lillianna, Jane, and Will traveling to Charleston to school each day. The girls enjoyed their studies and meeting new friends. As her horizons were broadening, Lillianna could feel herself maturing rapidly. The three young people enjoyed a lively exchange of ideas as they traveled to and from Charleston. They shared all their youthful hopes and dreams and profound philosophies as intelligent young people are wont to do. A special bond seemed to be growing daily between Will and Lillianna. In his maturity, Will recognized it for what it was becoming; however, she, in her still youthful mind, found it a little disquieting. He was prepared to give her all the time she needed. After all, he was nineteen; and she, only fourteen, albeit a very mature fourteen. Will learned that Lillianna agreed with him on the subject of slavery. He was relieved to know that her feelings were as strong as his. He knew that if and when they should marry, and he felt sure that they would, it would be absolutely imperative that they share the same feelings on this basic Southern tradition, which they both abhorred.

Back home at Fairlawn, Lillianna had finally devised a solution to the problem of continuing Mattie's education. With her new studies requiring so much of her time, she complained that she didn't have much time to spend with Sheba. Zeke had finally turned her horse over to her about two years before, and she usually rode everyday. Under the guise of combining study time and time with Sheba, she asked if she could transfer her studies to the stable tack room. She could ride Sheba, or in inclement weather, spend some time with her; then she could study in the tack room. John agreed to this arrangement, and thus she solved the problem of Mattie's continued education. Weekdays when she came home from Charleston, she donned a casual riding habit, had an afternoon snack, gathered her books, and headed for the stable. She then crept stealthily from the stable down to Mandy's house. There she and Mattie studied in Mattie's room in the front of the house facing the river.

After her first busy year at Miss Hockaday's school, Lillianna welcomed the brief freedom of the summer vacation. She was looking forward to celebrating her fifteenth birthday that summer, was riding Sheba everyday, and attending races at Washington Race Course every time one of the Fairlawn horses raced. John always rode Selam and usually won. Abel, Fairlawn's new jockey and Seth's younger brother, always rode the other horses. He was very good at it, and always placed well. All this racing whetted Lillianna's appetite to participate herself. She began to hatch a wild plan, which no one would ever have believed. She recruited Abel to join in her plan, over his frightened protests. She even let Jane and Will in on the plan, with the admonition that she would need their assistance later. In spite of the skepticism of her three cohorts-in-crime, she could not be dissuaded!

Each day, she and Abel would take Sheba and one of the other racehorses to a remote access road to one of the fields which was lying fallow that summer. She didn't use her side saddle, instead she rode astride Sheba. She and Abel would race the two horses. She always won when she was riding Sheba; but when Abel rode Sheba and she, the other horse, Sheba would lose. Abel didn't really believe that she was a better jockey than he; but he just couldn't understand why he couldn't ride Sheba to a win.

Lillianna, sensing his puzzlement, explained, "Abel, there's no question that you are a much better rider than I. It's just that Sheba doesn't run to win; she just runs because I ask her to run. She is my horse, and she loves me. I believe that I could win with her at the Washington Race Course; I really do!"

"How you gonna manage dat, Miss Lillianna? Mistuh John ain't never gonna allow it!"

"We can do it, Abel; if we plan it right!"

"My Paw's gonna beat de hide off me if I help you do dis!"

"No he won't; he will never know. If he should find out, I won't let him beat you; I'll tell him that I made you do it! Will you help me?"

"I reckun so."

"Good, here's how we'll do it. We'll come down here to race each morning. I'll ride Sheba, and you ride one of the other race horses. Ride a different one from day to day so that Sheba will get accustomed to racing against different horses. I'll get Papa to agree to let you race Sheba during Racing Week in February. The last time that I run Sheba each morning, you won't ride; you will stand well down the road, on the edge of the woods, with a lump of sugar to give her as a reward. She'll start counting on the sugar reward ;

and on the day of the race, after she wins she'll head straight for where you are with the sugar. On that day, the last place she will have seen you will have been the stable; so she'll head for the stable. On the day of the race, you will wear your jockey outfit to the track and sneak an extra one along for me. I'll come to the stable before the race on the pretense of wishing you luck. Then I'll change clothes in a hurry and mount and ride Sheba while you hide in the stable. As soon as I ride Sheba back in after the race, you will mount immediately and return to the track. I'll change back into my clothes in a hurry, return to mix in the crowd, and no one will ever know! Will and Jane will help cover for me."

The more Lillianna revealed of her scheme, the bigger Abel's eyes grew! "It ain't gonna work, Miss Lillianna! I just knows it ain't!"

"Yes it will; you'll see!"

"They ain't never gonna mistake you for me; your skin is too light!"

"Just don't you worry; I have a plan to take care of that too. You're not all that much darker than I am anyway."

During all of June, Lillianna and Abel pursued their plan. She finally talked John into letting Abel race Sheba in February. Each day after lunch she would go down by the river with a quilt and a book, as if to read. Then, in the privacy of Mama's nook, she removed her bonnet, and stretched out with her face turned up into the sunshine and her hands outspread, palms down at her sides. Her face and hands gradually took on a golden glow as the summer wore on.

It was John's habit to ride Selam over the whole plantation frequently. He especially enjoyed riding him into the woods where he found natural obstacles—fallen trees, narrow brooks, and ditches—over which he could jump the graceful Arabian. It was on one of these rides that he happened upon Lillianna and Abel racing. They, busy racing and talking about the plan, were unaware of his presence. He heard enough to know that some devious plot was afoot. He spied long enough to devise their basic plan. He realized, that if he wished to avert an embarrassing disaster, he must take some drastic steps to do so!

One morning in late July, Lillianna and John were having their usual breakfast together. "Princess, you must not be wearing your bonnet or using your parasol to shade your face and hands. I have been noticing that you are beginning to look more like a mulatto than my Lillianna."

"Oh Papa, the sun just feels so good; guess I forget to be careful sometimes. I'm enjoying lots of kisses from Mama, remember?"

"Yes, of course, how could I forget," he answered smiling. "But try to be more careful; that brown face isn't exactly ladylike."

"I shall, Papa, I promise."

"Oh, by the way, Princess; I have a surprise which I think will please you. I knew how very much you would like to race Sheba yourself; so I have talked with the other members of the South Carolina Jockey Club regarding the possibility of a Ladies' Race. It seems there are several other young ladies who have horses which they would like to race themselves. The club finally agreed to a Ladies' Race, preceding the main event, on the last day of Race Week in February. This is to become an annual tradition. A trophy cup will be awarded the winner. It will be inscribed with the name of the rider, the horse, and the year of the race; and will be so inscribed each year. It will, however, remain in the possession of the first winner until some other young lady and her horse succeed in winning it away."

"Papa, Papa, how wonderful!" Lillianna exclaimed, hopping out of her chair and dancing around the room, hugging Delilah and John gleefully. "That trophy is mine for good," she added confidently.

"Best not count your races before they are even run, my girl! Remember, 'Pride goeth before a fall'!" John warned.

"Oh I'm going to win; no doubt about it," she insisted.

"At any rate, it seems there will be ten young ladies riding in the first annual Ladies' Race at the Washington Race Course. The Jockey Club has set some ground rules, however: 1. All participants must be unmarried ladies between the ages of fifteen and twenty; 2. All participants must ride ladies' sidesaddles and be properly attired in formal riding habit; 3. A riding crop may be used, but is not compulsory; 4. Good sportsmanship and ladylike conduct will be observed before, during, and following the race, regardless of the outcome; 5. In the event of an extremely close finish, decision of the Jockey Club Judges will be final."

"It all sounds fair and proper to me. I can't wait to tell my Sheba girl!" As soon as they had finished their breakfast and Lillianna had dressed, she ran to the stable to find Abel to tell him the good news. He was so relieved he almost wept. They continued their morning racing routine with three changes: Lillianna changed to her sidesaddle; the sugar lump decoy was eliminated; and with no further need for secrecy, they did their racing along the River Road. Will and Jane were also relieved to learn that the big doubtful scheme would no longer be necessary. Will was especially happy that his beautiful auburn girl was going to be allowed to fulfill her dream of racing, and he entertained not the slightest doubt that the trophy would be hers. Later, Lillianna would look in retrospect at this time as the happiest period of her young life; and, indeed, as the end of naivete and innocence.

The summer, fall, and early winter of 1831 found Lillianna busy with preparations for the big Race Week in February. In the fall, she and Jane would begin their second year at Miss Hockaday's finishing school; and would no longer be lowly first year plebeians in the pecking-order of the school hierarchy. Most exciting of all, her fifteenth birthday was pending in August. She had always exhibited a maturity beyond her actual years, so she had passed that gawky age of adolescence sooner than most. She was gaining the full blown beauty of womanhood and feeling all the wonderful awakenings that go with that time. This period should have held some of Lillianna's happiest memories, and it would have except for two deeply traumatic occurrences which would change her life forever. The first would force her to face the deepest grief she had experienced thus far. The second would truly mark an end to her childlike innocence and would result in her *coming-of-age*.

August brought the hottest weather Charlestonians had experienced in years. With the heat, came the dreaded yellow fever. It soon reached epidemic proportions, and few families were spared the loss of one or more members. Among the victims stricken at Fairlawn, were John's youngest son Luke, and the older of Warren and Martha's two sons, Warry, as well as Samuel and Mattie. Although Samuel and Mattie survived, Luke and Warry died. At Pink Hill, they were even less fortunate. Eight people died—one entire tenant family, father, mother, and five children. Most tragic of all, the Pinkstons lost the younger of their two remaining children, the gentle and fragile Jane. The Prendles and Pinkstons, though grief stricken, had borne great loss before. The Prendles, of course, had lost their beloved Becca. The Pinkstons had lost their two younger sons during the previous yellow fever epidemic. So, stoically, the two families buried their dead and prepared to go on with their lives.

However, such was not the case with Lillianna. The deaths of her beloved brother Luke, her precious nephew, Warry, and her dear friend Jane were the first deep, gut-wrenching losses Lillianna had ever experienced. Her grief was so deep that she had been unable to shed even a tear, and it had cast a pall over her entire world. She lapsed into a deep melancholia and languished in her room most of the time. As the opening date for school approached, she had no enthusiasm for it at all and had determined not to return. John and the family tried to reason with her that death is always a part of life, and that when it occurs, those who are left must go on with life. All their efforts were to no avail.

Realizing that Lillianna was growing worse daily, John grew increasingly desperate to find someone or something that could help her. Knowing that having grown up together Lillianna and Mattie had always been very close, John went to Mattie to ask if she had any ideas which might help. She told John that in their many long talks, Lillianna had frequently spoken of her deep affection for Will Pinkston and how much she admired and respected everything about him. Realizing that in revealing this to John, she had violated Lillianna's confidence; nevertheless, though she regretted having to do so, she also realized the importance of getting help for her friend in any way that she could.

Finally, knowing the Pinkston family's own loss and grief, regretfully, John went to Pink Hill to ask Will to visit Lillianna to see if he could say or do anything that might help jolt her back to reality. As he was ushered into the study where Will sat reading, John immediately apologized for his intrusion upon the Pinkston family during their time of mourning. "Will, were we as a family not at our wit's end in trying to deal with Lillianna and her depression, I would never have considered calling on you for assistance at this time. I realize that you and your parents have suffered as grievous a loss as ours; but I am truly afraid that if a way is not soon found to turn her around, we might indeed lose her as well. I know of the deep respect she has for you, and I have learned of the great influence you have upon her. I am here to ask if you would be willing to come visit her to see if you might be able to prevail where we have failed."

"Mr Prendle, no apology is necessary, sir. I can't imagine that I might succeed where all of her loving family have failed; but I shall be more than happy to come and try to help."

Will arrived at Fairlawn midmorning the following day.

His drawn face bore witness to the depth of his own grief. Not only had he lost his dear friend Luke; but Jane's death had left a tremendous void in his life. He had always been big brother and guardian angel to his baby sister. Lillianna had eaten breakfast with John in virtual silence and had immediately returned to her bedroom. From the foyer, John pointed to the door of Lillianna's room on the balcony above; and, setting aside all the protocol of propriety, he asked Will to go up alone. Will took the steps hurriedly, two at a time; and when he reached Lillianna's door, he knocked softly, saying, "Lillianna, it's Will."

"Come in," came her almost inaudible reply. She sat beside the front window in her dressing gown, brushing her hair absentmindedly as she looked out over the lawn and down toward the river. The sun shone across her auburn hair; and Will thought it quite the most beautiful picture he had ever beheld. As he stored the scene in his treasure chest of precious memories, she turned to face him. His heart wrenched at the lifeless and terribly sad look in her brown eyes.

He rushed over to her as she stood; he took her in his arms, cradling her head to his chest. "Oh, my beautiful little auburn hair, where is the sparkle in those brown eyes that always warms my heart?" The words came pouring out, quite beyond his control. "I know I shouldn't say this now; you are still so very young. But I believe you know, and have somehow always known, that I love you. I love you with all my heart." As he held her ever closer, stroking her hair, he pleaded, "sweetheart, allow yourself to weep; let your tears purge the pain!"

She sobbed, "Oh Will." Clinging to each other in their grief, they both wept.

After a long time, Will stepped back; and holding her at arm's length, he wiped her tears as he said, smiling through his own tears, "Now little one, we have some things to talk about."

"First, remember you are not alone in your grief. You have many people who love you and share it. We must all help each other through this. Secondly, if you don't go back to school, neither will I. I can't face that ride alone each day. I have only one young lady to cherish and protect now; I need you, Lillianna. You must be my sunshine. Will you?"

"Yes Will, I promise I will. I . . ."

Putting his fingers to her lips, he said, "Hush now, my little Auburn. It isn't necessary to say more. My words, although sincere, came unbidden and at a very inappropriate time. Just keep them in your heart and think about them and all that they imply for our future. There will be plenty of time to speak of all the things we feel later."

After Will's visit, there was a marked change in Lillianna. As her enthusiasm for life gradually returned, she seemed to be moving forward with a maturity the family had not seen before. She returned to her training with Sheba and Abel for the big race in February. With Delilah's help, she surveyed her school wardrobe and had it readied by the time school reopened.

She and Will returned to school with a new closeness, so subtle that it went unobserved by their families; but the two of them were keenly aware of the change. On that first day of school, Will had arrived at Fairlawn at the usual time to pick her up. As they pulled away from the house, she noticed a secretive little smile just behind his eyes. He circled the oval and drove up the long driveway. However, when they reached River Road, instead of turning right toward Charleston, Will turned left and pulled into the little alcove beside the river. "What are you up to Will Pinkston?" Lillianna asked, looking around directly into his eyes.

"I have a little back-to-school gift for you that I purchased in Charleston on the day after I visited you in your bedroom," he replied, handing her a small package done up in beautiful paper and tied with a perky bow. "That day you were brushing that beautiful auburn hair in the sunlight as I entered your room. The sight took my breath away; I shall never forget it! The next day, I went into town in search of this gift."

Lillianna opened the package with her typical delight and found a lovely pair of mother-of-pearl combs for her hair. "Oh Will, they are so beautiful; thank you so much," She said giving him a quick kiss on the lips. As their lips parted, she looked into his eyes as her own filled with tears. "Every time I put them in my hair, I shall remember this moment; and I will cherish them forever!"

As Will pulled out of the alcove and back onto River Road, Lillianna moved closer to him and linked her arm through his. They didn't talk at all on the ride into Charleston; they had no need for conversation. In those beautiful moments of silence, there was an intimate communication between them on a far deeper level—a level which transcended mere conversation.

The second traumatic occurrence, mentioned earlier, was even more difficult in many ways than the tragedy of the epidemic. It created as great a change in Lillianna as had the first; and it sealed forever her *coming-of-age*.

After school started, she resumed her home schooling for Mattie as before. It was early in October that the two girls were studying in Mattie's bedroom one afternoon. They heard Delilah and Mandy coming up the walk to Mandy's house. They sat down in the rocking chairs on the front porch. The windows of the bedroom were open; so the girls signaled each other to be silent. As the two women talked, the girls could hear their conversation clearly.

"Honey has you thought anymo' 'bout what we was talkin' 'bout?"

"What's that Mama?"

"'Bout if you gonna tell Mattie 'dat Matthew is her papa. She be fifteen now, and I think she got a right to know, 'dat's what!"

"Mama, she has never asked me anything about her papa.

I think she probably just believes he's one of the slaves down in the quarters."

"She be smart, Mandy. Don' you 'spose she wonduh why you so black and she be so light. Ain' no light slaves down there."

By this time, Lillianna and Mattie were looking at each other mystified. "Mama, I don't know how Mattie would take it. Mister John would never accept it. Miss Becca was always good to me. She risked a lot just educating me secretly; she was there to help me herself when Mattie was born; then she saw to it that Mattie and I were freed and given a home. She did enough for us. If she had felt it should be told, she would have told Mister John herself." The two girls in the bedroom sat looking at each other wide-eyed, with the direction this conversation seemed to be taking. "I don't want to ever cause Matthew any trouble. We are deeply in love; and we have enough just the way things are, even though everything has to be done in secret. I'm just not willing to risk losing that. Matthew loves Mattie, and she loves him. He's always careful of what's best for her; he was terrified she would die when she had the fever. He and I know she's our child, and we love her. That's enough; isn't it?"

At that revelation, the stunned girls embraced each other in tears. Barely able to maintain the silence they both knew was necessary, each had her own inner feelings of shock, indignation, and even anger. Nevertheless, both shared a measure of happiness at realizing their kinship. "Lord," Lillianna whispered, "Mattie, I'm your aunt!" At that, both girls had to suppress a giggle.

Delilah said, "Mandy, what I'se hearin' soun's lak pure selfishness t'me. She still got a right t'know!"

"Mama, I'll have to think about it some more, and talk to Matthew about it. The two of us will decide what's best."

"'Das up to yaw'l, but you knows how me an' yo' papa

feels 'bout it. Now, Ah ain' nevuh gonna say nuthin' to you 'bout it agin!"

As Delilah and Mandy sat rocking on the porch in silence, Lillianna motioned to Mattie that she was going to sneak out the back way and go home. She kissed Mattie's cheek, gave her another hug, turned, and tiptoed out.

CHAPTER FOUR

DARK SECRET

As she headed back to the house by way of the stables, her mind was a-tumble with a hundred thoughts; and her heart raced at the thoughts. By the time she reached the stables, her thoughts had jelled into an overpowering anger at Matt, the gentlest and most loving of all her brothers, always her favorite. As she entered the tack room, the sobs came; and as fate would have it, there stood Matt! "Matt, how could you keep this secret all these years? Why weren't you man enough to stand up and say, 'I love Mandy, and Mattie is my child'? How could you allow them to feel like slaves all these years? I know it's true; Mattie and I were in her bedroom; and Mandy and Wilah were talking on the porch about it. We heard it all! I'll always love you, Matt; but I can never respect you again!"

"Lillianna, I . . ." but his words were lost to her, as she turned and ran out of the stable and up to the house, sobbing.

Stunned, Matthew closed the tack room door, and sat down. He sat there for a long time, numb and unable to even think, with his hands clasped, head down, and gazing at the floor. Finally, when he was able to start to think again, his mind traveled back to the earliest time he had become aware of Mandy as more than a slave. At the time, he was eighteen; and she was twenty-seven.

It was early spring at Fairlawn; and planning to take a horseback ride before time to get down to the day's work with his Father and four younger brothers, Matt Prendle arose very early. He went down to the kitchen out back for a quick breakfast that morning. Delilah and Mandy were busily preparing the breakfast fare for the family. Only dinner at Fairlawn was a formal, family-sit-down-together meal. Delilah spread the breakfast and lunch fare, buffet style, on the dining room sideboard; and everyone ate as their daily schedule permitted. As Matt entered the busy kitchen, he apologized, "I know I'm a mite early for you ladies this morning; so if the grits are ready, I'll just have a bowl of grits with butter, a biscuit with a little honey, and a cup of coffee."

"It's perfectly all right, Mister Matt. I'll be glad to fix it for you," Mandy replied, smiling.

Matt watched her as she moved about the kitchen preparing the breakfast he had requested and thought, "Mandy is truly a fine figure of a woman." She served him and he relished the food, and the view, as he continued to watch her work while he was eating. He finished his breakfast, thanked the two slaves for a "delicious breakfast," and headed for the stables, his favorite place on the plantation. Even in his boyhood, the tack room had been one of his habitual retreats, especially in the early morning or after dinner in the evening.

After Matt returned from his ride that morning, he went back up to the house and to his room to change into clothes for his workday. As he approached the door to his bedroom, he could hear someone humming a little tune inside the room. He approached quietly and saw that Mandy was making his bed, dusting, and cleaning the room as she did each morning. Enjoying her singing and admiring her tiny waist, encircled by a sparkling white apron, he noticed the way her hips swayed back and forth beneath her skirt as she moved rhythmically around the room; and he was surprised at the unexpected stirring he felt within himself. As she stood beside the window reaching up to dust the frame, her cap of black curls, her beautiful profile, and the curve of her rounded breasts made Matt's breath catch in his throat. He thought that she looked like an African princess. "My God, Matt," he thought, "pull yourself together, and forget it!"

As Mandy turned to pick up her cleaning equipment, she saw Matt. "Oh, I didn't know you were there, Mister Matt. I'm all finished; I was just leaving. Your room is all ready." She came out and moved down the hall toward Luke's room to continue her morning cleaning. Matt went into his room, closed the door, and leaned against it trying to gather his composure before he dressed for work.

In the weeks ahead, Matthew couldn't get the thoughts of Mandy out of his head during the day, nor out of his dreams at night. He tried in vain to reason with himself that it was wrong as well as impossible. He thought, "I could just take her; she wouldn't resist—couldn't, after all she is just a slave!" However, he had to admit to himself that what he was feeling was more than lust—much more! She would have to want him too. "Oh, dear God in heaven, I'm falling in love with her," he had to admit. "Forget it Matt, it can never be!" For a few days, he struggled to get her out of his mind; and it seemed it might be working. Then the nights and his dreams would bring her back.

He found himself arising very early each morning in order to eat his breakfast in the kitchen where she would be working. Late in the evening after riding, he stayed in the tack room, cleaning and treating his saddle and boots until it was dark. He would return to the house by way of a path that took him past the household slave quarters behind the kitchen. The window of Mandy's room was in clear view from the path. At this time of the evening, she had finished her day's chores and was taking her bath in a big oaken tub in her room by the dim light of her oil lamp. No matter how he tried to resist, he found himself stopping to watch her through the slats in her shutters as he stood quietly in the darkness. He watched her bathe her beautiful ebony body, watched how the rivulets of water trickled down between her perfect breasts, watched until she stepped from the tub, dried off, and put on her nightgown—thin enough for him to admire her body as the lamplight shone through the fabric. The beautiful sight of her body always brought to his mind the Song of Solomon, "I am black, but comely . . . look not upon me, because I am black, because the sun hath looked upon me . . . while the king sitteth at his table, my spikenard sendeth forth the smell thereof. A bundle of myrrh is my wellbeloved unto me; he shall lie all night betwixt my breasts . . . Behold, thou art fair, my love; behold, thou art fair; thou hast doves' eyes. Within thy locks: Thy hair is as a flock of goats, that appear from Mount Gilead. Thy teeth are like a flock of sheep that even shorn, which came up from the washing; whereof every one bear twins . . . Thy lips are like a thread of scarlet, and thy speech is comely: thy temples are like a piece of a pomegranate within thy locks. Thy neck is like the tower of David builded for an armoury, . . . Thy two breasts are like two young roes that are twins, which feed among the lilies." As desire rose in him, he turned away and walked slowly to the house, feeling dirty for his lust and hating himself for his weakness and for his blasphemous perversion of God's Holy Word. Although Matt had been taught that the Song of Solomon made reference to the Church's love unto Christ and of His, unto Her, he had never quite believed that it was anything but a beautiful love song between a man and a woman. What's more, he had never thought that there was anything evil or dirty about such a book's being a part of the Bible!

One night, desire overpowered his reason; and he went into the breezeway between Mandy's room and the kitchen.

He tapped lightly on her door. When she opened it, he stepped inside, took her in his arms, and kissed her. "Mandy, I've wanted you for so long; I had to come."

She didn't resist; she just closed the door behind him and started to remove her gown, saying, "You know I'm yours for the taking; you own me."

Matthew stepped back in shock and more than a little shame. "Mandy, I love you; I mean it; and I will never take you until and unless you feel the same way." As he turned to leave, he asked, "May I come in some night for a visit—just to talk, and to get to know more about each other and how we each feel about everything, not just about each other?"

"Come anytime; I'd like that too," she answered, with a smile, as she stood on tiptoe to give him a soft kiss on the cheek as he turned and left.

Matt resigned himself to the fact that he had reached the point of no return in this; and in spite of the fact that he saw all the problems ahead, his heart was singing as he went to sleep in peace for the first night in many weeks.

For weeks, Matt stopped to visit in Mandy's room nearly every night. They grew closer and closer as they came to really know each other. He was amazed at the extent of her education and at her profound thinking on subjects which he had never imagined she even considered. When he inquired how this had come to be, she said, "Your mother has seen to it that I was fully educated and that I had access to the entire library at home when we were girls. I might add that she did this with no regard for the consequences to herself. You are well aware that my education was against the law. I have always been more thankful for my education and the opportunities she gave me than for any other single thing in my entire life—until now. These long talks which you and I have had, the depth of feeling you obviously have for me, but most of all the respect you show me, all mean more to me than anything ever has." Although they sometimes held hands as they talked, Matt waited for her to offer herself in love to him. He never touched her more than a brief good night kiss; but he realized, somehow she had also begun to fall in love with him. Then one night as he started to leave, she put her arms around his neck and kissed him passionately. "Stay," she whispered.

"Are you sure?" he asked.

"Yes, Matt, I'm sure; I love you."

When it was done and their passion had ebbed, he still held her close in his arms for a long time. He whispered, "My darling Mandy, I had no idea you were still a virgin."

She answered, "Yes Matt, I have been waiting to find love."

"So have I, my love, so have I," he replied. "Have I ever told you that in all those weeks I watched you secretly, in my heart I could hear ringing the words of the Song Of Solomon? Could that have been blasphemy, when I love you so much?"

"No, Matt, not in any way," Mandy began to quote—now again the Song of Solomon, "My beloved put in his hand by the hole of the door, and my bowels were moved for him. I rose up to open to my beloved; and my hands dropped with myrrh, and my fingers with sweet smelling myrrh, upon the handles of the lock. I opened to my beloved . . . My beloved is white and ruddy, the chiefest among ten thousand. His head is as the most fine gold, his locks are bushy, and black as a raven. He eyes are as the eyes of doves by the rivers of waters, and fitly set. His cheeks are as a bed of spices, as sweet flowers: his lips like lilies, dropping sweet with sapphires. His legs are as pillars of marble, set upon sockets of fine gold: his countenance is as Lebanon, excellent as the cedars. His mouth is most sweet: yea, he is altogether lovely. This is my beloved, and this is my friend . . ."

Matt responded, "How beautiful are thy feet with shoes, O prince's daughter! The joints of thy thighs are like jewels, the work of the hands of a cunning workman. Thy navel is like a round goblet, which wanteth not liquor: thy belly is like an heap of wheat set about with lilies. Thy two breasts are like two young roes that are twins. Thy neck is as a tower of ivory; thine eyes like the fishpools in Heshbon, by the gate of Bathrabbim: thy nose is as the tower of Lebanon which looketh toward Damascus . . ." As he spoke he began to caress her body again, lovingly, reverently, "Thine head upon thee is like Carmel, and the hair of thine head like purple; the king is held in the galleries. How fair and how pleasant art thou, O love, for delights! This thy stature is like to a palm tree, and thy breasts to clusters of grapes. I said, I will go up to the palm tree, I will take hold of the boughs thereof: now also thy breasts shall be as clusters of the vine, and the smell of thy nose like apples; And the roof of thy mouth like the best wine for my beloved, that goeth down sweetly, causing the lips of those that are asleep to speak. I am my beloved's, and her desire is toward me. Come, my beloved, let us go forth . . ." Matt quoted, as they again reached the peak of their desire and kissed passionately. "If it be blasphemy, God please forgive us! I will love you forever, Mandy."

"And I, you, Matthew!" They stayed in each others arms until near dawn, when Matt left quietly for the house.

Unknown ever to Matt, was Delilah's conversation with Mandy the morning after that last visit to Mandy's room. "Honey, 'dese walls is thin; your papa and me heard it all last night. Be careful; 'dis cain't go nowhere but right in 'dat room; you knows 'dat! Mistuh Matt cain't never be hurt; and nobody else can know, never!"

"I know Mama; I know," Mandy replied, her eyes filling with tears.

For five years, Matt and Mandy continued like this—only in her room, except for a few stolen kisses here and there when they were sure no one was around to see. Delilah and Samuel never gave any indication to Matt that they knew anything that was going on. Late in the fifth year of their relationship, Mandy discovered she was pregnant. She and Delilah discussed the situation at length and decided to let everyone believe it had been fathered by some slave down in the quarters, pretending that it could be one of several and that they didn't know which one. When she told Matt of her condition and of the decision she and Delilah had made, he protested violently; but Mandy persisted. Matt finally agreed to her plan, but insisted on telling his mother the whole story. He was very close to Becca, and he knew she would understand.

When Matt told Becca, she wept, embraced him, and agreed to go along with their plan. "Son, I will do everything I can to help Mandy with this. I promise you that I will see to it that John gives Mandy, Delilah, Samuel, and your child their freedom. I know him; he will honor my request without question. I'll also see to it that he gives them jobs with a wage, some land, and a furnished house. No name will be revealed as to the identity of the father. Mandy, Delilah, and Samuel will insist that they have no idea. It isn't very flattering to Mandy; but under the circumstances, we have no other choice. Your father could never accept the truth, and we certainly don't want a lie on the birth records." Matt was crushed at the thought of what he regarded, and what he knew Mandy would regard, as a terrible shame. Although this kind of birth situation was recorded frequently among plantation slaves, he hated the thought of it for his and Mandy's child and blamed himself for putting them in this position. Little did Becca know that she would soon be pregnant again and that her requests of John would have to come so soon!

When Mandy went into labor, Becca, already pregnant with Lillianna, stayed with Delilah, by Mandy's side until the time came to summon the midwife. She sent Matt to get her; and when they returned, she asked him to wait outside in the breezeway. It was a long labor and a difficult delivery; and Matt, sitting helplessly outside, could hear Mandy's screams. With tears coursing down his face, he suffered his own agony.

When Mandy's little girl had finally been delivered and her room put back in order, Becca went out and sent Matt to tell Samuel about his new granddaughter and to ask him to drive the midwife home. She had also asked Matt to return to Mandy's room after he had spoken to Samuel. When he returned, his mother was sitting in one of the rocking chairs in the breezeway; and she sent him into Mandy's room. When he entered, Delilah placed his baby girl in his arms, smiled, kissed his cheek, and left the room, closing the door behind her. She sat in the chair beside Becca's; and the two of them sat there talking, rocking, and keeping watch to assure the little family in the room complete privacy.

Weeping, Matt gazed at his baby girl in adoration and kissed her. He placed her in Mandy's arms. "She is almost as beautiful as her mother," he said. "Thank you, darling, for my beautiful daughter.

Matt kissed her tenderly; and smiling through her own tears, she said, "Matt, I want to name her Mattie, if that's all right with you. When you get married, you can still use your name for your first son."

Matt replied, "I'd love for you to name her Mattie; and as for marriage, I am already married, my sweet, to the only woman I'll ever love or marry!"

Mandy smiled at his words, "Oh Matt, I love you so; and I always will. Nothing could make me happier than knowing you consider me your wife."

Matt said, "It's time we made it official before God, each other, and our mothers." He went to the door and asked Becca and Delilah to come in to witness something he and Mandy were about to do. They entered, and Matt closed the door. He went back to the bed, knelt beside Mandy, and took her hand in his. They looked into each others eyes; and with their baby between them, they exchanged the tender and traditional marriage vows.

When they had finished, Becca said, "What God hath joined together let no man put asunder."

"Amen," she and Delilah closed in unison.

In the tack room, Matt reluctantly snapped back from his warm reminiscence to the present and to cruel reality. "Oh Lord, help me to know how to handle this situation. Mandy, Delilah, Samuel, and I should talk about what we must do next with regard to what Lillianna and Mattie now know to be the truth." Late that evening he went to Delilah's and Samuel's room and asked them to accompany him to Mandy's house. They all had something important to decide he told them. When the three arrived at Mandy's house, Mattie had already gone to bed; so they went to the kitchen, closed the door and sat around the kitchen table to hear what Matt had to tell them. He took Mandy's hand and started," Apparently, Mattie and Lillianna were in Mattie's bedroom this afternoon when you and Delilah were talking on the porch. They heard the whole conversation. Lillianna is quite angry with me and terribly upset that I've allowed this to be kept a secret all these years. She feels I've let you and Mattie feel like slaves all this time, even though you're both free. I must admit that inside I agree with her in a way." He hung his head in dejection as the other three protested his words.

Mandy said, "Matt, we've done it the only way we could for everyone's sake, ours included." Delilah and Samuel nodded in agreement.

Delilah said, "Well, Mistuh Matt, they knows now, and we cain't change it!"

Samuel spoke, for the first time, "We must get 'de girls and talk to 'em as soon as we can, before Miss Lillianna tells anybody. We got to tell 'em it cain't go no further. Mistuh John, cain't never know; he just would never accept it. Ain' no tellin' what would happen if he knowed!"

"You right Samuel," Delilah added, "Mandy go git Mattie

up, and I'se goin' to 'de house to git Miss Lillianna now. We gotta talk tonight!"

They all agreed as Delilah rushed out the back door, thinking all the way to the house that she hoped Lillianna hadn't already told John. Delilah crossed the small outside dining terrace and entered the house through the door to the small breakfast alcove. She tiptoed through the dining room and foyer and up the stairway to Lillianna's room. She opened the door quietly, entered, and closed it behind her. She went over to the bed and gently shook Lillianna, "Wake up, honey, and don' say nuthin'. Put on your robe and come with me; tiptoe all de' way."

Lillianna, though puzzled, did as she was told. Delilah closed the door as they came out; and they both retraced Delilah's steps back out onto the terrace on tiptoes. When they were outside, Delilah whispered that they were having an important meeting down at Mandy's house. Suddenly Lillianna thought she knew what this meeting was going to be about, but she said nothing.

Matt had not arrived for dinner earlier that evening, but the family had just thought that maybe he had gone for a ride and hadn't yet returned. Saying that she had some reading she needed to do, Lillianna had eaten lightly, asked to be excused, and had gone to her room. She had dressed for bed early; and after she had said her prayers, she had climbed into bed and had cried herself to sleep.

When Lillianna and Delilah arrived at Mandy's house, the others were waiting for them in the neatly furnished parlor. Lillianna went over and sat beside Mattie, taking her hand in her own. The girls sat there waiting for someone to speak. Finally, Mandy spoke, "We know that you both heard Mama and me talking this afternoon; and that you know that Matt is Mattie's father. What you may not realize is that Matt and I are deeply in love and that we both love you dearly, Mattie. It was never Matt's idea to keep this a secret. In fact, he insisted on telling your mother, Lillianna. For this reason, Mattie and I were freed; and Mama and Papa were offered their freedom; but they didn't want to accept the offer. Mattie and I were given this nice piece of land with this lovely furnished house, at your mother's request on her deathbed. Mister John didn't ask why; he just honored her request. She never wanted him to know because she knew he could never accept it. For that reason, Mama and I refused to let Matt tell anyone else ever; and he has honored our wishes. It is best for everybody, probably especially for Mattie and for me, that this secret never got beyond the people in this room. Lillianna you must not blame Matt. He is an honorable man and a wonderful father and husband. You see we spoke our wedding vows before God on the night you were born, Mattie. Mama and Miss Becca were our witnesses. In fact, your mother spoke the final words after our vows, 'What God hath joined together, let no man put asunder. Amen.' Now Mattie, give your Aunt Lillianna a hug, your grandma, grandpa, papa, and mama a good night kiss; and let's all go to bed and get some sleep; it's late. Girls we trust that you both understand and agree that we must all let this remain a secret from everyone except the six of us. Agreed?"

"Yes ma'am," the girls replied.

On that night, Lillianna made her peace with it all. Before she left, she kissed Matt and said, "I didn't understand, Matt. I'm so sorry for the ugly things I said this afternoon. I didn't mean them."

"It's all right, princess. I know how you must have felt. You and I love each other and always will. We both know that, and that's all that counts. Isn't it?"

"Yes, Matt, it is; and you're still my favorite brother," she said, smiling.

The subject was never broached again, and the daily routines went on as usual. No longer just best friends, but aunt and niece, Lillianna and Mattie felt an even stronger bond for the rest of their lives.

School resumed the following week uneventfully. Lillianna wanted so very much to share with Will the things she had learned about Mattie. She knew that he of all people would understand and keep her confidence; but she had given her word, which was, throughout the rest of her life, inviolable. She knew that the time would come eventually when she would be free to share all things with Will.

Although it was mid-semester, Will had been turning something over in his mind that he had been considering ever since the yellow fever epidemic. Over the years, he had seen so many people die of that horrible plague while all the forces of known medicine were forced to stand by helplessly. The Medical School of Charleston, founded by the local Medical Society, had been open since 1821 and was thriving. The Pinkston plantation, always run primarily by tenant farmers, could operate very efficiently without his assistance. His father, still in very good health, was more than able to manage it alone. Will found himself thinking about switching from an academic course of study to medicine. He already had an excellent academic background; and he felt a strong desire to educate himself for a place of real service to mankind. Dr. Gilmore was getting up in years, and would soon be needing an assistant who would be able to assume his practice eventually. Will had talked to him about his thinking, and Dr. Gilmore was in full agreement. In fact, he offered to let Will study with him while he was attending medical school. Will's father was not only in full agreement, but was very pleased with his plan. Will knew there was one more person who must agree, or he would never pursue the plan further. When he talked with Lillianna about it, she agreed enthusiastically. "Will, I want you always to be and do everything that will make you feel fulfilled. Any woman who is ever fortunate enough to become your wife can count herself blessed with a truly noble and selfless husband."

As they rode into Charleston and continued to discuss

the subject, no longer a woman but once again a girl, Lillianna asked rather shyly, "Will, if we ever marry, after you are a doctor, would I be Mrs. Dr.William Pinkston?"

"No love, you'd just be Mrs. William Pinkston; wouldn't that be enough?"

"Quite enough!" She responded, with a coy smile.

"Oh my little Auburn Hair, you make my heart smile always. One moment you have the wisdom of a woman, and the next you're again a girl. Please promise me you'll never quite grow up—even when we are old and gray!"

Will took the steps necessary to switch over to medical school immediately. With this change, his studies became much more demanding; so Lillianna was unable to spend as much time with him. In fact, their time together consisted almost solely of the rides to and from school. She missed their long talks, but she understood the importance of his studies. The Christmas holidays and the gala New Year's Ball came and went; then came the inevitable lull that brings winter depression to everyone. Final preparations for Race Week in February brought welcome work and a frenzy of excitement due in large part to the advent of the Ladies' Race. Lillianna could hardly wait for the big day to arrive. The third week of February finally arrived; and with it, the highlight of the winter season for all of Charleston, Race Week! Each day of the week, preliminary races were held; and each evening, dinner parties and dances were held in the fine homes of Charleston's elite. The climax of the week, Trophy-Race Day, fell on the last Saturday. Lillianna awakened that morning excited beyond all reason. She arose very early; and after her prayers, her talk with Mama, and breakfast with Papa, she headed for the stables. She personally attended to every detail herself, from Sheba's currying to the soaping and buffing of her saddle, bridle, and reins. As soon as Sheba measured up to her requirements, she went to the house for a light midmorning snack, her bath, and her own dressing preparations. Her riding habit had been hanging in her room all week, with the gray plumed hat on the hat form on her dressing table, and her highly polished riding boots on the floor underneath. When she had finally bathed, dried off, powdered, perfumed, and donned her undergarments, she paused to admire her beautifully maturing figure in the mirror. "Not bad, Auburn Hair, not bad," she said as she smiled at her usage of Will's name for her. "Oh Will, I hope you'll have time away from your studies to be at the race today. It wouldn't mean a thing without you!" She was startled to hear herself say such a thing, and even more startled to realize the truth of it. "Oh Lord, Will, how I've come to love you!"

Delilah came in about that time to help her finish dressing and caught her admiring herself in the mirror. "Betcha I know what you thinkin," she said chuckling, "and it ain't 'bout no hoss race; and yes ma'am, he'd be thinkin' you a beauty!"

"Oh Wilah, no such thing; I was just wondering if my riding habit will still fit," Lillianna fibbed.

"Uh huh!" Delilah grunted.

When she was fully dressed, every auburn curl in place, and the plumed hat perched saucily on her head, there was a knock on her door. "Princess, may I come in?"

"Yes, please do come in, Papa."

"Oh my goodness, you take my breath away; you look gorgeous," he raved.

"Thank you, Papa; I am ready to go. May I take your arm, kind sir?"

"I would be honored, Miss Prendle," John replied, offering her his arm.

"Well I tell ya' one thing, ain't gonna be no riduhs there as handsome as yaw'l is," Delilah complimented them with pride.

When they reached the track, the first person she saw was Will as he parked his buggy. She ran over to him, gave him a hug and quick kiss on the cheek, and bubbled, "Oh

Will, I'm so glad you could come. I'm so excited I could burst!"

"I wouldn't have missed this for anything in the world," he replied as he went to the back of his buggy and took out a big bouquet of magnolias and wisteria.

"Will, where in the world did you . . . how?" she trailed off as she covered her mouth with her hands in disbelief and with her eyes as big as saucers.

"Remember my promise on your tenth birthday? Well, I'm not your husband yet; but I was determined to give you the bouquet I promised. Mrs. Bracken's Flower Shop had them brought in by packet from New Orleans; so I am counting on you to win this race! By the way, you are absolutely beautiful, Miss Prendle."

"And you, Mr. Pinkston, are quite the handsomest and most wonderful gentleman I have ever known," she replied, with stars in her eyes, as she kissed his cheek again, her lips lingering there for a moment.

The secondary races were run first; and Abel placed well with the Fairlawn horse he rode. John won the Main Race with Selam; and then it was time for the big Ladies' Race.

As the ladies and their mounts lined up at the starting gate, a hush fell over the crowd; and everyone who could, found a place along the rail. Will pushed his way in right at the starting gate. One could feel the tension in the air; in fact, truth be known, this was in actuality the main race of the day. Just before the starting gun was fired, Lillianna's eyes met Will's, and he threw her a good luck kiss. She caught it with a kiss back to him with puckered lips. The gun was fired; and the horses were off, throwing up a cloud of red dust. Lillianna and Sheba stayed abreast of the other two horses leading the field. The competing two riders whipped their horses frantically with their riding crops; Lillianna, leaning forward and speaking into Sheba's ear said, "Just stay with them, my sweet," and stay she did. About two thirds of the distance around the track, Lillianna decided to make her move. "Now, Sheba girl, now! Let 'em eat your dust!" she shouted, flicking the reins. Sheba pulled away and was leading the field—one length, two lengths, three lengths—and as she crossed the finish line, they won the race by a full four lengths. No contest!

Lillianna was presented the trophy at the judges stand, and was promised the plaque for the trophy as soon as it could be engraved. John lifted her down from the saddle with a proud hug and a hearty congratulations as she whispered in his ear, "See Papa, I told you I would win!" However, she accepted all other congratulations with a properly modest, "Thank you, I thought all the ladies rode an excellent race. I was just the lucky one today." John was hard-pressed not to laugh aloud at this fake modesty. Lillianna went to Sheba, pulled her head down, and kissed her nose, saying, "Thank you, Sheba girl. I love you!"

At the end of the line of well wishers stood Will, smiling broadly. He presented her the beautiful bouquet, took her in his arms, and gave her a far more than brotherly kiss, full on the lips; then he whispered, "Congratulations Mrs. Doctor William Pinkston to be." Lillianna blushed with pleasure, as her Father observed it all with more than a little apprehension.

That night after she was in bed, Lillianna thought back over the exciting events of the day. She was somewhat surprised that the highlight of the day was not the race, not winning the trophy, not all the congratulations and attention, but was Will's bouquet, his kiss, and above all, his final whispered comment. She drifted off to sleep smiling at the memory.

Back to the routine of school the following week, Lillianna felt anew the loss of Jane's companionship. Will was ever busier with his studies; consequently, she and Mattie were spending more and more time together. The girls shared their thoughts and deepest feelings on all the weighty subjects that teenage girls find important. Of course, love and romance were subjects that surfaced almost daily.

One afternoon as the girls sat talking on one of the marble benches in the oval across from the piazza, Virgil came out, crossed the piazza, and carefully polished the brass trim on the blackamoor and then all the brass trim on the front entrance. When he had finished, he reentered the foyer and disappeared. "Lillianna, isn't he absolutely the most handsome man you have ever laid your eyes on?" Mattie asked dreamily.

"Mattie, are you meaning what I think you're meaning?"

"Yep, that I am!" They dissolved into giggles.

Lillianna added, "By the way, to answer your question Mattie, no he's not the most handsome man I've ever laid my eyes on. As handsome as he is, he can't touch Will!"

"Well, I might have known you would think that!" Mattie answered petulantly.

After Virgil had gone back into the foyer, he peeked out at the two girls talking in the oval out front. Actually, he found Mattie as appealing as she found him; and he was gratified to know that the feeling was mutual. His face spread into a big grin as he overheard the girls' exchange.

As Virgil moved about his pre-dinner duties, his thoughts lingered on Mattie and the fact that she was free. His mind flashed back to the day of his arrival at Fairlawn, the morning after John had purchased him at the Slave Market in Charleston. He was delivered to Fairlawn by the auctioneer early that morning, and Samuel met them as they arrived in the auctioneer's wagon. After the auctioneer had departed and the two slaves had introduced themselves to each other, Samuel led him into the foyer and knocked on the study door where John was looking over the plantation books. "Mistuh John suh, de' new slave is here."

"Good, bring him in, Samuel, bring him right in!"

"Good morning, it's Virgil isn't it?" John greeted the big man with a smile.

"Yes sir," Virgil responded as he stood, head erect, looking John in the eyes.

"Have a seat, Virgil, while we get acquainted." Surprised and pleased at the offer, Virgil took a seat opposite John. "Tell me about yourself; you sound like a man who has had some education."

"My former owner was also the owner of my parents. In fact, we were the only slaves he ever owned. His name was David L. Lineham, a kind and very generous gentleman. He was a lifelong bachelor, owner of a very successful mercantile business and a lovely home in Savannah. He purchased my parents in New Orleans when he was a young man, when they were but a bit older than he. He educated them both—my father to be his bookkeeper and business assistant, my mother to run his home and to manage his household staff. The third floor of his home was their apartment, always very nice, nearly as nice as his own quarters actually. I was born a few years later. When I was old enough, I was trained and educated to assist both my parents in their duties. As my father's health failed, I assumed his responsibilities. Two years ago there was a yellow fever epidemic in Savannah. Mr. Lineham, my mother, and my father died of the fever. Mr. Lineham had one nephew, his only heir. He sold the entire estate, of which I was a part. I ended up on the slave block in Charleston, and you know the rest. I understand I was purchased to train as Samuel's replacement. Very little training will be necessary, and I shall be glad to assist you with the books if you so desire."

"Well, it seems you were a far greater bargain than I realized. Actually, my son Matthew has done most of the book work in recent years. However, I shall make him aware that you will be available if he should need you. I think you will find that running a household of this size will require most of your time. Samuel is getting on in years; and I would like for you to assume all the heaviest of his household duties—always being careful of his pride. He must feel that you are his assistant and not the reverse."

"I understand, sir; I deeply respect you for that. Be assured that I will honor your wishes."

"One question, Virgil. As good as your life has been, nevertheless, have you not wished for freedom?"

"I would be lying, sir, if I didn't admit to you that eventual freedom has ever been the greatest dream of my life, and I am sure that it always will be."

In the following months, Virgil had settled into his household duties with ease, and soon Samuel had felt him indispensable. He carried most of the burden of managing the household while still allowing Samuel the dignity of feeling that he was in charge. The whole Prendle family and especially Delilah, Mandy, and Mattie, could see what Virgil was doing. They all respected him for his unselfishness and sensitivity. In spite of his education and refinement, he had the unique ability to deal with the uneducated slaves without making them feel inferior.

Although Mattie had duties to perform, for which she was paid, Mandy and Matt had always arranged for her to be able to finish her assigned duties by early afternoon. They wanted to allow her as much freedom as possible to have the adventure of the childhood and teenage years. She worked under the tutelage of Virgil in the main part of the house rather than out back in the kitchen. Therefore, her contact with Virgil was very close and daily. Of course, they were both delighted with this arrangement; although neither admitted it to the other.

Mandy had begun instructing Mattie at the age of nine in proper household cleaning procedures. Mandy was an immaculate housekeeper and accepted nothing less from Mattie. By the time Virgil arrived when Mattie was fifteen, she was fully adept at every phase of cleaning the big mansion. When he was assigned the duty of assuming Mattie's training, he felt it necessary to observe her cleaning abilities for himself in order to ascertain her level of proficiency. He needed to make this evaluation to decide the level at which he should start her instruction. Virgil observed Mattie as she worked; and long before he said it, he was satisfied that indeed she had been thoroughly trained to properly clean the mansion and was ready to move to the next phase of her training. However, as he moved with her through the house as she performed her daily duties, he enjoyed watching her work too much to end it. He found himself admiring her trim and beautiful figure more each day. The graceful way in which she moved about her tasks, with a sensuous rhythm, stirred his manhood more than he liked to admit. Mattie was very much aware of his admiring glances and had to admit to herself that she was deliberately trying to provoke his attentions, for she was already completely smitten with this big and handsome young man. Actually, although neither of them fully realized it, there was a mutual attempt at gradual seduction taking place.

In late April, Virgil finally admitted that he could no longer justify the delay in moving Mattie on to the next level of her training. One morning he said, "Mattie, today you graduate to the butler's pantry."

"I have been cleaning the butler's pantry for years," She answered, somewhat resentfully.

"Cleaning the pantry will be no part of what you will be learning. First you will learn how to keep the pantry completely and properly stocked. Next you will learn to clean and polish all the fine silver flatware and serving pieces as well as the best imported china and crystal, of which there are several sets. You will also learn to care for the dining room linens to assure that they are in proper repair and impeccably clean and pressed. Then you will learn to properly set the table for every conceivable meal, from a breakfast to a full banquet. When you have learned all that, you will learn to properly serve all meals. Once you have mastered it all, the dining room will be your domain."

By the time Virgil had finished detailing her impending schedule, she stood there wide-eyed and terrified. He could see her fear and felt a little sorry for her. He could understand why she was overwhelmed by it all. "I know it all sounds insurmountable to you at this point, but don't worry. We shall take all the time you need until you are completely comfortable with it. Even then, you may be sure I'll always be nearby if you should need me."

"Thank you, Virgil, that makes me feel much better," she replied, with obvious relief.

As the weeks rolled into months, Mattie looked forward more and more to meeting Virgil very early each morning in the butler's pantry to begin the day's work. By the time Mattie was fully trained, she was sixteen; and she and Virgil had acknowledged to each other the truth that they were hopelessly in love. However, Virgil insisted there could be no future for the two of them. He vowed never to tie Mattie, a free woman, to a husband who was a slave.

"Virge, I love you. It doesn't matter to me that you are a slave. I don't want to live my life without you," Mattie insisted, as she moved into his arms.

"My sweet Mattie, you know how much I love you," Virgil replied, cradling her head against his massive chest and caressing her beautiful body, knowing all the while that he could not allow it to go further. "If we were to marry and have children, do you realize that under the law, they would be slaves? Neither of us would want that for our children," Virgil said, with tears in his eyes at the futility of it all.

"There has to be a way; we'll think of something. We just have to," she replied, as they kissed there in the early morning darkness of the butler's pantry.

As their passion rose, he stepped back, as he had so many times in the past weeks, saying, "No darling, we can't. We just can't," and he left the pantry quickly while he still could. Mattie buried her face in her hands and sobbed.

At this point, another summer had passed. Lillianna had turned sixteen and was in her third year at Miss Hockaday's School. Will was in his second year of medical school. Their relationship, like Mattie and Virgil's, had progressed to a deep and passionate love, kept within the bounds of propriety only by Will's determination to treat Lillianna as a lady.

Lillianna and Mattie still continued their studies in the afternoon down in Mattie's bedroom. On the afternoon following Mattie and Virgil's discussion of their problem, Lillianna noticed how despondent Mattie seemed. "I know something is wrong, Mattie; what is it?" At that, Mattie burst into tears; and the whole story poured out. Lillianna and Mattie had each confided to the other their deep love for Will and Virgil. However, that Mattie and Virgil had such a serious dilemma had never entered Lillianna's mind; for Mattie had never mentioned it to her before. "Don't worry, Mattie; you all are not alone in this. I'll talk to Will about it. I am sure that the three of us can think of something that can be done! Don't mention this to Virgil until after I talk to Will. He doesn't know Will as well as you and I do, and he might be afraid to trust him."

The next morning on the way into Charleston, Lillianna told Will of the situation with Mattie and Virgil; and asked him to try to help her think of a possible solution. By afternoon when he picked her up at school, Will's analytical mind had come up with several possible solutions. As he stepped down and went around to help Lillianna up into the buggy, he said, "My mind has been preoccupied with Mattie and Virgil all day today. I was hard-pressed to give medicine much attention. I have come up with a couple of possibilities which might be worth considering."

"That is wonderful, Will. I knew if anybody could think of a solution, you could."

"Well, there are no guaranties that they will work, but I think they could be worth a try. First, given the fact that your father did grant Mandy and Mattie their freedom at your mother's request, maybe if you told him the whole story and asked him to, he might grant Virgil his freedom and just hire him to serve in his same capacity for a salary, just as Mandy and Mattie do. If he refused that, maybe he would be willing to allow Mattie to work without pay and Virgil to work a longer schedule each day; and in so doing, they could work to earn Virgil's freedom. Should he even refuse that, my last suggestion, although it could not take place immediately, would be that as soon as we are married, we could ask to purchase Virgil. And we could grant him his freedom. If your Father refused all of these proposals, my last suggestion is drastic and fraught with danger for all concerned. However, with careful planning, I believe we could successfully manage to help Virgil and Mattie to run away to safety in the North. He and Mattie are both educated; they should have no problem in finding employment there."

"Oh Lord, Will, surely it won't come to that! I believe I can get Papa to agree to one of your first two suggestions. I don't think he is ready to even hear any discussion of my marriage anytime in the near future. Thank you so much for helping me try to solve this problem for Mattie and Virgil. That you would be willing to take the risk of helping them to run away makes me love you even more; and I didn't think that possible!" Lillianna said, as she turned his face toward her and kissed him.

"Oh ho! We can do better than that," Will said, as he pulled the buggy over to the side of the road, reined in the horse, took her in his arms, and kissed her passionately.

Lillianna savored the kiss, then straightened her bonnet and admonished, laughing, "Why Will Pinkston, what will the neighbors think?"

That afternoon as Lillianna and Mattie started their

studies, Lillianna told Mattie of her conversation with Will and of Will's suggestions. Mattie was somewhat frightened at what John's reaction might be to any of them. She asked Lillianna to delay speaking to her Father at all until she and Virgil had discussed it all fully and had, had the time to think it all through carefully. "Once you start, Lillianna, there is no turning back for any of us; and we have no idea what Mr. John would say or do. It just might be best for us to go on and get married, then pursue Virge's freedom later. Once he has heard all Will's suggestions, he might be willing to go ahead and get married."

On the day following her conversation with Lillianna, Mattie told Virgil that she had confided in Lillianna their dilemma. He expressed no concern, because he knew that Mattie could trust Lillianna with anything. He and Mattie had frequently talked about Lillianna's strong feelings against slavery and all its implications. However, when she told him of Lillianna's discussing it with Will, he was not only angry, but a little frightened. Even though it was common knowledge that the Pinkstons owned no slaves, Virgil knew very little about Will except that he and Lillianna were very much in love. Mattie assured him that Will shared Lillianna's aversion to slavery and that he could be trusted completely. "In fact, he has come up with some very good suggestions as to possible solutions; one of which would involve financial sacrifice on his part, and another which would actually pose danger to both Lillianna and himself," she said in defense of Will.

"I didn't mean to make you angry, sweetheart. I just feel the need for us to be very careful. If you say that Will is trustworthy, that is assurance enough for me," Virgil responded apologetically. After the two of them had fully discussed all of Will's suggestions and had considered them carefully, Mattie was able to convince Virgil to agree to move ahead with marriage plans, albeit reluctantly. Virgil made it clear to Mattie that their marriage would definitely commit them to securing his freedom as soon as possible, by whatever means necessary.

Virgil knew that final permission for him to marry Mattie must ultimately come from John, as his owner. First, however, he felt that he must properly ask her parents for her hand in marriage. He had been reared to believe in such proper amenities. Mattie had shared with Virgil everything about the well-kept secret of the situation surrounding her birth. Now he would be compelled to reveal his knowledge of that secret to her parents. He asked Mandy and Matthew to meet him down at her house late one evening to ask for permission to marry their daughter. He assured them that he realized the importance of keeping their secret and that it would always be safe with him. They both held Virgil in highest esteem and trusted him as a man of his word, and they gladly granted him and Mattie their blessings. Virgil was somewhat more concerned about approaching John with his request, but he need not have been. John was very happy that these two young people, whom he considered an excellent match and both of whom he was very fond, had fallen in love and wanted to marry. In fact, he had hoped that this might eventually happen, when Virgil was assigned the duty of becoming Mattie's mentor.

Wedding plans were soon well underway. Matthew suggested to John that their wedding gift to the couple might be the wedding itself. "Papa, I think it would have pleased Mother for us to go all out to give them a lovely wedding."

Mention of pleasing Becca was all it took to convince John. "What a splendid idea, Matthew. I'll tell Mandy and Mattie immediately to solicit Lillianna's assistance in planning and to spare no expense to make it exactly the kind of wedding Mattie and Virgil would like."

At Lillianna's request, the date was set for mid-June following the end of the school year. She wanted to be completely free to take an active part in the preparations. The wedding would take place on Mandy's front porch. The marriage altar would be centered on the porch facing the Ashley River. The guests would be seated on benches on each side of the walkway, which would serve as the aisle. Samuel was to give the bride away. At Virgil's request, Matthew, the oldest Prendle child, would be his best man. Of course, at Mattie's request, Lillianna, the youngest Prendle child, would be her maid-of-honor. The wedding was planned, as nearly as possible, to emulate traditional weddings in the white community. This was very unlike the usual black wedding held down in the slave quarters. There, the couple, holding hands, with all the residents of the quarters gathered around, merely jumped a broom placed on the ground in front of them. When they had "Jumped the Broom" they were considered officially married. There was then a big celebration with dancing, eating, and singing, which lasted into the night, well past the time when the happy newlyweds had retired to their own cabin. Usually, the celebration drew to a close with a chivaree, a noisy mock serenade to the newlyweds. The custom of holding a chivaree was occasionally practiced in the white community, however, only among tenant farmers and the like, but never among the higher levels of society!

The big wedding day finally arrived. The porch and walkway were resplendent with white baskets filled with magnolias and wisteria. Mandy's upright piano had been moved onto the porch and had a lovely arrangement centered on top. In the center of the porch stood the altar, a white archway draped with wisteria, under which the wedding party would stand. White benches were lined up in the yard on either side of the aisle. The whole scene was truly beautiful, especially when viewed from the altar with the graceful Ashley River as a backdrop.

Early that morning, Mandy went into Mattie's room to awaken her to come share the light breakfast she had prepared.

Her beautiful daughter slept peacefully, the sleep of an innocent child, who would today become a woman. The simple white dress trimmed in tatting, made lovingly by Delilah for her granddaughter's wedding, hung there in readiness. She heard the back door open and close and looked down the hall to see Matthew standing in the kitchen. She pressed her finger to her lips to urge him to be quiet and motioned him to join her at Mattie's door. He tiptoed down the hall and kissed Mandy good morning They stood there in each other's arms gazing down at their precious child. As Mandy bowed her head, Matthew did also; and Mandy prayed a little prayer for God's blessing of happiness for Mattie and Virgil for all the years to come. "Amen," Matthew ended the prayer.

With that, Mattie awakened to see her mother and father looking at her with tears in their eyes. "Oh no, no crying on my wedding day, Mama and Papa, just smiling."

They both smiled at her words; and Mandy said, "All right, now you two come on into the kitchen for breakfast. I have a surprise for you, little bride-to-be." They all sat down around the kitchen table, and Matthew blessed their repast. As they ate, Mandy revealed her surprise. "Mattie, since your papa and Mr. John are giving you and Virgil your wedding as a wedding gift, my wedding present to you two is this house. Following your wedding, the cake cutting, serving of the cake and punch to all the wedding guests, and the departure of everyone, you and Virgil will honeymoon right here in your own home instead of in Virgil's small quarters out behind the kitchen as you have planned. I have already packed all my things and moved them up to Mama's and Papa's quarters. I will move into Virgil's quarters, and he will move down here. The two of you can move into the master bedroom tonight; it is already freshly prepared for your wedding night. As Mattie started to protest that the gift was far to generous and was much too great a sacrifice on Mandy's part, Mandy silenced her. "Not another word; I will not hear it! I have been planning this ever since Virgil asked for your hand in marriage, and my mind is made up. Besides, I'll be much closer to your papa up there!" she said as she kissed Matthew. "Right Papa?"

"Right Mama, whatever you say. Seems your mind is made up anyway," Matthew replied with a smile.

Mattie hopped up and ran around the table and kissed them both. "Thank you so much, Mama; I'm so lucky. I have the best parents in the world!"

The wedding was scheduled for 2:00 p.m., and at 1:30 p.m. everything was in readiness. Jay's wife, Martha, who was an accomplished musician, had agreed to play the piano. The music started promptly at 1:30 p.m., and the guests started to arrive. Soon the benches were filled. The Prendle family, the Pinkstons, and a few other invited guests were seated on the right, starting on the third row. The household and stable slaves were seated on the left. The minister, robed in black, and Virgil and Matthew, dressed handsomely in new black suits with vests, came out of the house and stood beneath the archway facing the river. Delilah, looking lovely in her best Sunday dress and hat in shades of pink and wearing a gardenia corsage, was escorted down the aisle by none other than Mr. John Prendle, who seated her on the second row. He returned up the aisle to then escort Mandy, beautiful as always in a yellow dress and hat, with a daisy corsage. He escorted her down and seated her on the first row, after which he joined his family on the third row, thinking how pleased his Becca, looking down from Heaven, must be. Lillianna, a vision of beauty in lavender and carrying a single magnolia blossom, proceeded down the aisle; and as she turned to face the guests, Martha began to play "The Wedding March." Mattie, absolutely gorgeous in her white dress with babies breath in her hair, entered on Samuel's arm. As they walked down the aisle, Virgil and Matthew smiled at her with tears running down their cheeks. The traditional wedding ceremony followed, and all who attended agreed that it was perfect. The happy couple cut the wedding cake, and the household servants served the cake and punch to all the guests. As the Prendles, Pinkstons, the minister, and the last of the guests were finally leaving, Mattie kissed Mandy, Delilah, Samuel, and Lillianna good-bye. Then looking around to see that everyone had gone, she kissed Matthew furtively on the cheek and whispered, "Bye Papa, and thank you so much for everything."

After all had gone out of sight and had left the bride and groom standing alone on their porch, she asked Virgil to come into the house with her. There she told him of Mandy's wedding gift to them. He broke down and sobbed in gratitude as he realized that for the first time in his life, he actually owned part of something. It seemed to him the first step toward freedom. When he had collected himself, he took her hand and led her back out onto the porch. As she looked up at him puzzled, he said, "I think this is customary." He swept her up into his powerful arms and carried her across their threshold, kissing her long and passionately as he closed the door with his foot. Then he took her into their bedroom. No longer would they be denied this passion that had been building within both of them like a volcano for such a long time.

After the excitement of the wedding, the rest of the summer of 1833 was rather anticlimactic by comparison except for Lillianna's birthday celebration. The third floor ballroom of the Fairlawn mansion saw its first activity since Becca's death. John held a "Coming Out Ball" in honor of Lillianna's seventeenth birthday, which was a customary milestone in the life of every young lady of high breeding. All of Charleston society was in attendance. Lillianna loved the music and whirling around the floor in Will's arms. She appreciated her father's generosity in honoring her with a ball. However, as she observed Mattie and Virgil's having to work as servants rather than being allowed to join in the dancing and other festivities, she voiced the thought again to Will, as she had so many times before, "Oh how I hate slavery and all that it stands for!"

"Try not to think of that tonight, Sweetheart; just enjoy your birthday."

When school resumed in September, Lillianna and Will talked frequently of the injustices of slavery on their rides to and from Charleston. One afternoon when Will picked her up, the subject came up again as a result of something he had heard at school that morning. "You know Lillianna, all slaves are not as docile and passive as your father's slaves are. Of course, many slaves are not treated as well as he treats his slaves—not nearly as well. There is great unrest among the slave population in Charleston, and there has been for years. You probably don't remember, I barely do; but back in 1822, a black man named Denmark Vesey, who had been able to earn his own freedom, headed a plot which led to a slave insurrection. The whole incident ended in failure. There were over a hundred people involved. Four of them were white, a German peddler, a Scotsman, a Spaniard, and another Charlestonian. Nobody seems to know why those four white men were involved unless it was a moral issue with them. At any rate, they were convicted and served prison sentences. Thirty-five blacks were convicted and executed, thirty-one were deported, twenty-seven were acquitted, and thirty-eight were questioned and not charged. The subject came up at school today in my anatomy class. The thirty-five blacks who were executed were given to the Medical School for use in the anatomy department. Since that time, there has been much covert, even overt, action among the blacks in Charleston—freedmen as well as slaves—poisonings, insubordination, and such. I can't say that I really blame them much. They are all considered less than second class citizens, even those who are free. From what I hear, the Charleston slave owners are well aware of the unrest and greatly concerned."

Lillianne listened raptly as Will told the story. "If I were black, I know I would be among the insurrectionists. I just know I would! Where is it all going to end, Will?" she asked.

"I don't know, sweetheart, but it appears to me to be like a keg of dynamite with the fuse lit."

"The terrible part is, Will, that when that keg explodes, I am going to be on the opposite side of the struggle from Papa and my family!" she responded distressfully.

"Just remember, my little Auburn Hair, whatever happens, you and I will always stand together!" he encouraged, squeezing her hand, as they turned into the drive to Fairlawn.

Lillianna thought all that night about their discussion on the way home that day. The next morning on the way into Charleston, she told Will that she had decided it was time to broach the subject of Virgil's freedom to John. Will agreed that the time was right before Mattie and Virgil had any children.

That night at dinner, Lillianna asked John if she might talk with him in his study after dinner. Although he could not imagine what her subject was to be, he said, "Of course, princess, you know you may talk with me anytime you wish."

After dinner, they went into the study; and John poured himself a glass of sherry; and much to Lillianna's surprise, offered to pour one for her. "No thank you, Papa," she responded.

"All right, little lady, let's hear your problem."

"Papa, I don't have a problem. I have a very important request. I am sure you are probably aware of the unrest among the slave population down in Charleston. Before anything, such as an insurrection should erupt, I want to ask you to grant Virgil his freedom, especially before he and Mattie have any children. I know that you granted Mandy and Mattie their freedom, and even offered Wilah and Samuel their freedom, at Mama's request. It is rumored that slave owners in Charleston are aware of all the unrest and are greatly concerned that there might be a slavery uprising. I don't know what might happen to all slaves should there be a failed uprising, even to slaves who took no part in it. I am afraid all slaves would be suspect, just as they were in the Vesey uprising in 1822. I am afraid for Virgil should that happen."

"My, my, princess, you seem very well-informed on this subject."

"Yes Papa, Will heard all about it at school yesterday."

"Lillianna, I have been aware of the slave situation in Charleston for years; and I share the concerns of the slave owners there. For that very reason, I cannot grant Virgil his freedom lest I cause unrest among our other slaves."

"*Your* slaves, Papa, I don't wish to share any part of their ownership," she replied, her anger beginning to rise. "Then would you consider allowing Mattie to work without pay and Virgil to work a much longer schedule each day, in order to earn Virgil's freedom?" she asked.

"Lillianna, I have told you before, this is a subject I do not wish to discuss with you. My answer is no, and the subject is closed!" John answered hotly.

"The subject is not closed, Papa; I refuse to let it be!" she responded angrily. In her anger, she completely lost control and revealed much more of Will's and her original plan than she had intended to reveal. "If Will and I have to marry now, instead of later as we have planned, we will. Then we will purchase Virgil and free him!" she screamed.

John was astounded and furious at her words. "Indeed you shall not marry Will Pinkston now or ever if I have my way. In the first place, you are still too young to marry without my permission. In the second place, the son of Leland Pinkston, with his philosophy concerning slavery, so diametrically opposed to all that is traditional in the south, is not an acceptable husband for my daughter. And in addition, under no circumstances would I sell Virgil!" John raged.

"No matter how long I have to wait, Papa, I will marry Will Pinkston someday. you can count on that. I shall never ever love nor marry anyone else!"

"Not another word, Lillianna. I will make arrangements immediately to send you away to a boarding school in Boston, of which I have heard good reports. Now go to your room!"

"Yes, Sire Prendle," she replied. "Answer this one question for me, if you can. If your skin were black and John Prendle owned your body and your soul, no matter how well he treated you, somewhere deep inside, wouldn't you hate him?" John gave no answer, but his icy gaze drove Lillianna, sobbing, from the study. However, John was destined to reflect on her question, with discomfort, time and time again in the years to come.

After Lillianna left the study, John gazed up at Becca's portrait. "Oh Becca, I needed you and your wise counsel and cool head to help me deal with our daughter tonight. I lost my temper and said everything in the wrong way. She has grown up to be so like you. She is a young woman with a brilliant mind, a set of values all her own, and a will of iron. That will cannot be bent, let alone broken. I knew that, yet I raged on! Now I fear I might have lost her forever! Oh God, please lead me to handle this thing in the right way. I cannot do it alone. Amen."

Alone in her room, after a long while, Lillianna gathered her composure and realized that she had gone much too far. Ironically, her thoughts also turned to her mother. "Oh Mama, how I wish you were here for me to talk to tonight. I just know you would be wise enough to tell me what I should do. You knew Papa so well, and always knew the right things to say to him. He loved you so. I know he always listened to reason when you talked to him." Lillianna knew that it would be useless to even try to defy her Father. She lay awake far into the night planning how she should handle this situation.

She decided to tell her Father tomorrow morning that she would obey his wishes and go to the school in Boston. However, she would ask that he please wait until after the Christmas holidays to enroll her there and to permit her to finish this semester at Miss Hockaday's. She needed to have time to talk to Will, and with his help, to lay out the plan of action she had in mind. As she prayed her bedtime prayer, she ended with, "Please Dear Lord, lead me in the path you would have me take. Please put the right words in my mouth to say to Papa in the morning. Amen."

The next morning, John and Lillianna had their usual breakfast; however, there was a palpable tension between them. She opened the conversation coolly but respectfully. "Papa, I am sorry I was rude to you last night. I lost my temper and said many things I regret. Of course, I shall obey your wish that I transfer to the boarding school in Boston. Under the circumstances, I think that it is probably a wise move. However, I would like to ask you please to wait until after the Christmas holidays to enroll me for the winter/spring semester there. If you would be willing to permit it, I would like to go on just as things are to complete this semester at Miss Hockaday's.

"Princess, an apology is also due from me. I also lost my temper and said much that I regret. However, my basic feelings remain the same. Yes, you may finish this semester at Miss Hockaday's. I think that a wise plan, since we need time to prepare your wardrobe, to see to all your packing, and to arrange your enrollment and transportation. This is a big move, and it cannot be accomplished on short notice. Besides, we wouldn't want you to be away during the Christmas holidays, would we? I am especially pleased to hear you say that you feel that the move is a wise one."

"I had better go get ready to leave for school. Have a good day, Papa,." she said as she kissed John's cheek and left the room.

"You too, princess," he called to her on her way out. After their big confrontation the night before, Lillianna was surprised and greatly relieved that John was permitting her to continue to ride to and from Charleston with Will. Apparently, a night's sleep on it and time to reconsider all the things that had been said in anger, along with their calm, although rather cool, discussion at breakfast, had set his mind at ease somewhat.

Will arrived to pick her up at the usual time, and Lillianna didn't really breathe an easy breath until they reached River Road and turned toward Charleston and had ridden out of sight. "Will, you won't believe all that happened last night between Papa and me! I am so relieved to be on our way to school. I half expected him to suddenly appear on the piazza, to send you on your way without me, and to drive me to school himself!" She recounted the entire, unpleasant episode and admitted that she had displayed far and away too much anger, causing her father to respond in kind. "Now that he is insisting that I go away to boarding school in Boston, I presume in the hope that I shall forget you, we must think of a plan to avert my going. I agreed to go and asked permission just to finish this semester at Miss Hockaday's merely to give us time to come up with a plan. Oh Will, what are we going to do?"

"Give me a little time to think about it, sweetheart. Rest assured we will think of something!"

In the days that followed, Lillianna and Will discussed all the pros and cons of several possible plans; but it finally all came down to only one sure way to avoid her transfer to Boston to school. They would have to elope. After they both had agreed on that, they had to formulate a detailed plan. They knew full well that they would require assistance; however, they had to be very careful to enlist only the help of those they could trust completely, and those who could help without having to fear retribution from John for helping them.

Their final plan was for Lillianna to appear to be cooperating fully with all the preparations to transfer her schooling to Boston right up to the time she was to board the packet on which she was to sail to Boston. She just had to find a way to convince John to agree to let her tell him goodbye at home rather than as she boarded the ship in Charleston. She felt confident that she could manage that if she utilized a tactic that had always worked with him . . . tears. She and Will decided to enlist the help of Matthew, Mandy, and Mattie only. Virgil could know all about the plan, but they feared his participation in any way might pose a problem for him with John later. Reasoning that a secret could be inadvertently revealed in all innocence, Lillianna and Will decided to wait as late as possible to share their plan with anyone. A secret not known cannot be exposed.

CHAPTER FIVE

DECEPTION

In the following weeks, Delilah and Lillianna planned a wardrobe, which was appropriate for the colder weather of Boston and which would be very packable. Once planned, a seamstress, who did alterations for Mrs. Connor at The Charleston Mercantile, was employed to make the clothes Lillianna needed which were not carried by or could not be ordered by Mrs. Connor. They even inventoried the trunks available in the storage room to ensure that everything they would need for packing was at hand.

John informed Miss Hockaday of the impending transfer and enlisted her help in getting Lillianna enrolled in Boston. Whether or not he revealed to her the true reason for the transfer, Lillianna never knew nor ever asked. More quickly than she thought possible, she was enrolled for the winter/spring semester at the Boston Seminary for Young Women, beginning January 20, 1834. Once he knew the date, John immediately investigated the packet schedules from Charleston to NewYork and on to Boston. In order to ensure her timely arrival in Boston, he booked passage for Lillianna for January 2nd.

While all the preparation was taking place for Boston, Will was making all preparations for the covert plan for elopement. Initially, he and Lillianna had thought that they would sail to Savannah, marry, and honeymoon there. However, the more they considered the proximity of Savannah to Charleston, they realized that was exactly what John would suspect they had done; and they knew his determination when he was angry. They finally decided to have the ship's captain marry them aboard the ship, sail to Savannah, and then sail on to New Orleans for their honeymoon. As soon as they had settled on this plan, Will went about checking packet schedules from Charleston to Savannah and then on to New Orleans. Fortunately, the timing of the schedules were in sync; so Will booked passage for two to New Orleans on the same date that John had booked passage for one to Boston.

One month before her scheduled date of departure, Lillianna and Will decided that they could wait no longer to tell Matthew, Mandy, Mattie, and Virgil of their plans. At first, Matthew had some reservations about the drastic finality of what they were planning. "Have you two fully considered all the possible repercussions of what you are about to do? God only knows how Papa will react!"

However, Mandy spoke up, "Matthew, what other choice do they have if they ever hope to have a future together? Think about it! Do they have any other alternative?" Mattie and Virgil completely agreed with Mandy.

"I think you are probably right, Mandy; but I am so afraid for my little sister," Matt replied, drawing Lillianna into his arms tenderly.

"I am not a child, Matt. I am a woman. I know what I want, and I am not afraid! Will you help us?" Lillianna asked emphatically.

"Yes, of course I will."

"We all will," Mattie added, as everyone nodded in agreement.

Virgil said, "Just tell us what you want us to do, and we will do it."

"Virgil, just be there with your moral support. Will and I feel that you are not in any position, being Papa's property, to safely take an active part."

"Lillianna, had you not tried so hard to secure my freedom, you would not have been forced into this situation. I will do anything I can to help. I am not afraid of the risk."

"Virgil, it was inevitable that it would eventually have come to this with Papa and me. Don't blame yourself. I am sure our plan can be carried out successfully without your active involvement, but thank you so very much for your willingness to help. That is the kind of moral support we need. Will has already made all the arrangements for our sailing. I just have to find a way to keep Papa from going to Charleston to see me off, and I am reasonably sure that I can do that."

"Just how do you think you can manage that little miracle?" Matthew asked.

"I shall just tell Papa that I would rather say good-bye to him here at home because I don't think I can bear to board that ship and leave him standing there on the dock. I shall ask him to allow you to take me to the ship, get me on board and into my stateroom, and just leave me there and come back home, no waving and crying as I sail away. If I say this just exactly right with a few tears streaming down my cheeks, he will say yes. He never could stand to see my cry. It always works!"

"You little vixen, you are probably right!" Matthew said laughing.

The next morning, Lillianna awakened early to begin her morning routine. When she entered the study for her talk with Mama, she set the scene for her coming performance at breakfast with Papa. Long ago she had realized that John sometimes eavesdropped on her talks from the little stairwell up to his bedroom. There were times when she was well aware that he was there, but most of the time she could not be sure. This morning she wasn't sure, so she took no chances. "Oh Mama, as I have been telling you for weeks now, I am transferring to a boarding school in Boston in January. The more I think about the move, I must admit that I am rather excited about the prospect of visiting Boston and meeting new friends. I understand it is an excellent school with a renowned faculty. It is really a wonderful educational opportunity for me. However, as my sailing date draws nearer, I realize how terribly I am going to miss all my family and friends here." At this point her tears began to flow. "Worst of all will be leaving Papa standing on the dock as I sail away. I have never been away from my papa before. He has really been my mama *and* my Papa all my life. All of my love for both of you has been rolled up into my love for him! I don't know whether or not I can bear it. I really don't!" At this point, she was truly crying. After all, she was actually leaving John forever, more so than she would be if she were going to Boston. As happy as she felt at the prospect of becoming Will's wife, there was a deep sadness at the way they were being forced to do this. She had always imagined she would be married in her mother's beautiful wedding gown in St. Michael's Episcopal Church, escorted down the aisle and given away in marriage by her father. Now she knew this would never come to pass. She wiped her tears and left the study to join John for breakfast.

"Good morning, Papa," She said, still wiping tears and sniffling as she took her seat at the breakfast table.

"Good morning, Princess, whatever is wrong? Why all the tears this morning?"

Lillianna repeated to John, almost verbatim, the words she had just spoken to her mother. "Please Papa," she begged, "would you consider allowing me to say good-bye to all of you here at home; and to let Matt take me to Charleston alone? Matt can escort me onto the ship to my stateroom and then come back home immediately. I will just stay in my stateroom for the departure. I just don't think I can bear standing at the ship's railing and seeing my loved ones, especially you, Papa, fade from sight as I sail away!"

"As hard as that would be for me, sweetheart, of course I shall permit Matthew to drive you to Charleston alone. If that is the way you wish it, that is the way it shall be. I understand completely," he answered, as he rose and came around the table to embrace her, trying to stem the flow of her tears with his handkerchief. As Lillianna said her prayers that night, she was feeling very guilty for deceiving Papa so blatantly. She asked God to forgive her and begged that He would help Papa forgive her for what she was about to do.

The beginning of the Christmas holidays marked the end of Lillianna's last semester at Miss Hockaday's School. As Will helped her up into the buggy on that last day, Miss Hockaday, the other faculty members, and her classmates were there on the lovely piazza of the old mansion that housed the school. There were tearful farewells and wishes for continued success in the Boston school. As they rode through the gates for the last time, she looked back and waved. She realized that she was waving farewell forever to life as she had known it.

Lillianna moved through Christmas, with all its festivities, almost as if she were floating outside her own body, observing herself and her family celebrating all their traditions for one last time. Then, suddenly it was New Year's Eve. John opted to forego the usual New Year's Eve Ball, which ended with the traditional toast to welcome in the New Year; instead he and the family decided to celebrate with an intimate family gathering. Following a light buffet supper, they all drove into Charleston to the majestic old St. Michael's Church to join in the Watch Night service, which was held there every year but was attended by only a few. Somehow they all felt the need to set aside the frivolity of their traditional New Year's

Eve celebration, and to welcome in the New Year with prayers of thanksgiving for the blessings of 1833, and to ask God's continued favor throughout 1834. Although the rest of the family thought this was merely the end of what they considered Lillianna's childhood and the beginning of her adult education, Matthew and Lillianna sat there in the beautiful old sanctuary, clinging tightly to one another's hand, aware of the magnitude of the change that would begin in only forty-eight hours.

Delilah awakened Lillianna very early on the morning of January 2nd and helped her dress in her new travel outfit. Before she went downstairs for her last morning talk with her mother and her last breakfast with her father, she took one last long parting look around her bedroom, picked up her gloves and bonnet, and walked out, closing the door with finality. She descended the stairs slowly, her hand gliding down the banister, so very aware of the beauty and smoothness of the old mahogany. Her eyes caressed the beautiful cut-glass doors and marble floor of the foyer. Her hand luggage stood beside the front doors awaiting her departure. Her trunks had already been loaded in the rear of the large family carriage, in which Matthew would drive her to Charleston. As she stopped to place her gloves and bonnet on the table in the center of the foyer, she turned full circle to survey it all, the stairway and the balcony above, one last time. Then she turned and walked into the study.

"Good morning, Mama," Lillianna said as she looked up at the big portrait above her. Somehow she sensed that John was not in the little stairwell listening this morning, and she was right. John realized that his emotions, already fragile at the thought of her leaving, could not endure the pain of hearing her last talk with her mother. "Today is the last morning talk that I shall have with you for a very long time, perhaps forever. My life is going to change completely today. Today I shall truly become a woman. I pray that God will guide me all the way and that He will lead Papa to come and sit here where I am sitting and to look up at you and find a way to deal with all that is going to happen this day. Always when I questioned the things I couldn't understand about heaven, I was taught, 'For now we see through a glass darkly, but then face to face.' Just the same, I have always believed that you have heard me and have helped me during all my life, my guardian angel so to speak. If this is true, please Mama, ask God to allow you to help Papa in some way in the weeks to come. I guess it's time for me to tell you how very much I love you and to say good-bye for now," Lillianna finished, as the tears streamed down her face. She wiped her tears and rose to go in to breakfast.

She entered the breakfast alcove; and in an attempt to appear much more light hearted than she felt, she said with a smile, "Good morning Papa."

John responded with the same forced bravado, "Good morning Princess. You look like a regular grownup world traveler in your beautiful travel outfit!"

"Thank you Papa, I feel very grownup this morning! I am so glad we had our farewell family dinner last night. It will be so much easier when I leave this morning just to say good-bye to you and Wilah and her family."

"I totally agree, sweetheart. I think that will make it easier for all of us." They finished breakfast, exchanging light conversation, as Delilah stifled her sobs in the butler's pantry.

As the time for her departure drew near, Lillianna walked down to the stable to tell Sheba good-bye. "I'll be back for you girl before you know it," she whispered to the horse as, on tiptoe, she hugged her neck and gave her a sugar cube. She walked back up to the house and entered the foyer. As she put on her bonnet and gloves, John slipped her cape around her shoulders. He and Matthew followed her onto the piazza with her hand luggage and loaded it into the carriage. With many hugs and tears, she bade farewell to Delilah, Samuel,

Mandy, Virgil, and her beloved Mattie. Then she spoke through her tears, "I love you all very much, and I shall miss you with all my heart. Now please, would you all go inside and give me a moment alone with Papa?" They did as she asked without a backward look. When the door had closed behind them, she flew into John's arms sobbing. She kissed him tenderly and clung to him in one last embrace. "I can't begin to tell you how very much I am going to miss you, Papa." Finally she looked into his eyes and said intently, "Always remember, no matter what happens, I love you very, very much."

"And I you, Princess," he replied as he helped her up into the carriage beside Matthew. Matthew flicked the reins, and the carriage pulled away. Lillianna never looked back.

As they rode into Charleston, they said very little. Lillianna was wiping tears. Matthew simply let his flow. "Remember little sister, I will always be here for you, always!"

"Thank you, Matthew; I know that I can count on that. You have always been one of the real constants in my life, and I thank God for you." As they arrived at the pier, they passed the packet *Lorelie,* which was headed for New York and Boston, and drove on to the *Destiny*, bound for Savannah and New Orleans. Will and his father were there handing down Will's luggage to the dock hands responsible for loading the Savannah passengers. Lillianna and Matthew greeted the Pinkstons warmly as Lillianna kissed Will, her heart now singing.

They loaded most of Lillianna's trunks into the Pinkston carriage for Mr. Pinkston to carry home with him. Her honeymoon trunk and luggage were turned over to the dock hands to be loaded along with Will's onto the *Destiny.* The four of them boarded the ship and joined the Captain on the bridge. Will had arranged in advance for the Captain to perform the marriage ceremony there in the harbor, with Matthew and Mr. Pinkston witnessing. "What God hath joined together let no man put asunder. Amen," the captain ended the service. "You may kiss your bride, Mr. Pinkston." Will kissed Lillianna almost reverently. Matthew and Mr. Pinkston both kissed the bride, congratulated and shook hands with the groom, and after a brief conversation, hurriedly left the ship, since the order to haul in the gangplank and cast off had just been issued.

CHAPTER SIX

WOMANHOOD

As the ship moved away from the dock, Lillianna and Will stood at the rail smiling and waving as Matthew and Mr. Pinkston waved from the pier. The happy couple stood and watched until Charleston and their world faded from sight. As he offered her his arm, Will said, “Mrs.Pinkston, would you care to join me in our stateroom?”

“Of course, Dr. Pinkston, of course!” she answered taking his arm.

Will ushered Lillianna into their stateroom. There before them was spread an intimate wedding luncheon, replete with candles and champagne. The little girl she sometimes couldn’t suppress squealed with delight, “Oh Will, you didn’t forget a thing; it is all so perfect!”

“I tried not to, my precious little girl,” he said sweeping her into his arms and kissing her with a passion he had never unleashed before.

“You are going to learn very soon now, my darling, I am no little girl at all!” she replied, returning his kiss in kind.

“I have arranged for us to have all our meals here in our stateroom rather than with the other passengers, if that meets with your approval.”

"Oh yes, I would much prefer that. As I said before, you didn't leave anything undone. What a thoughtful and romantic husband I have! Shall we get out of these warm travel clothes and into something more comfortable?" she suggested, with a lift of the eyebrow.

"By all means," Will replied with a knowing smile. Their cabin steward had already unpacked their luggage and had stowed everything in its proper place. Lillianna went into their dressing room first. She found her beautiful white gown, negligee, and satin slippers neatly stored away in one of the small closets. This wedding night ensemble had been a private Christmas gift from Mattie and Mandy. Mandy had, had Mrs. Connor order it ostensibly as a gift for Mattie. It was seductively demure and quite beautiful. After Lillianna had donned the gown, she assessed the overall picture in the mirror. It nipped in snugly just below her ample bosom and down to her tiny waist, and emphasized both. The sheer negligee, full sleeved and tied demurely at the neck with white satin ribbon, revealed just enough to remain virginal, yet, extremely seductive. She stepped into the satin slippers, opened the door, and reentered the stateroom. Will again swept her into his arms and kissed her as he slipped his hands beneath the negligee and encircled her waist. As his hands moved upward in his first tentative caress of her body, he stepped away quickly, saying, "I had better go change myself before this gets out of hand. Our luncheon is getting cold I'm sure."

"I don't mind a cold luncheon," Lillianna said, as her arms encircled his neck, and her mouth sought his hungrily.

"Wait sweetheart, let me change. Then let's have a champagne toast to our future and eat our lunch. We've waited so long already. I'm sure the anticipation will only add to our pleasure." Will went into the dressing room and returned in a few minutes in his trousers, robe, and slippers. Then he poured the champagne. They toasted their future, kissed again, and sat down to enjoy their wedding luncheon. Afterward, Will set the luncheon table outside their door in the passageway as Lillianna stepped into the dressing room to freshen up following lunch. She was in the dressing room only a few minutes; and when she came out, Will went in.

While Will was in the dressing room, Lillianna removed her negligee, turned back the bed covers, and crept between the sheets. Will came out clad only in his trousers to find her peeking over the sheet and smiling coyly. Her eyes moved from his eyes downward, taking in his massive chest with its black hair, and still downward as he removed his trousers. She was surprised to see that he had already removed his undergarments. As her eyes caressed his body, she said, "You are quite a man Will Pinkston and quite beautiful!"

"Men are not beautiful, my love. That word is reserved for ladies."

"On the contrary, darling, they are beautiful when they look like a classic statue sculpted by some great artist like Michelangelo!"

Taking one step over to the bed, he threw back the sheet, "All right, Mrs. Pinkston, now it is my turn to admire!" Lillianna rose and stood before him. He loosened the ribbon at her waist and slipped the gown over her head, held her at arm's length, and admired her young body, every inch, head to toe; and as his eyes traveled back up slowly, he pressed her body to his and whispered in her ear, "You are gorgeous, my little Auburn Hair!" As he picked her up and laid her on the bed, he dropped to his knees beside her. His hands moved gently over her body, and she trembled with passion as his lips caressed it all.

As He moved onto the bed beside her, she returned his caresses with her hands and lips without inhibition. She laughed a throaty laugh, "I knew you were a big man, but I had *no idea* how really *big* you are. It's a little frightening for a small girl, but it's a challenge to which I have looked forward for a long time."

"Oh my, it looks as if I married a hussy," he teased.

"And I, a stud; so prove *it!*" she replied, as they kissed.

Their passion mounted until at last he gently and gradually penetrated as she lifted to meet him and cried out in ecstasy. When all was spent, Will kissed her long and lovingly. "My Auburn Hair, for the rest of my life I shall remember this moment and the precious gift you have given me," he murmured, as he buried his face in her hair.

During the following days of the cruise, like most honeymooners, the bride and groom could hardly get enough of each other. More than just the intimate acts of love, they enjoyed watching each other, as if trying to memorize every move lest something be stolen away which could never be regained. Lillianna watched Will shave, dress, and undress, devouring every move, every detail of his body. Will did much the same, watching her bathe, dress, undress, comb her hair, caressing her with his eyes. They were like two starving animals allowed at last to suckle. Lillianna summed it all up, "Will, if God created anything more beautiful than what we have, He kept it for Himself!"

The *Destiny* arrived at Savannah very late in the afternoon. The newlyweds went ashore for dinner. Following an elegant meal, they took a romantic, though chilly, moonlight tour of the beautiful city. In each others' arms, bundled beneath the warm robes of a rental carriage, they felt no discomfort as they gazed up at the stars and moon and took in all the sights beneath the street lamps of Savannah. This experience they would relive time and again in reminiscence in the years to come.

Back on board ship, Lillianna and Will enjoyed the days that followed, coming up on deck more frequently as they sailed southward into the warmer weather around the tip of Florida and into the Gulf of Mexico. Upon reaching New Orleans, they spent two idyllic weeks honeymooning in the beautiful city. They stayed in two of the travelers' rooms above the popular "Old Absenthe House" on Bourbon Street. They tried creole food and loved it; but most often, they enjoyed the excellent cuisine of the tavern.

Like all visitors to the fascinating and busy city of New Orleans, with its diverse cultures, they wanted to see it all. Carriage rides were a popular mode of touring the city and surrounding area; consequently, the carriages all had full schedules. Finally, Will and Lillianna had to settle for a tour in a well-worn and creaky carriage owned and driven by an enterprising black freedman, Jonah LaFitte. As it turned out, Jonah was one of the nicest discoveries of their honeymoon. He put his carriage and his in-depth knowledge of New Orleans and environs at their disposal. They had mornings and evenings to themselves to honeymoon. However, each afternoon they scheduled Jonah's rig for guided tours of the city and for rides into the surrounding countryside. His knowledge of everything, from voodoo folklore to what the latest building projects in the city foretold, was amazing. They saw the Cabildo, built in 1795, which had housed the government under French, Spanish, and now American rule. They saw and enjoyed Mass at beautiful St. Louis Cathedral, completed in 1794. They wanted to visit the busy French Market, located on the site of an old Indian trading post. On the way, they passed a lovely residence, with a beautiful iron lace balcony. Lillianna inquired, "Who lives in that charming home?"

Jonah replied hesitantly, "Uh, that's called Madame John's Legacy. Uh, a large family of, uh, ladies live there. Actually that is the oldest building in New Orleans." He hurried past without further comment.

They saw Lafitte's Blacksmith Shop, which, according to Jonah, had served as a front for pirates, Jean and Pierre Lafitte (no relation to Jonah), who had fought with Andrew Jackson in the Battle of New Orleans. They saw the Convent of the Ursulines, completed in 1734. They were interested to learn that it had housed young women who came from France to be wives of the early colonists. "My goodness, what a terrible way to begin a marriage!" Lillianna exclaimed. Then she and Will looked at each other and burst into laughter. Jonah looked at them, puzzled.

"It's nothing, Jonah, sort of a private joke," Will said still laughing.

Along the way, they passed two buildings under construction. One was to be the Medical College of Louisiana, especially interesting to Will; the other was to house the United States Mint.

It was wonderful to completely absorb themselves in each other and in this lovely city. Then all too soon it had to end, and they were sailing back home to Charleston. It had been a perfect honeymoon in every way, shadowed only by the thought of what awaited them when they arrived back in Charleston.

As the ship approached Charleston harbor on the return voyage, they both dreaded the unpleasant scene which probably was about to take place as soon as they walked down the gangplank. They were astonished and, strangely, somewhat dismayed that such was not the case! By now, John had, of course, learned of the elopement. He was inconsolable and unforgiving. He had made it clear to his family and household that he would never again see or speak to Lillianna or to Will. In spite of the efforts of his entire family, there was absolutely no reasoning with him.

Knowing the expected date and time of their arrival, Matthew and Will's father had arranged a big welcome home for the newlyweds. All the members of the Pinkston and Prendle families, along with Delilah, Samuel, and their family were on the pier in Charleston when the ship dropped anchor and docked. Lillianna and Will scanned all the faces of the large group standing on the pier smiling and waving to welcome them home. When she saw that John's was not among them, Lillianna's heart froze. For a moment, she was frightened as the thought crossed her mind that something tragic might have happened to him. "Oh how foolish," she realized, "if that were the case, my family would certainly not be here greeting us so cheerfully. Oh Papa, could your reaction be so terrible that you refuse even to see me?" She was crushed when she learned the full extent of her father's anger and resentment toward her and Will. Nevertheless, she felt confident that after she and Will had settled in at home at Pink Hill, she could, without a doubt, visit Papa at Fairlawn and all would be well.

In the week following their return, Lillianna and Will were busy settling into their private quarters on the second floor of the beautiful old Pinkston home. What it lacked in the elegance that graced Fairlawn, it more than exceeded with its wonderful atmosphere of freedom. All household servants were salaried employees of the Pinkstons rather than slaves.

On the first floor to the right of the foyer were located the formal parlor and the large formal dining room. To the left of the foyer were a large study and the master bedroom. Between two beautiful stairways curving upward to the balcony above, was a broad center hallway leading from the rear of the foyer. To the left of the hallway were two guest bedrooms with a small private sitting room between. To the right of the hallway, were the butler's pantry and the more intimate family dining room. The hallway led to the breezeway at the rear of the house. Beyond the breezeway, the large detached kitchen and storage rooms were located.

The entire second floor, composed of four large bedrooms, had been designated as Lillianna and Will's private quarters. She was to redecorate it as she chose. Jane's old bedroom had already been outfitted as a study for Will, so Lillianna left his private haven as it was. Will would return to his medical studies in February and would graduate at the end of the following semester in December, 1834. He would be spending many hours in his study as Lillianna would soon learn. However, redecorating the rest of their quarters and adjusting to the responsibility of becoming mistress of Pink Hill would completely fill the days of the young woman, who wouldn't mark her eighteenth birthday until August. She would find little time to feel lonely or neglected; moreover, such had never been the nature of her personality.

As they prepared for bed several weeks after their return home, Lillianna went into the dressing room to undress. In a few minutes, she stood in front of the mirror gazing at her nude body. The woman who looked back at her was a new and different person, almost a stranger. Will, already undressed, came up behind her and encircled her completely with his arms. The reflection in the mirror seemed to magnify the vast difference in their sizes. "Oh Will, I think I have just realized why I finally feel whole for the first time in my life. Look at us. You are so big, and I am so small. I am the rest of you, and you are the rest of me. I think God must have made you and saved your leftovers. Then five years later, He used those leftovers to make me! Do you think that could be what happened?"

Will laughed and turned her toward him, pressing her body to his. "Well, I don't know. Let's see, you certainly fit perfectly; and I love the idea. Oh how you do make my heart smile, my little Auburn Hair!" he said, as he kissed her and buried his face in her hair.

As at Fairlawn and most of the finer plantations of the area, the third floor of Pink Hill housed a beautifully appointed ballroom. Although it had rarely been used in recent years, William Pinkston, Sr. was now planning a reception and ball in honor of the happy newlyweds. Plans were busily being put in place since it was scheduled for late March. Compiling of the guest roster for the reception was placed in the hands of the bride and groom. Of course, all members of the Prendle and Pinkston families, the closest friends of both families, as well as the remainder of Charleston's elite were invited.

As he wrote the final name, Will said, "That should just about do it. Can you think of anyone we might have overlooked?" Lillianna, sitting there beside him, made no response. Will looked at her downcast eyes and troubled expression. "Sweetheart, what is it? What's the matter?"

"Will, we haven't included Mandy, Mattie, and Virgil. They are part of my family too."

"Darling, I just felt that they would be terribly uncomfortable if they came. I don't believe your Father would even consider coming if he knew they would be here, but we shall invite them if you wish. You know that as far as Father and I are concerned, they would be more than welcome."

"Oh Will, I know that you are right. I doubt that they would accept, but I feel compelled to make the gesture. Would you please add their names to the list?"

"Of course, I understand your feelings; and I agree completely."

With those names added, the roster was complete. Engraved invitations to the reception were delivered to all those invited. As always, the formal invitation requested an RSVP; and responses indicated that all of Charleston was looking forward to the gala with great anticipation.

John received his invitation and destroyed it without responding, an indication of the depth of his anger and pain. Ordinarily, common courtesy would have forced him to at least send his "regrets".

On Saturday afternoon after the invitations were delivered on Friday, Matthew, Mandy, and Mattie paid Lillianna and Will a visit at Pink Hill. Will had spent the morning in his private study preparing for Monday's classes. He took a break for lunch; and as they were finishing the meal, he suggested that Lillianna and he have their dessert on the piazza and enjoy a few minutes of the beautiful afternoon alone together before he resumed his studies. They had finished their dessert and were sitting there chatting about the upcoming party when the serenity of the afternoon was interrupted by the clatter of buggy wheels coming up the long marl drive. Lillianna looked and clapped her hands in delight at seeing the Prendle buggy with Matt, Mandy, and Mattie aboard. She and Will, all smiles, were waiting beside the blackamoor by the time Matt reined in. They greeted the trio warmly as Lillianna gave Pegasus, the dependable old Prendle buggy horse, a fond pat.

"The afternoon is so warm and pleasant, let's visit here on the piazza for a spell," Will suggested. "Lillianna and I have just finished our dessert. May we offer you all some refreshments?"

"No, thank you," they declined politely.

When the little group was settled in the comfortable peacock chairs, Mandy began gently, "This isn't just a social call, we have some important things we need to discuss with you. First, let me tell the two of you how very much Mattie, Virgil, and I appreciate our invitations to your reception. We love you both for including us; however, you must realize that our attending is out of the question."

"Mandy Ma, (Lillianna reverted to her babyhood name for Mandy), we sent the invitations in all sincerity because we both want you there," she insisted. "You are part of our family!"

"My sweet girl, we thank you; but you know that I am right. You both must know that no one else in attendance would understand or accept our being there. Will is going to be a doctor, practicing here in Charleston. He must consider his professional future. And once Mr. John learned of our attending, that would end forever any hope that he will relent and forgive you. And finally, and of least importance, is the fact that we would feel very uncomfortable. This is something the South is not ready to accept now, nor indeed may ever be! In short, our attending would completely ruin your reception. We could never forgive ourselves if we caused you all the kind of problems this would inevitably bring. Please try to understand and accept our decision."

After a few moments of thoughtful silence, Lillianna answered with resignation, "Of course, we both understand and do accept your decision. We know you are right, especially where Papa is concerned. He is so bound by his bigoted Southern tradition. He probably would turn on his heel and walk out if you all came, and that would only serve to embarrass you. It also might cause some serious repercussions for Virgil. I hadn't really considered that possibility until now."

Now for the first time, Matt spoke, "Lillianna, I'm afraid we have come with some even more disappointing news for the two of you. Papa is not even considering attending your reception."

"Oh yes he will, Matthew. I am certain he will. If nothing else, his beloved Southern courtesy will require it; and he will not want all of Charleston to be aware that there is a breach within the Prendle family!"

"Lillianna, you've known Papa long enough to know that nothing supersedes his stubborn pride! This Southern courtesy you speak of also demands a response to a formal invitation, but have you received one?"

"Well—no, but I still believe he will come," she insisted.

After their guests had gone, Lillianna and Will sat discussing the situation. Will tried his best to convince Lillianna of the strong possibility of John's not coming and to prepare her for the terrible disappointment she would have to face and accept. But she persisted, "I know that even though he is not planning to attend at this point, at the last minute he will relent and come." Will knew that it was pointless to say anything more.

As the day of the reception drew nearer, all the preparations were nearing completion. With Will's highly valued advice, Lillianna carefully selected her attire for the evening. On the evening before the ball, everything was finally in readiness.

The next evening as Lillianna and Will were dressing, she commented excitedly, “I can’t wait to see Papa. I hope he arrives a little early so that we can have a visit with him before the other guests arrive.”

“My optimistic little Auburn Hair, please prepare not to be too disappointed if your father doesn’t come. I’m afraid that’s a distinct possibility, and I don’t want you to allow that to ruin the whole evening for you.”

“Will, I am sure he will come. But, in the event he should not, I promise to take it in stride and enjoy all the festivities. I am a tougher little magnolia than you think!”

“On the contrary, I think you are a very fragile little magnolia when it comes to your papa!” Then changing the subject, he said, “You look completely ravishing in that beautiful beige ball gown with your mother-of-pearl combs lifting my auburn curls.”

“It isn’t beige; it is ecru; but thank you very much, handsome, for the compliment! Now please fasten Mama’s emerald necklace for me. I think the emerald earrings you bought me in New Orleans match it perfectly; don’t you agree?” she asked, putting them on and admiring the effect in the mirror.

“Completely. While you finish your final preening and perfuming, I am going on downstairs,” he said, as he fastened the cross around her neck. “I love to watch you descend the stairway, the young mistress of Pink Hill Plantation; it stirs my blood!” he added, and kissed her with considerable passion.

“Go on now before you start something we don’t have time to finish,” Lillianna said laughing.

A few minutes later, Will stood in the foyer looking up in anticipation. As Lillianna appeared at the top of the stairway, his heart skipped a beat. He marveled, as always, when he looked at her. "This beautiful creature actually chose me, just plain old Will Pinkston! Oh my little Auburn Hair, you are a woman beyond your years in many ways; yet still a vulnerable child in many others. I fear, no I feel almost sure, that you are going to be terribly hurt tonight. How I wish that I could in some way spare you that pain!"

When she saw Will, Lillianna smiled that radiant smile that could light up a room and Will's entire world. "Papa hasn't arrived has he by any chance?"

"No sweetheart, it's too early for any of the guests to be arriving," Will replied, as he vowed inwardly to give up trying to warn her further and just to be there for her when John failed to come.

The guests began to arrive promptly at 8:00 p.m. and among the first, were Lillianna's brothers and their families. She and Will greeted them with hugs and smiles. "Papa will be along soon won't he?"

"Oh little sister, will you always be such a trusting, vulnerable child, wearing your heart on your sleeve for the breaking? Papa isn't coming; give it up!" Matt said sadly as he embraced her.

Lillianna clung to her brother for only a moment; then she stepped back, squared her shoulders, in typical John Prendle fashion, and smiled radiantly. "Go into the ballroom, have some refreshments, and enjoy the music. Will and I shall join you presently when all the guests have arrived. Then we shall get on with the ball. After all, this is the official debut of Dr. and Mrs. William Pinkston, Jr!"

Will and Lillianna danced the first waltz together, alone on the floor; and the ball was officially underway. As he guided her gracefully around the ballroom, he gazed into her laughing eyes and thought, "She is quite the most beautiful woman in the room—probably in the world!"

The party was a rousing success as the handsome young couple twirled around the ballroom floor with Charleston's elite talking and laughing gaily. Will noticed that Lillianna kept looking hopefully toward the door, but her smile never faded. All in all, it was a perfect night. Lillianna enjoyed the last dance with Will's father. As she thanked him for the beautiful evening, he guided her to her smiling groom and turned her over to him to complete the final dance.

After they had said good night to the last of their guests, they returned to the empty ballroom; and Will asked the orchestra to play one last waltz. As they waltzed around the floor, Lillianna finally allowed the tears to come. Will held her close to him and continued to dance; no words were spoken at all; none were needed.

Will awakened very early next morning after sleeping fitfully. He had spent most of the night worrying about Lillianna's grief. He lay there in bed looking at her lovingly. He felt as if his heart were in a vise at the memory of her pain as they had waltzed that last waltz the night before. He wondered what he would say when she awakened. As he reached over and caressed her cheek gently, she opened her eyes, smiled, and said, "Good morning, darling, wasn't our reception wonderful?" And as she looked over at the sun streaming in the window, she added, "What a beautiful morning it is!" Then looking back at Will, she pulled his head down to her and kissed him tenderly.

He lay there propped up on his elbow, "You never cease to amaze me! I was afraid last night that your father's not coming might throw you into a deep melancholia; now this morning you're greeting the day with a smile!"

"You know, Will, I have learned that there are only two ways to handle a problem. You can surrender, crawl into a shell, and weep; or you can confront it head-on by thinking it through, deciding your strategy, and proceeding to attack that problem. After lunch today, we are going to pay Papa a visit."

"We? I take it you want me to accompany you. You do

realize don't you that your chances for positive results might be better without me?"

"Oh no! I definitely want you with me. We are going to see him on a matter of business. The purpose of our visit is to ask him to sell us Virgil."

She had that look of determination he had come to know so well; so, without arguing, Will replied, "Whatever you wish, my girl; the worst he can do is to refuse! Don't you think we should let him know that we plan to visit?"

"Indeed not! I know Papa so well. I don't want him to have a chance to devise a counter strategy, for he surely would. We'll catch him off-guard."

"I repeat what I said before; you never cease to amaze me!" With that, Will bent to kiss Lillianna again, this time not just a good morning kiss but a passionate kiss, which always led to more.

"Will, wait. You know that refusing your embrace is as hard for me as it is for you, or even harder; and I promise, later Sweetheart, I promise. But we are running late this morning; we must have breakfast and dress if we hope to make it to early services."

"We can go to late services for a change you know," he said as he traced the line of her cleavage with his finger and cupped her breast in his hand as he kissed her again.

"Papa always goes to late service, and I don't want to run into him at church. He would just avoid us, and I don't want to give him that opportunity."

"Oh, all right, but I'm going to hold you to that promise, Miss Auburn Hair!"

"Count on it; it will definitely be my pleasure," she replied as she left the bed looking back provocatively.

That afternoon they set out for Fairlawn in the buggy. For Lillianna's sake, Will was apprehensive about what might lie ahead; but in anticipation of once again visiting her home, she chattered happily as they rode along. As they turned in the drive and approached the mansion, Lillianna said, "I had almost forgotten how truly beautiful it is, Will!"

As the buggy crunched down the long drive, they saw Virgil on the piazza shading his eyes to better see who was arriving. As soon as he recognized them, he rushed inside; and in a matter of moments, he and Matt returned to the piazza and waved to them. As they drove around the oval, Matt stepped down beside the blackamoor and was there to help Lillianna down when Will drew the buggy to a halt.

"Hello little sister and brother, it's wonderful to see you all," he said, hugging her and swinging her around. He set her back on her feet and gave Will a big hug as he clapped him on the back.

Virgil shook hands with them both greeting them warmly, "You all don't know how good it is to see you! I'll go fix some refreshments; Delilah has baked one of your favorites, sweet potato pie," he said as he turned to go into the house.

"Sounds wonderful, Virge," Lillianna replied.

"Lillianna, is Papa expecting you?"

"No, Matt, this isn't a social visit. We are here on business. We've come to ask Papa to let us purchase Virgil," she said, getting right to the point. "Will you tell him we are here?"

"Honey, are you sure you want to do this now? Don't you think you should give him a little more time?"

"No, Matt, I have considered it carefully and at length. We've all known for months that this was the plan; you know that. Will and I feel that it is pointless to delay any longer."

"All right, I hope you're not making a big mistake. Have a seat here on the piazza. He's in the study. I'll go talk to him."

John was reading in his comfortable chair beside the window and had not only heard the buggy approaching and witnessed their arrival, but had overheard the conversation. When Matt tapped on the study door and entered, John said, "Send them away. I don't want to see them, and tell them that Virgil is not for sale at any price. They are not welcome here!"

"But Papa . . ."

"Matthew, I will not discuss this further, "John shouted as he turned on his heel and went out, slamming the little door to the stairway up to his bedroom.

"Oh, Papa, you are so stubborn," Matthew said to the closed door. "You're causing yourself as much or more pain than you are causing her!"

Matt returned to the piazza. "Lillianna sweetheart, I'm so sorry; but he refuses to see you at all. He told me to say that Virgil is not for sale."

"Matt, didn't you ask him at least to see us and listen to our offer?"

"Lillianna, he wouldn't let me say anything. He said Virgil was not for sale at any price, stalked out, and went up to his bedroom!"

"Well, I'm going up to his room to see him and force him to see me. He must at least allow me that!" she said, crying as she started to go inside.

"Will, please reason with her. Lillianna, don't force me to hurt you even more! He said you all are not welcome here!" Matt cried in desperation.

She seemed to freeze in her tracks and then collapsed on the piazza sobbing hysterically. "Oh my God, Will, he truly has come to hate me!"

"Darling, you know that's not true. Your father loves you. I think he just feels we betrayed him and is suffering from an acute case of hurt pride. We need to give him time. I feel sure he will come around in time. I think we should go now, don't you?" Will asked, as he lifted her to her feet, held her close, and kissed her hair.

"Will's right, honey. I'll keep trying to reason with him, and I promise to keep you abreast of how things are going," Matt tried to reassure her.

As they climbed into the buggy to leave, Lillianna said, "Matt, please thank Virgil and tell him we are sorry we couldn't stay for Delilah's potato pie, and please give everyone our love," Lillianna said, as she kissed him good-bye with tears still streaming down her cheeks.

Matt watched as they drove away. Lillianna leaned her head on Will's shoulder, and he could see her body shaking with sobs as they drove out of sight. Now in an uncharacteristic rage, he said through clenched teeth, "That's it, John Prendle, you are going to listen to some things I have to say to you!" He turned, slammed in through the front door, took the stairs two at a time, and burst into his father's bedroom without knocking!

John looked up startled and started to speak, "Matthew, I . . ."

"No! Close your mouth and listen for a change! I have some things to tell you, and you probably should sit down!"

John stood erect, fists clenched, barely maintaining his self-control as he said, "I prefer to stand. I expect this conversation to be brief. I have never tolerated insolence from my children, and I don't intend to start now!"

"I am not a child. And if this be insolence, now is exactly when you shall start! No one knows but Mattie, Mandy, and I, that Mattie is pregnant. You had better sell Virgil to Lillianna and Will, who plan to free him, or free him yourself unless you want your great-grandchild and my grandchild to be born into slavery!"

Suddenly, like a creature without bones, John collapsed into a chair, his face ashen as his eyes widened in puzzlement and disbelief. Matt was shocked; for the first time in his life, he was seeing his father totally unmasked, stripped of the last vestige of self-control.

For one brief moment he thought, "I can't do this. I'll destroy him," but he knew that he had revealed too much to turn back. The whole story must now be told.

He began with that morning so long ago when he watched Mandy move about the plantation kitchen as she prepared his breakfast before he took an early morning ride. Without sparing a single detail, he told John everything, right down to the vows he and Mandy had spoken before Rebecca and Delilah on the morning of Mattie's birth. He then told how Lillianna and Mattie had inadvertently learned the truth and of Lillianna's determination to see Virgil freed after he and Mattie had fallen in love and married.

When Matt, completely exhausted, had finished telling everything, John sat slumped in his chair, his face expressionless, his demeanor that of a man who has been completely defeated. As Matt waited for what seemed an eternity, John finally gathered his composure, rose, walked over to the window, and looked out across the lawn at the peaceful, unchanging river. Matt still waited, saying nothing.

After a long while, John said, "Seems no one, not even my Becca, had much faith in the strength of my character; so I was kept totally in the dark all these years. Matthew, have you any idea how that makes me feel?"

"Papa, we all knew the strength of your principles on the subject of slavery. We knew you to be a man who never compromised his principles! That should tell you in what high regard your entire family has always held your strength of character, especially Mother! Our intent was never to hurt you, only to render you our respect. Lillianna alone was willing to try to introduce the subject by speaking to you about Virgil's freedom before she ever married Will. Look at what your reaction was to that. She is the only person in this family who is as strong as you are and as unwilling as you are to compromise her principles, which just happen to be diametrically opposed to yours! For the stand she took, she has lost her father!"

"She inherited that strength and those principles from Becca. Becca was and is the strength in this family! Those are the things I always cherished most about Lillianna's character! It was not the difference in our principles that ended our relationship; it was the treacherous, duplicitous manner in which she went about exercising them! That decision was hers, not mine!

"Now, have papers drawn up giving Virgil, Delilah, and Samuel their freedom immediately. If he will agree to it, arrange for Virgil to continue in his present capacity, with a salary, of course. If they are willing, send Delilah and Samuel to Pink Hill to live."

"Papa, won't you go with them and see Lillianna and Will?"

"No, I never intend to discuss that subject again!"

Matt knew there was nothing left that he could say. As he rose to leave the room, his father said, "Ask Delilah and Samuel to take Sheba with them to Pink Hill.

"I'll do that, Papa. I'm sure Lillianna will appreciate the gesture. I shall also attend to everything else as you have instructed—immediately!"

When Matt had made everyone in the Prendle household aware of all that had taken place and of the pending results of it, he experienced paradoxical personal feelings. On the one hand, he felt grief for the pain he had caused his father; and on the other, he felt a tremendous sense of relief and happiness that there was no longer anything to hide.

First Matt had gone downstairs to tell Mandy what had happened. She looked at him in shocked disbelief. Her primary concern was for him. "Are you all right, darling? I know it must have been awful for you!"

"Not nearly so awful for me as for Papa, but I'm relieved for all of us that we no longer have to live a lie," he said, as he took her in his arms right there in the foyer and kissed her openly for the first time.

They went down to Mattie's and Virgil's to tell them the wonderful news. Hardly able to believe it, the happy pair danced around the living room, drunk with delight. Matt laid out John's proposal for Virgil's future employment, and Virgil accepted it with gratitude. "Mandy and I need to go back up to the house to tell Delilah and Samuel; but I'll be down first thing in the morning, Virge. You, Delilah, Samuel, and I will go into Charleston and have the papers of freedom drawn up for all three of you. See you about 8:00 a.m. All right?"

"Thank you, Matt. I'll be ready."

When Matt and Mandy had gone, it all suddenly swept over Virgil, "I'm free, Mattie, I'm free! Thank God, at last, I'm really free!"

"I know, darling, I know. Now I have something I want to tell you. Something wonderful that I've wanted so much to share with you! Brace yourself, we are going to have a baby, Virge!"

"We're going to have a baby? Do you mean it?" he asked, his heart tightening into a happy knot as he jumped from his chair and swept Mattie into his arms.

"I mean it, Papa, I really do!" she laughed, as her mouth sought his. She kissed him passionately, fumbling with his belt buckle as her hands caressed him.

He picked her up and started toward their bedroom; then he stopped abruptly. "Will this be safe for you and our baby?" he asked, looking down at her belly.

"Virgil, I'm just pregnant, not an invalid! It's a long time yet before you have to go to the 'gander pasture' and then not for too long," she assured him laughing.

Later as Mattie lay in his arms, her body pressed to his, Virgil said, "Matts, we have something very important to discuss. I want us to choose a surname of our own to record on my papers of freedom tomorrow."

"We could always take Prendle, Virge; that is actually my real name."

"Well, that is a possibility; but I have a story I want to tell you which might influence our decision."

"A story like what, a folk tale or a fairy tale?"

"No, sweetheart, it is a true story about my life. You know most, but not all of it. I have told you before about my life in Savannah, about my education and training, and about my former owner. Well, there is also something important which I haven't told you," he began, as Mattie looked into his eyes, puzzled but listening intently.

"Remember, I told you about the yellow fever epidemic that struck Savannah several years ago when my parents and my owner died. I also told you that his only heir, a nephew, sold the entire estate, of which I was a part. You know how I was sold to Mr. Prendle on the slave block in Charleston. What you don't know, and what I didn't learn until he was dying, is that Mr. David Lineham was actually my father."

"Oh Virge, how could he have kept you in bondage all those years knowing that you were his son?"

"Mattie, he and my mother didn't know what to do. They knew how it would hurt my papa to learn that he wasn't really my father. They both loved Papa very much; but without meaning to, they had fallen in love. When I finally learned the truth, I wasn't at all angry with Mr. Lineham or with my mother. I completely understood their feelings and shared them! However, he wanted to set things right before he died. He dictated a document to me from his deathbed and signed it. It gave me my freedom, acknowledged his paternity, and bequeathed two-thirds of his estate to me and the other third to his nephew. He told me to take it to the Rector of his church and to ask him to see to its administration. After he died, but before I could carry out his wishes, the Rector came down with the fever himself and died. I didn't know what I should do. I finally decided to present the document to Mr. Lineham's nephew and to rely on his southern integrity to honor his uncle's wishes. He took the document, called me a liar, accused me of forgery, and shipped me off to Charleston and the slave block, so much for his southern integrity! I have encountered few men who have had the integrity of my father, the Prendles, and the Pinkstons!"

"You were so very close to having your freedom, not to mention a sizeable fortune! How is it that you're not eaten up with hatred for this man?"

"What good would that do? It would only reveal weakness in my character. That would hurt me, and now you, far more than it would hurt him! 'Vengeance is Mine saith the Lord.' After all, as a result of all this, I found you, the greatest treasure of my life!"

"My dearest love, how fortunate our baby is to have such a truly noble father. At some point, I must have done at least a little something right to deserve you!"

"Mattie, my sweet, you look at me through eyes filled with love, thank God. I think that might cloud your vision more than a little! Now to get to the meat of what I wanted to say. If you will agree, I would like to take Lineham as my surname, our family name."

"Absolutely, Virgil, I couldn't agree more. Lineham it shall be!"

"Now, just to completely clarify for you our baby's paternal bloodline, not that it is important at all, my father was white; and my Mother was part creole, an octoroon."

"Well, as you know, my father is white and my mother is black. However, you are right; it really isn't important at all. As far as the people in our world are concerned, one drop of black blood makes a person a negro. Little do they know, I'm not ashamed of my black blood. On the contrary, I am just as proud of it as I am my Prendle blood! Cut any of us—black, white, or mixed—we all bleed red!"

"Amen," Virgil agreed.

After they had left Mattie and Virgil's house, Mandy and Matt had gone home, almost dreading to give Delilah and Samuel the news of their pending freedom and of why they were being freed. They knew how the old couple felt about having their freedom at this time of their lives. Most of all they feared what their reaction might be when they learned that they were to move to Pink Hill. Their lives had been so uncomplicated for years, and Fairlawn was home. Contrary to all logic, the idea of freedom was far from exciting to them; and moving was the last thing they wanted. When they were young and strong and able to meet the world on its terms, they longed for freedom. Now when they had grown old and tired and worn down by all the years of bondage, they were being offered freedom. Even though their lives and treatment had been good compared to the circumstances of many slaves, bondage is nevertheless bondage. If it weren't so sad and frightening, it would be almost laughable! However, without complaining, they accepted the move stoically as was the custom of slaves.

Matt asked them to join him and Virgil for the trip into Charleston the next morning. They agreed, and assured him they would be ready at 8:00 a.m.

The four of them left Fairlawn promptly at 8:00 a.m. By 1:00 p.m., Delilah, Samuel, and Virgil were free; and Matthew felt wonderful about it all! On the drive back, he and Virgil chatted pleasantly about the future; but Delilah and Samuel rode in silence, holding hands, each occupied with private thoughts.

When they arrived at Fairlawn, Virgil happily headed for home and Mattie. The old couple went to their quarters, with heavy hearts, to pack their meager belongings, clothes and every little bit of treasured memorabilia accumulated over the last sixty years of their lives. "Samuel honey, it sho' don't take much room for a slave to pack a lifetime o' livin' do it?"

"Sho' don't. Ah can 'membah a time when we'da been happy as larks at the thought of freedom. Now, without no edicashun, what can we do but what we allus has done; an' listen to us tawk! I hates it; I allus has! We's got pride; we thinks and feels. We ain't dumb jus' cause we soun's like it!"

"Aw come on; we cain't change all dat now. Lets go wid a smile," Delilah said, "we's gonna be wid our precious Miss Lillianna an' Mistuh Will! Life's gonna be good!"

Mid-afternoon, Matt drove the wagon up to the end of the kitchen breezeway to load their belongings. He had already loaded Lillianna's saddle and all of Sheba's gear into the wagon. He helped Samuel load the wagon and went back to the stable for Sheba. Delilah and Samuel were to drive in the wagon to Pink Hill, and Matt was going to ride Sheba.

The old couple went into the house to thank John for everything and to say good-bye. They went to his study, and Samuel tapped lightly on the door. John opened the door and came out into the foyer.

"Well, I see you folks are about ready to leave. At least you have a pretty afternoon for the drive," he said, as he looked out the front door.

"Yassuh, yassuh, we sho' do," Samuel replied. "We jus' come in to thank you, suh, for everthin', all dese years, an' to tell you g'bye."

"I'm the one who should be thanking you for all these years of excellent and dedicated service! There really is no way to adequately thank you; but I would like you to accept this small token of my regard for you both!" John took a small locked box from the foyer table and presented it to Samuel. "It's only money, my dear friends; and money could never express the gratitude I feel. And by the way, this isn't good-bye. We'll never say that. You know you are welcome here anytime you can come. And I shall be expecting to see you both—often!"

"Thank you, suh, for the gift and for everthing!" Delilah sobbed, as she turned and rushed from the foyer. Samuel followed, his head down and his eyes filled with tears. They went into the breezeway; and Matt, sitting astride Sheba, was waiting for them. They slowly climbed up into the wagon; Matt handed Samuel the reins; and the little party left for Pink Hill.

John stood looking out the study window. He watched until the wagon drove out of sight. "Well John, your world is growing smaller and smaller," he thought sadly. However, never a man to indulge in self-pity, he immediately busied himself poring over the plantation books, looking for ways to operate more efficiently.

Lillianna was at the little writing table in her bedroom working on thank you notes for the many wedding gifts that she and Will had received. When she heard the wagon coming down the drive, she hopped up and ran to the window. Delighted to see the little group coming up the drive, she raced downstairs to greet them. She ran out on the piazza, all smiles, "You all have made an otherwise dreary and boring day burst into sunlight with a rainbow! I can't think of any visitors I would rather have than the three of you, and Sheba! I needed this visit so!" she exclaimed, running to hug them all as they climbed down from the wagon.

After Matt had helped Delilah and Samuel down, he said, "Lillianna, could we all go inside to the parlor to talk? We have so much to tell you, most of it excellent news, some of it not so good, but all of it shocking!"

"By all means, I'll ask Ellen to bring us some hot tea and ginger cookies."

"Don't go to no trouble for us, honey," Delilah insisted.

"No trouble at all, Wilah. I was about to have some myself when I heard you all driving in." She went back to the kitchen and asked their cook, Ellen, to prepare the tray."

She returned to the parlor and rejoined the three of them. "All right, my curiosity is killing me! Come on, tell me what has happened!"

Matt began, "Is Will here? I would like for him to hear this too." "No, he went to work with Dr. Gilmore after classes today. I don't expect him until much later this evening."

"Well, I'm sure I can count on you to relay the news to him when he gets home. I'll proceed with the best news first.

Virgil, Delilah, and Samuel are now freedmen as of this morning; and Delilah, Samuel, and Sheba have come to live here at Pink Hill. Virgil will remain employed in his same capacity at Fairlawn. He and Mattie will now be completely responsible for running the household, and Mandy will assist them and will continue doing the cooking. All of this took place under explicit orders from Papa. Now I'm sure you're wondering how and why all this came to pass. That is the part of the story that isn't so pleasant." Matt looked at his sister sitting there in stunned silence. "Lillianna, I've never in your life seen you completely speechless. Are you all right?"

"I am speechless. I don't know what to say! I am delighted, but completely mystified and absolutely terrified! Is Papa all right?"

"Yes, he is all right physically; but he has tremendous emotional adjustment to make! It is almost impossible to believe that our whole world could turn completely around—indeed, upside-down—in little more than twenty-four hours. No one slept at Fairlawn last night. We have all been very busy!" He then proceeded to tell her everything that had happened since she and Will had visited the afternoon before, omitting only their father's final comments about her.

"Well, you were absolutely right! Most of this news is wonderful beyond believing, but the rest is worse than 'not so good'. It had to have been hell, not only for Papa, but for you. I must go to him!"

Silence hung in the air as Matt reached over and took her small hand in both of his. "Honey, there is more. I had hoped I could spare you this. However, if I have learned nothing else, it is that no one is really spared from pain by secrecy. It is only delayed to hurt even more when it does finally come out!" He told her all the wonderful, complimentary things their father had said about her and her strength of character; but he was forced to also tell her John's final word on her betrayal and of the futility of her hoping for a future relationship with him.

When Matt had finished, Lillianna, sat there dry-eyed, as only Delilah wept silently for her pain. "It may be futile, Matt; but I shall never give up hope that he will someday forgive me!"

"Now I haven't even stopped to rejoice that Virgil and Mattie have their first baby coming. Please tell them how delighted I am for them and ask them to come to Pink Hill with you and Mandy for a visit. We all have a lot of celebrating to do," she said happily, as she hugged Delilah and Samuel again.

Matt rose, "I need to head for home as soon as we get the wagon unloaded. Mandy will be expecting me."

"Honey, we don't wanna be no bothuh to you and Mr. Will," Delilah said frowning.

"Bother? I'm delighted you'll be here with us, and Will, will be too! We have the nicest little tenant house at the end of the back lane that will be all yours. We have been looking for an older tenant couple to hire for light housework to assist Ellen a little with her duties."

"Hire? We don't 'spect no money!"

"Now listen to me, you two are freedmen now! People who are hired at Pink Hill receive a fair wage, and you will also! I'm sure you will be able to find some things you might like to have, perhaps a new hat, Wilah, and a nice store-bought pipe, Samuel."

When they all went back outside to the wagon, Lillianna had a chance to really greet Sheba for the first time. "Hello my beautiful lady, welcome home. You're going to love it here, and I'm going to love having you. Come on, Matt, you, Wilah, and Samuel follow me in the wagon. I'll lead the way to their house." She mounted astride Sheba; and with a click-click of her tongue and a nudge of her heels, she trotted the horse gracefully around in front of the wagon. She waited while the trio climbed aboard; then, led off around the house and down the lane.

In the days and weeks that followed, both Pink Hill and Fairlawn underwent landmark changes. Every person in both households had tremendous adjustments to make—all happily so, except John, who chaffed under the harsh bit of departure from southern tradition. Of course, as always, news traveled and the story grew on the wings of gossip. All Charleston was abuzz and indignant with the what and why of the happenings within the Prendle/Pinkston family. Little did any of the principal characters involved realize the far-reaching reverberations of all that was taking place.

At Fairlawn, Virgil's and Mattie's lives and duties changed very little. However, as Mattie's pregnancy progressed, Mandy spent more and more time helping to carry her workload. The rapid increase in her size soon made it evident that the possibility that she was carrying more than one baby was very likely; a fact which was later confirmed when Dr. Gilmore discovered the presence of two fetal heartbeats. Everyone was delighted at the prospect of the arrival of two precious new babies!

Aside from sharing the excitement of becoming grandparents twice at one time, Matt and Mandy experienced very little change in their lives. Mandy continued to live in the household slaves' quarters off the back breezeway. Her primary responsibility was to oversee and help with the cooking and to help Mattie and Virgil supervise the rest of the household staff. Matt continued to sleep in the room he had occupied all of his life and to assist John in managing the business affairs of the plantation. Although John was aware of their personal relationship, out of respect for him, they were always discreet and never showed outward affection where anyone else in the household might observe them.

The rest of the boys and their families were aware of the whole story, but it was never discussed. No one ever expressed a personal opinion, pro or con. The closeness of the family and their upbringing demanded this loyalty.

As John progressed through a series of changes, they evoked many paradoxical emotions in those who observed his gradual metamorphosis. They felt anger, yet, a measure of understanding when at first he became reclusive. Except for meals, he remained in the private world of his bedroom and study, communicating only as plantation business required. After a few weeks, he seemed to awaken suddenly as from hypnosis. They observed the old John stride forth again, master of his domain—but something was missing of the old gentility, the old courtesy. They were all disappointed at this change, but still relieved that they had not lost him. And they admired the strength that had kept him from losing himself. Then finally, after some six months, he came full circle, accepting the inevitable changes with the dignity and kindness that had always personified his nature. They respected him more than ever when they stopped to consider the long and difficult journey he had made successfully. In the end, their only disappointment lay in the fact that he was still unable to forgive Lillianna.

At Pink Hill, the transition took place more smoothly. Although Matt kept them informed of the general happenings at Fairlawn, he softened the details for Lillianna in order to protect her from things that would cause her pain. Delilah and Samuel were delighted with their new house. The furnishings were nicer than any they had ever had; and with great pride, they cleaned, polished, and painted until it was sparkling. They planted flowers in their yard, and Lillianna saw to it that they had whatever they needed to complete the job. With the very first wages they were ever paid, they purchased two porch rockers and a swing to match. They were prouder of these possessions than anything they had ever owned. The two of them stood in the front yard looking at the whole picture, "Ain't dis' sumpin', Samuel, my, my!"

"Yassum', honey, it sho' is!"

Every afternoon, Lillianna rode Sheba down the road to her nook beside the Ashley River and then around to Mattie's house for a visit. The two girls, never seeming to run out of things to discuss, would sit on the porch and talk for hours. As she headed back toward home, she would pause again beside the river and gaze longingly across the broad expanse of lawn, rolling in green velvety waves up to the mansion. On many afternoons, her father gazed longingly back at her from the curtained window of the study.

Virgil, Mattie, Mandy, and Matt frequently visited Delilah and Samuel in the evenings. Will and Lillianna would usually join them all for dessert. Except for John's absence from her life, Lillianna was happier than she had ever been.

Will would be graduating from medical school in June rather than December, as initially expected, because he had accelerated his courses after he and Lillianna had married. In mid-May, he was extremely busy preparing for final theoretical and practical exams as well as a battery of orals with Dr. Gilmore. He and Lillianna had very little time for themselves since the big reception. Finally, in late May, all the exams were finished; and the only pressure remaining was the wait for exam results. Will was an excellent student and had been very dedicated to his work with Dr. Gimore; so as he gathered with the other students at the board where grades were posted, he felt fairly confident that his exam results would be acceptable. When he finally worked his way through the group to see his grades, he was delighted to find them not only acceptable but excellent; in fact, he led the class.

He raced to the stable where he boarded his horse during the day when he was in class. He didn't wait for the stable attendant; instead, he went to Lancelot's stall, saddled him, mounted, and headed for Pink Hill. He could hardly wait to tell Lillianna the good news.

When he arrived at home, he dismounted, tied the horse

to the blackamoor, turned, and ran inside and up the stairs, seemingly in one fluid motion. When he reached their bedroom, he dashed inside, lifted Lillianna off the floor, swung her 'round and 'round and fell on the bed with her in his arms, gasping for breath and laughing. "Mrs. Dr. William Pinkston, Jr. you are now lying in the arms of the Valedictorian of the Charleston Medical College Class of 1834!"

"Will, do you mean it? That's wonderful! I am so proud of you; however, I am not at all surprised. You have earned it! We have to celebrate. Let's go down and tell your father the news."

They found Mr. Pinkston in the study. Unable to wait for Will, in his reserved and modest way, to tell his Father the news, Lillianna bubbled it out proudly. Mr. Pinkston congratulated the happy couple and went over to the wine cabinet. He brought the tray with the brandy snifters and brandy and set it on the table. "I think a toast to our honor graduate is in order. What do you think young Mistress of Pink Hill?"

Lillianna flushed with delight that Will's father had now conferred this title upon her himself. "Yes, Father Pinkston, I agree wholeheartedly!" she replied.

Mr. Pinkston smiled with pleasure at this new appellation as he hugged her with one arm and poured the brandy with the other.

That night Will and Lillianna were in their dressing room preparing for bed. Will watched her as she turned and looked at her full body profile in the mirror, running her hands over her abdomen. Then she walked over to him, and encircling his neck with her arms, she said, "Dr. Pinkston, I have a graduation present for you."

"Although graduation is still ten days away, I shall accept that present in installments, the first tonight and several more before graduation!"

"Oh, my dear, that goes without saying, countless times for the rest of our lives! That is not my gift."

"Oh? Then pray tell what is this mysterious gift?"

"What would you think of—say—a baby?"

Will's eyes widened, and his mouth was agape as he stepped back and surveyed her from head to toe and back. "What—how—?" he stammered.

"In the usual way, I imagine," she responded laughing.

"Oh, of course, I know that! But how could I not have known? After all, I am a doctor."

"I guess you have just been too busy to keep track of things. At any rate, Dr. Gilmore confirmed it today."

Will pulled her to him and kissed her. He buried his face in her hair, as he did so frequently, and murmured, "My sweet Auburn Hair, next to the day you became my wife, this is the happiest day of my life!"

Lillianna kissed him back. Then wriggling out of his arms, she turned again to look at her profile in the mirror. Rubbing her still flat abdomen, she inquired, "Will, do you think I am getting fat and ugly already?"

"No sweets, I think you're absolutely beautiful. Not only that, by the time our baby comes, I shall think you are gorgeous!"

"You think you really will?"

"Count on it!"

Ten days later, Will graduated. The Prendles and the Pinkstons turned out in force for his big day—that is everyone except John. He ignored it completely. Five months earlier, Lillianna would have been devastated. Now his absence didn't surprise her at all and hurt her very little. It was a perfect day. Lillianna's usual morning sickness didn't manifest itself; and seeing Will receive his diploma was one of the proudest moments of her life—surpassed only by the pride she felt at his Valedictory Address, which was masterful. Following the ceremony, Mr. Pinkston hosted a surprise dinner for both families in honor of Will's graduation.

That night, after an exhausting day, Will and Lillianna

retired early. When they were in bed, they lay in each others arms and talked. "I guess you'll be going to work with Dr. Gilmore immediately?" Lillianna asked.

"No, as a matter of fact, he insists that I take a vacation and spend some time with you. I'll start work the first of July. Until then, we'll relax and enjoy each other. Perhaps we'll get the nursery ready for the baby and shop for a layette. Would you like that?"

"I would love it! You know, Will, this is such a wonderful time. Mattie and Virgil's babies are due in September, and ours is due in December. History seems to be repeating itself. I was born three months after Mattie was born, and our baby will be born three months after hers." Lillianna lay there silent for a moment; then she shuddered and snuggled closer to Will.

"What is it, sweets, why the shudder?"

"It just crossed my mind that Mama died when I was born."

"Oh, sweetheart, don't even think those thoughts. Everything is going to be fine. You are in perfect health, and you have one excellent doctor and one learning to be."

"Of course, I'm just being silly. Guess I'm somewhat like the Orientals; everything is so perfect that I wonder if our beautiful bubble might burst."

"My Auburn Hair, you are so kind and caring. You have the soul of an angel, and you deserve every happiness God has granted you. So bask in its light and enjoy it."

Just before she went to sleep, Lillianna murmured drowsily, "Poor Papa, he's missing so much by refusing to share all the happiness of our families. Say some little prayers for him, Will. He needs them so."

"I have been, love; and I promise to continue," Will replied, his face in her hair as they both dropped off to sleep.

Will started practice with Dr. Gilmore in July. They always found their days full. It was a large practice, which was growing larger every year. Will was happy to be out of the classroom at last and to actually be practicing. Dr. Gilmore was an excellent diagnostician, and Will was gaining experience and medical insight with each passing day.

Lillianna celebrated her eighteenth birthday without great fanfare. A simple family dinner with the Pinkston and Prendle families was really a baby shower for Lillianna and Mattie rather than a birthday party for Lillianna.

Lillianna's pregnancy was advancing normally and according to schedule. Mattie, being three months ahead of her and carrying twins, was, of course, growing larger and more uncomfortable each day. The intense low-country heat and humidity didn't help matters at all. Although she was no longer riding Sheba, Lillianna drove the buggy to visit Mattie several times each week. Their conversations revolved around everything pertaining to babies—pregnancy, childbirth, possible names (for both sexes), nursing, rearing, et cetera. As they sat on the porch rocking and fanning one afternoon, Lillianna asked, "Mattie, of all the character traits what one would you most want your babies to possess?"

"I don't know. I really haven't given that any thought. How about you?"

"I'm not really sure either; but I think strength of conviction, followed by—hummm—loyalty would lead my list."

Mattie thought for a minute and finally said, "The two 'I's I think, integrity and intelligence."

"Good choices, Mattie. Is there a reason you chose those?"

"That's easy, my babies are going to be boys. I want them to be like Virgil, and these are two of his strongest characteristics."

"How do you know they're going to be boys?" They just might be girls. I've always heard that women carry girls high and boys low, and your babies are right under your ribs."

"I tell you my babies are going to be boys! I don't know how I know it, but I know it!"

"All right Miss Clairvoyant, but you are going to be surprised if they are girls or maybe even a boy and a girl."

"Just wait and see!"

"By the way, have you considered what you're going to name these boys you're so positive you're going to have?"

"Oh yes, Virgil and I have already chosen their names. Of course, you know our surname is Lineham. One of our sons will be named Louis Samuel Lineham; and the other, Julius Prendle Lineham. The man who was actually Virgil's father was David Louis Lineham, and the man Virgil knew and loved as father was named Julius. We shall call them Louis and Julius."

"The names are perfect, Mattie. I love them. Will and I have talked a little about names, girl's and boy's; but so far, we have no favorites. Well, I had better leave for home. Since the sun is getting a little lower, maybe the drive won't be quite as hot."

As Lillianna drove along River Road, John was watching from the study window. Of course, he had been told that she and Will were expecting their first baby; and he thought to himself, "Oh Becca, our little baby is going to have a baby herself. She is so young and so small, and I am so afraid for her!"

He was too absorbed in thought to hear Matt enter the study. Suddenly, over his shoulder, he heard, "Papa she longs to see you too. She is always waiting in the hope that you will come. She loves you so very much. With the baby coming, this is the perfect time. You have the perfect excuse to bury your pride and go to her without losing face!"

Without turning from the window, John replied, "Matthew, it has never had anything to do with pride or face or love. It is a matter of principle!" Then he turned without even looking at Matt and went out through the stairwell door.

Matt looked after him thinking, "Oh, Papa, how you insist on torturing yourself!"

Lillianna arrived at Pink Hill to find Will waiting for her in their bedroom. "Where have you been off to my little vagabond?" he asked laughing.

"I've been down visiting Mattie. Lord she's getting so big, Will; and she isn't due for six more weeks!"

"That isn't surprising; she's carrying twins. Dr. Gilmore and I dropped by to check on her just a few days ago. Everything is fine."

"I guess I'm just a worry wart. Do you think maybe women worry more when they are pregnant?"

"I have never read anything in the medical books to support that theory scientifically; but from my personal observation of you, it seems a strong possibility," he said, putting his hands on her hips and drawing her to him.

"Wait, Will, did you feel that?" Lillianna asked wide eyed.

"Feel what?"

"That—that, didn't you feel it?"

"No, I'm sorry, sweets, I didn't feel a thing."

Lillianna pushed Will away gently and bent down to pull up her skirt and petticoats to expose her underpants. Taking Will's hand, she placed it on her abdomen and said, "Wait a minute, maybe she'll move again."

Will waited a few seconds and said, "I still don't feel a thing."

"Shhh, be quiet and wait. There! Did you feel that?"

"Maybe, I'm not sure. How does it feel?"

"From inside, it feels like what the fluttering of a little angel's wings must feel like. It's wonderful! There, there it is again! Did you feel it?"

"Yes! Yes, I definitely felt it then; and it is exactly as you described it!"

The two of them stood there not daring to move. With tears streaming down their happy faces, they waited for their baby to move again; but it didn't happen.

"She must have gone back to sleep," Lillianna whispered.

What's this she business? Is that prediction or a wish on Mama's part?"

"Oh no, I don't care whether our baby is a boy or a girl as long as it is normal and healthy. It's just that Mattie is so positive that her babies are both boys that I figure odds are against our also having a boy."

"I'm not sure that odds figure into this sort of situation. I wouldn't think they do. Besides, why is Mattie so sure their babies are boys?"

"I don't know, but she doesn't seem to have a doubt. I told her that I've always heard that girl babies are carried high and out front, and boys are carried low between the hips. If that is true, hers are surely girls because they are right beneath her ribs and way out front!"

"I believe that is actually backwards from the way I heard it; but I think it's probably an old wives' tale anyway. I have been working with Dr. Gilmore ever since I started medical school; and we have seen and delivered mothers who carried boys and girls, high and low. Seems you and Mattie have covered babies in depth in your conversations."

"That shouldn't be surprising since we are both in our first pregnancy; and yes, we have. We have discussed everything, some extremely profound things. For instance, tell me, Will, if you could choose only one characteristic you most wanted our baby to possess, what would it be?"

"My, my, your subjects have been profound haven't they? You might be surprised that your question requires very little thought for me. Far above all other qualities, I would choose compassion. All the most important qualities would follow naturally—love, loyalty, principle, et cetera. What would you choose first?"

"Well, I told Mattie my first choice would be strength of conviction, followed closely by loyalty; but your choice has changed my mind. I think you are right. Will, how did you grow so wise at such a young age?"

"On the contrary, I don't consider myself wise at all; but I have so often witnessed the terrible things to which a lack of compassion can lead. Now, I am curious, what was Mattie's answer to your question?"

"Her answer didn't surprise me at all; it was so—uh—'Mattie'! She had two equal choices. She called them the two 'I's, integrity and intelligence. I am sure you know her reasons without my telling you. These are two of Virgil's greatest strengths; and Mattie, more than loves Virgil, she worships him!"

"They are wonderful attributes, and I understand her mindset. Had my life experience been the same as hers and Virgil's, I would want my children to have an impenetrable fortress which bondage could never breach—integrity. I would want them to possess a weapon which would conquer bondage, or at the very least, make it endurable—intelligence."

"I repeat my question, Dr. Pinkston, how ever did you grow so wise, so soon? Life with you is really going to be an education!"

After they were in bed that night, Lillianna said, "Will, I was just thinking about how near Mattie's delivery time is. I hope you and Dr. Gilmore aren't planning to allow that new young midwife to deliver her babies. Although I am sure she was well-trained, I want you and Dr. Gilmore to be there with Mattie."

"Darling, we have every intention of being there. We've assured Mattie and Virgil that we shall both be there. It's not every day a doctor has the opportunity to help deliver twins this early in his career. This delivery will be a great training experience for me; and, after all, this is our niece Mattie!"

"Ah Will, how I do adore you!" Lillianna said, as she kissed him and snuggled down in his arms saying, "By the way, I'm going to be there, too."

"I'm not sure that would be wise with your facing delivery in just three months."

"Will, I am going to be there!"

"We'll see, sweetheart; we'll talk about it, all right?"

"I am going to be there!" she continued to insist.

Will opened his mouth to protest again; but he smiled as he saw Lillianna, in retrospect, on her tenth birthday declaring adamantly, ". . . I'll race her myself and I'll win; you'll see!" Then in his mind's eye, he saw her and Sheba cross the finish line, winning the first ladies' race at Washington Race Course by four full lengths.

"All right, 'Mrs. Dr. Pinkston', it shall be as you wish."

About four weeks later in the wee hours of the morning of September 18, the Pinkston household was startled awake by the clatter of hooves and Matt's voice shouting, "Will, Will, wake up, wake up; Mattie's in labor; and it's moving fast! Jay has gone for Dr. Gilmore."

Will had bounded from the bed at the first sound of the horse's hooves and Matt's frantic shouts. He had opened their window overlooking the piazza and was looking out by the time Matt reined in at the blackamoor. He could see Matt clearly in the light of the moon.

"You head back, Matt. I'll get dressed, saddle up, and be right behind you." Looking up at the full moon, Will said, "Should have thought it might be tonight with that full moon; always seems to trigger labor."

"Hurry, Will, we'll be waiting for you," Matt called back. "Like I said it's moving fast!"

As Will rushed to dress, Lillianna got out of bed. "Why Dr. Pinkston, full moon triggers labor? And you talk to me about old wives' tales!" she laughed, pulling on her robe and stepping into her slippers. "You go on; and I'll dress, waken

Delilah and Samuel, and tell them the news. I'll be right along in the buggy."

Will didn't stop to argue. He knew it would be useless. "All right sweets, but take your time and be careful."

Looking out the window, she responded, "I'll be fine. With the full moon, it's almost like daylight outside. Besides, I am sure Delilah and Samuel will insist on coming with me. Will, do you suppose it would be safe for me to ride Sheba just this once? I could get there so much faster."

"Forget it; that is out of the question!" he said firmly as he grabbed his bag, gave her a quick kiss, and ran out the door.

When Lillianna, Delilah, and Samuel arrived at Mattie's and Virge's house, the sun had just peeped over the horizon sending a ribbon of gold up the river. Lillianna turned and looked at her river smiling, "What a beautiful day for our babies to be born. Oh Wilah and Samuel, I'm going to be a great-aunt; and you two are going to be great-grandparents. Isn't it wonderful?"

When they entered the living room, they were surprised to see Dr. Gilmore settled comfortably in a chair as Virgil paced the floor. They could hear Mattie's groans as Mandy encouraged her, "Push, honey, push!"

"What's going on, Dr. Gilmore? Why aren't you in there?" Lillianna asked frowning.

"This is Will's case. I thought it a good one for his first solo delivery."

"Oh Lord, Dr. Gilmore, that scares me witless! Is everyone all right with that decision? I mean Will is so young, so new at this; and these are Mattie's twins he's delivering!" Lillianna exclaimed, obviously distressed.

"Of course!" Virgil answered her question. "I haven't a doubt in the world! I am confident that Will Pinkston could do anything to which he set his mind and do it well! How could you of all people wonder?"

"I have no doubts about Will's ability either, but I wonder about his objectivity. He is so close to this case personally."

Dr. Gilmore spoke up, "If Will had any doubt himself, he would never have agreed to this; but, on the contrary, he welcomed the chance. So rest your pretty little auburn head; he has everything under control."

"May I go in to be with her?"

"Under the circumstances, as your doctor I don't advise it."

"Wait a minute! Dr. Gilmore, you know how I love you; but Will is my doctor!"

"And you were questioning his objectivity here? No ma'am, he knows it wouldn't even be ethical. I'll be delivering your baby."

"I am sure you are right, sir. I guess there is much I haven't learned yet about medical ethics."

"They heard Will's voice, "Here he comes, Mattie, one last push—PUSH! Good!" They heard a smack followed by a strong newborn cry. "All right! Young Master Lineham number one has arrived. We're halfway home, Mattie Girl! Are you hearing me out there, Virgil? Your first son is beautiful!" Will called out.

"Yes, Will, we're all hearing you out here and thanking God!" Virgil answered through happy tears. They all remained where they were unmoving, waiting as children wait, transfixed, anticipating the last half of a suspenseful drama.

The wait seemed interminable. Finally Lillianna said, "Lord this is frightening; that silence in there is ominous. What do you suppose is going on, Dr. Gilmore?"

"Just be patient; a time lapse between the delivery of twins isn't at all unusual," he answered.

Some ten minutes later, they knew from Mattie's cries that her labor had resumed. This time it progressed much more rapidly; and in about six more minutes, Will again called for that last push. They heard Mattie groan with the push followed in rapid succession by the smack, the strong cry, and Will's laughing comment, "Welcome, Master Slow Poke, what took you so long?"

They all moved to the closed bedroom door waiting, hugging, crying; then Mandy opened the door smiling, "You all come on in and see our beautiful babies!" They all waited to let Virgil go ahead to the bed where his exhausted but smiling Mattie rested between their sons.

"Thank you for my beautiful sons, sweetheart. I've never loved you more than I do at this moment," Virgil whispered as he kissed her. He then looked at the babies proudly as he kissed each little nose. "I'm your papa, boys, and I love you."

Mattie reached up and caressed his face lovingly, "Thank you, my love, for granting me the privilege of being the mother of your sons. I am so very honored."

Virgil turned to the group waiting at the door, "These young men are waiting to meet their family; come on in and let their mama and papa introduce them to you. Mattie, we forgot something. We haven't decided which is which!"

Mattie started to laugh, "Oh my Lord, Virge, how could we have forgotten that?" she said as she began to laugh even harder.

"Come on, Mattie, this is serious!" Virgil responded with distress in his voice.

Mattie struggled to regain her composure, a smile still lurking behind her eyes. "Of course, Virgil, you are right; this is serious. So let's make that decision right now. Let's look at them and decide which one looks like a Louis and which one, a Julius."

"Well how are we going to do that? They look exactly alike!"

"You are right again, so let's choose another way to decide. Let's see, I wouldn't want to draw straws or toss a coin. That would imply one was a winner and one, a loser; and that would be misleading to them when they grow older and hear this story. How about naming them alphabetically, based on order of birth. The one born first would be Julius, and the one born second would be Louis."

"That sounds like a good idea to me, so which is which? You'll have to tell me."

"On my right is Julius, and on my left is Louis."

"Good, now we are ready for the formal introduction to your family." As everyone crowded around the bed, Virgil said to the babies, "Julius Prendle Lineham and Louis Samuel Lineham this is your family, the people who will always love you and help us to guide you. These two with tears running down their faces are your grandma Mandy and your grandpa Matthew. The two standing there grinning like cheshire cats are your great-grandma Delilah and your great-grandpa Samuel. This fellow, who brought you into the world, is your great-uncle Will; and the lady in his arms is your great-aunt Lillianna. This handsome gentleman with gray hair is Dr. Gilmore; he taught your great-uncle Will everything he knows! There are many more folks you will be meeting later."

Will said, "Now, I think it is time for us to go and to allow this new mother and her sons to get some rest and to give their papa some privacy just to dote a little!"

Virgil saw them all to the door and waved goodbye as they left for home. Mandy said, "I'll go home and get some things together. I'll be back later to stay awhile. You four are going to be needing grandma's help for a few days."

"Thank you, Mandy. I'm sure you're right. We'll need and appreciate your expertise!"

Will was on horseback on the ride home to Pink Hill, so Lillianna rode back in the buggy with Delilah and Samuel. Of course, all conversation was about the new babies. "Ain't 'dem 'de most beautiful babies you ever seen, honey?" Delilah asked Lillianna.

"Yes, they most certainly are! Do you think that they

look like Virgil and a little like their grandpa Prendle too, around the eyes?"

"Well, I see Virge all right, but I don't see Mistuh Matt much."

"Oh I don't mean Matt. I mean Papa. I should have said great-grandpa."

"They still too little to tell who they gonna look like; but they sho' do look a lot like Virge 'thout a doubt."

"I agrees, and they sho' is handsome boys, 'dat 'dey is!" Samuel chimed in smiling.

"Maybe I just want to see Papa in them," Lillianna said. "I hope he goes down to see them. Surely he will. They are innocent babies and haven't done anything wrong."

The next morning as soon as Lillianna and Will had finished breakfast and Will was about to leave for work, she kissed him goodbye and said, "As soon as I can dress and get the buggy hitched-up, I am going to Mattie's to see if I can help today."

"That's no surprise to me at all. I know you can hardly wait to get your hands on those babies, so go on over and enjoy your day. Just don't overdo it. Remember your own condition and take it easy," Will replied, giving her one last kiss.

"I promise not to overdo and not to be too late getting home. You and Dr. Gilmore have a good day. I'm sure I'll be seeing you two when you come by to check on Mattie and the babies today," she said as she turned, completely forgetting her condition, and bounced up the stairs in her usual way.

Following her with his eyes, Will just shook his head and smiled. "I might as well face it, my little Auburn Hair is going to bounce as long as she can!"

Within an hour, Lillianna was on her way to Mattie's house. As she drew abreast of her nook beside the river, she stopped for just a moment to gaze at the sunlight on the water. She started to flick the reins to move on as she glanced down the road at Mattie's house and saw a familiar figure walking up the front steps. "Oh, my Lord, it is Papa; and he is all dressed up!" Selam was tied to the hitching post at the end of the walkway. Lillianna knew her Father so well that she had always been able to sense his every mood by simply observing the various nuances of his body movement. "Thank God he is elated at the prospect of seeing his great-grandsons. I can see it in that youthful, jaunty step of his. I can't go in now and ruin this for all of them. I must go home and come back later." With paradoxical emotions, she laughed with delight that John was coming to see the babies; yet, wept that she could not be there to be part of it. She turned the buggy about and headed back to Pink Hill.

In the weeks ahead, Lillianna was a frequent visitor at River Bend, as Mattie and Virgil had named their little place. She adored the precious little boys; and as they grew cuter, chubbier, and more alert, she looked forward with greater and greater anticipation to the arrival of her own baby.

As the time drew nearer, the weather grew colder, and Lillianna grew larger, she was forced to stay close to home. She and Delilah busied themselves with the Christmas decorations and with putting the finishing touches on the nursery. When they had finished hemstitching the last of the receiving blankets and pre-laundering and ironing the entire layette, all was in readiness for the coming of the baby. Mandy and Matt were in and out almost daily monitoring Lillianna's progress and bringing messages of encouragement from Mattie and Virgil.

Early on the morning of December 24th, Lillianna awakened with a backache. "Will, if it is all right with you, I think I'll rest in bed a little longer this morning and eat a light breakfast later. I might have overdone it yesterday when Delilah and I gave the nursery a last thorough cleaning. I have a slight backache," she said as she went into their dressing room to use the chamber urinal. She was startled to see a spot of blood when she looked into the urinal. "Will, come here quickly. I'm bleeding!"

Will bounded out of bed and into the dressing room. When he looked into the urinal, his smile put Lillianna's fears to rest. "You have had what we call 'the show,' that little spot of blood. It usually means you're going into labor, especially in your case since it is accompanied by that backache. I think we're on our way, little mother. Although there is probably no real hurry, I'll go for Dr. Gilmore right after breakfast."

"But Will, today is Christmas Eve. I don't have time to have a baby today. There is still so much left to do to get ready for Christmas tomorrow!" she protested.

"Sorry, love, babies don't ask if today is convenient. I am sure you have heard 'When the apple's ripe, it will fall'. Well ours is ripe I'm pretty sure!"

As Will saddled up and rode out for Dr. Gilmore, he acknowledged the fact that his stomach was in a knot and had been since the moment he had looked into that urinal. He had helped deliver so many babies and had delivered Mattie's twins on his own. Why was he so frightened at the prospect of Lillianna's delivering their baby? She had, had a perfectly normal pregnancy with no problems at all; yet he was feeling panicky. Now he understood why Dr. Gilmore insisted on handling this delivery alone. He knew he would not be able to handle it himself. Nevertheless, he also knew he could not leave the room to allow her to go through it without him. Now that he had settled in his own head what his role in this case would be, only that of husband and father, he allowed himself to surrender to the usual husband's panic and spurred his horse to a gallop as he rode for Dr. Gilmore.

After filling Dr. Gilmore in on everything that had happened to Lillianna that morning and with Dr. Gilmore's assurance that he would be along shortly, Will headed back home, still at a gallop, thinking to himself, "This is ridiculous! After all, you are a doctor!"

When he reached Pink Hill, Delilah met him in the stable. "Mistuh Will, things is movin' along purty fast with Miss Lillianna. She be so much like her mama was it scares me. I hope it's all right with you; I done sent Samuel for Mandy to come help."

"That's fine Delilah. I am sure Lillianna will want both of you here," Will said as he ran inside and up the stairs to their bedroom. "I'm here, darling," he said as he entered the room. "How are you feeling?"

"The pain comes in a wave then leaves just as you and Dr. Gilmore said it would. They are a half hour or more apart I think, but each one is worse than the one before. Tell you one thing, they're no picnic; and I know they are going to get worse—much worse. Tell you something else, I'm not scared; but I'm not the type to bear this stoically like Mattie did! I am going to do some yelling when that pain comes, and anybody who doesn't want to hear it better get out of the house. Oh, Lord, here comes another one! Before this gets any worse, Will, no matter what ugly thing I might say to blame you for causing all this, pay no attention to it. I won't really mean it. I adore you and our baby; but like I said before, this is no picnic—yeeoow!"

"I know, little Auburn Hair, I've heard it all before. I am well aware it truly is no picnic, and you yell all you want to yell!"

And yell, yowl, and scream she did! Lillianna had babies just like she did everything else—wide open! No respecter of persons, for some twenty hours, whoever was trying to console or offer encouragement was the one she "lit into"! Whatever thoughts or words came into her mind came out of her mouth—uncensored! Had she not been suffering so terribly, it would have been hilarious.

As Will stood there mopping her perspiration between

contractions and hanging onto her through each one, he wept openly. “Yes, Will Pinkston, you ought to weep; you are a doctor; you knew exactly how this was going to be! You didn’t tell me when we were making this baby so ecstatically, just how bad it would be to get it out. No wonder! You knew that I would be spread out here, before God and everybody, having it! Yeeoow, I’ve got to PUSH,” she screeched through clenched teeth!

“Yes, you do, little hell cat; one more should do it; the head is coming, PUSH!” Dr. Gilmore urged. With one more tremendous push, the baby came. Dr. Gilmore gave the baby a whack on the rump; and as the baby gave a lusty cry, he flipped him up onto Lillianna’s stomach.

“What is it, what is our baby?” Lillianna asked breathlessly.

“Just look down and you will know. All his equipment is right there for you to see! He’s a whopper! He’s a boy, and if I am not mistaken, he looks just like his papa!”

Suddenly, Lillianna was as docile and apologetic as a lamb to everyone in attendance. “Oh Will, I’m so sorry. You know I didn’t mean any of those horrible things I said. Lord, I am so embarrassed! I didn’t even know I knew some of the words I said. I certainly didn’t sound much like one of the young ladies who attended Miss Hockaday’s School, did I? But look at our precious son. Isn’t he beautiful, Will? He does look just like you!”

“Yes, he is beautiful, my Auburn Hair; and you know, to be so beautiful, I must admit he really does look a lot like me. Now you don’t give another thought to anything that you said during your labor and delivery. You did have a long, hard delivery, and it’s no wonder with a small mother like you and a baby this big. We all understand, right folks?”

“Right!” they all echoed.

“Yes ma’am, little mother, you may rest assured that anything said in a delivery room never goes beyond those walls!" Dr. Gilmore reassured her. "That's a personal rule, upon which I have always insisted."

Gathering up his instruments, Dr. Gilmore turned them over to Mandy and Delilah to take them downstairs to clean them up. "I'll just go along with you ladies and wash up down there. Do you suppose Miss Ellen might have some hot coffee in the kitchen?"

"Yassuh, you can be sho' of dat," Delilah assured him.

"Then let's leave and allow this little family some privacy," said Dr. Gilmore as he opened the bedroom door. He stepped back startled, "Privacy indeed, I'd say someone really special has been born at the size of the crowd waiting out here on the balcony. How long you folks been here?"

"Mr. Pinkston, Samuel, and I have been here about eight hours I guess," Matt answered. "Jay and Martha, Davey and Ellen, and Gilly and Prudence all came directly from Christmas Eve Midnight Service at St. Michael's."

"So you all must have been here at least a couple of hours," Dr. Gilmore said as he passed through the group with Mandy and Delilah on their way down to the kitchen. Taking out his pocket watch, he stopped on the stairs and projected his booming voice toward the open bedroom door, "I logged this young man in at 3:55 a.m., December 25, 1834. A Christmas baby! Not too smart at picking birthdays was he? Now he can count on getting birthday and Christmas gifts combined every year!"

Lillianna hearing his comment, although she was weak and exhausted, nevertheless, managed an emphatic, "Oh, no he won't either!"

Will went over to the door and asked the little group, which was impatiently waiting outside to see the baby, for just a few minutes alone with his wife and son. Of course they agreed and settled in for a few minutes which proved to last about an hour!

"My beautiful Auburn Hair, you look like some Madonna

by Titian, propped up there with your Christmas baby in your arms! Another one of those precious pictures of you I'll store in my treasure chest of memories."

"He is adorable isn't he, Will? Look at that black hair would you. He looks exactly like you. No one would know that I had anything to do with him! Looks like we do make beautiful babies doesn't it?"

"Indeed, and we make them so ecstatically!" he answered with a sly grin.

"Oh hush up, Will, you're not supposed to mention that again!"

"I'm just teasing you, sweets. I promise that I shall never mention it again, just couldn't resist. Now don't you think we should give this young gentleman a name so that we can properly introduce him to his family?"

"I have been thinking this last week about what I would like us to name our baby if it should be born Christmas Day. If you agree, Will, I would like to name our Christmas son Noel Parker Pinkston; and I want to call him Noel."

"I think that name is splendid. I am in full agreement. Now Master Noel, brace yourself; I am going to bring your family in to meet you!" Will said as he opened the door.

The hearts of all those who waited on the balcony wrenched at hearing Lillianna say, "Will, please ask Father Pinkston to come in alone first to meet his grandson. After all, our children will be his only grandchildren; and Noel is the first; and, unfortunately, it appears now that Father Pinkston will be the only grandfather our children will ever be privileged to know." This was the first time Lillianna had ever acknowledged the fact that she no longer believed there was hope that her father would relent or that she would ever again have a relationship with him at all.

Later, after all the family had seen the new baby, had offered congratulations to the proud new parents, and had left for home, Will and Lillianna were at last alone in their room with their son sleeping in the Pinkston family cradle and with his mother resting quietly in their big bed. Taking her hands in his, Will kissed them, and then her lips, as he said, "Darling, I know this has been for you, as it has for me, one of the happiest days of your life, but also one of the saddest. I am so sorry that your father failed to come share this day with us and with all the family."

Dry-eyed she replied, "Will, I think I have finally emptied what I had considered a bottomless well of tears over Papa's rejection. I thought surely when he learned that I was in labor, especially on Christmas Day, that he would come. Christmas Day has always been very special for our family. Then when Dr. Gilmore opened that door and everyone was there on the balcony except Papa, as you stood there holding our precious, innocent Noel in your arms, I thought, 'All right, Papa, you win. I close the book on us, on you and me. If it is ever to be reopened, you will make the first move! I am dedicating the rest of my life to being the best wife, the best mother, the best person that I can be and all with a happy heart! No more tears on your account, Papa; and the pity is, you are the great loser!'"

Will made no reply. Later that night, he held Lillianna in his arms, snug and happy in his love for her and for their son. As always, he was amazed at the strength of his tiny wife. It would be years before they would ever again discuss John or she would ever again mention her papa.

Although the subject was officially closed at Pink Hill, such was not the case at Fairlawn. The day of Noel's birth, when Mandy and all the Prendles left for home, Delilah and Samuel went along with them in the Pinkston buggy. When Delilah said that she wanted to go tell John all about his new grandson, Matt and Mandy promised they would go directly to Fairlawn and give John the good news. "Nassuh Mistuh Matt; I dont mean no disrespect; but I wants to tell Mistuh John myself about my baby Lillianna's fust baby!"

Hearing Delilah's words, words spoken with a vocal inflection which said, "Go home and let me and Samuel do this alone!" The Prendle boys and their wives did just that. They said goodbye and went to their own homes, foregoing the usual Christmas dinner at Fairlawn.

Matthew and Mandy entered the quiet mansion, beautifully decorated for Christmas, and went directly to the butler's pantry to find Virgil and the kitchen servants preparing to serve Christmas dinner. "Virgil, there is great news from Pink Hill. Lillianna and Will have a beautiful baby boy, Noel Parker Pinkston, born early this morning. All the Prendles and the Pinkstons were there to welcome him except Papa, of course. Mother and baby are fine."

"That is wonderful news! I can't wait to tell Mattie," Virgil said with delight.

"Where are Mattie and the babies?" Matt asked.

"They are in Mandy's quarters waiting for you all to bring news from Pink Hill. She's going to be relieved to hear the baby is here and all is well," Virgil answered.

Matt continued, "There will be no one here for Christmas dinner. Ask the other servants to clear the dining room and to set up the breakfast alcove to serve dinner for Papa and me a little later. Then please go inform Papa that Delilah and Samuel are waiting in the foyer and would like to see him. We'll wait for you in Mandy's quarters with Mattie and the boys to tell you all about our Christmas boy!"

Virgil, though puzzled, went to the foyer to greet Delilah and Samuel and to show them into John's study. He then hurried to Mandy's quarters anxious to hear all about the new baby.

When Delilah and Samuel were seated comfortably on the love seat opposite John, who was settled in his big chair where he had been reading, she looked up at Rebecca's portrait; and with tears in her eyes, she began. "Mistuh John, when I was a young woman and my Samuel was a young man and our Mandy was just a young girl, we see'd you come courtin' dat beautiful creature, my Becca baby. Yaw'l fell in love, and I was so proud she done found a fine man like you. 'De day yaw'l walked down 'de aisle, I was so proud. I never see'd no bride and groom handsome as yaw'l was. We come to 'dis home with yaw'l and watched yaw'l build it into 'dis fine mansion, and agin I was so proud. I helped while she screamed your five fine sons into 'dis world. I was proud of all of 'dem and her and you for makin' such a fine family. 'Den I watched her die bearin' your last baby, and I was proud of 'de brave way she went through it all. I remembers holdin' 'dat precious baby in my arms and watchin' you square your shoulders and, without a tear, go down 'de stairs to tell your sons 'dey mama was gone. I ain't never been no prouder of nothin' or nobody 'dan I was of you at 'dat minute! Today I watched 'dat precious baby scream her fust son into 'dis world. All 'de Pinkstons and 'de Prendles was 'dere waitin' to welcome 'dat beautiful, innocent Chrismus baby boy. His name be Noel Parker Pinkston, and Mistuh John, you knows whut? I ain't never been no more ashamed of nobody 'dan I is you, right now; and I b'lieves my Becca baby would be too! Good as I loves 'dis place, I won't be back here no more, never agin! Let's go home Samuel."

John sat there listening in stunned silence through it all and watched unmoving as the old couple walked out of the house and drove away in the buggy. He sat there for hours, his mind filled with thoughts of the past. Finally, he rose slowly and walked over to the window and looked out. Then as the early darkness of the December night pushed the light of this Christmas Day behind the trees at the river's bend, he turned and looked up at Rebecca's portrait in the fading light. "Becca, God forgive me for the stupid and proud fool that I am; but this damnable pride seems to be all I have left. I know that it is my master and I, its slave; and I can't find the strength to conquer it! I am truly sorry, my darling." Then he closed the stairway door behind him as he went up to his empty bed.

At Pink Hill that night, Leland Pinkston sat alone in the formal parlor, but he felt no loneliness. Upstairs in their bedroom was the little family upon which the mantle of Pinkston destiny had fallen on this day. Looking up by candlelight at the serene face of the wife he had cherished so, he thought, "Dearest Janie, I think the time has come for us to turn our page. My father brought my mother to this house as a new bride. It was nothing like it is now. They both worked hard for years to make it the lovely old country home it is today. They acquired a few slaves to help run the place. Year after year they grew a little more prosperous, and they were able to add to their acreage by purchasing a parcel from their neighbors the Gilmores. Only one happiness eluded them, the blessing of children. When they had given up all hope, they learned that Mother was indeed going to have a baby. Mother was forty-three years old when I was born, what folks call a 'change-of-life' baby. As it turned out, as you know, I was her 'end-of-life' baby. She died when I was born.

"Father wrapped his life around me. He saw to it that I was educated, was properly instructed in the tenets of the Episcopal Church, and was taught everything there was to know about running a plantation. However, on one occasion, we went into Charleston to the slave market to purchase four new field hands; this was all a part of my training. There I witnessed a spectacle so brutal that it was destined to alter the core philosophy of my entire life. I had worked slaves and dealt with them at home for years, but this was a new and unutterably revolting experience for me. I was filled with revulsion at the sights and sounds of the whole procedure. I knew in my soul that our entire society and way of life existed on the degradation of a whole race of human beings, not livestock, not chattel, but children of God, just as surely as we are. I vowed then and there that if I ever owned this plantation, they would all be freed.

"Then I found you, and we fell in love. Miraculously, you shared my philosophy on the subject of slavery; so we married. I brought you home, and you became the new young mistress of Pink Hill. The Pinkston mantle of destiny fell upon our shoulders; and Father, realizing this, wisely turned his page; and Pink Hill began a new chapter, our chapter.

"Now history has once again repeated itself. Our one remaining child has found and married a wonderfully strong and intelligent young woman. She has filled this house with laughter and happiness; and on this blessed Christmas morning, she presented our Will with a beautiful son, Noel Parker Pinkston. So I repeat, it is time for us to turn our page. Now my sweet girl, tonight your portrait goes to our bedroom, above the mantel, where your lovely face will be the last thing I see each night and the first thing I see each morning," Leland said as he took the portrait down from the place of honor it had held for so many years. "Tomorrow I shall ask Will to commission an artist to paint a portrait of Lillianna, new mistress of Pink Hill."

CHAPTER SEVEN

MOTHERHOOD

Very early in the morning, January 1, 1835, Lillianna sat up in their big bed to nurse young Noel, who had awakened right on schedule, 2:00 a.m., ready for his first feeding of the New Year. Will had gotten up and brought the baby to her. Since he would only be one week old in a couple of hours, Lillianna was still confined to the bed for a few more days. Will sat in the rocker beside the old cradle and watched, absorbing another of those beautiful pictures. "Darling, I thought you could never be more beautiful than you were the night we married; but framed in our big bed with my son at your breast, you are more than a beautiful new and young bride; you are gorgeous,a woman in the full bloom of motherhood."

"Speaking of the day we married, do you realize that tomorrow will be our first anniversary? I haven't gotten you an anniversary gift yet, and now I won't be able to get it on time. I bet you already have mine, haven't you?" Lillianna asked.

"You will have to wait until tomorrow to find out about yours; and if you haven't decided on one for me, I have a request," he said as he took the now sleeping baby, tenderly kissed the fullness of her exposed breast, and kissed Noel as he tucked him back in the cradle.

"Tell me what it is; and as soon as I am able, I shall find the best and nicest one in all of Charleston."

"This is a gift that Papa suggested, and it is for the formal parlor," Will said, as he crawled back into bed and drew her into his arms.

"How would Father Pinkston know what you would like for an anniversary gift?"

"Well, he didn't actually suggest it as my anniversary gift; but I think that it is exactly what I want. The morning after Noel was born, we were having coffee in the parlor after breakfast."

"Coffee in the parlor after breakfast!"

"It was Papa's suggestion. You haven't been able to go downstairs since Noel was born, or you would have noticed the same thing missing from the parlor that I immediately missed when Papa and I had coffee there the morning after Christmas. Mama's portrait was gone from above the mantle. At first I thought maybe he was having it cleaned or re-framed for some reason. When I asked him where it was, he said, 'That is my reason for asking you to join me in here for coffee this morning.'

"That place above the mantel in the parlor has always been reserved for a portrait of the mistress of Pink Hill. My grandmother's portrait hung there first; Mother's has hung there as long as I can remember; and now Papa has moved Mother's portrait to his bedroom; and it is his request that a portrait of you be commissioned to hang there as the new mistress of Pink Hill. I am in full agreement, and I can't begin to tell you how very proud I am of the woman you are."

"Oh, Will, I can't begin to tell you how much this honor means to me; but I am not at all sure that I deserve it now or ever shall," Lillianna said tearfully.

"Papa and I both agree that you do indeed. It is what we

both want, and it is exactly what I want you to grant me for my first anniversary gift from you. As soon as you are up and around and feeling up to it, I plan to commission the most highly regarded artist in the South to come here and begin the portrait. From what I hear, he resides in Savannah; so he will be staying here with us until it is finished. I have been told that he will need a period of time to study you and to get to know something about you before he will even begin his work."

"Will, I have to have time to get my figure back in shape, to decide what I shall wear, and to select a setting. I just don't know if I am ready for this."

"Yes, you are ready. I know exactly what I want you to wear and the exact setting. I want you to wear the ecru dress you wore the night of our reception with your emerald cross and earrings and your hair swept up in your mother-of-pearl combs. I want you standing there at the top of the stairs as you did that night. At that moment, your beauty and elegance were breathtaking; you were the epitome of all that the mistress of Pink Hill should be."

"Darling, I am so very honored that you and Father Pinkston both want my portrait to hang in the formal parlor where the portrait of the mistress of Pink Hill has always hung. As soon as I am able and looking like myself once again, you may go ahead and commission the portrait. I want you both to know that I shall never regard this honor lightly, and I shall always endeavor to deserve it."

When the portrait had finally been completed and was hanging in the parlor, it was everything that Will and his father had hoped it would be and more. "What an elegant young lady you married son; I know you are as pleased with Lillianna's portrait as I am."

"Absolutely, Papa; and I think Mother would be too."

"I am sure she would have been delighted, Son."

The next four years rolled by rapidly. Noel was a copy of

Will and a totally trainable and well-behaved child. They were very careful not to spoil him the way a first child is frequently spoiled, especially when he is the only child for over three years. Among his many playmates were the children of the employees there on the plantation and those of the tenant farmers also. He was extremely close to Julius and Louis, Mattie and Virgil's twins. Dr. Gilmore's son's children, a twin boy and girl, Beau and Barbara, born in April following Noel's birth in December, were also close friends. He went to the homes of his friends frequently, and they also came to his. He also visited his cousins on their plantations with Lillianna, but he never went to Fairlawn itself.

Matt and Mandy would catch John peeping out from the study as Noel and Lillianna would ride by in the buggy to visit Mattie and the boys, but they never mentioned it. With his heart in his eyes, he would look at the small handsome child and mentally measure the rapid progress of his growth.

When Noel was two, Dr. Gilmore suffered a heart attack. Albeit minor, Will's schedule was impacted tremendously. For weeks he had to carry the full load of their combined practices. Even after Dr. Gilmore was able to work again, he decided to work only part time; and he planned to turn the entire practice over to Will in a few years. Although it was a wonderful opportunity for Will to become head of one of the largest medical practices in the area, his time with his little family was curtailed; and he missed many of the treasured moments of Noel's babyhood. Lillianna did permit the baby to stay up somewhat later in order for Will to have a papa/son visit with him each night after dinner.

Lillianna and Will had originally planned to space their children only two years apart, but they lost their second baby early on in the pregnancy. Will thought it wise for her to wait at least a year, or perhaps two, following the miscarriage before they tried again. As it turned out, it was a year; and their third pregnancy was uneventful. The baby was born

September 13, 1838. They named her Lydia Barton Pinkston for Lillianna's maternal grandmother. She was another little brunette; and just like Noel, she looked very much like Will.

This delivery was somewhat more subdued than Noel's had been; however, in Lillianna fashion, not silent by any means! Since Will had another baby to deliver in another part of the county at the same time, he couldn't be with Lillianna. Dr. Gilmore, with Delilah's and Mandy's help, delivered Lydia. Perhaps Will's absence and the fact that Lydia was much smaller then Noel had been, accounted for her somewhat calmer demeanor. Lillianna missed him terribly, but doctors' wives soon learn that there is a measure of sacrifice required of every doctor's wife.

She and Jeanette (Nettie) Gilmore, Dr. Gilmore's genteel wife, had become very good friends. Just as Dr. Gilmore was Will's mentor, Nettie was Lillianna's. Nettie was a lady who devoted her life entirely to running their home, rearing their one child, James (James Alan Gilmore, Jr), and being the epitome of what every doctor's wife should be. She made no demands for herself and was always there to support him in every way. Lillianna admired her tremendously and vowed to try to pattern herself as the same kind of doctor's wife. Her vow was put to the test during Dr. Gilmore's illness, and she had passed the test with honors!

It was dark before Will got home on the day of Lydia's birth. Anticipating that he would be anxious to visit with his wife and new daughter, Ellen had prepared a cold plate for him to take up to his bedroom to eat later. He thanked her, took the plate hurriedly, and took the stairs two at a time. He rushed in, hurried over to the bed, and kissed Lillianna tenderly. "Darling, I am so sorry I couldn't be here with you."

"Will, you are a doctor. I have known that from the beginning. A little sacrifice here and there goes with the territory. Besides, having Lydia was as easy as falling off a log compared to having Noel; she is so small. Look at her, sweetheart; she is absolutely beautiful, like a little doll."

As he went to the cradle and gathered the little bundle in his arms, surprised, he said, "Lord, she is so tiny; she's no bigger than a peanut!" From that time forward, Will called Lydia, Peanut. "She is truly beautiful, so petite and dainty, just like her mother. Her big brother will have to take care of her; he'll love that. More black curly hair; it doesn't look as if I am ever going to get me another little Auburn Hair. I guess the Lord must know I have about all the Auburns I can handle."

As Will sat in the rocking chair rocking his little Peanut, Lillianna said, "You're going to spoil her. If you rock a sleeping baby, you will surely spoil her."

"Oh, please, little mother, just this once, let me rock her for a few minutes more," he said, his eyes misting over at the sweetness of his baby girl as he kissed her forehead.

"All right, just this once," Lillianna conceded. "I must admit that she is pretty irresistible."

As Will sat there rocking, Lillianna said, "Mattie came over this afternoon. It was good for us to have a few quiet minutes to chat. That's rare for us; our three boys are so rambunctious. She told me something that she had never mentioned to me before. She said that she and Virgil have been trying for two years to have another baby. Did you know that?"

"No, I didn't. Why would I?"

"Well, you are their doctor. I thought maybe they had consulted you. I knew if they had, your medical ethics would never have allowed you to mention it.

"You're right, but they haven't consulted me. Maybe they just thought I couldn't help, or maybe they were too embarrassed or proud to mention it to me."

"I felt so sorry for her. She held Lydia and cried. She wants a little girl so very much. Somehow she feels that she has let Virgil down. Do you think you could help them?"

"First, not unless they come to me. Even then there is no assurance that I could help them. You know, sometimes there is no organic reason; it just doesn't happen. At any rate, as far as we are concerned it is a moot question. Unless they come to me, my hands are tied. I do understand Mattie's tears at holding our precious baby." As he put her back in the cradle and kissed her good night, he added, "Our Peanut would make anybody want a baby girl!"

"Will, surely you are not going to call our pretty little girl Peanut?"

"Yep, 'spect I am."

Several weeks later, Mattie and Virgil did ask Will to stop by for an important talk with them; so he did. After their conversation, he suggested that he check Mattie out first. After examining Mattie, he told them that he thought he knew the root of their problem. Mattie's womb had somehow become inverted. Will told them that it was not impossible, but was highly improbable that she would become pregnant. They were terribly disappointed; but, of course, had no choice but to accept it and go on with their lives.

However, Lillianna had no problem conceiving. Scarcely a year had passed when they learned that she was pregnant again. This was completely unplanned; and from the beginning, there were problems with the pregnancy. She experienced not just morning sickness but debilitating nausea, vomiting day and night, spotting every time she tried to be up and around, and completely disabling headaches. Dr. Gilmore and Will agreed that chances were slim that this baby would go to full term.

As the sixth month approached, Lillianna had not yet felt the baby move. She was extremely weak and in very poor physical condition when she went into labor during the first week of her sixth month. Her labor began with bleeding, much more profuse than the usual spotting of what is referred to as "the show." The labor and bleeding continued with no progress toward delivery. As her temperature climbed and her physical condition weakened, she slipped into delirium as the stillborn child was finally delivered. Dr. Gilmore and Will worked frantically to stop the bleeding and succeeded, but Lillianna's temperature continued to climb. Delilah and Mandy were in constant attendance trying to help the two doctors save her life, but they were all helpless as her condition worsened. She had a form of childbed fever, almost always fatal and the most common cause of death of mothers and babies during childbirth. The best they could do was to try to keep her as comfortable as possible and wait.

The family all gathered at the word that the situation appeared hopeless. They prayed for a miracle and waited for what seemed to be inevitable. Will was at her side day and night, inconsolable in his grief, as she drifted in and out of her delirium. At times she knew them all; and, true to character, she tried to console them all in their grief. For in the moments of lucidity, she was aware that she was dying.

In her delirium, she dwelt in the past. "Now Sheba girl now, let 'em eat your dust. See, Papa, I told you I would win . . . Mama, I wish I could talk to you. I'm ten today; oh, of course, you know that . . . Thirty-two kittens. So many kittens running over my bed . . . I'm sorry, Mattie, so sorry you can't play . . . No, Papa, no please don't bid on him; look at their baby . . . So many beautiful ships in the sunshine . . . Will, Will, where are you? It's so dark . . ."

"Here I am, darling, right here," Will answered as he held her close and kissed her hair.

"I think I was dreaming, Will. It got so dark I was frightened for a moment. Please don't cry. I'm going to be all right."

"Of course, you are, my Auburn Hair; of course you are," he reassured her. "Just try to rest, sweetheart."

She slipped away again into delirium, "Oh Mandy Ma, Wilah's mad with me because I slid down the banister . . ."

"Oh, no, baby, I was never mad with you, not never. Oh Lawd not agin, please not agin," Delilah prayed.

"My handsome Will, guess I'm just leftovers huh? . . . Dr. and Mrs. Dr. Pinkston had a little Christmas boy and now a teeny raven-haired girl, just a little peanut . . . Smell the wisteria, what a beautiful garden. It's so warm and sunshiny here and smells so sweet. Oh, Lukey and Jane, I'm so glad to see you. Oh hello, Mama, you're so beautiful; but where is your emerald necklace? Oh, it's so beautiful here! No, no I can't stay; I have so much to do. I have to find a way . . . Oh, Papa, please forgive me, please.

"Oh God, I can't bear this; I don't want to live without her," Will sobbed.

Delilah, on her knees at the foot of the bed, suddenly rose. "I got something I gotta do. She done seen heb'n and her Mama and cain't let go and stay there!"

"Delilah, she is just hallucinating; it's just the fever talking," Will said.

"You believes what you believes; and I believes what I believes; and I believes she's seen heb'n and her Mama and Mistuh Lukey and Miss Jane. I said I was never gonna go back to Fairlawn, but 'dis baby ain' gonna die without she hears her papa's forgiveness! I ain' gonna have it!" she raged as she rushed out of the room and down the stairs.

Samuel hitched up the buggy, and they fairly flew to Fairlawn. When they arrived, Delilah didn't stand on protocol or wait to be announced. She raced in through the front door. Seeing Virgil there in the foyer, she asked, "Where's Mistuh John?"

"He's in the study. I'll tell him you are here," Virgil answered.

"Never mind," she said as she burst into the study without knocking.

John was sitting at his desk poring over the books and looked up startled at the sudden intrusion. "What in the . . ."

"Git your coat and go git in 'de buggy! My Becca baby's last baby is dyin'. She got 'de childbed fever, and she ain' got long. She done seen heb'n and talked to her mama and Mistuh Lukey and Miss Jane. I see'd her see 'em. Mistuh Will, he think it 'de fever talkin'; but I know it ain'. She told 'em she couldn't stay 'cause she still had to git her Papa to forgive her. An' you is gonna forgive her! So git your coat and git in 'de buggy, now! 'Dis baby is gonna die in peace. And by de' way, you's got a dead grandson too, if 'dat make any diffunce to you!" she finished, sobbing between every word.

Without hesitating, John stood and headed for the buggy, "I don't need a coat. It's upstairs, and we don't have time." The three of them crowded into the buggy as John took the reins and urged the horse into a gallop. He prayed aloud as he drove, "Oh, God, let me get there in time, please!"

When they arrived at Pink Hill, John handed the reins to Samuel, jumped from the buggy, ran into the foyer and up the stairs to the balcony where all the family was gathered outside Lillianna's door. About that time the door opened, and Dr. Gilmore came out. "Oh, John, I don't think I have ever been happier to see anyone than I am to see you at this moment. She is about the same physically; but right now she is, at least, lucid. Go right in."

When Will saw John, a look of immense relief and gratitude shone in his eyes. "Mr. Prendle, thank you so much for coming, sir. I can't tell you how much this means to both of us," he said as he rose and shook John's hand warmly. "Mandy, let's you and I give Lillianna and her father some time alone." Will and Mandy left the room and closed the door behind them.

Her hollow eyes were closed, and John's heart tightened as he looked at her colorless face. Taking her small hand in both of his and kissing it, he whispered, "Lillianna, princess, it's your papa. Please try to open your eyes, darling."

Slowly she opened her eyes. Her voice barely audible,

she spoke, "I can't believe you came; thank you so very much. I just had to tell you how very sorry I am for having deceived you. I know I can't have much time left. Papa, at the time, we thought we had no other choice. Please tell me you forgive us, before . . ."

"Shhh, my precious princess," John said placing his fingers on her lips. "Save your strength and let me do the talking. First, know that long ago I forgave you and Will for the deception. But above all, know this, I have done much, much more for which to beg your forgiveness. You tried in every way you could to seek my forgiveness; but pride, my stupid, bullheaded pride stood in the way of my even telling you when I knew that I had long ago forgiven you. That stupid pride robbed us all of more than five years. Five years in which I could have shared in your happiness, and I could have enjoyed my two precious grandchildren. Instead, I watched you and them from behind the curtains of my study, longing to touch you, to put my arms around you, to hold and kiss your beautiful babies. What a fool I have been! Can you ever forgive me?"

"Oh, Papa, there's nothing to forgive. I have never stopped loving you, respecting you, longing for your wise counsel all during these years. And now there is no time left for us. But please start now; be there for Will and for our precious Noel and Lydia. Promise me you will."

"Listen to me, princess, you are your mother's daughter. You have her beauty and so much more; you have her strength and her wisdom. I am prouder of you than I ever have been of any other child we had. I am so very proud of the sense of justice and Christian love you have always possessed, even from childhood, of your high principles and the courage you have always had to speak-up for those principles, even at your own expense, no matter how great the cost! Lillianna, the lamp of your mother's life was always the guide for our family. When she died, I despaired that there was no one who could ever be worthy to become guardian of that lamp. Now I know that you are. Listen to me, princess, you are not going to die. There is too much good left to be done that only you have the wisdom, strength, and, more than just courage, the guts to do! I am somehow sure that the Lord is not ready for you at Home yet; and all those people outside this door, who are praying for your life, believe that too!" With tears streaming down his face, John went over to the door, opened it, and motioned Will, Dr. Gilmore, Mandy, and Delilah back into the room. From that moment, the tide began to turn for the better.

No one knew whether it was a miracle, or whether John was the magic medicine Lillianna needed, or whether she would have recovered anyway; but a few hours later, her fever broke. That evening she was able to take some light nourishment and to see her children for a few minutes. The rest of the family was allowed brief visits with her, one or two at a time. At Will's request, the Rector of St. Michael's, who had been a faithful visitor and intercessor in Lillianna's behalf all during her illness, came to Pink Hill and held a special service of thanksgiving for her recovery. All the family and many close friends attended the service.

Her recovery was very slow, and Dr. Gilmore insisted that she limit her activities drastically for months to come. It was no surprise to anyone that Lillianna followed his instructions only under protest. For a few weeks, while she was still feeling poorly, she didn't complain; but when she started to feel and look much better, she wanted to be out and around. Only Will's insistence and Delilah's watchful eye and sharp tongue kept her under control.

John came nearly everyday. He visited with Lillianna every minute he was allowed in her bedroom when she was still in bed then on the piazza after she was able to negotiate the stairs. They hungrily made up the missing years and laughingly reminisced about her childhood. Slowly the color returned to her cheeks and the sparkle to her eyes, due, no doubt in large part, to John's attention. As soon as she was able, John came in the buggy and took her home to visit Fairlawn, to her brothers' homes to visit them, and down to Mattie's to visit with her and the twins. On especially pretty days, Ellen would pack them a picnic lunch; and Lillianna, Noel, Lydia, and John would have lunch in the nook beside the river. These were extra special days for all of them. To paraphrase Robert Browning, God was in His heaven; and all was right with the world.

The one thing John seemed to enjoy as much, or maybe even more than his visits with Lillianna, if that were possible, was getting to know his grandchildren, Noel and Lydia. He always arrived with gifts for them, notably Lillianna's childhood pony cart and a new pony.

"Papa, you are going to spoil them rotten," Lillianna said as he drove back up to the piazza after riding them up and down the drive in the pony cart. "Just having you be Grandpapa, at last, is more than enough."

"Princess, please, this is all for me as much as for them. Please don't deprive me of this pleasure. I promise to back off on the gifts though. I know that to overdo isn't wise. After all, I am not exactly new at this fatherhood routine you know."

"How well I know, Papa; how very well I know!" she answered, kissing him on the cheek.

That night as she lay in Will's arms running her hands over his bare body, she said almost shyly, "Will, it has been almost three months now. When, darling, how long do we have to wait?" She continued, kissing his chest and then his mouth hungrily.

"No longer, my beautiful Auburn Hair; I have been lying here night after night on fire for you, knowing that we had to wait until I was sure it would be safe for you. Now I am sure," he said as he swept her body to his. They were as lost in their passion as they had been on the night they married.

Later as they lay there, their sweating bodies still locked in embrace, they talked into the night. "Lillianna, when I thought I was going to lose you, I didn't want to go on living without you. I didn't think about Noel or Lydia, my practice or Pink Hill or Father, only that you and you alone were, and had been for years, my sole reason for living. I know that was selfishness. Do you love me less for my selfish weakness?"

"Love you less for loving me so much? Never, my sweet! Would it surprise you to know that I feel the very same way about you? You are the center of my universe! Will, if you died, I would want to die, too."

"You think that, but you underestimate your strength. I don't! You would go on, fulfilling every responsibility, upholding every principle, fighting to try to make the world what it should be, and rearing our children with their mother's strength."

"My beloved Will, don't you know yet that I learned all that from you and that I draw all my strength from you?"

"Do you think that perhaps we draw our strength from each other?" he asked.

"I think that is a strong and very beautiful possibility. God has truly blessed us, Will; and at the same time, He has given us a big responsibility to live up to that blessing."

"Yes little Auburn Hair, I know." he answered, drawing her even closer as they drifted off to sleep.

Christmas of 1840 was the best in years. Lillianna had fully recovered, and all of the Pinkstons and Prendles enjoyed the holidays together. That year a tradition was established that would continue through all the years to come. During the holidays, there were three parties held which included the entire family circle. Christmas Eve dinner was always held at Pink Hill with Lillianna and Will hosting. A huge dinner was served, buffet style, followed by caroling in the formal parlor with Jay's wife Martha at the beautiful grand piano and Mr. Pinkston, an accomplished harpist, at the harp.

The party usually broke up about 10:00 p.m. to allow each family time to make it to Midnight Mass at St. Michael's in Charleston, if they chose to go; and usually, everyone went. Every individual family observed the Christmas morning tradition of Santa Clause and Christmas breakfast at home. The second big family party was held early Christmas evening at Fairlawn. John and Matthew hosted a huge, seated Christmas dinner, followed by the exciting exchange of gifts by all the family. Needless to say, other than Santa Clause, this was the highlight of all the holiday festivities for the children in the family. The final party was held on New Year's Eve. The three remaining Prendle brothers and their wives took turns hosting this late night buffet to welcome in the New Year.

Now that life had changed, Delilah, Samuel, Mandy, Mattie, Virgil, and the twins were included in the family circle and were always a part of the holiday festivities within the confines of Pink Hill and Fairlawn. Certainly a very unique situation in the South. However, for the safety of the blacks, they didn't flaunt their *togetherness* in the faces of Charleston society. In fact, the blacks, realizing the impact it might have on Will's practice, wouldn't permit it.

In August, 1841, Lillianna had celebrated her twenty-fifth birthday. She was at the peak of her young womanhood and was lovelier than ever. She had two beautiful and intelligent children, a successful husband, who adored her, a fine home, and a loving, and now complete, family circle. Life was more idyllic than she could ever remember its being.

One morning in early September, she, Will, and the children were enjoying a leisurely breakfast. As was his practice, Mr. Pinkston had eaten earlier and had already ridden out to attend to plantation business. They were startled to hear the sound of galloping hooves coming down the drive and a frantic voice calling, "Will, Will, come quickly, Father has had a heart attack!"

Will raced to the front door and was alarmed to see that the rider was Dr. Gilmore's son, James. By the time Will had talked to James about his father, Lillianna was standing there waiting with his medical bag and his coat in hand. Will always left both in the foyer in readiness for emergencies such as this. "I'll saddle my horse and be right behind you!" Will assured him.

Lillianna followed Will to the stable and asked Richard, Ellen's husband, who handled the animals and all stable duties, to ready the buggy for her and Delilah. "Will, Delilah and I will be right along to see if we can be of any assistance at Meadows."

"Thank you sweetheart. I am sure they will appreciate that," he said as he kissed her good-bye, mounted, and rode out at a gallop.

When Will arrived at Meadows, Dr. Gilmore was lying on a chaise in a small downstairs family parlor. They had taken him there when he had collapsed during breakfast. He was conscious but obviously in pain, and his breathing was labored.

James gently led his mother from the room as Will started to examine Dr. Gilmore. "Mother, I am so glad I was here when this happened," James said, holding her close to his chest. He managed the large Gilmore plantation with a full complement of slaves and one overseer. He had breakfast with his wife and children at his own home each morning and then preceded the beginning of his workday by having coffee with his parents at their home. Fortunately, on this particular morning, he had arrived earlier than usual.

As Will started his examination, Dr. Gilmore said, "It is pointless, my boy, this is it. I have been a doctor too long not to recognize the symptoms. Please call Nettie and James back in. I want them to hear this." Will did as Dr. Gilmore asked.

When the three of them were gathered in the little parlor, with Nettie sitting on a low stool beside the chaise, her hands in his, Dr. Gilmore began, "Nettie, my darling, you and James know that I have a legally drawn will leaving everything that I own to the two of you. However, I have something to say to Will that I want both of you to hear. Will, I bequeath to you our entire medical practice. No one knows better than you that this bequest is a dubious boon. Our practice has grown tremendously, thanks in very large part to your expert medical talents. My advice to you is to do what I did, find yourself a talented medical student, or better yet a graduated doctor, and become his mentor. I only hope you come to hold him in the same high personal regard that I hold you. No one could be prouder of a son than I am of my James and the wonderfully strong man he has become; but I want you to know that if I could have had a second son, I would have wanted him to be like you. Good luck, dear boy, today and every day. And, Will, *carpe diem;* life is so very short! Now would you excuse us and allow me some time with Nettie and James?" he said squeezing Will's hand.

"Of course, sir, and thank you, thank you so very much . . . for everything. I'll be outside if you need me," Will answered as he left the room, tears welling up in his eyes.

When he went into the foyer, Lillianna and Delilah had just arrived and were waiting. "How is he, Will?" Lillianna asked.

Will broke down and sobbed as he moved into her arms. "He's dying, darling; my partner, my mentor, my best friend is dying. I just can't believe it. I guess I always felt he was indestructible. What will I do without him? He advised me to become mentor to a young doctor, but who will be *my* expert consultant."

"Oh, Will, I'll say to you the same words that you said to me when we lost Lukey, Warry, and Jane, when I was lost in my own grief. First, you are not alone in your grief. You have many people who love you and who loved him. We must all help each other through this. Secondly, as far as your need for an expert consultant, you are that expert; and moreover, you will make a wonderful mentor because you have had the best!"

So they passed through the painful crisis of the next weeks and months together. They were always there for Nettie, James, and the Gilmore family, supporting them in every way. Will, as always, found relief in the loving arms of his beautiful Auburn. They had always been able to leave grief, care, fatigue, indeed the entire world behind in the intensity of their love and the heat of their passion.

In a few months, Will had to admit to himself that Dr. Gilmore had been right. Their medical practice was too big for him to handle alone. He went to the medical college to inquire about recent, top quality graduates who might possibly be interested in coming into a successful practice as a junior partner. They gave him the names and addresses of several, and he immediately started to make the contacts.

After contacting and interviewing all the candidates, some of them twice, he selected the one he felt most suitable for the size and type practice he and Dr. Gilmore had built. Young Dr. Nelson Rogers Bradner was from Ripley, Ohio. He had chosen to study medicine at the Medical College of Charleston due to its fine reputation. He liked the area; therefore, he was delighted with Will's offer, which enabled him to settle there. Will was equally delighted. Nelson's ability, confidence, personality, and, most of all, bedside manner meshed perfectly with his own. All in all, they made a great team, much like Will and Dr. Gilmore had been. Will was surprised at the fulfillment he experienced in serving as mentor for a young doctor. At the same time, he came to appreciate the strong sense of responsibility Dr. Gilmore must have felt at taking him on when he was a young medical student.

With Will's medical practice moving along smoothly and with John's growing closer each day to Noel and Lydia, Lillianna was glowing with health and blooming with the happiness of life when the summer of 1842 arrived. In June, she strongly suspected that she was pregnant again. By the time her twenty-sixth birthday arrived in August, there was no doubt that she was. Quite naturally, with the serious problems of the previous pregnancy still fresh in his mind, Will was more than a little concerned about this one. However, Lillianna, with her usual optimism, was looking forward with delight to the arrival of another baby. She loved everything about motherhood with the possible exception of the delivery itself.

Noel, who would be eight years old on Christmas Day this year, was very precocious. One of his favorite spots in all of his world was John's study. The large collection of books attracted him to that particular room. He and Lydia were both exposed to books and music from babyhood. Lydia's talents and preferences were toward music. The grand piano and Mr. Pinkston's harp in the parlor at Pink Hill seemed to draw her almost hypnotically. Having two highly intelligent parents, it was natural that Noel and Lydia would be very bright. However, that was no doubt enhanced by the fact that from the age of three all the children at Pink Hill were tutored, including those of employees, along with Julius and Louis Lineham, and Beau and Barbara Gilmore, the twins of James Gilmore from Meadows. Lillianna had converted the third floor ballroom into two temporary classrooms separated by a small library, to be used until the children were old enough to enter more formal schools in Charleston. She hired two tutors who came out from Charleston five days a week. One tutor taught the three through five-year-olds; and the other, the six through nine-year-olds. At the age of ten, they would enter schools in Charleston.

One Saturday afternoon in late August, at Noel's urging, Lillianna took him, Lydia, Barbara, and Beau Gilmore to Fairlawn to visit "Pagrand Prendle's" big library. When Lillianna had first told the children who John was, as habit would have it, she had said, "This is Papa, Grandpapa Prendle." Repeating her verbatim, but shortening it slightly, Noel immediately started calling him Pagrand Prendle; and it stuck. So the children called their grandfathers, Grandpapa Pink and Pagrand Prendle. Both grandfathers loved the distinction.

John was sitting on the piazza having a glass of lemonade when Lillianna and the children arrived. As they came down the drive in the carriage, he called, "Virgil, will you ask the girls in the kitchen to bring some more lemonade and cookies to the piazza? Lillianna and the children are coming."

Virgil replied, "Yes, sir, Mister Prendle, right away." Mattie was working on a flower arrangement up on the balcony above the foyer. "Mattie, Lillianna and the children are coming," Virgil called up to her. Mattie put the finishing touches on the arrangement just as John was helping Lillianna down from the carriage. The children all jumped down from the carriage and ran to hug their grandfather. After greeting Lillianna with a hug and kiss, he welcomed each of the children with a swing-around hug and picked Lydia up and headed for the piazza with her in his arms. About that time, they heard a scream from the foyer and rushed inside to see Mattie as she landed at the foot of the stairs.

"I'm all right. I'm fine," said Mattie as she sat up straightening her clothes. "I slipped on the top step in my rush to come down to greet you all."

"Are you sure, honey?" asked Virgil, as he and Lillianna, in their concern, ran to help her up.

"I am fine; don't fuss over me. See?" she answered, as she flexed her limbs and swiveled around from the waist to prove it.

"Nevertheless, you come out on the piazza with me for some lemonade, a visit, and a little rest," Lillianna insisted. As they went out, Noel, Barbara, and Beau had finished their refreshments in gulps in their eagerness to head inside to the study and the wonderland of its library.

"Come on with us, peanut," Beau said to Lydia, "I'll read you a story."

"No, I'm going to play the piano for Pagrand Prendle; and don't call me peanut!" she answered, taking John's finger and pulling him toward the front door.

"All right, my little virtuoso; I can't wait; so let's go," John answered, laughing as she pulled him inside and into the parlor.

Virgil returned to his duties, but came back to the door to peek out to check on Mattie several times.

"I am fine, Virge, go on with your work and stop worrying about me. Lillianna and I have to catch up on all the news."

"And I do have some news, Mattie," Lillianna said with a chuckle. "It has happened again; I'm pregnant. Seems every time Will hangs his pants on the bedpost, as the saying goes, this happens; and I am delighted. However, Will is very concerned because of the problems with my last pregnancy."

"Oh, I am sure everything will be fine, honey. I just wish it would happen for Virge and me, but I guess that would take a miracle."

"Don't give up hope. I'll be praying for that miracle for you," Lillianna said, squeezing Mattie's hand.

They continued to sit, chatting pleasantly and fanning as sounds of the piano floated out the door. Lydia played all the beginner's tunes, which Grandpapa Pink had taught her. John applauded enthusiastically after each tune. The three older children chatted quietly in the study as they browsed through the shelf of books for young readers.

"Just listen, Mattie," Lillianna said, stopping in mid-sentence, as she listened to the music and the chatter of the children, "What a peaceful and perfect scene this is!"

After awhile the four children came outside and set out to play a favorite game, "Let's Explore." John joined the ladies on the piazza. "Don't stray too far children. We must leave in about an hour or so," Lillianna said as the children ran off in the direction of Mattie's house to find Louis and Julius.

Lillianna, Mattie, and John spent a pleasant hour catching up on all the news and were discussing this year's cotton crop when the six children came racing around the house laughing, with Lydia, the youngest of the group, bringing up the rear. "Hurry up, peanut. Last one on is a rotten egg," Beau shouted in an effort to encourage her.

As the other five circled the back of the oval heading for the center of the piazza, wily Lydia simply ran onto the end of the piazza nearest them shouting, "Ha, ha, ha! I'm first! Now who's the rotten egg, Beau? And I told you not to call me peanut!"

Lillianna, laughing, sat there thinking how much they sounded like Will and her when she was a little ten-year-old girl. "We had better go children. They will be expecting Beau and Barbara at Meadows pretty soon."

As they all said their good-byes, Noel asked John, "Pagrand, may I spend the night with you tomorrow night?"

"I'd like that, Noel, if it meets with your mother's approval. Come early and have dinner with us."

"May I, Mama? I have some things I need to talk to Pagrand about. Please let me come," Noel begged.

"My this visit does sound important. I suppose it will be all right. We'll bring you over late tomorrow afternoon."

"That won't be necessary. I'll ride Selam over to pick him up; and he can ride back with me on Sheba if that's all right with you, princess. We'll enjoy the ride back together."

"That will be fine, Papa, if Will doesn't object; and I don't think he will."

That settled, Lillianna and the children climbed into the carriage and headed for home waving a last good-bye as they turned from the oval into the avenue of live oaks leading to the main road.

After attending church the next day, followed by a late

lunch, Noel packed his little overnight valise, set it out on the piazza, and headed for the stable. "Noel, where are you going so early? It's only two o'clock," Lillianna said.

"I'm going to the stable to get Richard to help me saddle Sheba."

"That's what I thought," Lillianna continued. "Just wait until Pagrand gets here. He'll probably visit with us a little while. You'll have plenty of time to get her saddled after he arrives."

"Mama, I want to be ready when he gets here. Besides I thought I might ride her around the drive a little just for practice."

"Oh, all right, just be careful. I know you have ridden her before, but she is a big horse, and you are still a little boy."

"Oh, Mama, I am a big boy for my age. I'm already taller than Beau is, and Pagrand thinks I'm big enough, or he wouldn't have suggested I ride her back with him and Selam!" he called back, as he ran around the corner of the house toward the stable.

John arrived about two hours later to find Noel riding up the driveway at a fast trot. When he saw John, Noel urged Sheba into a canter as he came to greet his grandfather. "Pagrand, I thought you would never get here. Let's race to the house."

"Oh no, young man. You have a lot to learn about riding before you start racing, and I am looking forward to teaching you."

"Can we start today on the way back?"

"I don't see why not, but first I want to have at least a short visit with your folks and Lydia before we leave."

After a brief visit with the whole family, Mr Pinkston suggested they all go inside to hear Lydia play the harp. "I find it quite amazing how quickly she has learned to play both the piano and the harp. She has a natural gift for music," he said. They all took a seat in the parlor, and Lydia settled behind the harp with Grandpapa Pink's help.

The tiny girl played a simple melody flawlessly, with her mentor behind her looking on proudly, the sunlight streaming in around them. Afterward, when the applause had ended, John said, "I wish I could paint. If I could I would capture this beautiful scene, and I would entitle the painting 'The Proud Maestro'."

Lillianna closed her eyes and thought, "Thank you, God, for this beautiful moment, for giving Papa back to us." Will reached over, took her hand in his, and kissed her palm.

Later that night after dinner, John and Noel sat reading in the big study at Fairlawn. Looking at his pocket watch, John said, "My, time really seems to fly. Don't you think it's about time we went to bed?"

"Yes sir, I do. I am feeling a little sleepy. Is it all right if I sleep in your big bed with you, Pagrand?"

"Yes, I think that would be fine provided you don't kick," John answered laughing.

"I'm not sure, but I don't think I'm a kicker," Noel replied seriously.

"Well, I am glad to hear that," John said, squelching a smile as he realized Noel had taken him seriously.

As they climbed the back stairs from the study to the master bedroom, John said, "I'll tell you what, Master Noel, let's get our nightshirts and robes on and go down to the kitchen for a glass of milk and some cookies. Sound good?"

"Yes sir, Pagrand, it sounds great!" Noel answered enthusiastically.

When Noel had retrieved his valise from his mother's old bedroom, where he thought he would be sleeping, and returned to John's bedroom, he found his grandfather donning his robe already. So he hurriedly undressed and was soon in his own nightshirt and robe.

Seated on high stools at the big work table in the kitchen, they were enjoying their milk and ginger cookies. "Pagrand, may I ask you a question?"

"Of course, Noel, what is it?"

"Yesterday afternoon when we were exploring, we went down to the slaves' quarters. I don't understand anyone owning people like he owns horses or cows or pigs. I guess what I really want to know is why *you* have slaves at all?"

John thought, "Oh, how very like your mother you are, Noel." But he said, "Noel, your mother asked me that same question when she was a girl. I'll tell you what I told her then. The South has an agricultural economy. A plantation is far more financially successful if it employs the use of slave labor. In other words, it makes more money. You'll come to understand it much better as you grow older."

"We don't have any slaves at Pink Hill, and Mama says we never have had and never will have. We have tenant farmers and hired hands. We may not be as rich as you are, but we have everything we need and most of everything we want. I don't like slavery, and I wish you didn't own any slaves. Mandy, Virgil, Mattie, and the twins aren't slaves are they?"

"No, of course not!" John answered uncomfortably.

"Why? They're not white."

"Ah . . . Noel . . . it's a long story . . . they're . . . different."

About that time, Mandy who had overheard their conversation from the breezeway, decided it was time she intervened to rescue John. She went into the kitchen and interrupted, much to John's relief. "What in the world are you gentlemen doing raiding the cookies and milk this time of night after I've already cleaned up my kitchen. Besides it is time you two were getting to sleep. I thought I would serve breakfast a little earlier than usual in the morning so that you two can take a ride on Selam and Sheba. Maybe you could ride down to the river. I'll pack you a picnic lunch."

John said, grateful relief showing in his voice, "That sounds wonderful, Mandy. What do you think, Noel?"

"Could we, Pagrand?" Noel asked enthusiastically,

forgetting, for the moment at least, their discussion about slavery. "I would love that!"

"Then off to bed with you," Mandy said, "I'll clean up these plates and glasses."

"Thank you, Mandy, for everything," John said meaningfully as he urged Noel ahead of him out of the kitchen.

After they had knelt on either side of the bed to say their nighttime prayers, they bade each other goodnight with a hug and settled into John's big bed. John lay there for a long time looking up into the darkness and thinking about the things Noel had said. In a few minutes, Noel was asleep. John listened to the deep easy breathing of the peaceful and innocent child. He thought, "Oh, my beautiful, idealistic grandson! I am so proud of you. Maybe I'm not too old to learn something of humanity from you. Perhaps, as William Wordsworth said, 'Child *is* father of the man' after all."

As they sat beside the peaceful Ashley River the following day and enjoyed their picnic, John said, "You know, Noel, I've been thinking about our conversation last night and your thoughts on slavery. I'm beginning to think you may just be right."

"Well, what can you do, Pagrand, sell them?"

"No, that wouldn't solve anything. They would still be someone's slaves. I could always grant them their freedom, and I want you to know I'm going to give that some serious thought."

"I'm glad, Pagrand; I'm really glad. I'll be so proud of you if you do!"

John hugged Noel impulsively, saying, "You're quite a young man, Master Noel Parker Pinkston!"

It was a Wednesday in late November. On Wednesday afternoons, Lillianna enjoyed sitting quietly in the parlor and listening as Father Pinkston gave Lydia her weekly harp lesson. While she waited for them to begin, she looked out the window at the beautiful, sunny, autumn day, the kind of day that shines down through all the red, orange, and golden hues of the season and touches the depths of your soul. She thought, "As someone once observed so graphically, 'It looks as if God reached His hand into the big-paint pot of heaven and splattered the world to create a landscape no earthly artist could ever touch!'" Then she saw a buggy round the curve of the drive. When it got close enough, she was delighted to see that it was Mattie. "Lydia and Father Pinkston, would you please excuse me today? I see Mattie coming down the drive for a visit."

"Of course, dear," Father Pinkston replied. "Lydia will play for you later I am sure. Right little peanut?"

"That will be fine, Grandpapa Pink. I'll play better after my lesson anyway," Lydia assured her mother.

"Good, I'll count on a private concert for your papa and me after dinner tonight," Lillianna said, hurrying outside to greet Mattie.

Mattie reined-in beside the piazza, all smiles as she stepped down from the buggy and hugged Lillianna, "Hello, oh-most-round-one! If you get much bigger, and you most assuredly will, there will be no hugging you at all! Is there a chance that you are carrying twins?"

"I asked Will that same question; and he doesn't think so, oh-most-humorous-one!" Lillianna answered laughing. "I'm so glad to see you. It has really been a long time since you paid me a visit. I was beginning to think you didn't love me anymore," she added, with a mock pout.

"On the contrary, I not only love you, I love the whole world!" Mattie said as she followed Lillianna into the study. They could hear the beautiful strains of the harp coming from the parlor. "Is that Lydia playing the harp?" Mattie asked incredulously.

"No, that's Father Pinkston. He is giving Lydia her harp lesson, but you would hardly believe how rapidly she is progressing. Father Pinkston says that he truly considers her a child prodigy at the harp! Now, come on, you never did tell me why it is that you are suddenly in love with the whole world!"

"Lillianna, you won't believe it. It seems that the fall down the stairs I had in August was a blessing in disguise. Will thinks it flipped my womb back into its proper position; and he confirmed this morning what Virgil and I had suspected, but had dared not allow ourselves to hope, I am pregnant! I couldn't wait to come share our good news with you!"

"Oh Mattie, how wonderful! Are you hoping for a girl this time?"

"Oh our baby will definitely be a girl, Annamarie Lineham. I just know it without a doubt!" Mattie replied confidently.

"You beat all I've ever seen with your positive predictions; but I do love the name; it is beautiful! When are you due?"

"June fifteenth, give or take a few days."

"I'm so glad you came to share your news with me. You couldn't have told me anything that would make me happier. Will would never have told me until you did. You know him and his ethics!"

"Yes, and I respect him tremendously for them."

"And, of course, I do, too. In fact, it is one of the things about Will of which I am proudest," Lillianna replied.

About that time, the ever-thoughtful Ellen brought in a tray of tea and sugar cookies; and Lillianna thanked her. The women spent the rest of the afternoon chatting about nothing and everything, just as they had done when they were little girls. It was a lovely visit.

Autumn slipped into winter. Thanksgiving and Christmas were celebrated with the usual traditions observed, and New Year 1843 arrived right on schedule. Then on February thirteenth, also right on schedule and with little more than the usual fanfare of labor and delivery, Master William Leland Pinkston III, the name Lillianna had already chosen, made his happily anticipated debut. Dr. Bradner, now a seasoned veteran, handled the delivery efficiently, with Mandy and Delilah assisting, as Lillianna screamed and Will paced up and down outside the door. Noel and Lydia sat quietly nearby; and, with wide-eyed, childish concern, they watched their father pace.

As Dr. Bradner opened the bedroom door, Will asked anxiously, "Nelson, is Lillianna all right?"

"Yes indeed. She and your son are both fine, but come in and see for yourself."

Will came hurriedly to the bed and dropped to his knees. "Darling, are you all right?" he asked Lillianna as he put his arms around her and kissed her.

"Of course, Will. I'm getting to be an old hand at this. Besides, I have an excellent physician," she answered, smiling at Dr. Bradner.

"That much I knew; but from the noise emanating from this room, it sounded pretty rough!"

"Oh, Will, you're a doctor. You've delivered enough babies to know that is an inevitable part of the birthing routine!"

"It is very different when I'm the father outside the door listening; and you, my little Auburn Hair, are doing the screaming!" he answered.

"Papa, speaking of auburns, aren't you going to look at your new son?" Lillianna asked, as she uncovered the blanketed bundle beside her to reveal a beautiful baby with a head full of red curls.

"Well, what do you know, we finally have us a carrot-top just like his mother used to be," Will laughed.

"Now don't you call him carrot-top like they did me when I was young. His hair will darken to auburn as he gets older just as mine did," she said confidently.

"Did that really bother you back then?"

"Yes, it did when anyone except you said it, but I loved the special attention from you," she answered, suddenly serious.

"Then I promise I'll never call him carrot-top again."

"Thank you, darling. I'm sure he will hear it enough from others."

Will took his son in his arms, kissed his button nose, and said, "Hello Master Leland, I am your very proud papa. There are some more folks outside who are waiting to meet you. We'll be back in a minute," he added as he settled the baby into the cradle beside the bed.

"All right, Miss Lydia and Master Noel, there's a young man named Leland in here who is anxious to meet his big sister and brother," Will said as he opened the bedroom door.

Wide-eyed and smiling the children rushed into the room and over to the cradle. As they stood there looking at the baby, their smiles faded. "He's wrinkled like a prune," Lydia said frowning, sounding somewhat disappointed.

"Yeah," Noel added, "He's really ugly!"

"Now don't you two go out there and tell them our baby is ugly!" their mother said.

"Well, what must we say if they ask?" Noel said.

"We just haven't had a chance to iron him yet," Will teased.

"Oh, Will," Lillianna reprimanded, "They might take you seriously. All babies are like that when they are newborn," she told the children. "He will smooth-out and pink-up in a day or so. Then you will think he is beautiful!"

"Maybe so, but I wonder," Noel answered doubtfully, as Lydia nodded her agreement and their parents laughed.

Sitting on the edge of Lillianna's bed, the children looked even more puzzled as they watched the reactions of the rest of the family who came in to see the new baby. They "ooo'd" and "ah'd" and said how perfectly beautiful he was. Lydia and Noel looked at each other and shrugged, raising their eyebrows. Noel decided they must not be able to see well in the dim light of the room; or, more likely, they were just fibbing. "That was it for sure.

Of course, they wouldn't want to hurt his mama's and papa's feelings!" he finally concluded.

When all the visitors had finally gone and only Lillianna, Will, and their children remained in the bedroom, Lydia and Noel ventured again to the cradle. "Lee boy, all I can say is you sure do have carrot orange hair," Noel said, rubbing the baby's head a little roughly, in typical big brother fashion, as he headed out of the room to pursue other interests.

"Don't be so rough, Noel, he's too little," Lydia chided, as he went out the door. She almost whispered as she touched his curls tentatively and gently caressed his little hands, "What teeny, tiny yittle fingees," she said to him in baby talk. "You pwecious baby Bubba, you dot curly fingees, Lee Lee," she cooed on like a little four-and-a-half-year-old mother. As he wrapped his little hand around her finger, she sighed with delight. "Oh Mama, you know he really is beautiful, a beautiful angel baby."

"Indeed he is, and he obviously loves his big sister," Lillianna answered, smiling at the sweet picture they made as her baby and knee-baby looked adoringly at each other. It set a precedent which would prevail for the rest of their lives. Lydia would ever consider Leland her angel baby.

The next months passed quickly, with life moving along peacefully and altogether pleasantly for nearly all the family. Mattie progressed satisfactorily toward her June delivery date. Young Leland was filling out and developing quite a unique personality of his very own. He was so cute that it was difficult not to spoil him. John alone was not at peace at all. He found disquieting thoughts disturbing his nights and intruding upon his days, thoughts of slavery and all of its ugly implications, remembrance of the words of a sensitive teen-age girl so many years ago, the words of his little eight-year-old grandson on the same subject, and his own tentative promise to Noel on the day of their picnic. Now with Mattie's baby on the way, he thought how easily her little one, his own great-grandchild,

Guardian of the Lamp

A Novel by

Laryce Henderson Rybka

About the Author

Laryce Henderson Rybka, a native Tar Heel, was born in Raleigh, N.C. and grew up in Reidsville. She and her husband, Bill, now reside in Raleigh. During her children's formative years, she was a stay-at-home mom and taught kindergarten. In 1975, she moved to Raleigh and accepted a job with IBM where she worked in worldwide videoconferencing. Since retiring in 1992, she and Bill have traveled extensively. Her hobbies include travel, volunteer work, ballroom dancing, and her favorite pastime, writing. For the past four years, she has devoted much of her time to writing this, her first published novel. The sequel, Legacy of the Lamp, is now in progress.

*Laryce is available for signings & readings. Call 919-782-5852.

Email:laryce@bellsouth.net.

Three Generations of Women Battle Slavery

New Novel Portrays Strong Women, Progressive Thought

~ Amidst Pre-Civil War Southern Tradition ~

It is said in the Book of Proverbs that the virtuous woman is a woman "...whose price is far above rubies," and whose "...lamp does not go out by night.' Placing this piece of scripture at the thematic center of *Guardian of the Lamp*, her first novel, Rybka paints a family portrait of three generations of such women, whose strength and determination help them overcome the stifling

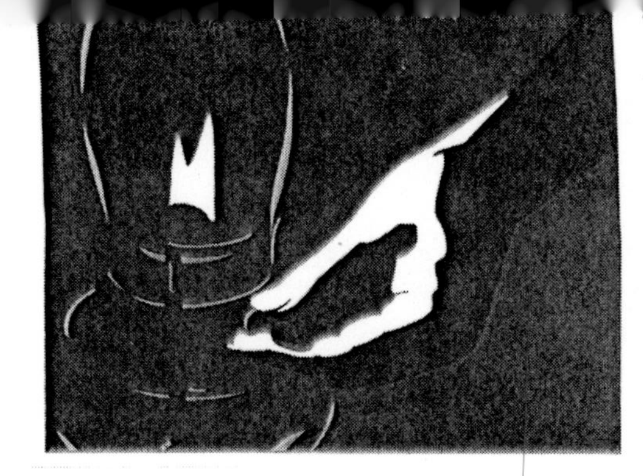

southern tradition of antebellum South Carolina.

Telling a story that inspires as well as entertains, she presents a different Old South, a departure from the timeworn tales of mincing Southern belles, foppish Southern men, and divisive Southern bigotry. The novel recounts the struggles of the women of the Prendle family as they cross the line into forbidden love, advance the cause of abolitionism, and work with the Underground Railroad. In their attempt to fight the injustice of the antebellum South, the Prendles battle not only slavery, but the "Southern Tradition," the prevalent manner, custom, and code of genteel plantation owners, a tradition that had been perpetuated by their own family.

Guardian of the Lamp is loosely based on the ancestry of Rybka's maternal grandmother, a native of Charleston, S.C. The author, a native North Carolinian, set the majority of the novel in the actual locales in which the women of her family were born and reared. Relying not only on their stories, but also on extensive research, Rybka's own story is also one of strength and determination. She began writing the novel at age 65, successfullly completing and publishing it at 69.

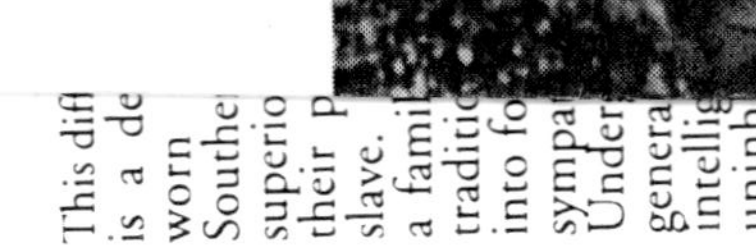

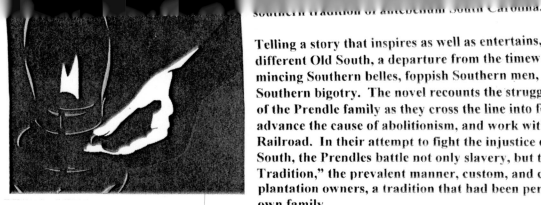

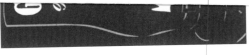

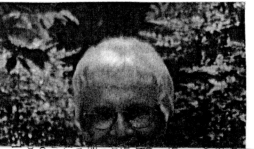

could have been born into slavery. The very thought made him shiver! "I must find a way, and soon, to honor the promise I made to my grandson and to my own conscience."

At about 7:00 a.m. the morning of June 15, Mr. Pinkston, as had recently become his practice, was attending little Leland out on the piazza to allow Will, Lillianna, Noel, and Lydia the time to enjoy a leisurely breakfast together. Suddenly, they could all hear the sounds of a horse's hooves and its shouting rider as they charged down the drive.

"That will likely be Virgil coming to tell you that Mattie's in labor; today is the day," Lillianna said matter-of-factly as she rose to get Will's bag from the foyer.

"And how, may I ask, would you know that?" Will asked.

"She told me long ago that it would be a girl, born on June 15. I don't know how she knows; but I'm confident she was right; so finish that last sip of coffee and get going!"

About that time, Virgil reined in at the piazza and called, "Will, Mattie's in labor; and it looks like it's moving pretty fast. Can you come right on?"

"I'll saddle up and be right behind you, Virge; you head on back," Will answered through the open door.

"Tell Mattie that Samuel, Delilah, and I will be along shortly," Lillianna called out to Virgil as he turned his mount and headed back home at a gallop.

"No big rush, Lillianna. Mandy is with her," Virgil called back.

When Lillianna, Delilah, and Samuel arrived at River Bend, John and Matt were sitting on the porch. Lillianna rushed up the steps, "Matt, how are things going; and what can I do to help?" she asked as Delilah started to rush right by her and into the house, expecting to help with the delivery.

"Whoa Ladies, it's all over! Have a seat and wait to be invited in to meet the latest addition to the Lineham family," Matt said.

Will strode out on the porch smiling broadly as he dried

his hands and rolled down his shirt sleeves. "Well, as always, our new mother was absolutely correct in her prediction, a girl born on June 15. It's uncanny; she must be clairvoyant. I'm her doctor, and I am never that sure!"

"A woman just knows these things," Mandy added as she came out on the porch and joined Lillianna on the swing. "Virgil and the boys are in greeting their new daughter and baby sister. I'm sure he will be out soon to invite you all in to meet her. She is perfectly beautiful; anyone can see that; although, I admit I might be just a little prejudiced, as grandma's tend to be," she finished.

In a few minutes, Virgil appeared at the door laughing, "All right, folks, her highness, Annamarie Lineham, is now receiving, at the specific invitation of her older brothers, Masters Louis and Julius Lineham!"

Virgil reentered the bedroom; and as all the family filed into the parlor, Louis and Julius waited outside the closed bedroom door. Louis requested that the family line up in the order he and Julius had predetermined. "We ask that you all don't stay too long. Mama and Annamarie have had a hard time, and they are both tired you know," Louis began seriously and in his most grown-up voice.

Drawing himself up to his full height, Julius continued his and Louis's very formal plan for introduction to their new baby, "Mama Delilah and Papa Samuel you may go in first."

Delilah and Samuel came over, opened the door and tiptoed in, almost reverently, as befitted the dignity of the occasion.

Louis chimed in, "Next comes Pagrand Prendle please, then Grampa Matt and Mandy Ma, and last Aunt Lillianna," he finished, taking her hand to lead her in.

Taking Will's hand, Louis said, "Uncle Will please come back in, too."

"I'd be honored, Louis," Will assured him.

Virgil sat on the bed holding Mattie in his arms and smiling broadly as Louis and Julius began the formal introductions.

Louis and Julius went over to the cradle where the baby was sleeping quietly. Julius stood at the head of the cradle, and Louis at the foot, like two guardian angels, roles they assumed on the day of her birth. They invited the visitors, two by two, to come forward to see and meet their beautiful baby sister. She lay there with long black lashes curling on her ivory cheeks and a cap of soft black curls framing her precious face.

As Lillianna and Will finally stood beside the cradle, Julius asked, "Uncle Will, she is so light colored. Will she always stay that way?"

Will replied, "Sometimes newborn colored babies are lighter than they will be later; but, on the other hand, she might stay the same light, creamy color. Look at all your family and their coloring—Mama Delilah and Papa Samuel, Pagrand Prendle, Grampa Matt and Mandy Ma, and your own mama and papa, all shades and skin tones. They are all part of you, Louis, and Annamarie. One thing for sure though, no matter what her skin coloring turns out to be, she will always be beautiful; and we shall all love her very much!"

"Yes, sir, you can count on that!" Louis said, bending over to kiss each little eyelid. "She's the most beautiful baby sister in all the world!"

After Annamarie's birth, little thought was given to the passage of time. Like the peaceful old Ashley River, time rolled languidly from 1843 through 1844 and into the summer of 1845. The only thing that seemed to move rapidly was the lightening-like growth of all the children.

However, the summer of 1845 was a scorcher. Even the oldest of old-timers could not remember a summer so hot. Suddenly everyone became acutely aware of the misery of the heat and the passage of time; more accurately the lack thereof; time seemed to stand still.

The children all escaped to the cool of the creek that wound through Meadows Plantation and on to Pink Hill and finally to Fairlawn before it flowed into the Ashley. They sought relief in its water and busied themselves all summer long trying to build a mud and rock dam across the narrowest part of the creek behind Pink Hill. They wanted a deeper swimming hole; however, they worked to no avail. Most days when they returned to continue their project, the prior day's work had been washed away. Determined, they refused to give up. Finally one day, when they returned to find three good days' work all washed away again, Noel said thoughtfully, "I guess we're just not supposed to dam-up this little creek, it wants to run free and refuses to let us stop it. I think we should forget the dam and just enjoy it like it is." All the rest agreed, and that was the end of their great engineering endeavor.

To cope with the heat, Samuel and Delilah spent a large part of each day rocking or swinging and fanning in the shade of their front porch. "Samuel did ya' ever wonduh what life was really all about?"

"What does ya' mean, honey?"

"Well, most folks thinks life all about winnin'. Slaves dreams about winnin' they freedom. The mastuhs thinks about winnin' money and riches. De' more we gits, de' more we wants, and still we don't feel lak winnuhs. We still wants more. 'Den we gits to de' end of our life, and we dies and has to leave all our winnin's behind when we actually just won de bes' prize of all, heb'n! I don't believe life's about winnin' at all. I believe it's about how good we's able to live with de' losin' 'til we finally wins when we dies." Delilah mused philosophically.

"Oh honey, 'das all too deep for us slaves to be worryin' about. I ain't nevuh give 'dat stuff no thought at all." Samuel answered.

"You is wrong, Samuel, us slaves, we knows bettuh 'dan anybody does. Slaves is always lookin' forward to dyin' and finally bein' free!" She insisted. "You just think about it.

Evuhbody think 'dem little babies is wigglin' and fightin' to git out when they's gittin' bawn. Did 'ya evuh think they might be fightin' to stay in 'dere where they's warm and close to they mama's heart?" Delilah asked.

Moving to join her on the swing, he put his arm around her shoulders and kissed her cheek. "Honey, you may be right. Nobody know but de' Lawd. Let's us jus' leave 'dat all up to Him and quit worryin' about it," Samuel comforted.

"Aw, Samuel, I knows you is right. I didn' mean to burden you with 'dese heavy thoughts."

"Don't worry about it, sweetheart; anything you's got on your mind, you can talk about to me always. You know 'dat."

They sat there swinging until the afternoon started to fade into twilight, and Delilah went in to get their supper ready. Samuel followed to set the table for her.

After they had eaten, they went back out on the porch seeking a little cool night air. As the two old folks sat there watching, the fireflies danced a ballet around their little yard to a random rhythm of their own.

"Honey, I'se a little tired tonight. I believe I'll go to bed a little early. Guess the heat's gittin' to me," Samuel said, patting her knee and kissing her forehead as he rose to go inside.

"Good night, honey, I'll be along presently."

The following morning, the sun shone in the window full in Delilah's face. She awakened with a start, "Lawd, what time is it? We ain't nevuh slept 'dis late before. Samuel wake up; we's done overslept." She reached over to shake him, but when she touched him her heart felt as if it shattered into a million pieces. His unyielding flesh told her that he had slipped away during the night and would never again awaken on this side of eternity. She rolled over, and putting her arm across his chest and her head on his shoulder, she wept. "Oh my dahlin' Samuel, now you has won . . . won de' biggest prize of all. Good night, honey, I'll be along presently."

The next days and weeks passed in a blur of grief for the whole family. Delilah, Mandy, and Mattie selected a secluded spot in the shade of a big live oak tree at River Bend for his burial place. Later Virgil built a picket fence around the plot and a comfortable bench where Delilah could sit when she came to visit. She always kept a fresh arrangement on his grave, in spring and summer, fresh flowers, and in fall and winter, autumn leaves or pine boughs and holly berries. Delilah was never again her old self. It was as if her only reason for living was gone.

CHAPTER EIGHT

AN UNEASY HORIZON

The next few years marked a growing uneasiness in the South, hard to define, gradual, but definitely growing and frightening. This was especially true in Charleston where for years there had been great restlessness among the slave population and, consequently, apprehension among the slave owners. Word of abolitionist activity gave the slaves new hope; and slave owners reacted with intense emotion. Their feelings ran the gamut from guilty half-agreement with the abolitionists to hate and violent anger. Among the most adamant and bigoted, strangely enough, were the poor non-slave owners. These angry and violent citizens were the most eager to go to war to protect the interests and traditions of slavery; perhaps because the slaves were the only people to whom they felt superior.

Their poverty drove poor white southerners to latch onto any means available for making extra money. This, coupled with their almost innate hatred of the black man, led them to become bounty hunters. They brought their guns and hounds and went about the business of hunting down escaped slaves for whatever amount was offered for them alive, since, of course, they were only valuable alive. However, before allowing a slave to escape, they would kill him.

Slaves attempting to escape from states north of the Carolinas, usually fled into Canada; those escaping from the Carolinas and south usually headed into Florida, the Caribbean, or southwest into Mexico. It was not uncommon to hear the sounds of hounds, gunfire, and the cries of the hunters and the hunted along the Ashley River Road and into the swamps to the south.

During one particularly noisy and disturbing night, Virgil and Mattie arose very early. Sleep was impossible. "Virgil, I never have been a slave; but the longer the noise of the hunt goes on, the more in bondage I feel. Oh, God, there but for His grace go we!"

"How very true, Mattie! I feel as if there were iron bands around my chest. I don't think that any man with a drop of black blood in his veins can ever feel truly free as long as slavery exists!"

When Virgil arrived to begin his day's work at Fairlawn, the central topic of conversation was the night's slave hunt. Matthew was saying, "The tension is growing greater with every passing day, Papa."

"Yes, and with every passing day, I can see the growing necessity for me to get off this fence-of-conscience I have been straddling and follow my little hero, Noel, and his parents!" John replied. "However, I must be careful how I accomplish it. I don't want to endanger my family in any way; but, on the other hand, I would like to make whatever I do count in some way on the side of abolition. I don't want to make the mere silent gesture of freeing my slaves. Virgil, you're an astute man. Do you have any ideas on how I might achieve both these goals?"

"No sir, Mr. Prendle, at this point I really don't. I recommend we all think and pray about it, sleep on it for a few nights, then turn it over to the Lord and follow His lead. We can always count on Him!" Virgil answered confidently.

"Gentlemen, I think I have come to the most eye-opening conclusion of my entire life," John said. "As much as I have bandied about, with conviction, that insidious expression, *Southern Tradition,* I have come to believe that our beautiful Southland is more in bondage to that expression, with all it implies, than our slaves are in bondage to us!"

It was several nights later, late in November 1846, Virgil and Mattie were sitting in the parlor relaxing and enjoying some quiet time alone; the children were all in bed and sleeping soundly. They were surprised to hear a tentative knock at the door. "My goodness, Virge, who do you suppose that could be at this hour?"

"Only one way to find out, Honey," Virgil answered as he rose to go to the door. He opened the door to see a man standing there, hat in hand. His features were hard to distinguish in the half-light of the shadowy porch, yet there was something strangely familiar about him to Virgil.

"Good evening, Mr. Virgil Lineham, I believe? I am sorry to disturb you at such a late hour, but I have been traveling from Savannah and have just arrived," he said.

"That is perfectly all right, sir; won't you come in," Virgil said pleasantly, as he stepped aside and gestured a welcome for the stranger to enter.

Mattie came forward to take his hat. "Won't you have a seat, sir? Is there anything I can get for you, coffee or maybe a cup of tea?" She asked, as he took a seat on the sofa.

"That isn't necessary. I wouldn't want to put you to any trouble, Mrs. Lineham," he answered, with a question in his voice as he spoke her name.

"Oh, I'm sorry, this is my wife, Mattie," Virgil answered apologetically.

"You probably don't remember me, Virgil. It has been a long time since we have seen each other, and it was a situation you probably would prefer to forget. In fact, it was a situation of which I am not proud and would prefer to forget myself.

However, I haven't been able to get it out of mind in all these years," the stranger said hesitantly.

"On the contrary, Mr. Lineham, the family resemblance is uncanny." Virgil answered. "Mattie, I would like you to meet my cousin, Mr. Percival Lineham of Savannah."

"This is your father's nephew, the one who inherited his estate?" Mattie asked, impending anger in her voice.

"That's right," Virgil responded, with no hint of resentment. "That was many years ago. Much water has passed under the bridge, and I have lived a lifetime since then—a wonderful lifetime!"

"Virgil, that is why I am here. I shall never forget the look on your face the day the slave brokers herded you, along with many other slaves, aboard a packet headed for Charleston and the slave block. I remember one particular couple with a new baby; their look of despair and terror has plagued my days and haunted my nights all these years. I have been trying to make amends ever since for what I did to you. I freed my own slaves and joined the abolitionist cause, but my conscience still gives me no rest. Especially during this last year since my own first baby was born! I had to come here and find you to tell you how very sorry I am for all I did to you and to beg your forgiveness. I have also brought all of the proceeds from Uncle David's estate to you."

"Percy, I am truly sorry for all the pain that you have suffered. I forgave you long ago; now you must forgive yourself. Coming to Charleston has brought me only happiness, the greatest happiness a man can know: freedom, the most beloved wife on earth, three precious children, and a big loving family! I am a rich man in all the things that are really important. Thank you so very much for the generous gesture, but I neither need nor want my father's money."

"Virgil, I anticipated your answer; so I have already arranged with the bank for the money to be held in trust for his grandchildren until they are twenty-one; said trust to be administered by you."

After a long silence, Virgil finally spoke, "Well, Percy, it seems you have me there. The privilege of refusing for myself belongs to me, but the privilege of refusing their grandfather's estate belongs to his grandchildren and not to me. Since they are too young to make that decision at this time, as "administrator of said trust,"—to use your terminology—I must place the trust on hold until they reach the age of twenty-one when the decision will be theirs. I thank you, on their behalf, for your generosity."

"Now, Virgil, I must confess I have only told you half the reason I came here. You might have heard of an organization which has recently come to be referred to by some as the Underground Railroad. It has actually been around since the earliest days of slavery in this country. It is a network of different routes to freedom for escaped slaves. Some routes go north leading to freedom in areas that don't allow slavery. Some lead as far north as Canada; others lead south into Florida, the islands beyond, and even west into Mexico. Fugitives generally follow the route that leads most quickly to freedom. These routes are well organized and have safe places referred to as stations. The stations furnish a brief respite, supplies, a hiding place, identification papers, and then help to the next station. These stations are run by anti-slave sympathizers or avowed and active abolitionists. I have been active in helping to recruit stations for the routes leading south and west through South Carolina and Georgia. I am here to ask you to consider serving as a stationmaster. Don't answer quickly. This is a very dangerous undertaking for you and your family, but you know what it means to the futures of the slaves you would be helping to set free. Until you have made a decision, don't discuss this conversation with anyone but your wife or those who would be directly involved. Our whole organization is jeopardized when anyone not personally involved knows about it."

"Percy, this is completely overwhelming. I am not remotely approaching a personal commitment to this, although I support all the things you and the network are striving to do!"

"Virgil, I have many contacts to make in the next few weeks," Percy said as he rose to leave. "I shall be back in about a month. Maybe you folks will have reached a decision by the time I return," he finished as he disappeared into the night.

Mattie and Virgil sat in the parlor in silence for a long while; each thinking his own thoughts. Virgil finally spoke, "Mattie, we can't take the chance on doing this; it's far too dangerous for our family!"

"Virge, I have been free my entire life; and now, you also know what that means; our babies are free. We can do no less for those who are still in bondage."

"Mattie, Mattie, my heart tells me you are right, but my fear for our children makes me hesitant to do what we both know is the right thing to do. We have to consider this very carefully from every standpoint! At any rate, we need to get to bed now; morning will be here before we know it. "

The two of them slept fitfully the remainder of the night. By morning they had both arrived at the only decision with which they could live in good conscience. Somehow it seemed to go without saying, as was frequently the case with the two of them, that the decision had been made; and they were both completely committed to it.

John and Matthew were finishing breakfast with a final cup of coffee when Virgil came out of the butler's pantry. "Gentlemen, if you have time, I have something important which I need to discuss with you this morning."

"Of course, Virgil, have a seat and join us for coffee," John answered.

"Thank you, sir," Virgil said as he poured himself a cup of coffee and took a seat. "First, I must have your assurance that anything discussed here will not go beyond this room."

"Of course, Virgil, you have our assurance. Right Matthew?"

"Most assuredly! Virge, you asked, and so it goes without saying. I would think you would know that!" Matt added incredulously.

"I didn't mean to offend you; but you are my family; and this could mean life or death to a member of our family at some point in time."

"We weren't offended, Virge, just surprised that you felt it necessary to ask. As you say, we are family," John answered. "Obviously something very important has happened that you do need to share with us."

"Yes sir! I'm sure you both remember our discussion not long ago about freeing your slaves. Something occurred last night that I believe might enable us to devise a workable plan which will allow you to free your slaves and also aid the abolitionist cause. Mattie and I had an interesting surprise visitor last night." Virgil told John and Matt all the events of the previous night. "Mattie and I agree that we have no choice but to go forth with my cousin Percy's request."

"I have a vague idea for a tentative plan," Virgil continued. "River Bend would become the station; and I, the stationmaster. You could free your slaves secretly but employ them to stay on and farm Fairlawn. They could assist us in helping lead the fugitives out. Gradually, should they choose, they could work themselves into the flight plans. What do you two think?"

John began, "First, Virge, after hearing all you have told us about your background and all the injustice you endured at the hands of Percy Lineham before coming to Fairlawn, let me say to you that my respect for you and admiration of you, which has always been great, has more than doubled!

Now, I like your plan, but I suggest a slight revision. I don't think we have a slave on Fairlawn who wouldn't be happy to help the cause of freedom, even at the risk of his own life, and who can't be trusted to keep our confidence. However, I suggest that Matthew and I share the stationmaster's duties and that our slave quarters become the station. That is the last place anyone would look for runaway slaves. I fear that your home would be the first place they would look. Your home and Pink Hill would be the most suspect places in or around Charleston. No one at Pink Hill nor any of the other children can ever know any of this!"

"Papa, I agree with you. I think your revised plan offers us greater hope for success."

"I must agree, Matt. Every point the two of you have made is valid, and Mr. Prendle's plan seems to be more logical."

"Speaking of logical, the planning, implementation, and logistics of all this is going to be a huge undertaking," John said.

"You are absolutely right, sir; and the sooner we get underway, the better!" Virgil continued. "Percy will return in a month or so. Meanwhile, we can proceed to collect clothes, food, and other supplies the fugitives will need. I am sure when Percy arrives he will have many suggestions for the things we need to do in order to establish an effective station. He has had much experience in setting up other stations which have been very successful."

"Virge, let me say again how much I admire the courage you and Mattie exhibit in accepting this dangerous challenge. I feel that we, as your family, can do no less than join you in this undertaking. I consider it a noble cause; although I must confess that I am terrified at the thought of the dangers which lie ahead for all the members of our family. However, even though covert, our efforts stand for the right; and in years to come, our children will be able to look back with pride. At this point in time, lack of action would shout loudly for the wrong; and we cannot allow this to be the heritage of our family. It took the principles of a small boy and of his mother before him, and the courage to speak-up for those principles, to serve as a mirror to the stubborn and guilty conscience of this old man."

Percy Lineham returned three weeks later and was delighted to hear of the plans which were already underway. Taking advantage of Percy's expert experience based knowledge, they moved along rapidly with their plans. Soon the organization of the station was ready to begin its work. According to plan, all was accomplished in complete secrecy. As expected, John's slaves were not only willing but eager to help in the cause. They were now freedmen and tenant farmers in the employ of their former master. In reality, their everyday lives had changed very little; but with the knowledge that they were finally free, their attitudes, incentives, and demeanors were completely different.

The station kept records; and, as is usually the case, success was measured in numbers. The numbers reflected the fugitive slaves who had been successfully led to freedom in the six years between November 1846 and November 1852. Remarkably, two hundred had been led to safety and freedom.

In these six years, the existence of the Underground Railroad station on Fairlawn was still a secret from everyone except Will. Early on they had called on Will for medical help for one of the fugitives. It had been difficult for Will to keep the secret from Lillianna. From the day they had married, it had never been their practice to keep secrets from one another. However, knowing her as they did, Will, John, and Matt knew that she would want to be actively involved in aiding the cause. For her own safety and that of the children, they all agreed that she must never know.

This six year period had also marked tremendous changes

in the Pinkston, Gilmore, and Lineham children. The older of the children: Noel, Barbara and Beau Gilmore, and Louis and Julius Lineham, were all seventeen years old. Young Lydia was fourteen; and the youngest, Leland and Annamarie, were seven.

When the older children had reached the age that they would transfer to higher education in Charleston, the Lineham twins, because of their race, were not permitted to enroll there. Mattie, Virgil, and Mandy saw to it that their education was continued at home. However, when they reached their seventeenth birthday, they felt the boys should have a more formal education. Since they were freedmen, Virgil and Mattie decided they should go north to Canada to attend school. Virgil sailed with them to Quebec and enrolled them in an Anglican school there. This was a heart-wrenching experience for the whole family, but everyone felt it a necessary move.

Noel was interested in engineering and business. His ambition was to ultimately help operate the plantations. He was well-versed in the various processes necessary to the successful production of cotton and sugar cane, since he had always worked in the fields industriously with his grandfathers and his Uncle Matt. He enrolled in the military college of Charleston, S.C., The Citadel, in 1852. The school had an excellent reputation for offering a good foundation in the arts, sciences, business, and engineering as well as the discipline of military training. Lillianna and Will felt, and Noel agreed, that an education at The Citadel offered a well-rounded curriculum that would be beneficial to the future Noel had mapped out for himself.

Gentle Beau had felt from boyhood that he wanted to follow in his grandfather's footsteps and become a doctor, so he enrolled in Charleston Medical College. Beau's twin sister, Barbara, wanted a general education in preparation for becoming a homemaker, a mother, and possibly a teacher; so she attended Miss Hockaday's School for Young Ladies, and subsequently, the recently added Hockaday Advanced Academy for Women.

For some time now, Mr. Pinkston had known that precocious Lydia had advanced musically beyond the point that he was qualified to teach her. She already knew at fourteen that she wanted to become a music teacher. After she gave an audition concert on the harp and piano, a master musician, the conductor of the Charleston Symphony Orchestra, agreed to take her on as a private student.

With all of their older siblings having moved on in pursuit of higher education, the seven-year-old cousins, Leland and Annamarie, remained behind still being schooled at Pink Hill. They were best friends and constant companions. Neither of them was a very serious student. Their interests lay in outdoor pursuits—riding, fishing, exploring, collecting rocks and arrowheads, bugs and butterflies and such—to the great dismay of their mothers.

The summer of 1853, much like the summer of 1845, was intolerably hot; but, unfortunately, it had an unwelcome companion, the dreaded yellow fever. The epidemic made tragic claims among the revered older generation. Pink Hill first lost adored Grandpapa Pink. He had for years suffered with a heart problem, and the yellow fever proved to be more than his heart could take.

Next they lost the beloved Delilah. At age ninety-four, she was a likely victim. Having lost Samuel, she seemed almost eager to join him. John delivered a beautiful and moving eulogy for Delilah as she was laid to rest next to Samuel at River Bend. "Dear God, we now commend to You the soul of one of the finest and most courageous Christian ladies who has ever graced our lives," John finished, weeping openly for the first time in years.

CHAPTER NINE

END OF AN ERA

The years between 1853 and 1860 rolled on rapidly. All the children who were pursuing higher education progressed toward accomplishing their goals and adulthood. The attraction between Noel Pinkston and Barbara Gilmore, as well as that between Lydia Pinkston and Beau Gilmore, moved toward romance. Both families had recognized this growing attraction for some time.

Since the Protective Tariff of 1832, which taxed imports, the South, and especially South Carolina it seems, started to harbor antiunion sentiments. The tariff, designed to protect American industrial interests, had a negative impact on free trade with other countries for the agricultural South. Even as early as the late 1830's, there was talk in South Carolina of secession from the Union. So in the late 1850's, when the political climate of the nation was volatile, with the lines of opposition forming based on the question of slavery, the old proponents of secession had an even stronger case. The Democratic Party, now concentrated primarily in the south, held very strong pro-slavery and states' rights convictions. On the other hand, the Republican Party, concentrated primarily in the north and west, held very strong anti-slavery convictions. Charleston, having had a disturbingly restless slave population for years, was becoming a veritable boiling pot.

In November of 1855, Noel graduated from The Citadel; and the following June, Barbara graduated from Hockaday's Advanced Academy for Women. They both graduated with honors at age twenty-two. At John's urging, Noel made his home at Fairlawn in order that he might observe first hand the day to day operation of a successful plantation.

Barbara, with an impeccable academic record, graduated at an opportune time. There was to be an opening next semester in the English Department of Miss Hockaday's School for Young Ladies, of which she was an alumna. Miss Hockaday offered the teaching position to Barbara; and she accepted, delighted with the opportunity. Like all the teachers in Miss Hockaday's schools, during the school year, Barbara would be housed in the Teacherage, a deluxe dormitory for teachers, on the campus. She would live with her Grandmother Gilmore at Meadows during the summer months.

During 1856 and '57, Noel and Barbara fell more and more deeply in love. By the summer of 1857, their love had ripened into a passionate relationship, impatient for consummation. When Barbara came home to Meadows following the end of the spring semester, Noel came, seriously courting, on the evening of the day she arrived home.

Barbara and Gran Nettie (as Beau and Barbara called their Grandmother Gilmore) were finishing their dessert on the piazza when they saw Noel approaching in the buggy rather than on horseback, as they had expected. "Looks like you two are going for a buggy ride, my dear," Gran Nettie said, as Noel reined-in and tied-up at the blackamoor. "Good evening, Noel. We're so happy to see you," she added, as he stepped up on the piazza.

"Good evening, beautiful ladies. I have never seen a lovelier picture than you two magnolias make, sitting there framed in the twilight's glow," Noel observed.

"Oh, Noel Pinkston, you and your silver tongue. I haven't figured which of two callings you missed, that of an artist or a poet!" Gran Nettie laughed.

"More likely a big old tale teller!" Barbara added. "Have a seat and let me serve you a dessert."

"I'll take you up on the seat, but I'll decline the dessert. I've just had dinner, and I'm full to the brim," he said, as he sat down beside Barbara in one of several peacock chairs arranged randomly on the broad piazza.

"Well, children, I'm not so old that I don't remember that about this time, young folks are ready for the old folks to make their exit; so I'll take the dessert tray, say goodnight, and leave the evening to you youngsters. It's always good to see you, Noel. Come back again soon."

"You may count on that, Mrs. Gilmore, and goodnight to you," Noel replied as he rose and hastened over to open the front door for her. As soon as Mrs. Gilmore was inside and the door closed, Noel rushed back to Barbara, pulled her to her feet and into his arms, and kissed her passionately. "Oh God, Barb, I'm so glad you're finally home. I thought this school year would never end!

Let's go for a buggy ride down to the river. That's all right with you isn't it?" Noel asked as he took her hand and led her to the buggy without waiting for an answer. As they rode down toward the Ashley, he drew Barbara near with one arm around her shoulders and holding the reins with his other hand, he slipped into a habit he had always had since he and Barbara had been courting. He had a nice singing voice, and he sang love songs into her ear as they rode along. She loved it, especially when he sang "Beautiful Dreamer" and substituted her name. In no time it seemed, they arrived at Lillianna's little alcove by the river.

Noel stepped down from the buggy, tied the horse to a tree, and helped Barbara down, holding her close to his chest as she stepped to the ground. "It seems we've barely seen each other since last summer. I came into Charleston to see you as often as I could; but the only time I was free to come on weekday evenings, you were nearly always busy preparing for the next day's class or grading papers; and the weekends seemed a hundred years apart! I'm ready for us to get married now! In fact, as you know, I was ready last year after we graduated.

"Noel, darling, you know how much I love you and have from the time I was old enough to realize what love was; but my better judgment tells me that we perhaps should wait another year for each of us to gain a little more experience at our work."

"Barb, my brain says maybe you are right; but each time I hold you in my arms, my manhood says I want you now, for my wife, in a home of our own, and in my bed and arms every night! I love and respect you and our upbringing too much for us to even consider satisfying our passions without benefit of marriage vows spoken before God and our families," Noel said as he kissed her a lingering and intimate kiss, fighting, in spite of all his noble words, to restrain his hands from caressing her beautiful body as he dropped his lips to the cleavage between her breasts. He stepped back suddenly to regain his composure, leaving her breathless, her own desire matching his. "Darling, the only time I can move forward honorably, without restraint, is in my dreams. If that is a sin, I have to plead guilty."

"Oh, Noel, you're not the only one who dreams with abandon. You don't know how many times you have kissed me goodnight the way you just kissed me. Then the desire you had ignited stayed with me through my bath, into my bed, and into my dreams where I found you waiting; and with my body on fire for you, we pursued our desires with passion. Then suddenly, without satisfaction, I would awaken frustrated, with my gown soaking wet; so you see, I have those same sins, if they are sins, to deal with also! From the way I feel right now, I must agree; I think we had better get married. It is probably dangerous not to," she said, melting into his arms again.

Suddenly Noel stepped back and dropped to one knee as he took her hands in his. "Barbara Anne Gilmore, would you do me the honor of becoming my wife, Mrs. Noel Parker Pinkston; and would you grant me permission to ask your father for your hand in marriage, immediately?" Noel asked, with great formality and in all sincerity.

"Noel Parker Pinkston, I, Barbara Anne Gilmore, accept with pleasure and humility, your beautiful and most eloquent proposal of marriage. I consider being your wife and spending the rest of my life with you, the greatest of all honors. I grant you permission to ask my father for my hand in marriage, immediately," Barbara responded, with equal formality and sincerity.

"Do you agree that we should plan for our marriage to take place as soon as possible so that we can be settled in somewhere before the time arrives for you to prepare for the fall session of school ?" Noel asked.

"Yes, I do, but I'm not sure it is possible. A wedding isn't planned overnight you know. So many other people are involved. We must select bridesmaids and groomsmen, set a date, and schedule the church; that's just for starters. The logistics are mind boggling!"

"Darling, I'm sure you have always dreamed of a big wedding with all the traditional frills that accompany it; but I'm not at all sure of the wisdom, or even the safety, of making such elaborate plans. With our political climate what it is these days, and with the open restlessness of the black population and the angry white opposition, I really think it might be well for us to plan a simple ceremony at home, with only our families attending. Would you be terribly disappointed if we did that?" Noel asked. "Please accept my word without question, there are other extenuating circumstances which make this plan a wiser one."

In the months Noel had spent living at Fairlawn since his graduation, it was inevitable that he would learn of the Underground Railroad activities underway there; and he felt that these activities, even though they were carefully guarded, might pose a threat for both families. Upon learning of the existence of the UGRR and his family's involvement, he was, of course, sworn to secrecy; and he agreed it was far safer for the women in the family not to be told about it. He knew he couldn't tell Barbara; he just hoped she would agree to his plan.

"Sweetheart, of course I agree. I could never be disappointed with any ceremony which ended with my being your wife. I trust your judgment always; I know whatever your reasons may be, they are valid. However, do you feel it would be too unconventional for us to hold our marriage ceremony right here in this little alcove beside the Ashley? It is so beautiful and peaceful, and we have spent so many happy hours here."

"I think that would be wonderful! As soon as possible, I will speak to your father. Then we shall set the date for the wedding, clear it with the rector's calendar, announce our engagement to our families, and invite the guests by personal note. Today is June tenth; how does July thirtieth sound to you for our wedding? That would give us almost two months to settle down before school starts again," Noel rushed on, in orderly fashion—no doubt a carryover from his Citadel training—organizing the details like some military campaign!

"That sounds like an excellent plan to me; although, it leaves my mind in a whirl! Since we have decided to keep it simple, the sooner the better I think. I would like Father to give me away, of course; and, Lydia to be my one bridesmaid, if you agree."

"I am sure Lydia would be honored that you have chosen her. I will ask Papa to be my best man, of course. We may get some argument from our mothers and from your grandmother;

you know how women are about weddings. After all, you are your mother's only daughter."

"I don't think either of the three will give us any problem. I believe, knowing them all as I do, they will want it to be just the way we want it. Oh, Noel, I am so happy at the thought of being your wife. I can't wait to tell everyone that you have proposed, especially Gran Nettie, Beau, and Lydia!" Barbara bubbled, clapping her hands.

"I'll tell you what, we will tell your grandmother when we get back tonight; and, I must confess, I have already told Beau that I was going to ask you tonight. After all, he has always been my best friend. I am sure he has probably already told Lydia, his precious 'peanut'; he tells her everything! Mama has always said Beau and Lydia are just exactly like she and Papa were when they were very young—in love before either of them even knew it. I don't think we will have to reverse the news unless your father surprises me with a refusal."

"My love, your asking Father is merely a courtesy. I am going to marry you regardless of his answer! You are, and always will be, the center of my life. If you but knew it, you have never had a chance. I have been determined all my life to someday be Mrs. Noel Parker Pinkston!"

"Really? You little fox, and all the time I thought this was my idea!" Noel said, pulling her back into his arms with that same smile behind his eyes that was so characteristic of his father.

"Noel, you and your silver tongue again. You have always known my heart belongs to you!" she laughed, as he pulled her hips to his and kissed her.

"I want much more than your heart, my girl. I want to unveil all of you, and then hold you close to all of me!"

"My goodness, what a carnal husband I am going to have!"

"You may count on that! Now let's go tell Gran Nettie our news," he said, helping her up into the buggy.

When they arrived at Meadows, Barbara's grandmother had retired early and was reading. "I guess we'll have to save our news for later, sweets, since Gran Nettie has gone to bed," Noel said, disappointed.

"Oh no, we'll go upstairs and tell her. She won't mind; she always reads late into the night," Barbara answered.

"Well, all right, if you think she won't mind," Noel agreed with some reservation, as Barbara led him upstairs to her grandmother's bedroom.

Barbara tapped on the bedroom door. "Gran Nettie, it's Noel and I, may we come in? We want to talk to you."

"Come right in children; I was just reading myself off to sleep. Come on in if you think you can stand the sight of an old lady in her nightcap," she laughed, as Barbara entered with Noel following hesitantly. "Come over here and sit on the bed with me," Nettie said, slipping over to the center and patting the bed on either side of her.

As the two young people sat facing her on either side, she sat propped up on a mountain of pillows with her gray spit curls escaping here and there around her white, lace-trimmed nightcap and her matching nightgown ribbon, tied closely beneath her chin. She started, "All right, what in the land is so important that you two come rousing an old lady out of her slumber!"

"Oh, Gran, we just couldn't wait! Guess what?" Barbara answered, clutching her grandmother's hand in both of hers.

"Well, my guess would be that I am about to have the honor of being the first to hear of a coming wedding. Right?"

"How did you know?" Barbara said, wide-eyed.

Noel looked at both of them lovingly, realizing for the first time how very much Barbara looked like her grandmother—the same beautiful blue eyes that seemed to be ever smiling, the spit curls around their faces, Barbara's a honey blond and Gran Nettie's, which had once been the same, now gray. He thought, "How truly beautiful you both are!"

"How did I know? It's something your grandfather Alan told me years ago. He said, 'There is one peak time for a young couple in love to marry. Not that their love would die; whenever they married, it would be good; but there is only one perfect level of intensity. If they fail to seize it, they will miss that moment in time when they would be more *one* than ever again.' He thought that was truer with your mother and father, Noel, than with any couple he had ever known. I believe that time has come for you two. Now, when is the big day to be? Knowing you two as I do, I'm sure the detailed plans are already beginning to gel; so tell me all about them."

"Gran Nettie, you're going to think we have lost our minds; but we want to get married next month. We don't want to wait to prepare for a big wedding; that could take as much as a year. We want to have a small, simple ceremony with just our families present, in that beautiful little alcove beside the river. That way, we could be all settled in before school starts again. Does it all sound too crazy, Gran?" Barbara asked, half expecting her to say that it did.

"Indeed not, you two seem to have planned it as you both want it to be, and that is exactly the way weddings should be. Now, speaking of settling in, where do you plan to live?"

"We haven't really discussed that. I think we just assumed we would stay on at Fairlawn for the time being. I feel sure that we would be welcome," Noel answered.

"I have an offer I wish you would consider," Gran Nettie said. "The little gatehouse here at Meadows is a nice little first home for a couple. No one has lived there for some years now. It needs some freshening up, but I want to offer it to you. I would love to have you living nearby. Think about it and let me know. If you decide to accept, I would love to have it refurbished to suit your tastes and to present it to you as a wedding gift."

"Your generosity is overwhelming, Gran Nettie!" Noel answered. "I can't think of anyone I would rather have as my closest neighbor. What do you think, sweetheart? I am all for it if you are!"

"I agree without hesitation. We accept most gratefully!" Barbara said, kissing her grandmother's cheek.

Surprisingly, both families not only approved, but did so enthusiastically. Plans went off without a hitch. Gran Nettie, with Barbara's and Noel's input, saw to the complete restoration and furnishing of the gatehouse. There was a rush to finish, but it was ready just in time for the wedding.

Barbara and Noel had decided to postpone a formal honeymoon until they had more time. Instead, they settled for spending a few days in seclusion in their own little home.

On July twenty-ninth, scarcely a month after the job was begun, the renovation was complete; and the furnishings were all in place. Noel and Barbara entered their front door with excited anticipation. "Oh, Noel, it's all so perfect. It looks like a beautiful playhouse, but on a larger scale," Barbara exclaimed, with tears welling up in her eyes.

"Oh, love, no tears today; it's a time for happiness. In just two days you will be my wife; so no tears my darling," Noel said, taking her in his arms and kissing her.

"My tears are not of sadness, but of happiness, dear heart. I can't wait to be your wife and to move into our new home. There are so many beautiful things here, so many things that Gran Nettie gave us from Meadows—old things that were part of my childhood memories. We are going to be so happy living here, Noel!"

"My goodness, aren't we moving along rather rapidly? You're skipping over a part that I am really looking forward to," Noel said thickly, as he allowed his hands to move dangerously close to caressing her body in ways still forbidden. He stepped back suddenly and said, "I think we had better get out of here before we lose control and do something we'll regret. We have waited this long; we can wait two more days!"

The next two days, time seemed to creep by on the one hand, and yet, paradoxically, in many ways it also seemed to fly. Finally, on July thirtieth, they moved as if through a beautiful dream. Suddenly they were standing in the serenity of the alcove beside the Ashley River where so many happy hours had been spent. "I, Noel, take thee, Barbara, to be my lawfully wedded wife . . ."

As Lillianna watched her beloved Will, standing as best man beside their firstborn Noel, and Lydia, standing as maid-of-honor beside his bride, Barbara, her eyes filled with happy tears. Memories of her little alcove came threading back to weave themselves into the fabric of this happy day, another beautiful memory in the making.

Every member of both families stood watching the ceremony, each with his or her own thoughts. Lillianna and Will saw Lydia's eyes meet Beau's as Noel and Barbara tenderly spoke their vows, and they looked at each other and nodded knowingly.

Following the ceremony, the little group trailed the bride and groom as they left the alcove and walked across the broad lawn and up to the beautiful mansion. A small reception was given in honor of the happy couple by Pagrand, Matthew, Mandy, Mattie, and Virgil.

When the reception was over and Barbara and Noel were saying their goodbyes on the piazza, around the house came a fine new carriage, festooned in ribbons and flowers and bells with Beau, Lydia, Louis, Julius, Leland, and Annamarie all crowded aboard and singing a little wedding song, composed by Lydia, which explained that the carriage was a wedding gift from all their old playmates.

Noel said laughing, "I knew you characters would pull something; but I had no idea it would in the form of such a generous and thoughtful wedding gift. We both thank you so very much, and we remind you that our fun days together aren't over. In fact, the best is yet to be!"

"Amen," Barbara echoed, her eyes sparkling with tears!

The happy couple said their goodbyes with many hugs and kisses and, in their elegant carriage, left for their new home at Meadows, cheered on by a cacophony of "good lucks" and "congratulations"!

As soon as they were out of sight, Noel reined in, took Barbara in his arms, and kissed her long and passionately. "Oh, Barb, at last you are mine!"

"Yes darling, and you are mine, forever. Let's go home now."

When they reached the gatehouse and drove around to their front door, Noel stepped down, went around the carriage, helped Barbara down and swept her up in his arms, seemingly in one fluid motion, for the traditional trip across the threshold. "Suddenly you seem so much smaller than I thought, like a beautiful china doll," he said, setting her on her feet and enclosing her in his arms as he finally caressed her body freely.

"Are you hungry? Gran Nettie had Trudy, her cook, one of the best anywhere around, prepare our wedding night dinner. It's in the kitchen, and I am sure it's delicious. Would you like to eat while it's still hot?"

"You don't really mean that, do you? We can re-heat it later tonight, or in the morning! We have waited so long; and I don't know about you; but I've reached the point-of-no-return!" Noel answered, as he started fumbling with the buttons on her dress.

"I have too," she answered, "and what I am hungry for isn't food," she said, kissing him passionately as her hands groped downward. "And I see you are ready," she added, smiling as she caressed him with a desire that equaled his own.

Noel picked her up and carried her into the bedroom. Trembling with desire, they finished undressing. Barbara lay back on the bed, as he devoured her beauty with his eyes. "You are gorgeous," he said, as he kissed her body. Moving upward from her abdomen, he caressed her breasts with his tongue and lips relentlessly until her passion reached the breaking point; and she begged breathlessly, "Noel, please, now, please!" He rose to his knees between her legs, encircled her waist with his hands, and drew her downward to him as he moved inward, slowly and gently. She cried out in ecstasy and pain, that wonderful paradox that comes in those first few moments of abandon that ultimately lead to fulfillment. They continued thus throughout the night, with no thought of eating or sleeping, completely lost in each other as wave after wave of desire, unleashed at last, seemed insatiable.

The rest of 1857, saw life settle into a very satisfactory pattern for the newlyweds and for all of the family. Lillianna and Will were ever busier, he, with his practice, and she, bent on being everywhere at once, driven to be everything she felt her family needed her to be. Rather than finding this burdensome, they both seemed to thrive on their frantic paces.

Beau and Lydia fell more deeply in love with every passing day and grew more impatient to move forward in their relationship. Observing Noel and Barbara as they seemed to grow happier everyday, just served to increase their restlessness. Naturally, this was of considerable concern to their parents. Lydia was very young; and it was obvious that they were like a train headed downhill, about to lose control.

The work of the Underground Railroad was curtailed to the point of a trickle of escapees. The situation in Charleston had the slave owning population ever vigilant of the activities of their slaves and highly suspicious of the non-slave-owning whites and their abolitionist leanings. Every faction concerned was living with the unrelenting fear that some nebulous, impending tragedy would trigger war.

John, unlike the rest of the family, was not able to relax, live one day at a time, and accept life as it came. Maybe it was due to his advancing years or, more likely, due to a personality which had always required that he be in control.

At any rate, it was beyond his capability to avoid acute stress, which was drastically affecting his health. In January 1858, he suffered a massive stroke which left him paralyzed and severely impaired. He was obviously able to think clearly, but unable to express his thoughts. It was so very sad for all the family to see this proud man, whom all had regarded as the big, strong oak under which they had taken shelter all their lives, reduced to this tearful, pitiful, helpless creature.

The family members took turns sitting with him and doing everything they could to make him comfortable and to keep him company. Lillianna would sit by the hour trying in vain to help him communicate. He tried so hard to find the words for which he was searching. Lillianna would try to guess, questioning him in an effort to help, but all to no avail; and he would finally break down sobbing in frustration.

One night as Lillianna and Will were preparing for bed, after a particularly grueling day with her father, she said, "Oh, Will, Papa is so pitiful. It would almost have been better if he had lost his mental capability along with everything else. At least, he wouldn't realize what was happening to him. I can't bear seeing him this way," she paused, bursting into tears. "Dear God, please have mercy on him," she prayed fervently, "Please release him from this hell in which he is trapped and take him home to be with Thee!"

Will drew her into his arms and held her as she cried herself to sleep. "Oh, my beloved little Auburn Hair, how I wish I could bear your anguish for you," he said, as he kissed her hair and drew her ever closer.

The following day when Lillianna went to visit, she noticed a tremendous difference in John. He was strangely still, completely relaxed and staring into space. She sat on the edge of his bed, turned his face toward her, and looked into his eyes. Suddenly his eyes came alive with joyful recognition. He said, "Becca, my beautiful Becca, it has been such a long time since I have seen you." He spoke clearly and with no hint of a speech problem. Then he closed his eyes; and with one big sigh, he was gone.

"Oh most merciful Father, I thank you for freeing Papa from his agony," Lillianna sobbed in prayer.

Jonathan Prendle was laid to rest beside his beloved Rebecca. As he would have wished, a simple graveside ceremony marked his passing. The rector of St. Michael's read Psalm I and delivered a brief eulogy based on those words. With tears streaming down his cheeks, Noel sang "Amazing Grace" as the closing prayer, amidst the muffled sobs of family and friends.

That night, as had become their custom, Lillianna and Will had a brief devotional period before retiring. "Psalm I, verses one through three," Lillianna began, as she read aloud the words from John's eulogy, "'Blessed is the man that walketh not in the counsel of the Ungodly, nor standeth in the way of sinners, nor sitteth in the seat of the scornful. But his delight is in the law of the Lord, and in this law doth he meditate day and night. And he shall be like a tree, planted by the rivers of water that bringeth forth his fruit at his season; his leaf also shall not wither; and whatsoever he doeth shall prosper.'" She paused for a long moment as she pondered the words. "What a perfect description of Papa; it is as if the psalmist knew him and wrote the words specifically for him."

"Yes, it certainly is," Will agreed. "He was all of those things and more."

"He truly was; and now with all that strong generation gone, first Papa Pink and now my papa, the mantle of that era falls on us. Are we wise enough, or strong enough, with roots deep enough to replace that 'Tree planted by the rivers of water'? It's frightening,Will, truly frightening!"

"Those are truly big boots to fill, but we are up to the challenge. After all, their blood runs through our veins. We cannot and we will not fail!" Will answered with conviction.

CHAPTER TEN

PRELUDE TO WAR

By 1858, the abolitionist cause was rattling the chains of slavery more and more. With new territories becoming a part of the country and disputes over whether they would or wouldn't be slave-holding, the question of slavery led to the alignment of two major political parties in the United States, the Republicans and the Democrats. The South was primarily pro-slavery Democrat, and the remainder of the country, antislavery Republican. As mentioned earlier, the southerners who espoused abolition were caught in the middle, with antislavery sympathies yet with traditional States' Rights loyalties, dating back to the Protective Tariff of 1832.

As time passed and the supporters of abolition grew more vocal and active, slavery soon became a part of the States' Rights issue. Finally, the line between slavery and the tariff blurred and disappeared; and the cause of States' Rights came to encompass both. Therein lay the dilemma of the Prendles, Pinkstons, and Gilmores.

War seemed inevitable; and when it came, it would end the way of life that southerners all loved. It was true that the South had a horrible disease, slavery, which did need treatment. However, the South also had a quiet, genteel way of life that was truly beautiful. But, as it often happens, the needed treatment, in this case war, would cure the disease, but would kill the patient. The pressures of the looming possibility of war seemed somehow to increase the pace of life, as if they were on a carousel that they hoped might outrun it all.

Noel and Barbara were so happy that they seemed insulated from the rest of the world and its problems. Beau and Lydia longed for this same kind of happiness. If only they could grab the brass ring now, before they missed boarding the runaway carousel. While Beau was attending the Medical College of Charleston, he worked with Will, who served as his mentor, just as Dr. Gilmore had served as Will's when he was in medical school. Beau graduated in June of 1858 and continued to work with Will and Dr. Bradner in their busy practice. Lydia had continued her musical studies under the esteemed conductor of The Charleston Symphony Orchestra and had also graduated from Miss Hockaday's School for Young Ladies. Miss Hockaday offered her a position on that faculty, teaching music as well as music appreciation. Now that they had both finished their education, they were eager to get on with their lives.

In January of 1859, at the invitation of Gran Nettie, they married in a very quiet ceremony in the once elegant ballroom at Meadows, seldom used for its intended purpose. After Lillianna had turned the Pink Hill ballroom into classrooms and a library for the children, Gran Nettie converted the Meadows ballroom into a giant playroom to be used by the children in inclement weather. She had equipped it with every imaginable toy and even pieces of playground equipment. At the time she had said, "There is nothing more maddening for a mother than to have bad weather corral the siblings within a beautifully appointed home to try to entertain themselves. This playroom will eliminate these problems and give a doting grandmother a chance to serve cookies and milk to a rollicking band of youngsters, who can't damage a thing!" So Beau and

Lydia married there, surrounded by their families, a few friends, all the toys they had once enjoyed, and many happy childhood memories. Their generous parents and grandparents joined forces and purchased them, as a wedding gift, a modest home in Charleston near Miss Hockaday's school. Lydia, of course, planned to continue teaching; and Beau, at Will's suggestion, was to take care of their patients who lived in Charleston proper. They set up a medical office in two rooms of their new home. Finally, Beau and Lydia had succeeded in boarding that enchanted carousel; and their happiness was complete.

This occasion was one of the last truly happy times shared by all the family. As mentioned before, the work of the Underground Railroad had ground to a virtual halt due to the vigilance of the determined pro-slavery zealots. Only a few even attempted escape and then at great peril to themselves and to any who attempted to assist them. There were five brothers who instigated several acts of sabotage on the Charleston waterfront. They were slaves of the shipbuilder who owned the company. During the last of these escapades, one of the brothers was injured; and they narrowly avoided capture. They realized that the time had come when they must make an attempt to escape and that the Underground Railroad was their only hope.

One of the UGRR agents in Charleston contacted Matthew on behalf of the brothers. He in turn, with Virgil's help, set about putting a plan in motion for their escape. That plan had one big drawback, the slave who had been injured had gone untreated; and his injuries had become infected. When they arrived at the slave quarters on Fairlawn very late in the evening, the injured brother was growing worse by the hour. "Yaw'l go on widout me. I'se jus' gon' slow you down," he begged his brothers.

"No way dat gon' happen, Bruh; we all goes or we all stays, and dat's dat!"

"I understand how you feel," Matthew interrupted, "I have brothers, too. We'll see what we can do to help you before we set out. My brother-in-law, who is a doctor, lives on the next plantation. We'll take you to him. The rest of you wait here in hiding until we return."

Matthew and Virgil loaded the injured man into a false-bottom wagon, the kind frequently used by the UGRR to transport runaways, and set out for Pink Hill. "I don't think we would have a problem anyway, but this foggy night with no moon or stars is in our favor nevertheless," Matthew commented.

"Right, but we do have a concern that has nothing to do with getting caught. It's Lillianna; she's likely to learn of the UGRR tonight," Virgil answered.

"You're absolutely right, but it's a chance we'll have to take. This escape plan has little chance of succeeding if this man doesn't get some medical treatment."

Following an exhausting day of house calls, Will had arrived home long after dark. Everyone had retired for the night except Lillianna, who, although dressed for bed, waited up for him in the kitchen where she was keeping a light supper warm for him. As usual, they talked of the day's happenings as Will ate. "I am much more tired than hungry tonight," he said, after eating only part of his supper. "I think I'll go on up and get ready for bed."

"I'll be along shortly, as soon as I straighten up here in the kitchen," Lillianna answered, giving him a kiss.

By the time she got upstairs, he was in bed and nearly asleep. She tiptoed in, and removing her robe and slippers, she knelt to say her prayers. When she had finished, she slipped quietly into bed beside him. In his semi-sleep, he reached for her and pulled her into the circle of his body. As they nestled like spoons, Will, who usually slept lightly, fell into a deep sleep. However, Lillianna wasn't sleeping soundly that night and was the first to hear the wagon coming down the drive. "Will, sweetheart, wake up. I hear a wagon; someone must be sick."

Will finally awakened reluctantly. He sat up on the side of the bed, rubbing his head, "Gee, seems as if I just got to sleep."

"You did," Lillianna answered with sympathy, "I'm sorry, darling; I know you're exhausted."

"Well, duty calls. No one ever said medicine was an easy calling."

"Are you ever sorry you chose it?"

"Never, not even for a minute," he assured her as he headed downstairs to answer the door. He was surprised to see Matthew and Virgil standing there. "What's wrong, Matt? Who is sick?" Will asked, alarmed.

Not seeing Lillianna coming down the stairs, Matt answered, "We hated to bring him here, Will; but we have an injured runaway about to start the first big leg of his escape; and we need to hurry as much as possible. There are four more, his brothers, waiting back at the station (as they referred to the slave quarters at Fairlawn)."

"What station?" Came Lillianna's voice out of the darkness behind Will. "What are you talking about, Matt?" she asked insistently.

"Oh Lord, I'm sorry; I didn't know she was behind you, Will," Matt said, startled.

"Don't worry about it, Matt. Bring him in and take him to that first bedroom down the hall. I'll take care of Lillianna," Will said.

"All right," Matt answered, "Then we had better move the wagon 'round back. We'll come back in through the back hall. You might need us to help you."

As Matt and Virgil went back to the wagon, Will turned back to Lillianna, "Sweetheart, please go back upstairs. I promise to explain everything to you as soon as I take care of this patient and they leave."

Lillianna hesitated and started to question Will further.

"Please, Lillianna, do as I ask," Will urged.

"All right," she answered, "but I shall still be awake when you come back up."

"Thank you, sweetheart," Will said, kissing her cheek. "I'll be there as soon as I can."

Will watched as she reluctantly climbed the stairs. When he heard their bedroom door close, he went down the hall to the injured man.

"Hello, son," Will said to the young man, seeking to reassure him as he started removing the soiled rag that served as a makeshift bandage. "Let's have a look at this leg. What's your name?"

"Shadrach, suh," he answered, wincing with pain as Will probed the wound.

"Well, Shadrach, I'm happy to report to you that your wound is not as serious as I was afraid it might be. I think we can treat this in short order and have you on your way."

"Dat's good news, Dr. Pinkston; I sho' do 'preciate yo' help."

"How is it you happen to know my name, Shadrach?"

"Lawd, Dr. Pinkston, all us slaves knows 'bout you and 'de help you gives us."

About that time, Virgil and Matt came in. "Will, could I do anything to help?" Matt asked.

"Yes please, would you hold the lamp close so that I can see to clean this wound? Now brace yourself, Shadrach, this is going to hurt." Will cut away the proud flesh and cleaned the wound thoroughly, finished treating it with a salve, and dressed it. Through it all, Shadrach clenched his teeth and bore the pain stoically.

"Good man," Will said patting the boy's shoulder. "Matt, he needs to rest a day if possible. Will he be at the station?"

"Yes, and we'll give him two days to rest if we can," Matt answered.

"Good, I'll come by to check on him and change the bandage tomorrow night. He's able to go now, but be careful—be very careful. Never know who might be out and about."

"Thanks, Will, sorry to rout you out in the middle of the night."

"Don't give it a thought. This is just regular routine for me," Will answered, seeing them out the door.

As he climbed the stairs, he prayed a little silent prayer that God would help him find the words to tell Lillianna about the work of the UGRR and his part in it all—something he had hoped she would never have to know. It was no surprise to Will that she was sitting propped-up in bed waiting for him when he entered their bedroom.

"How is your patient, darling? Is his injury very serious?" she asked, as he went over to the bed and kissed her.

"No, his injury was really not serious at all; it had just been neglected. It was fairly simple to clean and treat. He should be fine in a day or so."

"Lillianna," Will started, as he sat down on the side of the bed facing her, "I have a rather long story to tell you; one that is going to make you feel very proud of your family. Please let me tell you all of it before you ask any questions."

"All right, Will; I'll do my best to listen carefully, but silently, to everything you have to tell me," she answered, settling into the pillows comfortably.

"This all started back in late November 1846," Will began his story at the very beginning, the night that Percy Lineham visited Mattie and Virgil. Some two hours later, Will finally finished with the story of Shadrach and his brothers. "Now, my little Auburn, fire away. I know you have a hundred questions."

"Oh, Will, I hardly know where to begin. I truly am so proud of all of you; Mattie and Virgil, Mandy and Matthew, of course, you, but especially of Papa. This had to have taken a great deal of soul searching on his part. Aside from the least important factor, the financial cost, there is the courage it took to undertake this project with all its risks. With all those pride-worthy factors considered, I am prouder yet of his ability, at that late stage of his life, to set aside his long-cherished *Southern Tradition* and do an about face to become the man he was at the end of his life. I just wish I had known at the time all that he was doing instead of finding out after it is too late to tell him face to face how proud I am of him. And there is one more thing I wish, I wish I might have had the privilege of being a part of it myself. I know that Mr. Lineham advised, and that you all agreed, that the fewer who knew, the safer it was for everybody concerned and the more successful the work would likely be. However, I shall always regret not having been involved in this noble undertaking—one that has always been close to my heart since childhood."

"I know, darling, after all the hours on end we have spent discussing slavery and its hateful implications, I understand completely. I have been, as you put it, privileged to be a part of it; so I know how you must feel. And it has been very difficult for me to keep it from you all these years. One of the things I cherish most about our marriage is the way we have always shared everything, with no secrets between us. I am relieved that you finally know."

Will finally crawled back into bed beside Lillianna and pulled her close again. Soon they were both sleeping soundly; and when the morning sun crept in to awaken them, they both felt as if they had just gone to sleep.

Will started to slip out of bed and let Lillianna sleep a little longer, but she pulled him back. "Stay with me a little longer," she begged, as she sought his lips and caressed his body with an expertise that always aroused an immediate response. They were soon lost in the passion that had never lessened with the years; and when it was spent, they lay, still locked in intimate embrace. "Please, easy out, darling; I wish that you never had to leave me—that this moment never had to end!" Lillianna said, clinging to him.

"Sweetheart, you act as if this is the last time we shall ever make love," Will laughed.

"Well, we can never really be sure, can we?" she answered thoughtfully. The memory of their morning threaded its way in and out of Lillianna's mind all day as she went about her duties.

CHAPTER ELEVEN

A BEND IN THE ROAD

On this particular day, at Beau's request, Will's workday began with a trip into Charleston to visit the clinic. He wanted to consult with Will on a particularly difficult case that he was treating.

Since it was a Saturday, Lydia was not teaching at Miss Hockaday's School, and although she was expecting one of her private harp students for a lesson early that afternoon, she prepared a light luncheon for Will, Beau and herself. After their consultation, the two doctors joined her for lunch. The three of them enjoyed a pleasant luncheon visit; then Will said his goodbyes and headed out River Road to make several house calls.

In view of the fact that Saturday was usually a fairly light workday for him, Will had planned to try to get home a little earlier to have a leisurely supper with Lillianna and Leland for a change. However, as Robert Burns observed, "The best laid schemes of mice and men often go awry"; and by the time he finally got around to making his promised visit to the UGRR station at Fairlawn to check on Shadrach, it was almost dark. He tied his horse to the hitching post at the cabin they used as headquarters, walked up on the porch, and tapped on the door. "Come in," came a muffled voice that Will recognized as Virgil's.

In the dim light of the room, he could hardly make out the faces of the six men sitting there. He surmised they were Virgil, Shadrach, and his four brothers. As his eyes became more accustomed to the darkness, he asked, "What are you all doing sitting here in the dark?"

"Will, we have had to step up our plans. One of our agents in Charleston has sent word that the slave hunters are hot on the trail of these men. The hunters have now traced the sabotage at the shipyard to them, and we must make their escape move immediately. We were just waiting for you to check Shadrach's wound and change the bandage. He says that he feels up to going tonight."

As he hastened to remove the bandage and examine the wound, Will answered, "Virgil, I don't anticipate any problem here. I'll medicate, re-bandage, and be finished shortly. As he worked, two of the station helpers, Isaac and Reuben, experienced in escape procedures, had entered through the back door of the cabin.

"Will, I have a favor to ask of you," Virgil said hesitantly. "It could be dangerous, and we'll understand if you refuse."

"Virgil, I hope that you know that I am always willing to help in any way I can. When we entered into this, we all knew there would be the possibility of danger. We accepted that possibility with our eyes wide open. Now, how can I help?"

"We might need you to be a decoy if the slave hunters are anywhere about. You hitch your horse to the wagon out front, take Isaac and Reuben with you, and head down River Road for home. We'll go out the back and try to escape southward through the swamps. With two black men in the wagon, you all will, hopefully, throw the hunters off track if they pursue. If you hear them, drive the wagon as fast as possible to give us more time. If they should catch up with you, tell them you had come to pick up these men to help with some work you had planned at Pink Hill tomorrow. If they should inquire what your hurry was, pretend that your horse, not accustomed to pulling a wagon, got spooked and bolted." Will nodded his agreement to the plan. "Wish us luck, and the same to you all!" Virgil finished, shaking Will's hand.

"Good luck, and may God be with us all," Will answered.

Will rushed out front prepared to hitch his horse to the wagon, but Isaac and Reuben had already taken care of it. "Virgil must have been pretty confident of my willingness to do this since he had these men hitch up my horse to the wagon," Will thought, pleased at Virgil's confidence in him. Will boarded the wagon and took the reins in hand as Isaac and Reuben climbed in back.

No sooner had the wagon reached River Road than they heard the baying of hounds in the distance behind them. "Virgil's source must be well-informed; sounds like the hunters are on the trail. All right men, let's throw out the bait and draw their attention to us," Will said, flicking the reins and giving a shout, as he urged the horse into a gallop. "Let 'em eat our dust boy," Will shouted, smiling as he thought of Lillianna, with the feather on her hat and her auburn curls blowing in the wind, on that race afternoon so many years ago. The trackers took the bait, as planned, and were soon behind them in hot pursuit, shouting for them to stop. The baying of the hounds and the shouts of the hunters grew louder and louder as they closed the distance between themselves and the wagon. Isaac and Reuben could almost make out the faces of their pursuers in the light of the torches they were carrying, and Will slowly reined the horse in and finally brought the wagon to a halt. The riders soon surrounded the wagon.

The man who appeared to be the leader spoke up, "Well, well, well, if it ain't the high and mighty, nigger lovin' Dr. Pinkston. Where you think you're carrying these boys in such a hurry tonight? We all know you love 'em. Hell, the way I hear it, you got some in your own family; but I didn't think you was stupid enough to use a main road as their escape route. Doc, we ought to just *love you to death* for makin' it so easy for us; but that ain't the way we do it, is it men? These boys are going to pay for the damage they did down at the shipyards; and since we know they ain't got no money, we'll take another kind of payment; and you, my nigger lovin' friend, are going to wish you never saw 'em!"

"Aw hell, Jed, cut the crap; and let's get on with it," shouted one of the men, who carried a torch in one hand and lifted a rope from the horn of his saddle with the other.

Will raised his hands, motioning for them to be quiet and listen to what he had to say.

Another man shouted, "He don't have nothing to say we want to hear, Jed. We can all see what he's up to. I'm with Hank, let's just get on with it! There's plenty of trees around here for our purposes.

The man named Jed interrupted, "Naw, let's listen to what he's got to say. It ought to be a good story; hell, we might even enjoy it. I always did like fairy tales."

The trackers all laughed and then got quiet enough for Will to speak. "The truth of the matter is, gentlemen, that we're undertaking a big project at Pink Hill tomorrow which is going to take more help than we have available. I stopped by Fairlawn to see if they might be able to lend me a couple of hands. Not being in my own buggy, but on horseback, I borrowed this wagon to bring them on home with me. My horse isn't accustomed to pulling a wagon; he got spooked and bolted. It took me all this distance to get him settled down. And as far as something that happened at the shipyards in Charleston, these boys are Fairlawn slaves. They wouldn't know anything about that at all! I'm sure you wouldn't want to be guilty of hanging innocent men.

The men obviously had no intention of listening to or believing Will, Before he had finished speaking, there was mumbling and growing anger among them. The mumbling became shouts, and the anger became rage. The organized band of trackers had become an unruly mob; and like a pack of vicious dogs, they had come for blood and were determined to have it!

Will understood that the situation was extremely grave. This was a bloodthirsty, unreasonable mob; and besides, he was in no mood to beg. He had no intention of giving them that pleasure. "If I only have a few minutes left, I must use them to some gain," Will thought. "These two brave men, who are probably about to die for the cause of freedom for their people, need and deserve to have someone tell them that their deaths will not have been in vain."

Isaac said, terror in his voice, "They's gonna hang us, Dr. Pinkston, you and Reuben and me; and there ain't nothin' we can do to stop it!

Will spoke calmly to his two frightened companions. "I think you're right, Isaac; but listen to me, please. I have something important to say to you before we die. Five men will go free, and three men will lose their lives for their freedom. You might say, and you would be right, that is taking five steps forward and three steps back! Surely, that *is* progress; but is it worth the price that will be paid, not only by the three of us but by our families? Indeed, I tell you it is worth it. You, Reuben, and I have known what it feels like to be free, you two for fifteen years or more, and I, for a lifetime. Freedom is more than a precious gift; it is the right of every living human being! Five men are going to experience that freedom, and, hopefully, the future generations of their families will inherit that freedom. This is the cause for which we are about to die. It is a worthy cause, even noble; hold your heads high, men; you are heroes!"

The mob had settled down somewhat; most of the men were listening intently; but their leader, Jeb, realizing that their determination was faltering, began again to try to renew their frenzy. "He's lyin' boys! Cain't you see the Doc gave this whole fancy speech to try to make us forget what we all know they done? He's just tryin' to save their sorry nigger hides. He don't really think we got the guts to kill a high and mighty Pinkston, so let's just show him!" he finished, taking his rope in hand and heading for a big oak tree nearby. "This is a stout limb here, looks like it was made for hangin' I'd say. It's so long, I think we can hang 'em all three at one time. What do you say boys? Bring that wagon over here and throw two more ropes over this limb." As Jeb made one noose, two of the other men made one each. When the nooses were finished and the rear of the wagon bed was in place beneath them, they lined Isaac, Will, and Reuben, side by side, across the rear of the wagon, placed the nooses around their necks, and tied their hands behind their backs. Jeb climbed up on the wagon seat and spoke to Will's horse, "All right you spooky hoss, let's see if I can spook you one last time." Then he yelled, "Git up." As he lashed the horse's hindquarters with the whip, the wagon lurched forward. One of the young men, hanging back on the edge of the crowd, shuddered, turned his mount, and retreated into the darkness.

In those last few minutes as they stood with the nooses around their necks, each man had pursued his own thoughts. An owl hooted somewhere in the darkness and Isaac thought, "I always heard that an owl a'hootin' in the night is mournin' for somebody a'dyin'. Is you mournin' for me Mr. Owl? Just don't bothuh, suh; I'se a'goin' Home!" Reuben, standing on Will's left, sang quietly, "Deep river, my home is ovuh Jordan. Deep river, Lawd; I want to cross ovuh into campground." Will closed his eyes; and to the sad sounds of the hooting owl and Reuben's song, he buried his face in a fragrant mass of auburn hair.

Lillianna and Leland had looked forward all day on Saturday to having supper with Will. However, supper time came and went and still, no Will. "I'm beginning to worry, Leland. Your papa was sure he would be home for supper tonight."

"Mama, you have looked forward to our having supper tonight as a family, and you're just disappointed. After all, we rarely have the pleasure of eating supper together. I'll tell you what, let's go on and eat, and have Emma fix a plate for Papa and keep it warm in the kitchen. I feel sure he will be here by the time we have finished eating," Leland reassured his mother.

"All right, you are probably right. It's just that I have had this terrible feeling of foreboding all day long," Lillianna said, as they sat down at the supper table. When they had finished the delicious supper Emma had prepared, they agreed to postpone their dessert and have it when Will had his. They went out on the piazza and sat in the peacock chairs to chat and await his arrival. They sat there until dark, and sensing his mother's growing tension, Leland said, "Maybe we had better go inside, Mama. It's getting a little chilly. I have been reading a book on The Citadel that Noel loaned me, and I would like to finish it tonight. I am seriously considering applying for admission there." He had not wanted to tell his parents about his plans until he had fully made-up his mind, but he felt the need to get Lillianna's mind off the subject of Will's late arrival.

"Leland, I had no idea you were considering such a move. I am delighted to hear it, and I'm sure your father will be too," she said enthusiastically, as he held the door for her to go inside.

"Mind you, Mama, I haven't decided definitely to enroll at The Citadel; I'm just thinking about it. Annamarie thinks I should. She said I should seize every opportunity I have—use every advantage I possess."

"Annamarie has a good head on her shoulders, but what does she mean by 'use every advantage' you possess?"

"She isn't planning to go beyond what education she already has. She can't go to any of the schools nearby; and she doesn't want to go to Canada to school like her brothers did. She says my big advantage is not the financial support I will have; but, my pure white blood. She says it is very difficult to live in the world when you have white skin and black blood. That is the way our world perceives her, and she resents it bitterly!"

"Oh, Leland, everyone doesn't perceive her in that way; she knows none of our family considers her as anything but one of us—our precious and beautiful Annamarie!"

"Mama, in many ways that makes it even harder. She grew up from babyhood thinking she was no different, surrounded by a big loving family. But the more she tries to venture away from the protection of her little sheltered world, the more she sees the world of the South as it really is—bigoted, cruel, vicious. I feel so angry for her sake. I'm not sure I want to stay in a world like this!"

"You can't run from it, son. I have always felt from childhood exactly the way you feel; but we are the only ones who can change it; and it is our duty to do so! You can only do this by staying right here, going on to get an education, then fighting to make the changes you would like to see in a peaceful and positive way!"

"I don't know, Mama; you may be right. I'm just not sure that would be possible. In fact, I am fairly sure it wouldn't be, not in my generation for sure and probably not in several generations to come!"

The clock struck midnight; and at the stroke of twelve, Lillianna said anxiously, "My God, Leland, it's midnight; and Will hasn't come home. I know something has happened."

When the echo from the chimes died away and the house fell silent, they could hear the lonesome hooting of an owl in the distance; and Lillianna shuddered.

"Mama, Papa is probably just tied up with a slow birthing. You know how unpredictable that can be. Let's go in the kitchen and have our dessert and a glass of milk; then we can get ready for bed. I know, I know—you have no intention of going to bed until he comes home," Leland said. "But we can do our nightly ablutions, as Lydia always used to tell me when I was little," he added, trying to channel Lillianna's thoughts away from her anxiety about Will—an anxiety he was beginning to share.

They went back to the kitchen, and Lillianna cut the sweet potato pie while Leland poured the milk. As they ate, he continued to make small talk, still trying to distract her, all to no avail; it was obvious that his mother was lost in her own worried thoughts

"Leland, why don't you go on up and get ready for bed. I know you want to finish that book on The Citadel so that you can return it to Noel tomorrow."

"I think I'll do that, if you're sure you'll be all right."

"Of course, sweetheart, I'll be fine."

"Goodnight Mama," he said, as he kissed her cheek and headed upstairs.

Lillianna went into the parlor and peered out the front window into the dark night. She stood there for what seemed an eternity, watching and waiting and wondering, "Where are you, Will? Then she saw the torches out on the road before she heard the sound of the horses as they made the turn into Pink Hill. She ran into the foyer and called up the stairs, "Leland, please come down; there are riders coming." Leland came hurriedly down the stairs, pulling on his robe. "Oh God, I know something terrible has happened," Lillianna said, beginning to weep.

"Calm down, Mama; don't start crossing bridges before

we even get to them," he said, sounding much more confident than he felt.

He rushed past her and out onto the piazza. She followed close behind, anxious to learn what had happened, yet terrified to know. As the riders reined-in in front of the house, Lillianna could see by the light of the torches that all the men had scarves tied around their faces to hide their identities. She thought—even hoped, "Maybe this is a robbery rather than news about Will!"

"What are you men after? What do you want?" Leland shouted.

"We don't want nothin', not a damn thing! In fact, we got a present for your nigger lovin' ma," the man in front growled, as he threw something rolled in a horse blanket on the ground at their feet. When the long bundle hit the ground, it fell open to reveal a body lying face down. Lillianna fell to her knees beside it, knowing that it must be Will. As Leland knelt beside her, they both reached to turn the man over. In the light of the torches, they could see Will's discolored face, his eyes open and staring, the rope still around his neck. Lillianna screamed and fell across his lifeless body. In blind anger, Leland sprang upon the man on the horse and dragged him to the ground. At that point, the other men dismounted and hurriedly came to subdue the boy. They beat him unmercifully; and as Lillianna ran forward to try to defend her son, one of the men backhanded her to send her sprawling across the piazza. The men then mounted their horses. "Boys let's burn 'em out," the leader shouted. "Get your torches and burn the whole damn place to the ground!"

"Jeb, we better get the hell out of here now," one of the men warned.

"Not 'til we finish what we came to do we ain't! Now get on with it!" Jeb shouted.

When Leland finally regained consciousness, the house,

the stable, and all the other buildings were ablaze. In the light from the fire, he saw his mother lying on the piazza, bleeding and unconscious, the house burning behind her. He ran to her, gathered her up in his arms, and carried her to the safety of the lawn. At first he was afraid that she might be dead; but she soon stirred from his arms and, sobbing uncontrollably, began to crawl toward Will's body.

Lillianna lay prostrate across his body, cupping his face in her hands and kissing his lifeless lips. "Why, God, why my Will?. He was the best of the best, the wisest of the wisest. Oh my love, how can I live without you?" she cried in agony.

Leland stood unbelieving, watching the flames devour his home. Anger mixed with futility fed his hatred, hatred not only of the ignorant men who had killed his father, but of a society that could produce this kind of action.

About that time, Richard and Emma came down the drive. From their home nearby, they had been awakened by the shouts of the mob and had seen the flames at Pink Hill lighting the night sky. They had come as fast as they could.

Leland tried to explain to them, as best he could, what had happened. "Please help Mama, Emma. She was beaten by the mob; they brought Papa here after they hanged him!" he sobbed.

Emma ran to help Lillianna. Seeing Leland's wounds, Richard said, "You're hurt yourself; let me help you to our wagon. We'll drive you and your mother to Fairlawn."

"I'm all right, Richard, just help me get Papa's body into the wagon. We must take him with us to Fairlawn. Uncle Matt will know what to do."

At Emma's urging, Lillianna finally stood and allowed her to help her into the wagon. Richard and Leland, carrying Will's body, lifted it into the wagon, and Lillianna cradled Will's head in her lap. As Emma and Richard drove them to Fairlawn, Leland sat beside his mother, his arm around her and her head on his shoulder. They both wept quietly. Lost in their grief, they never looked back at Pink Hill.

Will was eulogized eloquently as he was laid to rest in the family plot at Pink Hill. Dr. Bradner, his partner, spoke of his excellence as a physician; Beau spoke of his loyalty to family and friends; and Noel spoke of him as the best of all husbands and fathers. Virgil asked to speak last. “I have known Will Pinkston since I first came to Fairlawn Plantation as a slave. He and Lillianna were instrumental in my becoming a free man. He was there when Mattie and I married, and he delivered all three of our babies. Never in all these years have I heard him speak in anger to another person nor speak ill of anyone. He was a good Christian man in every sense of the word. He once said that if he could choose only one characteristic for his children, that characteristic would be compassion; and if I had to choose the most precious of all Will Pinkston’s many attributes, that attribute would be his compassion. If I had to measure the success of his life, the yardstick would also be his compassion. He was the wisest, the best, and the most compassionate man that I have ever been privileged to know. Dear God, may he rest in peace.”

In the weeks that followed, Lillianna, though immersed in grief, became increasingly concerned for Leland and the extreme changes in his attitudes—even in his personality. One morning at breakfast, she noticed that Leland, who had always enjoyed a hearty appetite, was just picking at his food. “A penny for your thoughts?” she said.

“They’re not worth even that much, Mama,” he answered dejectedly, not looking up.

“What is it, son? I have been noticing a restlessness in you—a disturbing change in your whole outlook on life. The whole experience of losing your father, the way we did, was earth-shattering for all of us. We have all been devastated; but there is more with you—some nebulous thing I can’t put my finger on, as if there's something unspoken you can't live with."

"Oh, Mama, you know me so well; I have never been able to hide anything from you. I don't want to burden you; you've been hurt enough already."

"Leland, I am your mother; you can tell me anything. Don't you understand? When it comes to her children, a mother's worrying about the unknown is far worse than her knowing even the worst. So talk to me, son, talk to me!"

He sat quietly for a moment, hesitating to speak. "It all started so long ago; I hardly know where to begin. When we were kids, Annamarie and I used to hunt arrowheads on the bank of the Ashley, down near Charlestown Landing. We met a boy our age, Samuel Flood, who also liked to collect arrowheads and other Indian artifacts. It was just a passing thing for Annamarie and me, but he was really a serious collector. His father was a dockhand at the Landing, and they lived in shantytown near there. The three of us became friends and remained so for several years. Then we somehow lost touch; you know how those things go. A couple of weeks after Papa was killed, Samuel came looking for Annamarie. He told her about an incident that he had witnessed—had really been a part of himself. It seems he was with the mob that hanged Papa. He had seen everything that happened that night and told it all to Annamarie—in detail! Mama, it was horrible; the atrocities that men are capable of committing in the name of justice are unbelievable! Samuel was part of the mob, but he was so horrified at all he saw that he ran away into the woods after Papa and the two black men were hanged. He's never been back home since."

"I want to hear it all, Leland."

"Mama, why torture yourself with hearing all the details? Let's put it behind us; let it be over and done with now," he urged.

"I must know, son; I don't really understand exactly why; but I must know. I can't allow you to carry this thing alone."

So he told her the whole ugly story, beginning with the chase and ending with the moment the wagon lurched forward and the men were hanged. He included the speech, almost verbatim, that Will had made to the two black men just before the three of them died. "That speech was the final straw for Samuel. It moved him tremendously; so much so that he determined to leave his papa and his home behind. All the values that he had been taught he finally came to hate! Samuel said that during Papa's speech, the whole crowd got quiet—listening; but Jeb, realizing that he was losing them, shouted out, ridiculing Papa, and succeeded in stirring-up their anger again. Mama, you're not going to believe this, Jeb is Samuel's papa, Jeb Flood!"

After a long, thoughtful silence, Lillianna spoke, "Leland, as hard as it all was to hear, I'll always cling to those courageous last words your papa spoke. They were so wonderful and so like him."

"But, Mama, it was all so futile, such a waste! Papa *was* courageous and wonderful and all those noble things; and what did it get him—a horrible death at the end of a rope! Take Samuel—he was supposed to be my good friend; but he was a part of it and didn't try to help at all. He just ran away—then unloaded his conscience on Annamarie! I don't want any part of this wonderful Southland, now or ever! I have to go; you just have to accept that!" he finished, his jaw set, his eyes cold.

"Son, if you will just stay here with us, we can all help you get through this. I'm not even going to try to rebuild Pink Hill. I plan to deed a parcel of land to Richard and Emma and one to each of our other tenant farmers. The remainder of the plantation will be divided equally among you, Lydia, and Noel."

"I don't want any part of it, Mama. I never did. I've never

had any desire to become a farmer. Give it all to Noel and Lydia. I want to leave; I would prefer to do it with your blessing; but, with or without, I *am* going!"

"I can see that nothing I could say would change your mind; so go, go with my blessing and with my love—always with my love!" she finished, with tears in her eyes.

Most of the family finally accepted Leland's decision to leave; but a few of them did so with serious reservations, expecially Lydia. "Lee Lee, you're so young. Where will you go; what will you do; how will you live? We'll all be worried sick about you! Noel, talk some sense into him!"

"Lydia, I am not a child. I am strong; I have two hands; and I can work. No one needs to worry about me. I can take care of myself. This is something I have to do. I *am going;* and that's that!" Leland answered.

"Little sister, the time has come for us to turn our baby brother loose," Noel said. "If he feels this thing he wants to do is a good thing, then I agree with him; it's a good thing. What's more, I intend to help him if he'll let me. What do you say, Leland?"

"I'd appreciate your input, Noel. I have some plans to make, and I'm looking for a direction in which to go."

"All right you two, I can't fight both of you. *I will be worried*, Leland; but I give up trying to talk you out of it. I know you too well to even think I could," Lydia said, ruffling his hair fondly then throwing up her hands in resignation.

In the next two weeks, things began to fall into place. Leland and Noel perused maps and books and did research at the newspaper office and around the waterfront in Charleston. By happenstance, Leland met a trapper named Carl McMurtry, who was there making arrangements for a shipment of animal pelts to England. Leland told him something about his plans and about his and Noel's research. In return, the trapper told him something about his life as a trapper in the mountains of North Carolina. Leland was interested to hear about the prospects of a trapper for making a living. McMurtry ended up by inviting Leland to join him on his return trip to the mountains. "That way, you can take a firsthand look at how I live. I wouldn't have any other life, but I know that it's not for everybody. You're welcome to come along if you want to."

"Thank you, Mr. McMurtry, I appreciate your offer. I'll think about it and let you know."

"Call me Carl, Leland. I plan to leave in a couple of weeks. If you decide to go, you will need a little time to provision out for the trip. I hope you will decide to go. I'd enjoy the company."

After more research and with Noel's encouragement, Leland decided that of all the prospects about which he had read and heard, that he wanted to try his hand at trapping. There was a big demand for animal pelts, and he believed the chances of his making a living at it were good. He notified Carl that he wanted to take him up on his offer and asked his advice on what provisions he would need. It took about a week for him to make ready to leave. They set July 9, 1859, as the date for their departure.

On the night of July eighth, Leland walked down to River Bend for one last visit with Annamarie. He knew that it would be difficult for both of them. They had been inseparable all of their lives. Little did he know *just how difficult* it would prove to be.

They sat on the swing on her front porch talking quietly about all the good times they had spent together over the years. It was a hot night, but there was a nice breeze off the river. "Leland, let's take a walk down by the Ashley. It's cooler there."

"Sounds like a good idea. Guess we're about to launch into "dog days" pretty soon," he answered. "Carl says it will get cooler the farther west we travel; says the mountains get downright cold at night."

"That should help make your trip easier, but you had better be sure to pack a blanket or two to keep you warm when you camp at night."

"I did. Carl told me the same thing. He always packs a coffee pot and plenty of coffee along with the other provisions. He says it warms your *innards* on a cold night. I never have cared much for coffee, but I expect I'll learn to appreciate it now."

"Leland, all this small talk is ridiculous; we're both talking all around what we really want to say." We both know that this *could* be the last time we'll ever see each other. I don't think that I could face the future if I knew that would be true!" Annamarie hesitated before she went on. "Lee, I might never again have the opportunity to tell you this; so I must say it now, before you leave. I love you; I always have loved you."

"Annamarie, of course, we love each other; we are more than just cousins; we are best friends. Time and distance can never change all that. We'll always love each other," Leland answered, as he put his arms around her in a brotherly hug.

"Oh, Leland, don't you understand what I am saying? I don't love you only as a cousin or a best friend, and I do believe that all truly romantic love is successful only if the lovers are also best friends, like our parents are. What I am trying to tell you is that I am *in love* with you! Couldn't you tell? Didn't you at least suspect?"

"I had no idea, Annamarie—truly; that thought never entered my mind," he answered, completely taken aback.

As he started to speak again, afraid that he was about to protest that, that kind of love could never be for them, she put her arms around his neck and covered his mouth with hers in a kiss so passionate that the hair on the back of his neck stood up. He returned her frantic kisses in kind and drew her body to his, caressing her passionately. Suddenly he pushed her away at arms length. "Annamarie we can't do this. I believe you really *think* that what you feel for me is love; but I don't know what I am really feeling except that my body wants yours at this moment. I'm not sure that it's anything more than lust. I just couldn't do that to you. I respect our relationship too much. Papa always said, 'If it's the real thing, it will simmer; just keep your head.' We have to follow that advice and not do anything for which we'll be sorry later. A time apart will help us find out what we really feel. We'd better head back to the house now."

They walked back in silence, holding hands. As they walked up the steps, Leland said, "I'd better go along home, get to bed, and get a good night's sleep. We're heading out early in the morning. Goodbye for now, little cousin. I'll be back this way again; you can count on it," he promised, giving her a quick kiss.

"Goodby, Lee; I'm going hold you to that promise," she answered, with tears in her eyes and voice. She watched him walk away into the night and thought, "I *know* what I feel, Leland. No matter what you feel, I *know* that I love you; and I always will."

CHAPTER TWELVE

LURE OF THE MOUNTAINS

The trip to the mountains was quite an experience for Leland. They were at the mercy of the weather, which wasn't always pleasant—hot days, cold nights, and rain, hard, wetting-to-the-bone rain. However, Leland would always remember it, in retrospect, as the greatest adventure of his life. He learned more under the tutelage of Carl McMurtry during that long trip than he had learned in all of his life up to that time—not only about trapping and mountain survival, but about life itself.

They traveled by day and camped out at night. Carl told him the story of his life; and Leland was surprised to learn that Carl wasn't a lonely mountain man at all, but a man with a family. He had a wife, who was a Cherokee Indian, and a daughter, who was eighteen years old. He had grown up on a farmstead, but wanted no part of farming. As a boy, his favorite companions were the young boys from the nearby Indian village. He was always drawn to the woods, tracking and trapping animals and just exploring. Leland was amazed at how much he and Carl had in common, at how very much alike they were. He told Carl about his childhood and roaming the woods with Annamarie, collecting rocks and arrowheads and the like. He told all about his father's death and about his own innermost thoughts on the subject of farming, slavery, and man's inhumanity to man. He even told Carl about the incident with Annamarie on the night before they left. And at the moment of telling, time and distance made him suddenly realize that he really wasn't *in love* with Annamarie; and he prayed that she would realize that she wasn't really *in love* with him.

By the time they arrived in the westernmost part of North Carolina, Leland had come to look on Carl like a second father; and Carl was just as fond of him. That night as they rode into the clearing and approached the McMurtry cabin, the lamplight from the cabin windows was a welcome sight to the two bone-weary travelers. "Well, we're home, lad, at last. Are you as hungry as I am?" Carl asked.

"Man, am I ever!" Leland answered, rubbing his empty stomach.

"I'm sure Grey Moon will have some leftovers from supper to stop this growling in our bellies."

Hearing them ride up, Carl's wife and daughter came rushing out to greet him. They were surprised to see that he wasn't alone. "All right, ladies, aren't you going to give this tired old traveler a hug? I want you to meet my young trapping apprentice, Leland Pinkston, from Charleston, South Carolina. He'll be with us awhile until I can teach him the in's and out's of trapping. Leland, this lovely lady is my wife, Grey Moon; and this is our daughter, Carlotta."

Leland was surprised to see that Grey Moon was wearing a blue dress and a gingham apron, much like the ladies at home wore. The only thing that was the way he had pictured her was her braided hair. Somehow he had expected her to be in fringed buckskin. Carlotta was beautiful, with deep skin tones touched with a tint that made her appear to be blushing, and with eyes that flashed black when she smiled, and with straight black hair, black as a raven's wing, which seemed to never have known the violation of scissors.

In no time at all, Grey Moon had a delicious meal on the table for them. She was a quiet and shy lady, but her warm smile made Leland feel welcome. Her love for Carl was evident in the way she looked at him when their eyes met in a quick caress. Carlotta was her father's daughter. She had a quick wit and a ready laugh that bubbled-up from somewhere deep inside. Leland found her enchanting.

Carl leaned back in his chair, rubbed his stomach, stretched, and yawned, "I don't know about you, my boy; but I'm about ready to turn in. We have a cot in the loft that we offer to our rare visitors; consider it yours while you're with us."

"Thank you, folks. I don't know how I can ever repay your hospitality. Mrs. McMurtry, your supper was delicious; and your apple pie is the best I have ever eaten," Leland said, as he helped Carlotta clear the table. "You go on and tuck Carl in; I know you two have a lot of catching-up to do. I'll help Carlotta with the dishes.

The young people chatted easily as Leland washed the dishes, and Carlotta dried and put them away. When they finished, he said goodnight and climbed the ladder to the loft. Looking around the small loft area, he was surprised to see that the walls were one continuous bookcase filled with books of every imaginable genre. He remembered also noticing bookcases full of books along the front wall of the big room downstairs. For a moment, his mind drifted back to Pagrand Prendle's big library back home at Fairlawn and to the times he had spent there sitting in Pagrand's big desk chair, spinning 'round just for the fun of it. As he browsed the shelves reading titles, his respect for Carl grew. There was so much more depth to this big *mountain man* than he had realized. After he had bedded down, he remembered the way Carl had introduced him. He hadn't really thought of himself as an apprentice; but a trapping apprentice was, in fact, what he was. He liked the sound of it. It implied that he would make upward progress, but to what—a master trapper? He knew that he was a long way from being that. He was pleased to think of being here with Carl and his family during his *apprenticeship.* He blew out the lamp; and as he dropped off to sleep, he remembered how the firelight played on Carlotta's beautiful hair.

In the days and weeks that followed, Carl was busy introducing Leland to the art of tracking and trapping animals, then to the killing and skinning of the animals, and finally to the proper method of curing the skins through a regular process of drying, cleaning, and packing them for shipping. There was so much more to becoming an expert trapper than Leland had ever imagined. However, he was an apt student and had such an affinity for trapping and all it required that he made rapid progress.

Although he and Carl were camping in the mountains for days at a time, setting traps and then checking them, they still spent most nights in the cabin. Leland felt more and more at home with the McMurtry family.

Sunday had always been a day of rest and worship for Carl and his family, and Leland enjoyed being part of their tradition. He and Carlotta usually spent Sunday afternoons together, either visiting in the Indian village of her mother's family or fishing in a nearby stream. They talked for hours on end about everything, and they shared their most private thoughts and feelings. They grew very close, as close as two friends could be; however, they soon realized that their growing fondness for one another was much more than just friendship.

One Sunday evening on their return walk from the village, they stopped by the stream for a cool drink of water and a rest. They sat on a rock talking and listening to the bubbling of the stream. "Autumn is so beautiful in the mountains. I thought nothing could be as beautiful as autumn in Charleston, but these colors are far more beautiful. I'm like a glutton who gorges on his favorite food. It's breathtaking, and I can't seem to get enough of it. And the breath of fall in the air is invigorating and intoxicating. Lord, I'm beginning to sound like a very bad poet," Leland said laughing. As the sun dropped behind the mountains, a full moon hung in the night sky above them. He gazed at Carlotta's black hair, shining in the moonlight, and leaned his face close to breathe its fragrance. She turned to face him and sought his lips tentatively. This was the invitation for which Leland had longed for weeks. Their kisses were passionate, so passionate that they led to intimate and groping caresses, which would inevitably lead to much more. "Carlotta, I love you. I'm so very much *in love* with you, and I believe you feel the same way about me. I want you so desperately, and that desire comes alive in my dreams every night."

"Leland, I do love you and desire you as much. I have desired you almost from the night you arrived, before I ever realized that I was in love with you. My people have that kind of passion, and our ways do not deprive us of satisfying that passion. Please darling, I am more than willing and ready; and I know that you are ready too. I feel the hardness of your desire against my belly. Please, Leland—now!"

"Oh my sweet little hot-blooded Indian girl, there is no way that I can tell you how much I want you. But the ways of *my* people—your father's people—demand that we wait for that fulfillment until we are one. Your father trusts me, and I respect him too much to violate that trust. But more important than that, I respect *you* too much to compromise your reputation. I want you to be my wife. I want to ask your father for your hand in marriage, as is the custom of our people."

"Leland, I have dreamed all my life of the man I want to marry; and I have always known that I would recognize him whenever I saw him. From the first week you were here, I have known that you are that man. But are you sure this is what *you* want?"

"Although we have known each other only a few months, I have never been surer of anything in my life, Carlotta!"

"Then let's go ask my father tonight. I am sure that he will say yes."

"How can you be so sure? I can think of at least a dozen reasons he might give that we should wait."

"I just know. It is a gift the Indians have been given," she answered, starting to rise to go.

"Wait, I want to always remember this moment; please give me a little longer to look at you in the moonlight and to hold you." She settled back and moved into his arms. After a few minutes, he asked, "Carlotta, what is your Indian name?"

"Promise you won't laugh if I tell you."

"You know I would never do that."

"My mother's people named me 'Little Moonbeam'," she told him shyly.

"Little Moonbeam, it's perfect; I love it! My beautiful Little Moonbeam." He stood and pulled her to her feet and back into his arms and kissed her passionately—yet, somehow with a reverence, a reverence he would always feel for her and for their love.

In spite of Carlotta's prediction of Carl's approval, when Leland approached Carl and Grey Moon to ask for her hand in marriage, he was, nevertheless, surprised when they happily granted their permission. "Leland, I have to admit that this possibility is what I had in mind when I asked you to come to the mountains with me. I have always felt myself a pretty good judge of men. And when I first met you and talked to you, I sized you up as quality, in the best sense of the word; and you have proven me right. Nothing would please us more than having you marry our Carlotta. Right, Mother?" Always a lady of few words, Grey Moon smiled her approval and hugged Leland and Carlotta enthusiastically.

The wedding was planned for January 28, 1860, six months to the day after Leland and Carl arrived. Leland sent word to the family in Charleston in a letter to Lillianna to be delivered by two trappers headed that way in November.

Carlotta and Leland felt that the wedding ceremony should include traditions of the Indians as well as those of the white man. Carl and Grey Moon both agreed, so the wedding plans went forward. Carlotta planned to wear the traditional white buckskin dress, white moccasins, and white headband. The dress would be fringed, and the entire costume meticulously made and intricately beaded by the bride with the help of her mother. The ceremony was to be held at the Indian Village with the circuit preacher presiding. Following the ceremony, the wedding party and friends would attend a reception hosted by Carl and Grey Moon at their home. They were also planning, as a surprise gift, to spend two weeks with Grey Moon's family at the Indian Village so that the newlyweds could have the privacy of the cabin for their honeymoon.

By December, several little skiffs of snow had fallen, but none had stayed on the ground more than a day. However, to a South Carolina lowlander, even a light snow transformed the mountain scenery into a wonderland. So when the snow started to fall in the wee hours of a Saturday morning and continued all that day, through that night and into Sunday, finally stopping at twilight, Leland was mesmerized by the beauty of it all.

Grey Moon kept a fire crackling in the fireplace all day, and Leland was drawn away from the window only by the enticing aroma which emanated from the seemingly bottomless pot of coffee simmering in the hot coals there. As supper time approached, a rabbit stew bubbled, a delicious smelling temptation, on the wood stove at the opposite end of the big front room. She had baked an apple cobbler, which resided in the warming oven above the stovetop, and fresh biscuits were baking in the big oven below.

Carlotta had busied herself with her usual Saturday cleaning routine on Sunday, since they had all been drawn to watch the snow fall all day on Saturday. She had cleaned every inch of the cabin thoroughly. Carl sat reading in his big chair in front of the fire. He took advantage of this rare day of leisure to finish a book which he had been reading.

It was the kind of day you don't want to see come to an end. You hold onto every golden minute like a miser, savoring every delicious smell and storing the whole scene in your memory to draw on later when life is less pleasant.

By the time Grey Moon called them to supper, everyone was more than ready. "Carlotta, would you set the table please; supper is almost ready."

"Yes ma'am. It smells wonderful, Mother.

"Let's eat, Leland," Carl said, as he closed his book. "I don't know about you, but I'm starving."

"You don't have to call me twice; my mouth has been watering all afternoon," Leland answered, following Carl to the wash basin to wash his hands.

When they had finished supper and the dishes were clean and put away, they all gathered in front of the fire to join in a period of family devotions, as they did every night before bed. Carl read a passage of scripture and closed in prayer. They all sat there talking about Christmas, which was just around the corner, and about the coming wedding. Carl finally stood and reached his hand out for Grey Moon. "Come, my love, let's go to bed and give these young folks some time to themselves."

After Carl and Grey Moon had retired for the night, Carlotta and Leland settled on the rug before the fire and sat for a long time just gazing into the flames. He pulled her into his arms; and as she nestled her head beneath his chin, he kissed her hair. "Well, I guess we should think about getting to bed. What do you think?"

"It's been such a perfect day," she answered. "I hate to see it end."

They sat quietly a little while longer, watching the fire die down. When only glowing embers remained, Leland stood and pulled Carlotta to her feet. "Let's take one last look at the moonlight on the snow before we head for bed." They walked over to the window and stood with their arms around each other looking out at the beautiful blanket of snow, glistening in the light of the full moon.

"It's so beautiful, Leland. I have looked at the snow all of my life, but tonight I seem to see it through different eyes. I think it must be that I love you so much I see *all the world* through eyes of love. The snow seems to shut us away, almost as if we were in another world—a quiet, white world, clean and serene," she said wistfully.

"My own Little Moonbeam, I do love you so. How I wish that I could sleep tonight with you in my arms, your body next to mine."

"It won't be long now, darling," she answered, rising on tiptoe to meet his kiss.

The snow lingered several more days, melting very slowly in the warm sunlight of each day, then re-freezing during the long, cold nights. A few days before Christmas, Grey Moon and Carlotta started to prepare for a big Christmas Eve dinner. The men went to the woods in search of the perfect Christmas tree. "Don't bring a scraggly one, and remember, it must touch the ceiling," Carlotta demanded.

"Yes dear," Leland answered, laughing as they went out the door.

It took a little looking, but they finally found one they liked and came home dragging it behind them. They shook the snow off the limbs and nailed wooden crosspieces to the bottom of the trunk for a stand. When they took the tree into the cabin and set it up in front of the window, the ladies were delighted. Everyone agreed it was quite the most beautiful tree they had ever seen. "All it needs is a little decorating," Carl said.

The decorating of the tree was scheduled to begin after supper. The dishes were no sooner put away than Carlotta began to assemble materials for making the decorations for the tree. They would need popcorn and holly berries for stringing into garlands, twine, pages from an old catalog to cut into strips for making a paper chain or into large triangles from which cone shaped cups would be made, to hold the delicious hard sugar candy Grey Moon always made to hang on the tree, pine cones Carlotta had collected to hold the small candles for the tree, flour and water paste for gluing, and most importantly, the candles which Grey Moon and Carlotta had been making all during the year. The four of them sat around the table working on the decorations and singing Christmas carols. It was the same Christmas tradition that the McMurtry family had played out year after year, with one happy addition—Leland, who loved being there as much as they all loved having him.

It was growing late when all the decorations were finally finished, the paste dried, and the garlands completed. They all joined in hanging the decorations on the tree. When they were all hung, Grey Moon lodged each small candle into a pine cone and hung these on the tree last. She carefully arranged a white sheet around the base of the tree to simulate snow and stepped back to admire their handiwork. Nodding and smiling she said, "Just perfect!"

"I think this calls for a glass of wine," Carl said. "I'll go down to the root cellar for a bottle of Grey Moon's elderberry wine, for which she is famous. You get out the glasses, Carlotta."

After Carl had poured the four glasses of wine, they each took a glass; and just as they were about to raise their glasses in a toast, Carlotta cried out, “Wait, I have to get something from my room.” She ran into her bedroom and came back carrying a corn-shuck doll, which her Cherokee grandmother had made for her years ago. “Here is an angel for our tree! Leland, would you put her on the top?”

Leland took the doll, reached up, and placed the doll’s skirt over the top of the tree. “How’s that?” he asked.

Once again, Grey Moon said, “Just perfect!” And they all agreed, as they lifted their glasses in a Christmas toast.

The few days left before Christmas, passed quickly. The cabin was filled with the aroma of Christmas cooking. They made mincemeat, sweet potato, and apple pies, candied yams, greens, beans, cornbread, biscuits, and turkey, dressing, and gravy. Carl brought in mistletoe and hung it above every doorway. Leland helped Carlotta arrange pine cones, hemlock boughs, and candles across the mantle piece, in every window, and in the center of the kitchen table. Under the tree, there were small gifts for everyone.

All the frenzied activity culminated on Christmas Eve. It was a perfect celebration. A waning moon hung above the cabin, and inside a yule log crackled in the fireplace. Candles burned warmly on the mantle, in every window, and on the tree; and a happy and loving family joined hands around the candlelit dinner table. With heads bowed, they thanked God for His bounty and for the most precious Christmas gift of all, His Son, the Saviour of the World.

A month earlier, Thanksgiving was being celebrated back home in Charleston. In spite of the best efforts of everyone in the family, including Lillianna, a depressing air of sadness pervaded the whole celebration. Everyone felt the void left, not only by Will’s death, but also by the absence of those who had always been a part of the family Thanksgiving tradition—ever happy Leland, Pagrand Prendle, Grandpapa Pink, Dr. Gilmore, Delilah, and Samuel.

That night, Lillianna stood at her bedroom window looking out at the night sky. "Things will never be the same again. How can I go on? Oh Lord, please help me to find some little ray of sunshine to use as seed for starting over again, something to which I can look forward with hope and happiness; or I'm afraid I shall be doomed to look ever backward to happier times."

CHAPTER THIRTEEN

NEWS FROM THE MOUNTAINS

The next morning, as if in answer to her prayer, the trappers from the North Carolina mountains arrived in Charleston. Seeking directions in town about how to reach Mrs. Lillianna Prendle Pinkston, they were directed to Fairlawn and arrived there in the early afternoon.

Lillianna was in the study reading when she heard a knock at the front door, so she answered the door herself to find two men standing on the piazza. The larger of the two removed his hat and spoke, "Are you Mrs. Lillianna Pinkston?"

"Yes, could I help you?"

"Ma'am, my name is Caleb McPherson and this is my nephew, Angus. We are trappers from out the North Carolina mountains. We're here in Charleston on business. We're friends of Carl McMurtry and your son Leland. He's a fine lad, ma'am; you ought to be right proud of him."

"Thank you, Mr. McPherson; I certainly am," Lillianna answered.

"Anyway ma'am, when Leland found out we were coming to Charleston, he asked us to bring this letter for you," he said handing her the letter.

"Thank you so very much. I appreciate your bringing this to me. May I invite you gentlemen in for some refreshments?"

"No ma'am, we need to get back to town and take care of our business. If you would like for us to take a reply or anything back to Leland, we'll be glad to. We'll be leaving day after tomorrow; and if you do want us to take anything, we'll be glad to come back by and pick it up."

"I would really love to send Leland a letter and maybe a small Christmas gift, but I wouldn't want to put you to the trouble of coming all the way back out here. Couldn't I bring it to you in town tomorrow?" she asked.

"We really don't know what we'll be doing or where we might be at any certain time tomorrow. It won't be any trouble for us to come back out; we don't mind at all. We'll come back late tomorrow afternoon to pick up whatever you want us to take."

"Then please come join our family for supper tomorrow evening," Lillianna said.

"We wouldn't want to impose, Mrs. Pinkston." Caleb protested.

"Nonsense, it would be no imposition; but, a pleasure to hear all the news about Leland and the McMurtrys and something about your part of the country," Lillianna insisted. "We usually have supper about 6:00 o'clock, so we'll be expecting you gentlemen anytime that's convenient for you prior to that time."

"Thank you, Mrs. Pinkston, we'll be here around 5:00 o'clock if that's all right."

"That will be fine," she answered. "We'll be looking forward to having you."

She went back into the study and sat at her Father's big desk to read Leland's letter.

November 15, 1859
North Carolina Mtns.

My Dearest Mama;

By the time you receive this, Thanksgiving will be past. I hope that it finds you and all the family well and happy. Everyone here is fine, and the McMurtrys all send their regards. (In rereading the previous sentence, I realize that I have made them sound like a whole tribe when, in fact, there are only three of them; Carl, his wife Grey Moon, and their daughter Carlotta, who is eighteen. Oh well, you know I have never really been the best at English Composition).

Mama, the McMurtrys have taken me into their home and into their lives and treat me like a member of their family. From the day that I left Charleston right up to the present, my whole experience has been a wonderful adventure! You could never imagine the beauty and majesty of these mountains. I love it here. This is my kind of country, wild and free. If I had to cite a scene at home that was even moderately comparable in beauty to a full moon shining on a snow covered mountain world, I would think of standing on the piazza at Fairlawn and looking across the Ashley River, glistening in the sunlight, with wisteria entwined trees on the far bank serving as a backdrop.

I have learned so much about trapping and about life itself from Carl and Grey Moon. Contrary to what one might think, Carl is a very wise and well-read man. He has a library of books on every imaginable subject. Grey Moon is a Cherokee Indian, quiet and shy; and you will be glad to hear, a wonderful Christian lady. She is a superb cook and an artist when it comes to needlework. I wish you could see some of her bead work. We often visit the Indian Village of her people. They are a kind and intelligent people and very proud of their heritage. I feel so much at home with all the people here and in these beautiful mountains. I think I must have been born to be a trapper, and I believe that God had a hand in my being here and in all that has happened. That brings me to the real reason for this letter.

Carl's daughter, Carlotta, is such a wonderful girl, Mama. Her Indian name is "Little Moonbeam," and it is perfect for her. She is tiny, like a perfect little doll. She seems to be perpetually happy and beaming. She has her father's sense of humor, a ready laugh, and a bubbling personality. She is as outgoing as her mother is quiet and shy. She reminds me in so many ways of you; and I feel that's the greatest compliment I could pay any girl. I hope you know that, Mama. You have probably figured out that I am in love with her; and the beauty of it all is that she is also in love with me. We plan to be married on January 28, six months to the day after we met. I wish that my family could be here and be a part of our wedding celebration. However, I realize that it is a futile wish, considering the great distance, the difficulty of the trip, and the uncertainty of what the weather will be at this time of year. I hope you will approve and will be happy for us. Carlotta is wonderful and beautiful. Her eyes are big and deep, deep brown—as trusting as a doe's. She has long hair, raven black, that glistens in the light of the moon or of a fire. She is all I have ever dreamed of in a woman—beautiful, inside and out! I just know you are going to love her, Mama. By the way, the Indians have given me a name too—"Flaming Hair"—better than "carrot top" don't you agree?

Guess I had better close for now with regards to all the family. This will be my first Christmas away from home. My feelings are mixed—sad to be away from home and all of you, but happy to be here with Carl, Grey Moon, and my own "Little Moonbeam"! My wish is that this Christmas will be a Blessed Holy Season for all, followed by the best of all New Years. God bless you, Mama.

My love always,
Leland

Lillianna sat for a long time rereading Leland's letter and shedding tears of joy for her son. She studied how best to word her reply so that he would understand just how much she did approve and how happy she was for him. She finally began to write; and when she had finished, she sealed the letter; and in typical Lillianna fashion, her mind immediately moved on to other things. "Now what would be an appropriate gift for each one of them for Christmas. Not too big and not too much, it would be presumptuous for me to expect Caleb and Angus to transport a large load. Perhaps a special book for Carl from Papa's library would be proper. Let me see, I could send Grey Moon some good old Charleston rice and Delilah's recipe for okra soup. That's not very personal though; I think I'll send her some embroidery floss in an assortment of colors, for her bead work. Now, something very special for Carlotta and Leland is in order. I know, I'll send each of them a Christmas and wedding gift combined. Leland is our last child to marry; I think it would have pleased Will for him to have his wedding ring. Now, what for Carlotta? Oh I know, as much as I shall miss using them myself, I think my mother-of-pearl combs will complement that raven-black hair," Lillianna smiled, satisfied with her decisions as she rose and walked over to the bookshelves to select Carl's gift.

The next night, Caleb and Angus arrived promptly at 5:00 o'clock. They enjoyed the delicious, Charleston low-country style supper. The family enjoyed hearing the trappers' inciteful views on Leland and the three McMurtrys. Lillianna smiled as she noticed that young Angus seemed to be directing everything he said to Annamarie, who was seated next to him at supper. She asked him lots of questions about Leland and listened with rapt attention to all of his answers. Lillianna had not yet told anyone of Leland's pending marriage; and when Angus mentioned it, Annamarie flushed as her eyes filled with tears. Always the romantic, Lillianna interpreted this to be a happy reaction for Leland's happiness. It was obvious that Angus was completely taken with Annamarie, and Lillianna *thought* that Annamarie was just as taken with him. She would have been distressed to know how very wrong she was.

Caleb had also been observing the two young people and thought he would put in a good word for the boy. "Angus here is my brother's son, over from Scotland to make a life for himself here in America. He's been here for four years now and has become quite a trapper if I do say so myself. He's a good lad from good stock, and I'm right proud of him!" he said.

"As you should be, Caleb," Matt spoke up. "If he is as fine as he is fine-looking, he'll be a good catch for some deserving girl." Angus and Annamarie both blushed, realizing what everyone at the table was thinking. And Lillianna almost laughed aloud.

Caleb was a born storyteller and held the family spellbound with his tales of the mountain country. They were all sorry to see the evening end. As Lillianna and the family all saw their guests to the door and out onto the piazza, she gave them her letter and the gifts, neatly wrapped for the trip. "We have enjoyed your visit tremendously. I want to thank you again for delivering Leland's letter to me and for taking my letter and package back to him," Lillianna said.

"The pleasure has been ours," Caleb answered. "We want to thank all you folks for that delicious supper and for your hospitality. If you are ever out our way, look us up; our latchstring will always be out for any of you."

"Thank you, Caleb," Lillianna answered, as they mounted their horses. "We'll remember your offer. You gentlemen enjoy a good night's sleep, and have a safe trip home."

Before they left, Angus spoke up shyly, looking all the while at Annamarie, "Mrs. Pinkston, after meeting you and the rest of Leland's family, I understand why he is such a fine man." That said, he spurred his horse and rode around the oval and out the drive as Caleb followed.

On Christmas Eve, Caleb and Angus reached a little place called Flat Rock in the North Carolina mountains. They stopped there at the cabin of Gus Mingus, Caleb's trapping partner in the old days. Gus invited them to stay the night and to join him and his wife and son for Christmas dinner the next day. As it turned out, they stayed two nights and continued their journey the day after Christmas.

They finally reached Carl's cabin on January third, exhausted and hungry. They delivered Lillianna's letter and the package, and told them all the news about the trip to Charleston and about their visit with Leland's family. After a few hours rest and some good food, they set out for their own cabin, which was about five miles farther west.

After Caleb and Angus had gone, Leland eagerly started to open his mother's letter.

Grey Moon looked at Carl meaningfully and suggested, "Carl, you look a little tired. I know that I surely am. Let's go lie down for a awhile before supper."

"That's a good idea, Mother; it has been a long day," Carl answered, as they went to their bedroom and closed the door behind them.

"I know they left just to let us read Mama's letter in privacy. That wasn't necessary; I want them to hear it too."

"They wanted us to have this special time alone, sweetheart," Carlotta said. "They can read it later."

They sat down at the table as Leland began to read.

December 1, 1859,
Charleston, South Carolina

My dear Leland;

I was so very happy to receive your nice letter. We all miss you tremendously, son. Thanksgiving was wonderful, but, of course, it was just not the same without you and your father. Everyone here is well, and all send their love.

By the way, I found no fault with your English composition at all. It is like you—direct, colorful, and from the heart. If you should ever decide to give up trapping, perhaps you should consider writing. You paint such beautiful word pictures. I bet you never thought you would ever hear me suggest that!

I don't know the McMurtrys yet, but I already love them. Anyone who could make my Leland as happy as this family has made you, has to be wonderful! Carl and Grey Moon sound like such wise and intelligent people; I couldn't wish for my son to marry into a nicer family. I have a mental picture of Carlotta that is breathtaking, rather like a tiny little angel doll. Of course, compared to you any small person seems tiny; you are such a big red bear of a man. You obviously love her with all of your heart, and she must love you just as much for you to be so in love with her. I am so very happy for both of you, and I approve wholeheartedly of your marriage. I wish that we could all be there to help celebrate your marriage, too; but you are right, it *is* a long, hard trip for cold weather. However, we shall all be there in spirit. If I may be so bold (you know I'm an incurable romantic) January 28 is a great date for a wedding and beginning a honeymoon—cold, cold nights, good for bundling and cuddling, *etc.*

I was interested to hear of your visits with the Cherokee Indians. They have been terribly deceived and mistreated by the U.S. government. Their treatment has been just as shameful as the treatment of the slaves has been. At times, I feel almost ashamed of being a member of the white race. The things we have done in the name of progress are an abomination! I know you must feel gratified to be marrying into such a noble heritage. I was also interested to learn your Indian names. It sounds as if Carlotta's *is* just perfect for her, and yours is certainly perfect for you. Her people have a poetic way with names.

By the time you receive this, Christmas might well be over; so I am sure we shall have missed you terribly. I am sending some gifts for everyone there. Yours and Carlotta's are combination Christmas and wedding gifts. I couldn't send a package so large as to be burdensome for the McPhersons. (They are delightful people. We enjoyed their visit so very much. With all their news, not to mention their perceptions of you and the McMurtrys and their tales of the mountains, we were completely taken with them). Now back to talk of the gifts I sent to you. I selected the gifts for each of you with a great deal of thought. I tried to choose things that suited the interests, talents, or physical attributes of each one, as you described them to me. I enclosed a personal note in each gift to explain my selections. I hope my choices were on target.

Now "Flaming Hair" and "Little Moonbeam," before I close, may I propose a wedding toast to you since I can't be there to do it in person. May you always love each other as you do today; may you always be each other's best friend; and may you ever remember to put God first in your marriage, turning to Him every day for guidance and *listening carefully* for His counsel. God bless you both, my precious children; my heart, thoughts, and prayers are ever with you. I do plan to come see those mountains of yours as soon I can, and you surely must know that a visit from you would be a special treasure for me. My fondest regards to Grey Moon and Carl.

Love always,
Mother

Oh Leland, I can't tell you how happy your mother's letter makes me. I am so relieved," Carlotta said.

"What do you mean, sweetheart? For what reason are you *relieved*?"

"I was so afraid she wouldn't approve. After all, we *have* only known each other for six months; and our lives have been so *different*. You are a southern aristocrat, and I am just a half-breed Indian girl. Our worlds are very far apart. She had so many reasons, which I am sure she could have felt were valid, for opposing our marriage."

"So you do understand how *I felt* when we were about to tell your folks that we wanted to get married," Leland said.

"Yes, I do," she answered. "But I knew my folks so well; I knew that they would have no objections. Moreover, I knew that they would be happy."

"I know my mother just as well, and I'm not surprised at

all at her reaction. Neither she nor my father has ever been in the least prejudiced against another race; nor did either of them ever believe in the so-called traditions of the southern aristocracy. They reared me with that same set of principles, and those principles are the very reason that I left Charleston and came here to the mountains to make a new life for myself. Mama knew that was my aim when I left home, and she gave me her unconditional blessing. Her principles are what led us to find each other. You're going to love her; just wait and see!"

"I don't doubt that for a minute, my darling," she answered.

"One more thing, don't ever again let me hear you refer to yourself as 'just a half-breed Indian girl!' I am proud—so very proud—to be marrying a girl I shall always consider a beautiful Indian princess, descended from a noble people," Leland said, as he took her in his arms, tenderly kissed each eyelid, the tip of her nose, and then her lips.

After they had finished supper that night, they all sat in front of the fire as Leland read Lillianna's letter to Carl and Grey Moon. When he had finished, Carl smiled and nodded his approval, "Eloquent!" he said.

Grey Moon wiped away tears, as she whispered, "Perfect, just perfect!"

"Now let's open our gifts," Leland said, as he rose to bring Lillianna's package over by the fireplace. Leland unwrapped the box and read the note attached to the lid. "Please open your gifts one at a time, and each one share the note from me with the others. Merry Christmas, and may God bless you all. Love, Lillianna.

The first gift bore Grey Moon's name. As Leland handed it to her, he said, "All right, folks, you heard what the lady said. Grey Moon the first one is yours."

Grey Moon carefully removed the wrapping from her gift and cried out in delight at its contents. There was a bag of rice, grown in Charleston, a recipe titled "Delilah's Okra Soup," and several skeins of embroidery floss in beautiful jewel toned colors. Finally, she removed the note from the little envelope and read, "'Dear Grey Moon, I understand you are a superb cook. This is high praise coming from Leland, who loves to eat more than anyone I know and who is considered by our family to be a man with epicurean tastes. Alas, I can't claim any real cooking expertise; but I am sending you Delilah's recipe for okra soup; and she was the best cook *I* have ever known. It's a Charleston specialty, and is traditionally served over this Charleston grown rice. Of course, you may not be aware of this, but every Charleston family serves rice at least once a day. I hope your family will enjoy this dish as much as we low-country folks do. Leland says you are also an artist at beadwork. I am sending you some embroidery floss in several colors, which I hope will complement your artistry. Thank you so much for all you have done for my son. He speaks very highly of you as a Christian wife, mother, and homemaker; I can hardly wait to meet you. May God bless you, my dear. My love, Lillianna.' How thoughtful and lovely her selections are, just perfect!" Grey Moon finished.

"Carl, you're up second," Leland said, handing him his gift.

Carl unwrapped his gift, a copy of Edward Gibbon's, *Decline and Fall of The Roman Empire.* He smiled broadly, delighted with Lillianna's choice for him. He opened her note and read, "'Dear Carl, Leland tells me that you are an avid reader and that you have a very eclectic library. I wanted to give you just the right book, so I went to my father's large library to make my selection since his tastes in literature were also eclectic. I chose this first edition copy of *Decline and Fall of The Roman Empire.* Father always said that every library of more than ten volumes should include this book. I hope you don't already own it, and I hope you will enjoy reading it. I love to read, too; so from one avid reader to another, I wish for you always a comfortable chair in front of a warm fire and a good book to read. Love, Lillianna. P.S. I think Leland regards you almost as a second father. Thank you for being his mentor and his friend.' Leland, I really appreciate your mother's selection for me! I don't have a copy of this book, and I shall always treasure it," Carl said, as he thumbed through its pages.

"All right, sweet, you're next," Leland said to Carlotta.

"No, you go next, Leland; please, let me go last," she begged.

"Anything that makes you happy, my sweet," he answered, as he started to unwrap his gift, which was in a tiny box. "I have always heard that the best gifts come in small packages. Just look at you, sweetheart!," Leland said, laughing. He removed the top of the little box to reveal a plain gold wedding band. As he examined the ring, he found an inscription inside. "'LP *to* WLP,JR. 1-2-1834'. It's my father's wedding ring!" he exclaimed. "Oh sweetheart, I can't tell you how much this means to me! To have Papa's wedding ring for *my own* makes me feel as if *he* has blessed our marriage." Leland opened his note from his mother and read, "'My beloved son, I send you your papa's wedding ring, along with a part of my own heart. I know that he would have wanted you to have it and use it for your own wedding ring. He would have been so very proud of you and happy for you and Carlotta. God bless you and your marriage. Love, Mother.'" Leland couldn't say more; the tears came in spite of his effort to control them.

"Leland, your mother is such a wonderful and unselfish lady; I am going to be very proud to be her daughter-in-law and her friend. Now, I think I'm ready to open *my* gift," Carlotta said, as she kissed him and took the last gift from the box. Childlike, she shook it, "Listen, it rattles. What could it be?"

"Well, why don't you open it and see?" Carl said, laughing.

She ripped the wrapping off the box and lifted the lid. Squealing with delight as she saw the mother-of-pearl combs, and unable to contain her excitement, she jumped up and danced around the room putting the combs into her hair and taking them out again to admire them. "Look at them, Leland, aren't they beautiful? There are flowers engraved on them. I am going to wear them for our wedding; they will be perfect with my dress."

Grey Moon echoed her favorite description of anything beautiful, "Oh yes, just perfect!"

"Yes, I have always thought they were beautiful. Those combs in Mother's auburn hair are among my earliest recollections. Papa loved her hair. His favorite pet name for her was 'My Little Auburn hair'. God, how he loved my mother; it was something close to worship. And she loved him in the same way," Leland reminisced. "Now, my little raven hair, read the note Mama wrote you."

Carlotta opened the note and read, "'My dear Little Moonbeam. May I call you that? I love your Indian name—that is the way I picture you. Leland has described you, adoringly, as an angel princess with lovely raven hair. I thought these mother-of-pearl combs would grace that hair beautifully. There is a sweet story behind these combs that I shall tell you sometime. But for purposes of this brief note, I'll just tell you that they are among my most cherished possessions. My Will gave them to me when I was just fifteen, and I have worn them all these years with the greatest pleasure. Now, they are yours; it is my very special privilege to give them to you with all my love. I hope that you will enjoy and cherish them as much as I always have. God bless you, dear one. Love, Lillianna.' I can't imagine how she could have given them up for me. I shall always cherish them and consider them among my most precious possessions," she said, clutching the combs to her breast.

CHAPTER FOURTEEN

THE WEDDING

In spite of the fact that the wedding was approaching rapidly, the January weather assaulted relentlessly. It snowed day after day; and by January 15, Leland and Carlotta were concerned that the weather might actually force them to postpone their wedding. However, during the pre-dawn hours of January 16, it finally stopped snowing. When the dawn came, the sun shone brightly and continued to shine every day, right up to their wedding day.

On the morning of January 27, Carlotta and Grey Moon packed all of their wedding attire, kissed Leland and Carl good bye, and set out for the Indian village. They would stay there until time for the wedding on the following day. Along with the women of the village, they would complete the pre-wedding preparations and would observe the customary tribal rituals.

As Leland and Carl ate the supper that Grey Moon had prepared for them, they talked about what was going on that night at the Indian village. "I know they'll just sleep tonight.

Why do they have to spend the night there? I can go get them in the wagon; I want to see Carlotta tonight."

"In the first place, there are rituals with the women of the tribe to be observed tonight and in the morning. In the second place, you know it's supposed to be bad luck for the bride and groom to see each other before the ceremony on the day that they marry. And finally, it's cold out there, son," Carl said laughing. "You don't want to go bring your bride-to-be out on a night like this and risk either of you catching a cold the night before your honeymoon do you?"

"Well, no sir, and that's for *sure*!" Leland answered, blushing at the implications of his reply.

The morning of the wedding dawned cold and clear. The sun shone brightly on the mountain tops, and the snow glistened like a blanket of diamonds. After breakfast, Leland stood on the porch drinking a cup of coffee and breathing in the crisp morning air. "What a perfect day for our marriage to begin," he thought. "Dear God, please bless us with health and happiness and prosperity, according to Thy will; and please help us to channel our life together in the direction You would have us go, ever offering You our humble thanks for all our blessings, amen."

Leland went back in the cabin to review his checklist of things he had to do before he and Carl set out for the Indian village. When he got down to "Give Carl Carlotta's ring," he took the ring, wrapped in a square of rawhide, and gave it to Carl. "Carl, when I received my father's wedding ring from Mama, I suddenly realized that I had no ring for Carlotta. I decided to carve a bone ring from the rack of that buck I shot back in December. I hope it will fit her and that she will like it. I want you to tell me honestly what you think of it. It's my wedding gift to her

Carl removed the little ring from the rawhide and gazed at it in amazement. It was engraved with tiny Indian symbols and polished to a high luster. "Leland, it is exquisite; I have never seen more intricate or beautiful work! Son, you are an artist!"

"Thank you, Carl," Leland beamed; "I just hope she will feel the same way."

"I am sure that she will; it is so obviously a work of love."

The wedding ceremony took place at 3:00 p.m. in the tribal lodge of the Indian village, and the circuit preacher heard their vows. When he asked for the rings, Grey Moon, Carlotta's only attendant, handed him Will's wedding band; and Carl, the best man, handed him the bone ring that Leland had carved for his bride. It fit her perfectly, and she was so surprised and touched that she finished the ceremony in tears. It was a beautiful wedding—to quote the mother of the bride, "Perfect, just perfect!"

Carl and Grey Moon invited everyone to their cabin for a reception in honor of the newlyweds. Some of the women from the village had gone on ahead to prepare for the reception. In the center of the table, was the wedding cake Grey Moon had baked. It was surrounded by a variety of delicacies, all beautiful and delicious. Rather than the traditional champagne toast to the bride and groom, Grey Moon served her famous elderberry wine. She had many bottles, which were heretofore untouchable. She had made and aged these bottles over the years in anticipation of her daughter's eventual marriage. Everyone was enjoying the reception; and mellowed by the wine, seemed to be settling in for an extended celebration. However, Carl had anticipated this possibility; and had a plan in mind to call a halt to the festivities. "Leland," Carl began, "I expect you and Carlotta had better go on to bed, so these folks can get on home!" The crowd all laughed; the bride and groom both blushed; and Carl opened the door and said, "This meeting is officially adjourned, folks." The women were already busy cleaning up behind the revelers and finished the job in short order.

The last of the guests, along with Grey Moon and Carl, said their good byes about 9:00 o'clock. "Come here you; I thought they would never leave," Leland said, as he pulled her to him. God, you are one gorgeous creature, and you are mine—*mine*!" He started removing the mother-of-pearl combs from her hair and loosening her braids.

"Here, let me do that while you go prepare for bed; I know you must be tired," Carlotta said, smiling coyly. With expert hands, she quickly loosened the braids as he stood watching. "Go on up and get out of those wedding clothes."

As he started up the steps to the loft, he said, "Who is thinking about bed! Let's just sleep here in front of the fire tonight. I'll bring that bearskin rug from the banister when I come back down; that will make it more comfortable."

"You go ahead; and since you're not interested in bed, prepare for whatever *it is* that *does* interest you," she teased.

In the loft, Leland hastened to undress and don his pajama pants. However, before he went down to Carlotta, he hung his wedding suit neatly and placed his shoes beneath the cot, which he would no longer need.

He took the bearskin rug and descended the steps. Not knowing what to expect, he was actually a little nervous, to his own surprise. The room was dark except for the light from the fire. Carlotta sat on the floor in front of the fire brushing her hair. Leland's breath caught in his throat when he saw her beautiful body glistening in the firelight with her black hair cascading over her breasts. "I almost hate to disturb her," he thought. "She looks like some Greek goddess, cast in bronze, sitting there." He walked quietly to the fireplace and spread the bearskin rug on the floor beside her. He took the brush from her hand, "Let me do that; I want to brush your hair," he said.

As he started to seat himself, she reached up and untied his pajama pants. "You won't need these," she said, as the pants dropped to the floor. As he stood there, the red hair on his massive chest glowing in the firelight and his red curls falling on his forehead, she rose to her knees and kissed his hard, flat stomach. Leland pulled her to her feet and pressed her body to his, kissing her passionately as he caressed her. Their desire reached the point of no return; and, with her arms around his neck, she wrapped her legs around his waist. He dropped to his knees and laid her back on the rug. Ever mindful of his size, he entered her small body slowly and gently; but locking her legs around him, she pulled him to her and lifted to meet his thrust, again and again, with abandon; and finally, at climax, she gave a primal-sounding scream of ecstasy. When their desire was spent, they lay locked in that last embrace and slept.

Sometime during the night, the silent snow began to fall again, and Carlotta awakened. The fire had died down to embers, and the room was chilly. She wanted to get up and put another log on the fire and to cover them with the blanket that always stayed folded in a basket on the hearth. But when she tried to withdraw from Leland's body, he awakened and pulled her hips close to his again. Soon they had no need for the warmth of the fire, nor for the blanket; and thus it continued throughout the night and into the morning.

When they finally got up to have breakfast, the snow was still falling. Leland built a fire in the wood stove; and while Carlotta cooked breakfast, he laid a new fire in the fireplace. By the time she had finished cooking breakfast and they sat down to eat, the fire was crackling; and it was snowing harder than ever.

"I'm so glad it is snowing again, Leland. We have plenty to eat and plenty of wood for the fire; and we have each other in a little world all our own. Could even Paradise be more perfect than what we have?"

"I can't imagine that it could, sweetheart," he answered, as he pulled her close and kissed her hair. "Let's sit by the fire, and I'll brush your hair. I never did get to brush it last night." They went to the fireplace and sat on the bearskin rug as Leland brushed her hair. This was a ritual they would repeat again and again over the coming years.

For the two weeks of their honeymoon, they were completely alone and totally absorbed in each other. They didn't spend a single night in the new bed which Carl and Grey Moon had given them. They elected instead to sleep on the bearskin rug in front of the fire. The warmth of the fire and the romantic glow of its light set the mood which ignited their passion night after night.

On the second night of their honeymoon, Carlotta had gone into their bedroom and had come out wearing the new gown Grey Moon had made for her. Leland had already undressed and was waiting for her in front of the fire. "I wanted you to at least see the pretty nightgown Mother made for me to wear on our wedding night," Carlotta said, as she came and stood before him in front of the fire.

He could see her body through the gown, silhouetted in the firelight; and his desire began to rise. Of course, for most new grooms, the boiling point is low; and Leland was no exception. He rose to his feet and ran his hands down the soft full sleeves of her gown; and taking her hands in his, he caressed each of her fingers with his tongue and then kissed the palm of each hand. Then he reached for the little bow at the neck of the gown and untied it. "This *is* a *pretty gown*, my little raven-hair," he said. As he ran his hands down the front of her body, he circled each of her nipples, hard beneath the gown, with his fingers, and said, "This is *truly* a *beautiful gown.*" And as he continued downward, caressing her body, over her belly and down her legs, he stooped as he reached the hem of the gown, and said, "Yes, this is *indeed* a *gorgeous gown.* Then taking the hem of the gown in his hands, he pulled it up and over her head and cast it aside. Then caressing her body, just as he did before, he said, "But no gown should ever touch, *could ever touch*, the perfection of this body that sets my manhood—my soul—afire! I want to sleep every night for the rest of my life with it pressed to mine, your heart beating in rhythm with mine, with nothing between us *ever!*"

"Then thus it shall ever be, my man with flaming hair, and magic hands, and magic mouth," she replied, kissing his chest again and again.

The halcyon days of their honeymoon ended all too soon, and they were back to life as usual. The cabin seemed so full, too full, after Carl and Grey Moon returned. Their love making became much more inhibited when they could hear the breathing of Carlotta's parents in the next room during the night. By mid-February, it had been decided; come April, they would begin to build their own cabin.

CHAPTER FIFTEEN

A CABIN BESIDE A STREAM

When April finally arrived, only the snow on the mountain tops remained; and according to plan, Leland began work on his and Carlotta's cabin. With help from Carl, some men from the Indian village, and the McPhersons, the work progressed rapidly. By the end of May, the cabin was nearing completion. Carlotta and Grey Moon had stayed busy cooking for the workers and doing anything else that they could to help. Everyone concerned was happy to see the job completed, and the young couple finally move into their new home. Although their furnishings were sparse, they at least had in their bedroom, a bed and chest, and a rocking chair. In their kitchen area, they had a stove, a table, and two benches; and in their sitting area beside the fireplace, they had two chairs. The cabin stood on a piece of land which overlooked the little stream and the rock on which they sat the night they had first declared their love. Carl and Grey Moon lived only a mile or so away, so they could visit often. The evening they completed their move, Grey Moon invited them to supper. When they were about to leave for home, Carl said, "Wait a minute; we have one more thing we would like to give you as a housewarming present." He went up the stairs to the loft, took the bearskin rug from the banister, and brought it down. "We thought this might make it a bit cozier when you all sit by the fire at night."

Leland and Carlotta burst into laughter. "Thank you," Leland said. "You'll never know how much this means to us!"

Carl and Grey Moon looked at each other, puzzled. "I don't think I even *want to know* what *that* is all about!" Carl said.

"Nor do I," Grey Moon echoed, knowingly.

"When they reached their cabin, it was dark. Leland laid a fire in the fireplace while Carlotta lit the oil lamp on the kitchen table. They spread their bearskin rug before the fireplace, and both sat on it looking into the fire. "Leland, I have a housewarming gift for you," Carlotta said.

"Oh sweetheart, I feel terrible; I don't have one for you," he answered.

"Don't feel badly, darling. My gift is actually one you gave to me. Brace yourself, big man, you're going to be a Father. I am almost sure that we are going to have a baby!"

"A baby! When . . . . *how?*"

"The best I can calculate, late November or early December; and in the usual way; you know I *have been exposed!*" Carlotta answered, laughing. "Are you unhappy about this, Leland?"

"Oh no, sweetheart. How could I be unhappy? I guess I'm just a little bit shocked. Are you all right? It frightens me; you know having a baby is dangerous. I couldn't stand it if anything happened to you," he said, drawing her close, as if his arms alone could keep her safe from all danger. "You are so tiny, and I am so big! What if our baby is big like I am?"

"Darling, you are talking silly. Women have been having

babies since time began, and babies are all tiny when they are born! I am healthy; don't borrow trouble."

"But there is no doctor for miles around!"

"Leland, the Cherokee women are old hands at having and delivering babies. I'll have plenty of help when the time comes," she answered, reassuringly.

"Well, we'll postpone our love making until after the baby comes. I don't want to do anything that will hurt either of you."

"Oh, no we won't! It's a long time until you have to *go to the gander pasture*! It's perfectly safe for us to make love. I'm not about to take *that* away from either of us until we absolutely have to give it up," she said firmly.

"God, I can hardly believe it! It's a wonderful miracle isn't it? You are actually carrying a little human being inside of you, a little human being that we made from our love!" Leland said, as he gently kissed her belly. "I can't imagine how anyone could know this and not believe in God! I don't even know what our baby will be; but I already love it almost as much as I love you, my little mother to be."

"Oh Leland, I am so glad that you are as happy as I am that this little one is coming!" Then she offered up a fervent prayer, "Lord, please keep our little *papoose* in Your loving care."

"Amen," Leland finished.

The months passed quickly as Leland and Carlotta worked to make their little cabin a home. Finding that he had a talent for carving, he built a new kitchen table and chairs and hand-carved each piece. He also built a long, hand-carved seat to place opposite the two chairs before the fireplace. The seat was hinged to provide storage beneath; it was somewhat similar to what is referred to as a deacon's bench. Carlotta and Grey Moon made a cushion for the seat, curtains for all the windows, a tablecloth and napkins for the table, a quilt, and other items, which made their cabin more attractive. When

Leland started to build a cradle for the baby, Carlotta started work on the layette. She quilted a coverlet, made a little pillow, and stitched little sheets and pillowcases to fit the cradle. Grey Moon made little gowns and hemstitched receiving blankets. With a November delivery date, everyone knew that baby blankets, warm sweaters and caps, and bootees would be needed to keep the little one warm. The women of the Indian village took great pleasure in making all these things.

Soon it was Thanksgiving, and the McMurtrys and the young Pinkstons all felt that they had more for which to be thankful than ever before. They invited the McPhersons, who insisted on providing the turkey. Grey Moon and Carlotta prepared a delicious traditional Thanksgiving dinner. Thanksgiving Day fell on November 27, and Carlotta's due date was drawing near. Nevertheless, she and Leland wanted to host their first Thanksgiving dinner in their own home. She and Grey Moon scrubbed every inch of the cabin until it shone. Carlotta had gone out and picked autumn leaves with which to make arrangements for the mantle and the table centerpiece. When the guests arrived, the cabin was bathed in candlelight, there was a warm fire crackling in the fireplace, and the delicious fragrance of, what can only be described as, a gourmet meal! "This place has the look of the home of an expectant mother who has far too much energy. I have always heard that a spurt of energy like that is the immediate forerunner of the birth of the baby," Carl observed. "And from the looks of you, my girl, it appears that you are more than ready for that apple to fall!"

"It should be at least another week before the baby comes, Father," Carlotta answered. "I feel too good to be on the verge of delivery."

"That frequently means that labor is impending," Grey Moon warned.

"Then maybe we should get down to some serious eating

while we still have time," Leland laughed, as he led the way to the table. When they were all seated, they joined hands; and Leland asked Carl to return thanks.

"May I suggest that each of us, in turn, name the thing for which he or she is most thankful this year; I shall begin and then end with a brief closing," Carl said. They all bowed their heads and prayed.

Carl began, "Dear Lord, I thank Thee for the addition of a fine son-in-law to our family this year."

Grey Moon continued, "Our heavenly Father, I thank Thee, in advance, for this little grandchild that will soon be joining our family."

Caleb McPherson, seated next to Grey Moon, prayed next, "Oh Master of the endless Universe, I thank Thee for another profitable year, which we have reaped from the bounty of Thy beautiful mountains."

Angus McPherson followed his uncle in prayer, "Almighty God, I thank Thee for allowing us to travel safely during this past year and for all those new friends and acquaintances we had the privilege of meeting on our travels. I pray that You will bless them and keep them in Your tender care and allow us to see them again, *soon.*"

Carlotta prayed next, "Dear Lord, there are so many things that Thou hast given to us during this past year. I could never just thank Thee for a single thing. I thank Thee for happiness beyond measure, for my husband and his love, for joining together the heritage of our two very different cultures, for blessing our union with a child of our love, and for our new home and the privilege of sharing it with our family and friends."

Leland continued the prayer, "Divine Father of our Saviour, I feel so blessed with having for my wife this woman, who has thanked You so eloquently for all the things nearest my own heart, and who will soon give to me the gift of fatherhood. For her and for this gift, I truly thank You, Lord.

Please make me worthy of the little life You are entrusting to our care."

Then Carl ended the prayer, "Oh Lord, I entreat Thee to hear all our prayers and to answer them according to Thy will. Now please bless this food to the nourishment of our bodies and us to Thy service, in the name of Christ we pray. Amen."

That first Thanksgiving in their new home was the embodiment of everything Thanksgiving should be. That night after their guests had gone, Leland and Carlotta sat before the fire reflecting on what a perfect day it had been. They had been talking for a long time when the clock on the mantle chimed midnight. "My goodness, I had no idea it was so late," Carlotta said.

It has been a long day, my very pregnant wife. It's time for us to get to bed," Leland answered.

"I think you are right. I didn't realize how tired I was," Carlotta said, as she rose and started toward their bedroom. Stretching her back, she added, "I'll tell you one thing, my aching back surely knows."

"You go on in and get ready for bed. I'll close up in here and be along shortly."

CHAPTER SIXTEEN

A NEW ARRIVAL

Carlotta lit the oil lamp on the table beside their bed, undressed, and was slipping into her warm robe when Leland came into the bedroom. As he started to undress, he asked, "Are you too tired for devotions tonight?"

"I'm not ever too tired for that, sweetheart," she answered.

"All right, you crawl into bed; and I'll read our scripture. We'll pray our evening prayer with you comfortable in bed. I'll kneel for both of us tonight," Leland said.

"No indeed, the least I can do is to kneel and honor the Lord," she insisted.

"Well, I am sure He would understand; but if you insist, all right."

Leland selected a very appropriate scripture for their Thanksgiving night devotion, Psalm 100. Following the scripture, they always knelt beside their bed; and each offered up a silent and private prayer to God. When Carlotta arose from her knees, she suddenly cried out, "Oh God, Leland, my water has broken; I think I'm going into labor!"

"Don't get excited, darling. Just get into bed; I'm going for Grey Moon!"

"I don't think there is any big hurry," Carlotta said. "First babies usually take a good while. It will probably be all right to wait until morning." She tried to sound reassuring, but Leland could tell that she was as anxious as he was.

"Get into bed, sweetheart; I am going for your mother, now! Please don't argue with me!" Leland said emphatically.

"Yes sir," she answered meekly, as he helped her into bed. He took the wet nightgown, brought a dry one, and helped her to put it on. He tucked the covers around her and kissed her.

"You stay right here in bed, and we'll be back before you know it," he said, reassuringly.

He ran quickly to their small stable. Putting only a bridle on his horse, he didn't take the time to saddle him. He mounted with a leap and rode bareback toward Carl and Grey Moon's cabin. When he arrived, he jumped from the horse and ran up on the porch. Banging on the door, he called, "Carl, Grey Moon, get up. Please, hurry and get up; Carlotta's in labor!"

Carl came to the door in his nightshirt with Grey Moon right behind him. Leland quickly filled them in on the situation at home; and Grey Moon said, "You get on back home to Carlotta, and we'll come on as fast as we can get there!"

"Thank you, folks; I don't know what we would do without you," Leland answered, as he remounted and galloped off toward home.

By the time Carl and Grey Moon arrived, Carlotta's labor had progressed from a nagging backache to minor contractions, spaced about thirty minutes apart. Grey Moon sent the men out of the bedroom and closed the door. She examined Carlotta to check on the progress of her labor. Then she helped to settle her comfortably in bed. "You relax as much as you can between contractions, sweetheart. I'm going to send Carl for Sahoni Kawi (blue deer) and your Aunt Gilohi (long hair). They both help deliver most of the babies in the village. In fact, Sahoni Kawi helped deliver you."

When Grey Moon came out of the bedroom, Leland and Carl were sitting by the fire. "Well, she's just getting started. It looks like it's going to be a long night. Leland, why don't you get a fire going in the wood stove, and I'll put on a pot of coffee. We'll need to get a pot of water on to boil after awhile; but there's no hurry. We'll have plenty of time. Carl, you had better go on to the village and bring Sahoni Kawi and Gilohi.

"I should be back within three hours," Carl said, as he left for the Indian village.

As Carl drove off in the wagon, Leland, obviously worried, said, "Three hours? Grey Moon, that's a long time; anything could happen in three hours!"

"That's not likely, Leland; but if it should, we'll take care of it," Grey Moon answered.

"We! What do you mean by *we*?" he asked, wide-eyed.

"Yes, *we*! Women have been bearing babies since the dawn of time; and believe me, your baby is going to arrive with or without our help. Now pull yourself together! If her labor starts to progress more rapidly than we expect, the last thing I need on my hands is an hysterical husband!"

And indeed, within the hour, Carlotta's labor *did* progress and did so rapidly. Her contractions were coming about ten minutes apart and became increasingly forceful. However, like all Cherokee women, she took pride in her strength and bore the pain stoically. Leland stood there watching helplessly with tears streaming down his face. He wiped her sweating body with cool cloths in an effort to give her some measure of relief. "Oh, sweetheart, I wish I could bear this pain for you. You don't have to be so brave, scream!" he urged.

As the contraction subsided, she reached up and touched his face, "My poor Leland, please don't look so distressed.

I'm all right. Why don't you go in by the fire for awhile and have a cup of coffee?"

"No, I am not leaving you, not even for a minute!" he answered.

Grey Moon interrupted, "Leland, I think it is probably time to go put the water on to boil. Get the scissors and some white thread out of my basket on the kitchen table. Look in the trunk and get some clean cloths, a gown, a receiving blanket, and some bootees. Then go outside to see if you see any sign of Carl's coming."

Leland left the bedroom to follow Grey Moon's instructions. "Now, that should keep him busy, at least for a few minutes," she said, smiling at Carlotta.

A few minutes later, Leland called, "Grey Moon, I hear Carl coming. Tell Carlotta to hang on; help is on the way!"

"Thank God," Grey Moon said, relief in her voice.

The next two hours passed in a blur for Leland—a blur of sights, sounds, and feelings, which proved to be an anesthetic, of sorts, for the guilt he was suffering. As the women, who were there to help with the delivery, came in and out of the bedroom, they seemed to be walking as if in quicksand, when he wanted them to run. As the birth of their baby drew near, Carlotta, at last permitted herself to scream in the agony of birth. Leland felt as if he were drowning in the screams, which rose above the background noise of conversation, the crackling of the fire, even the subtle sound of the water still boiling, unnoticed, on the stove. These sights and sounds came to Leland like an echo through a long, dark tunnel. He said over and over, "I did this to her. It is all my fault. God, forgive me; it's all my fault!"

Carl had heard all he could take, "Leland, pull yourself together! You didn't make this baby alone. Carlotta was right there enjoying it with you and cooperating fully. You have done nothing wrong. Babies are born every day in this same way. And God willing, the two of you will soon be making another one. Believe me, tomorrow you will book back on this night in an entirely different way."

Suddenly, the scene came into focus for Leland; and he heard a voice from the bedroom, "Now, Carlotta, squat and push!" There was one more scream, silence, and then a squawking cry.

Leland and Carl looked at each other and smiled. "Well, it sounds like you're a father. And I'm a grandpa. Lord, have mercy, I just realized that I am going to be sleeping with grandma!"

About that time, Grey Moon came out of the bedroom. "Leland, you have a beautiful little daughter and a tired, but very happy, wife; and they are waiting for you. Carl can visit with them later. Right now I think poor grandpa probably needs comforting. After all, from now on he has to sleep with grandma!" she said.

Leland was still laughing as he opened the bedroom door. "And what is so funny, Papa?" Carlotta asked as he entered.

"Oh, your mother is out there teasing *grandpa* about having to sleep with *grandma* from now on. They are a couple of characters.

"Well, come on over here and meet your daughter," she said, as she uncovered the little bundle resting in her arms.

Leland went to the bed and dropped to his knees beside them. First, he kissed Carlotta. "Darling, you look so tired; are you all right?"

"Of course. I admit I'm a little tired, but I am fine," she answered.

Then he pulled back the receiving blanket, and his breath caught in his throat as he gazed adoringly at his little girl. "Oh, my God, she is so beautiful. Would you look at those auburn curls?"

"She's her papa's daughter; no doubt about that," Carlotta said. "What would you think of naming her *Auburn? Auburn McMurtry Pinkston.*"

"I would love it. It's a beautiful name for our beautiful

little girl!" Leland answered. "Her Grandma Pinkston would surely love it."

"Then Auburn McMurtry Pinkston it is, and she is ready to meet her Grandpa McMurtry. Papa, would you ask grandma to come back in and to bring grandpa with her?"

When Carl and Grey Moon came in, she took the baby from Carlotta and put her into Leland's arms. "I don't know how to hold a baby. She's so little. I'm afraid I might hurt her," he protested, holding Auburn with his fingers tight together as if she were liquid and might run through them.

"Papa, you're a big strong man. I don't think you'll drop her; she's not a china doll; and she won't break," Carlotta said laughing. "Sit here beside the bed in the rocking chair and rock her. Babies love to be rocked, so you might as well get used too it. Now, Grandma and Grandpa, we would like you to meet Miss Auburn McMurtry Pinkston, your granddaughter."

"And a beautiful granddaughter she is," Carl said, with tears in his eyes at the magic of this precious baby.

"Auburn, what a perfect name for this little girl with her father's flaming curls!" Grey Moon said. "But she has her mother's dark skin."

"And she has her mother's flashing black eyes," Leland said, as he looked lovingly into Carlotta's eyes.

"All I can say is that with this combination, she's going to be a heartbreaker for all the young swains around," Carl said.

"Yeah, and I'm going to be a *head breaker* if any young upstart comes fooling around her!" Leland countered.

"My boy, you have a lot to learn, I fear," Carl answered.

Christmas arrived, marked by all the things that would make it a holiday to be remembered. They had snow, a tree with all its decorations, good food, gifts, Christmas carols, peace on earth, and best of all, a newborn baby. Unfortunately, the entire nation was destined to view that Christmas, in retrospect, as the last happy holiday for a long time to come.

Leland had always kept the family in Charleston abreast of the news from the mountains. He was especially happy to send the announcement of Auburn's birth. However, the letter that he received from Lillianna in return was very disturbing. A frightening incident had occurred in the Charleston Harbor on January 9, 1860. A supply ship, *Star of the West*, attempting to bring supplies to the Federal Garrison at Ft. Sumter, was fired on by cadets from the Citadel, under orders from the South Carolina Militia. The ship was turned back and forced to put out to sea.

Leland had followed the political news with interest and was aware that Abraham Lincoln, Republican candidate for President, had been elected. He had known that if Lincoln should win the election, South Carolina would probably secede from the Union; so he was not surprised when that happened. South Carolina had always been an advocate for States Rights; and to a majority of South Carolians, and all southerners for that matter, secession appeared to be the only way to preserve those rights. Although abolition of slavery was a big plank in Lincoln's campaign platform and was widely publicized as the primary reason southern states seceded from the Union, such was not the case. Not to say that southerners weren't interested in the preservation of slavery, for it was important to the economy and to the social order of the South. However, the sovereign rights of the individual states were the primary concern. They felt that the United States was a union of individually sovereign states, bound together by mutual agreement, and not subject to the will of that union.

Of course, Leland knew, from personal experience, of the racial unrest in Charleston; but he was upset to learn from his mother's letter that the unrest had accelerated considerably. Now, with this latest incident, he was extremely concerned for all his family, especially for Lydia and Beau, who were living in the center of the city. But, in spite of his concern for his family in Charleston, he was very thankful that his own little family was so far removed from the scene of all the turmoil there.

Lillianna had ended her letter with a chilling observation. She wrote, “Long ago, when Will and I were still very young, we were riding home from school one afternoon. We were discussing the racial tension which existed in Charleston at that time and which had been escalating for years. Will made a statement that I have never forgotten. He said, ‘It appears to me to be like a keg of dynamite with the fuse lit.’ Now, I am terribly afraid that the burning fuse is growing shorter by the hour. God help us all when it finally blows; and mark my words, *it will blow*!”

Much to the disappointment of young Angus McPherson, his Uncle Caleb had decided that they would postpone their usual fall trip to Charleston until the spring of 1862 when they should have on hand a larger supply of skins for shipment. Angus, who had been so smitten with Annamarie Lineham on their trip the previous year, had begun corresponding with her; and they had established a close friendship by mail. They were both disappointed that Angus wouldn’t be visiting Charleston as they had expected. When Angus learned of the incident in the Charleston Harbor, he decided to go there immediately.

“Angus boy, whatever could you be thinking to consider setting out for Charleston in the dead of winter?” his Uncle Caleb asked.

“Uncle Caleb, I have found a woman with whom I am in love; and with things there developing the way they are, I am afraid she could be in grave danger. I am going to try to persuade her to come back here with me,” Angus asserted.

“Angus, this is idiotic; you hardly know the girl. What if she doesn’t share your feelings?”

“I doubt seriously that she does, certainly not to the extent that I love her. Still, I must try to bring her out of harm’s way. I am going to stay there until I can persuade her to come with me. She will come to love me, of that I am sure. I knew from the first time I saw her that we were meant to be."

"Son, think this over carefully before you take this step. What will you do if she refuses to come with you?" Caleb asked, obviously very concerned.

"Then I'll stay there until she will!"

"This is sheer folly! How will you live?"

"Uncle Caleb, I am young; and I am strong. I will find a job of some sort."

"Well, if you are hell-bent on going, I am going with you!" Caleb said.

"No, this is something I have to do alone; but I appreciate your offer."

"But Angus, I promised your folks . . ."

"The subject is closed, Uncle Caleb. Please don't say anything more. I'll be leaving in the morning."

To say that Leland was surprised when Caleb brought the news of Angus's departure for Charleston would be an understatement. Then when he learned that Angus planned to bring Annamarie back to the mountains with him, he was more than a little worried. Considering his last visit with her, Leland was concerned about the impact that her coming might have on his life. He need not have worried, it would be a very long time before he would again see Angus or Annamarie.

CHAPTER SEVENTEEN

BLOODY CONFLICT

The next letter which Leland received from Charleston brought terrifying news. That letter would prove to be the last direct message he would receive from his mother.

April 15, 1860,
Charleston, South Carolina

Dearest Leland,

I am afraid I have distressing news for you. Three days ago, Confederate forces in Charleston bombarded the Federal Garrison at Fort Sumter. That keg of dynamite I mentioned in my last letter, has finally blown; and I believe that life, as we have known it, will be forever changed.

Noel, as a graduate of the Citadel, has been offered a commission in the military organization of South Carolina by an act passed by the Legislature. Under the same act, the Cadet Corps of the Citadel and

Arsenal academies were organized as "The Battalion of State Cadets" to serve as "Public Guard;" so it seems they are even planning to use our children in this war. Noel says that he has no intention of fighting in an army which will be perceived by most of the country and the world to be waging a war to preserve slavery. On the other hand, he could never fight in an army that would attack his home state. It is truly a dilemma for him, Leland. At this point, he has only one conviction. He will do whatever it takes to defend his home and family.

You will be excited to hear that Barbara and Noel are expecting a baby in October. Ordinarily, I would consider this to be wonderful news; but now, with a war underway, I wonder what sort of life we can offer this new little one. God help it and all of us.

People in Charleston are trying to go on with their lives and businesses as usual. Lydia and Beau are still living in their home in Charleston, and the clinic continues to prosper. As always, Lydia is busy with her teaching. However, the situation in Charleston is volatile; and no one knows what lies ahead. I wish they would move out here and drive in to work each day, but they are hoping that won't be necessary. As I said before, on one has any idea what lies ahead.

I am sure you know that Angus McPherson has come here to Charleston. We knew that he was quite taken with Annamarie when he visited last year. We also knew that they had been corresponding and had become good friends; however, we had no idea of the depth of his feelings for her. Leland, he is deeply in love and wants to marry her! Annamarie is very fond of him, but she is not in love with him. He just won't take no for an answer. He has taken a job on the docks in Charleston and is living in a boarding house. I feel sorry for the boy. He's courting Annamarie with determination. They are seeing a great deal of each other, but I'm afraid that he is wasting his time.

Actually, ever since you left, Annamarie has been spending time with Samuel Flood. You remember, he is the boy who used to explore with you and her when you were children and who witnessed your papa's murder. I think that at first, she just felt sorry for him; but now, I am beginning to wonder if she feels more than just pity.

I guess that about covers all the news of any importance. All here send their love. Leland, stay where you are, there in the mountains. As anxious as I am to see you, Carlotta, and my precious granddaughter, I wouldn't have you come here for the world. Keep your little family as isolated from this war as possible. Please keep us all in your prayers, and be assured of our prayers for you. My regards to Carl and Grey Moon. God bless you all.

Love always,
Mother

As everyone had feared, the war came; and it would prove to be one of the costliest wars in history with respect to the number of lives lost. The bloody conflict raged in Pennsylvania and Virginia; it covered North Carolina from the mountains to the sea; nor was South Carolina spared the horror. The reports from Charleston were frightening. Being, in the words of General Robert E. Lee, " . . . the South's second largest port . . . the 'Cradle of the Secession' . . . the symbolic mother city of the Confederacy," Charleston was a high priority target for the Union. It was shelled from land and sea. The harbor was blockaded by the Union Navy, and only the blockade runners served as lifeline for the South. The Union constructed fortifications with all guns trained on Charleston. Fort Sumter was bombarded relentlessly from land and sea. The decision was made early on that Charleston would " . . . be defended at any cost of life or property." Lee passed the order to General John C. Pemberton, commander of Confederate forces in Charleston, to fight "street by street and house by house as long as we have a foot of ground to stand upon." And fight courageously they did! The Battle of Secessionville in June, 1862, was won by the Confederates, with heavy Union losses. Then followed a period of " . . . relative calm, interspersed with some Confederate victories." But on April 7, 1863, the terrible siege of Charleston began. And as much as Leland had hoped to isolate his family from the war, such was not to be the case; for during these tumultuous years, the war raged all around the area designated as the Indian lands of western North Carolina. The lives of the inhabitants of that area were in chaos. As concerned as Leland was about the news of the siege of Charleston, he was hard-pressed to handle the needs of his own little family.

Charleston had been under siege for seven months when Auburn celebrated her third birthday. Bubbling with a personality like her mother's, she was a precocious and beautiful little girl.

In the mountains, they received only the news of the war; but there was no news from Leland's family in Charleston. There life moved forward precariously. As a matter of fact, it seemed to be moving much too rapidly. Like reflections in a kaleidoscope being turned in the hands of a small child, everything was changing too fast and was all a-jumble.

Noel and Barbara had a baby boy, Noel Parker Pinkston, II, in October, 1861. Though life on the family plantations, Fairlawn, Pink Hill, and Meadows, was difficult, it was, nevertheless, far easier then the lives of those in Charleston. Beau and Lydia remained in their home there. Beau felt that he was needed there at the clinic, and Lydia refused to move home without him. Only when he was recruited to go work in the Confederate field hospital in Columbia, did she finally agree to move home to Fairlawn. Not long after he left, she learned that she was pregnant.

Just after the Union Navy blockaded the harbor, Angus McPherson was employed aboard a blockade runner. In spite of the danger, the money was good; and the adventure stirred his young blood. Unfortunately, after several successful runs, their luck ran out; and the boat was sunk, there in the harbor, killing all hands on board. Annamarie never forgave herself for not going with him to the mountains. She always felt that if she had, he would still be alive. Samuel Flood was there for her during those first painful months, trying to convince her that it was not her fault. She found comfort in his attention and married him a few months later. One of those spur-of-the-moment decisions that she would live to regret. At the time of her marriage, Virgil signed over to her, her share of his father's estate. He had given the twins their shares to finance their move to Canada, to pay for their educations, and set up a law practice in Quebec. Unfortunately, Samuel Flood was a ne'er-do-well, who would soon run through Annamarie's entire inheritance.

Lillianna's brothers, Jonathan and David, both lost sons. Jonathan lost his two remaining sons, Jonathan, III, and Theodore, who were both killed defending Battery Wagner on Morris Island in July, 1863. David's two older sons, Lucas and Marcus, were both killed. When Lucas, older of the two, was conscripted into the Confederate Army, Marcus, unable to support the cause of the Confederacy, went north and joined the Union Army. Lucas died in the Battle of Tulifinny Creek, protecting the railroad between Savannah and Charleston. Ironically, Marcus was killed trying to perform a humanitarian gesture for a Confederate soldier. On the last day of the Battle of Gettysburg, Major General George E.

Pickett led 12,000 Confederate soldiers across an open field against Union forces positioned on Cemetery Hill. The charge, which would come to be known as Pickett's Charge, was futile and tragic. Only one-hundred and fifty Confederate soldiers actually made it across the stone wall in an area known as the Bloody Angle. They fought for forty-five minutes before they were finally repulsed. Thousands of dead and wounded were strewn over the field. In the heat of that July day in 1863, the wounded lay screaming in agony. Marcus, who was positioned behind the stone wall, could see one young soldier, just a boy, begging for water only a few yards away. Overcome with pity, Marcus crawled over the wall to the boy and was giving him a drink from his own canteen. Another wounded Confederate soldier, a few feet away, fired point blank at the back of Marcus's head, killing him instantly.

The tragedy of Will's death and all the useless carnage of the war, had taken a heavy toll on Lillianna's health. One February evening in 1865, she bundled up in warm clothes and walked down to River Bend to visit Mattie. As they sat on the porch swing, arm in arm and wrapped in a blanket, Lillianna rested her head on Mattie's shoulder. "Mattie, I am so very tired. Everything is moving so fast. Even the Ashley, usually so tranquil, seems to be in a hurry. I feel like a squirrel, running 'round and 'round in a cage. Sometimes I feel I must stop running and just ride the cage!"

"Maybe that wouldn't be a bad idea, my little Lilli," Mattie answered, kissing her forehead.

"Why, Mattie, you've never called me that before."

"I know. It has never been permitted, but I have always *thought* of you that way," Mattie admitted.

"I love the *sound and feel* of it. At this moment, I could almost believe that the war is far, far away. I wish we could stay here like this forever," Lillianna said.

"Me too," Mattie agreed.

The bombardment of the lower part of Charleston had

long since driven most citizens to move north of Calhoun Street and along the Ashley River where the hospitals and prisoners were located and where the shells did not reach. Battery Wagner had been evacuated, and Fort Sumter lay in ruins. On the evening of February 17, 1865, the Confederate flag was lowered for the last time. Later, the soldiers started to leave under cover of darkness. A fire was lit near a stockpile of powder left in the railroad station by the Confederates. A great fire began to burn near the Cooper River; and on the other side of town, the Ashley River Bridge was burned deliberately. Soon, the fires met in the center of the city. With evacuation in progress, cotton was piled in the public squares and burned. The whole city was ablaze in an effort to leave nothing of value for the approaching Union Army.

Word of the fire spread; and when Lydia heard it, she was panic-stricken. At her home in Charleston, she had left many treasured possessions, among which was Grandpapa Pink's beautiful old harp. She was reconciled to losing everything else, but she was determined to rescue the harp. She asked Zeke, the stable manager, and his son, Seth, to hitch-up the horse and the wagon and to take her into the city to get the harp. When they reached the city, horror and chaos reigned. Roving mobs of looters roamed the streets, and explosions rocked the entire city. When Lydia, Zeke, and Seth reached her street, she was relieved to see that her house was still standing. She went in ahead of the two men; and just as she stepped inside, the house took a direct hit. There was little of the house left standing; and Lydia, along with her unborn child, was killed.

Zeke and Seth were horrified. "Seth, we gotta' get out of here and get back to Fairlawn. I sho' do dread to take this news back to 'em!" Zeke said. They raced back across the Ashley River Bridge just before it fell and headed for home.

When Lillianna learned of Lydia's death, she collapsed. Dr. Bradner was summoned; and when he finally arrived,

Mattie had put her to bed in her room upstairs. She was conscious, but having severe chest pain, and was in a cold sweat. Dr. Bradner examined her and confirmed what he had feared; she had suffered a heart attack. He gave her laudanum for the pain, and soon she was resting, but only fitfully. By the next day, she was somewhat improved, but the doctor had left orders for her to have complete bed rest until further notice. The family saw to it that someone was in attendance with her day and night. In order that she not feel so isolated, Matthew had her bedroom moved downstairs to the study. However, in spite of all their efforts, Lillianna's recovery was coming along very slowly; and April found her still unable to get out of bed.

Noel decided that the best medicine for his mother would be a visit from Leland. However, the responsibility of the struggling plantations, Pink Hill and Meadows, would not permit his going to the mountains to bring Leland home. Noel's cousins, Robert and Franklin, sons of his Uncle Gilmore, volunteered to make the trip for him.

On April 9, 1865, the war officially ended with Robert E. Lee's surrender at Appomattox Court House. And, even though the trip to the mountains was less dangerous now that the war was over, it was, nevertheless, very difficult. Robert and Franklin were not prepared for the kind of horrible death and devastation they would see along the way. They were relieved to finally reach the Cherokee country.

Leland was terribly upset at the news of his mother's heart attack, but he was completely devastated to learn of Lydia's death. He agreed that he was needed at home and that it was imperative that he return to Charleston immediately with his cousins. "Carlotta, I'll return as soon as possible. You and Auburn can stay with your folks while I am gone."

"Leland, Auburn and I are going with you."

"Darling, it will be a long and hard trip. And from what Robert and Franklin have said, the things we will have to see will be very unpleasant. Besides all that, you and Auburn will only slow us down," he protested.

"I am very sorry for all that, Leland; nevertheless, we *are* going with you. I refuse to discuss it further!"

"Well, gentlemen," he said to his cousins, "it looks like the lady is determined to go with us."

"We have no problem with that, Leland," Robert answered.

"Good," Carlotta said. "Let's see, it's Friday afternoon. I can be ready to leave Monday morning."

"Are you sure you can get ready that fast?" Leland asked.

"Oh yes, you just worry about your own packing. Auburn and I will be ready. Right, sweetie?" she asked Auburn.

"Mama, are we going to go see Gaama Liddy?" The four-year-old asked. Auburn had long since stopped baby talk, but the baby talk name she had given her grandmother had stuck.

"Yes, ma'am, we surely are!" Carlotta answered.

"Then I'm ready to go now!" Auburn said, her brown eyes sparkling.

CHAPTER EIGHTEEN

THE LAMP PASSES

They made the journey to Charleston much more quickly than they thought possible. The spring weather was beautiful. The rhododendron and mountain laurel were in bloom; and, in spite of all the devastation they were forced to witness, all in all, the trip was pleasant.

They arrived at Fairlawn mid-afternoon on a Wednesday. At word of their arrival, the whole family turned out to greet them, that is, all except Lillianna. She was taking her prescribed afternoon nap, and Leland wouldn't allow them to disturb her. "Let her rest; we'll have plenty of time to visit later."

Everyone was delighted to finally meet Carlotta, and Auburn was the center of attention. She loved every minute of it; and was especially taken with Noel's little boy, Parker. They were about the same age, and were soon happily playing on the piazza.

Leland took Carlotta's hand and said, "Come with me, sweetheart; I want to ride over to Pink Hill and visit the family cemetery." To the rest of the family sitting there, he said, "If you folks will excuse us, we'll be back in a little while."

"Take all the time you want," Noel answered.

They walked down to the stable, and Leland hitched-up the buggy. They took a short ride down to the river first. "Leland, it's so peaceful and beautiful here," Carlotta said.

"I spent so many hours here when I was growing up. Annamarie, Samuel, and I explored every foot of these riverbanks. Nothing escaped our collection of arrowheads, rocks, and anything else that took our fancies."

"I know who Annamarie is, but who is Samuel?" Carlotta asked.

"He's her husband now," Leland answered, a little disdainfully.

"What is it, Leland? I get the feeling that you don't like him."

"Oh, it's not exactly that I don't like him. It's a long story. I'll tell you all about it later," he answered. "We'd better head for Pink Hill so that we can get home in time for supper. You'll likely get to meet them then."

"Please, darling, let's sit here for just a few minutes more. I love being here. I can just picture you as a little boy roaming along these banks, barefooted, skipping stones across the water, and maybe dreaming of being a riverboat captain when you grew up," Carlotta said, kissing him lightly on the lips. For one fleeting moment, he thought of the last kiss he had had here beside the Ashley; and he took Carlotta in his arms and gave her a lingering, passionate kiss. Then he turned the buggy around; and they rode on to Pink hill, in silence, enjoying the scenery.

When they reached the little cemetery, they walked through the gate and found Lydia's grave. They sat on a nearby bench; and Carlotta took Leland's hand and sat there quietly beside him. He wept silently for the loss of his beloved

Lydia, who had been his guardian angel since the day he was born. And Carlotta wept at his grief.

When they got back to Fairlawn, Noel and Barbara were sitting on the piazza watching Auburn and Parker play. "Isn't it wonderful to see these two playing together?" Barbara asked.

"Yes indeed, it surely is," Carlotta answered.

"I take it Mama is still napping," Leland said.

"Yes, but she should be awakening anytime now. You know she didn't know you were coming; we wanted to surprise her." Noel said.

"Was that a good idea?" Leland asked. "The shock might be too much for her."

"Oh, we checked it out with Dr. Bradner. He didn't think there would be a problem," Noel assured him. "Let's go in and rouse her; it will soon be time for supper."

They called the children and went into the house. Noel motioned them all to wait outside the study door, and only he went in. "Wake up, sleepy head," he said, kissing her cheek.

Lillianna opened her eyes; and, still half asleep, she looked up at Noel and smiled. "Noel, I had the most wonderful dream. I dreamed that Leland came home and that Carlotta and Auburn were with him. I hated to wake up; it was such a happy dream."

"Well, Mama, I'm sorry I had to awaken you; but you have visitors," Noel said, with mock sympathy. He helped her to sit up in bed, plumped her pillows, and saw to it that she was comfortably settled.

"Noel, please hand me my comb and mirror before you show them in," she said. He did as she asked and stood there watching as she combed her hair and arranged it on her shoulders. "Do I look all right?" she asked.

"You look beautiful, as always," he answered.

"Well, show them in! No, wait, you didn't tell me who has come to visit."

"I'm not sure myself, so I don't think you know them either. They're apparently not from around here," he said, as he went over and opened the door.

Auburn, smiling her special little smile, peeped around the door smiling. "Hello, Gaama Liddy, I'm Auburn. We've come to see you!"

"Oh, my Lord, my dream has come true! Come here to me, my precious darling," Lillianna exclaimed, holding out her arms to welcome Auburn. With that, the little girl ran over to the bed, stepped up on the step stool, and threw her arms around her grandmother's neck exuberantly.

Concerned for Lillianna, Carlotta rushed over to the bed behind Auburn, "Whoa, be careful, darling," she said, reaching for the child.

Lillianna pulled the child closer in her arms. "This angel could never hurt me," she said, kissing Auburn's forehead, nose, and both cheeks. Then she reached up for Carlotta and pulled her into the circle of her embrace. Then looking up at Leland, who was standing beside the bed with tears in his eyes, she said, "Leland, your girls are as beautiful as you told me they were." Carlotta took Auburn from Lillianna's arms and stepped back so that he could greet his mother.

Leland sat on the side of the bed; and his mother, putting her arms around his neck, cried as she pulled him close to her. "Oh, Mama, I've been so worried about you and *all* the family. And now, we have lost our sweet Lydia," he said, sobbing.

"I know, I know, baby boy," she said, trying to comfort him as she kissed him, first on one cheek and then the other.

Little Auburn looked on with concern, for she had never before seen her father cry. "Mama, is Papa going to be all right?"

"Yes, sweetheart, he is with *his mama* now. He is going to be fine," Carlotta assured Auburn.

"Mama's can always fix things, like you always do for me," Auburn observed wisely.

"Well, mama's certainly do always try to fix things, darling." Carlotta answered.

As Noel had predicted, the arrival of Leland and his family seemed to be just the medicine that Lillianna needed. She started to improve rapidly. In a few weeks, she was able to be up and around for a little while each day.

One day after lunch, Lillianna and Leland were sitting on the piazza chatting and relaxing. "Mama, where is Beau? Noel said he was in Columbia working at a Confederate field hospital when Lydia was killed."

"Yes, he was in Columbia; but he came home a few days after the surrender at Appomattox Court House. He knew nothing about all that had transpired with Lydia. The last he knew, she was safe at home with us. He didn't know that she was pregnant; she didn't learn that she was until after he had left. It was ironic that the only time she had been back to their home in Charleston in weeks was the moment that fate chose to strike it. Beau was completely devastated. He went to live at Meadows, with every intention of resuming his medical practice. But his grief was more than he could bear. He just couldn't stay here surrounded by all the memories of Lydia, so he left."

"Where did he go?" Leland asked.

"We don't know; he didn't even know where he was going."

"Oh, Mama, I can understand how he must have felt. I can't imagine life without Carlotta. I don't believe I would want to go on living."

"Believe me, son, going on living after you have lost the person who has made your *worth living* is not easy. However, that choice is not ours to make," Lillianna said, her eyes filling with tears.

"I know, mama. *I know,*" he answered, taking her hand and kissing it.

About that time, Carlotta and Auburn came out on the piazza. “Well, we have finished up in the kitchen; and Auburn came out to tell you that it’s time for your afternoon nap, Mother Pinkston. The time you two spend together each afternoon is the highlight of her day,” Carlotta said.

“I think you are right, Auburn. I seem to be more tired than I had realized. Perhaps I have stayed up a bit too long,” Lillianna said, as she rose unsteadily.

“Here, Mama, I’ll carry you in,” Leland said, as he started to pick her up.

“Leland, don’t bother. I’m sure I can make it on my own with the help of my trusty cane,” Lillianna insisted.

“Bother indeed! As if you could ever be a bother,” he countered. Gently sweeping her up in his arms, he took her inside. “I think I can manage a little feather like you, Mama.”

Carlotta helped settle her into the big bed. “You try to take a good nap now. I’ll check in on you in a little while,” she said, kissing Lillianna’s forehead.

“Thank you, sweetheart. Nappy night, as my Delilah used to say; I love you.”

“Nappy night, dear heart, I love you too,” Carlotta replied.

Just before Lillianna dozed off, Auburn peeped in the study door. “Gaama Liddy, can I come in and kiss you nappy night?”

“Of course, you may, sweetheart. In fact, you may climb up here in bed with me; and we will just nappy together!”

“All right,” she agreed, delighted to be invited. Her favorite thing to do was to go to sleep counting the kittens on the canopy above, as her grandmother said she had done when she was a little girl. She stepped on the step-stool, climbed up onto the high bed, and backed up to Lillianna. “Snuggy me up, Gaama Liddy, like spoons.”

“All right, my little pumpkin girl, come here,” she replied

laughing, as she wrapped her arm around Auburn and drew her close.

Looking up at Becca's picture, Auburn said, "Know what Gaama Liddy? Your mama was a really pretty lady."

"Yes Ma'am, your great-grandmother was a beautiful lady. And do you see that pretty necklace that she is wearing? That will be yours someday when you are all grownup. Then they will make your picture with you wearing it."

"Do you think that I might be that pretty?" Auburn asked.

"I feel sure that you will be, darling!" Lillianna answered, kissing her cheek.

Gaama Liddy, your hair is her same color, but it looks like it's snowed on yours a little bit."

"Indeed it has; and you know what? Your hair is that same color."

"I know. It's called auburn. That's why they named me Auburn, Papa said. He said that Grandpa Will used to call you 'my little auburn hair.' If he were here, do you think he would call *me* 'little auburn hair'?"

"I am *sure* he would, darling. He would absolutely adore you!" Lillianna's heart tightened at the thought that Will would never see their precious grandchildren.

"I wish *you* would call me *your* 'little auburn hair,' Gaama Liddy. Would you?"

"I would love to, my little auburn hair, just love to!"

"I'm so glad," Auburn murmured sleepily. "Nappy night, Gaama; I love you."

"Nappy night, my little auburn hair; I love you too." With that, they both dropped off to sleep.

Much later, Carlotta peeped in to check on them. They were both sleeping quietly, still snuggled up like two little puppies. "How beautiful that picture is!" she said. She went out on the piazza to call the rest of the family to see the sleeping pair before she awakened them. All the family had gathered there, enjoying the peace of the late afternoon, waiting for supper time to arrive. "If you want to see a beautiful picture, come look in the study," Carlotta said. They all rose and followed her in, tiptoeing into the study behind her. "Now, as Leland likes to say, doesn't that make your hearts smile?" Smiling and blotting tears, they all agreed. Carlotta said, "Wake up you two sleeping beauties; it's almost supper time. Besides, if you don't, you won't sleep a wink tonight."

Auburn opened her eyes and rubbed them sleepily. She asked, "What are you all doing in here?"

"Your mama just wanted us to come in and see how pretty you two girls looked all snuggied-up asleep," Leland answered. "Time to wake up, sweetie."

Lillianna didn't move at all. Auburn said, "Gaama Liddy needs some more cover; her arm feels cold."

"Oh no, please Lord, no! Not Mama, not now!" Noel cried. Leland went over to his brother and put his arm around his shoulders, drawing him close.

Matthew ran over to the bed and felt for Lillianna's pulse. Struggling to maintain his composure, he picked Auburn up, turned, and placed her in Mandy's arms. "Take Auburn out of here, Mandy!" When Mandy had taken the child out into the foyer, Matt sobbed, "She's gone! Oh, God, our Lillianna is gone!"

The family was devastated; they took little comfort in the fact that she had passed so peacefully. Although they knew in their hearts and minds that she was in a far better place, with all those she loved most, they were inconsolable in their grief for their own loss. Added to all the tragedy that the family had endured, this was more than they could bear.

They arranged for the wake and went through it mechanically, almost as if in a terrible dream. They chose the scripture and the music for the funeral, lovingly. Then, considering her personality, her strength of character, and the unselfish life she had lived, they chose what they considered the perfect inscription for her gravestone. That it echoed, almost verbatim, the inscription on her mother's stone, seemed entirely appropriate. After all, Lillianna had become the guardian of Becca's lamp. More than that, she had made it her own.

As family and friends gathered within the white picket fence that surrounded the Pinkston family plot, Lillianna Prendle Pinkston was laid to rest beside her beloved Will. The rector conducted the graveside service. As an ending, he read the inscription on the stone. When he started to read, almost as if led by an unseen hand, Auburn walked to the stone alone. Dropping to her knees, she placed her tiny hands on the words engraved there. "What a tiny little girl to have to become the guardian of the lamp," Leland whispered to Carlotta, through his tears.

"Until she is ready to carry it alone, darling, you and I will be here to help her," Carlotta replied.

"'Who can find a virtuous woman, for her price is far above rubies . . . her lamp does not go out by night . . . Many women have done excellently, but you surpass them all . . . ' amen, the rector finished.

And a tiny little voice echoed, "amen."

EPILOGUE

If the reader has perceived this work as *different, inspiring, and has enjoyed the reading of it,* I feel that I have succeeded in what I set out to accomplish. However, my story is but half told; there is more . . . .

Laryce Henderson Rybka

ACKNOWLEDGEMENTS

There are so many people to whom I owe a debt of gratitude for supporting me during my years of work on this book. First my beloved husband, Bill, who has suffered neglect for the many hours I have sat working, closeted away in the office in front of the computer. At times, he jokingly threatened to place his wedding band on top of *the monster* as I seemed to be more married to *it* than to him. Nevertheless, he was more than willing to read, critique, and suggest changes as my work progressed. Thanks, Honey, it is great to know that I can always count on you.

Along with my mother, my children and grandchildren find it difficult to be truly objective. They believe that I can accomplish anything to which I set my mind. That kind of confidence is contagious and has kept me going at times when I might have given up.

My daughter, Lillianne McDonald, went even further with her enthusiastic support. She pushed, prodded, and lovingly *nagged* until I finally finished. She, in effect, has become my agent and has no intention of backing off until my book is a success. Thanks, Lilli, you are, among other things, our family sunshine and *heir to the lamp*.

My stepdaughter, Judy Rybka, has spent hours editing for me. She has proofread, offered advice on changes in punctuation, sentence construction, grammar, and literary content, that have added much to the quality of my work. She is an avid reader, whose informed opinions I value highly. I am forever in her debt for her dedicated work and unfailing support. Judy, when it comes to daughters, there can never be a *step* in what I feel for you.

My stepson, Mark Peterson, a very talented, professional graphic artist, created the cover graphics. He read the book; and with keen insight, succeeded in capturing the beautiful images I held in my mind's eye. He offered his talent and support lovingly. Mark, I shall be forever grateful; and there again, *step* is a misnomer.

I would be remiss if I failed to thank my Godson, Mike Martin, who installed my computer, set up all programs, warned me of all the pitfalls, and serves as my systems guru. He is always available, at the other end of the phoneline, to bale me out when I get in over my head. Mike, thank you a thousand fold. Your technical know how and loving support is the primary reason that I have been able to complete this book.

I could go on and on, but I shall conclude with a thanks to *all* my family and friends who have supported me and who had the confidence that I could bring this work to a successful conclusion.